ROYAL MAGES

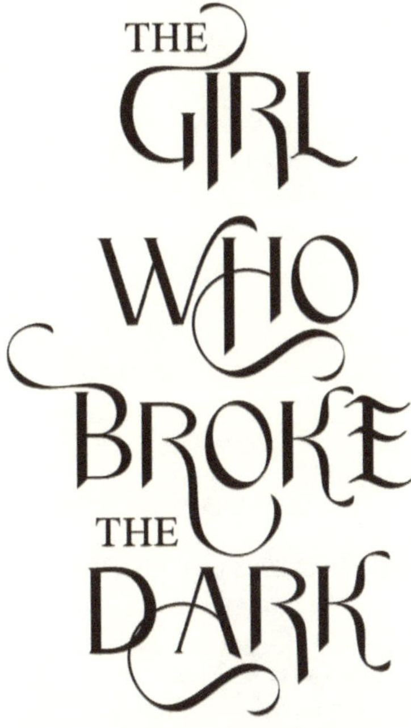

THE GIRL WHO BROKE THE DARK

*Sleeping Beauty
with
a deadly twist*

EVELYN PUERTO

THE GIRL WHO BROKE
THE DARK

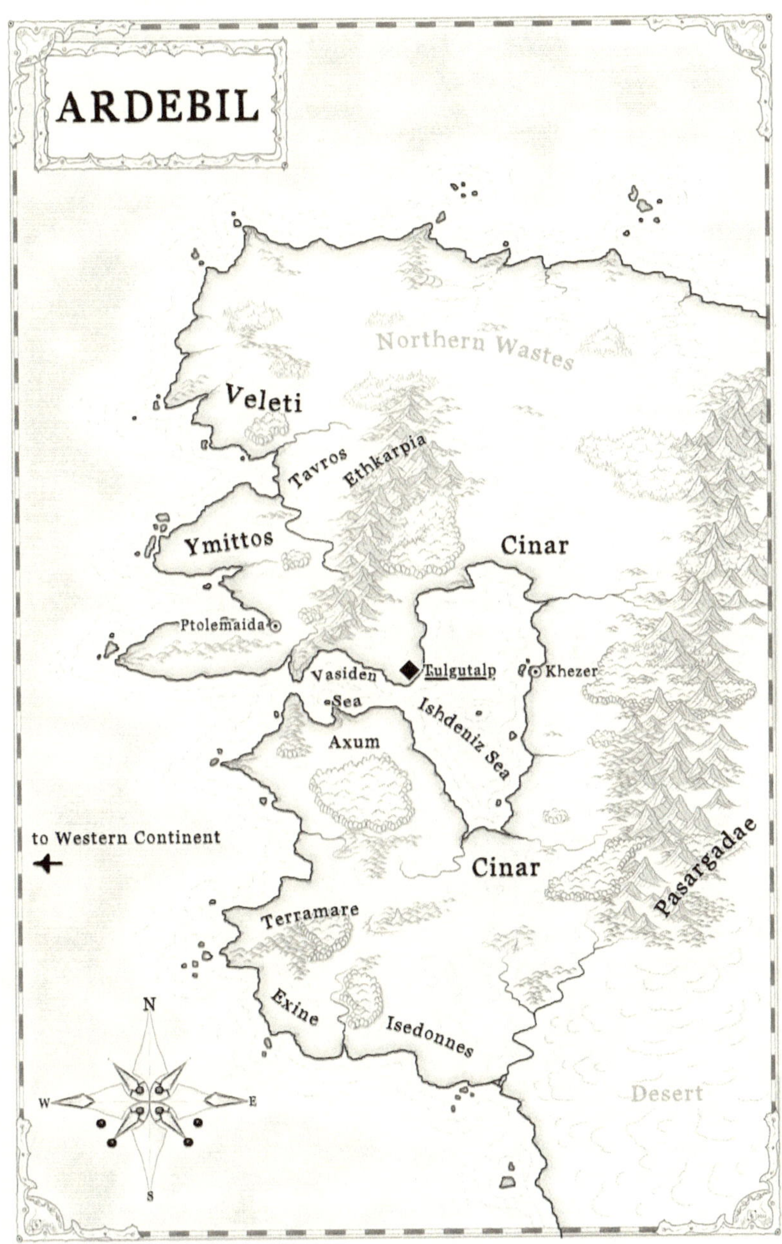

ARDEBIL
Northern Wastes
Veleti
Tavros
Ethkarpia
Ymittos
Cinar
Ptolemaida
Vasiden
Sea
Tulgutalp
Khezer
Axum
Ishdeniz Sea
to Western Continent
Cinar
Pasargadae
Terramare
Exine
Isedonnes
Desert
N
W
E
S

CONTENTS

1

Princess Eliana of Ymittos wondered if using her magic to strangle the Heir of Cinar would cause a war. She sighed and forced her lips into a smile. Just one more sacrifice royalty demanded. If only the fate of the realm didn't depend on her friendship with a visiting princess. The girl riding a chestnut mare beside Eliana surveyed the city streets with the air of a conquering empress who condescended to allow the rabble to witness her magnificence.

Eliana's cheeks ached from the effort of hiding her true feelings. To relieve the pain, she closed her eyes and tipped her face into the cool breeze blowing in from the sea. *Merciful winds, spare me.* Straightening in her saddle, she made another attempt to engage. "In a few minutes, we'll pass the library. You can see the towers already. Right now, Ymittos is hosting an astronomy symposium, with participating scholars from all over the continent of Ardebil. I believe some are from Cinar."

Her companion made no reply.

Princess Derya, heir to the throne of Cinar, and her entourage had arrived two weeks before. For those two long weeks, Eliana struggled to entertain the other princess, choking back the sarcastic ripostes she wanted to hurl at

Derya and her supercilious sneering. Even the previous evening's lavish celebration of the winter solstice had, in Derya's words, failed to impress.

Before Derya's arrival, Eliana's parents lectured her endlessly on the importance of making the Heir of Cinar her friend. They didn't know if the Emperor of Cinar planned to absorb Ymittos into his empire or simply wanted a stronger alliance. Eliana needed to win Derya's confidence and find out the emperor's intentions. The queen had arranged dinners and dances, theatrical spectacles and concerts. Eliana had done her best to make sure that Derya enjoyed them all. But Derya made her disdain for Eliana's country and everyone in it quite obvious.

This morning, the drizzling rain and sleet that had fallen continuously since Derya's arrival had ceased and the weak midwinter sun peeked through the clouds. Eliana proposed a ride through the city, thinking that once Derya saw the spectacular architecture of Ptolemaida, she'd find something she wouldn't deride.

Their horses paced slowly through the crowded streets. Two guards preceded them. One was a burly man clad in Ymittos's colors of navy and white. Somehow his livery looked drab compared to the hues of Derya's guard—brilliant turquoise against somber black.

Street vendors hawked their wares, shouting the praises of their wine, sausages, and clams. The smell of baking flatbread mixed with the odor of manure from the stables connected to a roadside inn. A breeze brought a whiff of rotting fish from the port. Eliana glanced at Derya, who was crinkling her nose. An icy wind blew the hood of Eliana's cloak from her head, teasing strands of her black hair into her eyes.

A scant half an hour into the ride and Eliana was berating herself for thinking the sights and sounds of the city would make Derya's presence less odious. At least they were out in the fresh air. But a canter through the countryside, when she'd be permitted to ride astride, would be better than this slow parade perched on an uncomfortable sidesaddle.

"Have you seen enough?" Eliana asked. "Ready to turn back?"

"Why? Are you cold?" One corner of Derya's mouth curled.

"No, of course not." Eliana flexed the toes she could barely feel inside her leather boots. "Are you?"

Derya snorted. "We'd call this autumn, not winter."

Eliana pressed her lips together. She'd already heard endless, tiresome tales of Derya's exploits with a bow and arrow hunting in the vast forests of the northern provinces of her father's territory, forests that were blanketed in snow many months of the year.

Snow rarely appeared in any part of Ymittos. Instead, a dreary drizzle fell through most of the winter. And while the spitting rain had ceased for the moment, gray clouds churned overhead, reflecting Eliana's own dark thoughts. How long would she be saddled with a companion whose every word made her feel inadequate and incompetent? Perhaps challenging Derya to compete with bows or swords might wipe the smirk off the other girl's face. Years of training with her cousin Evander had given Eliana skills few girls had. Besting Derya in a duel was a tempting thought. *Better not try it.* It was her duty to sacrifice her feelings for the sake of the alliance with Cinar. Eliana didn't want to risk a diplomatic incident, or worse, embarrass herself if Derya won.

A white marble building came into view on their right. Wide steps led to a portico whose roof jutted three stories above its mosaic flooring, supported by a row of towering statues of the former kings of Ymittos. "That's the King's Theater. A new play will open next week. If you're still here, we could go see it."

Holding her breath, Eliana waited for Derya's reply. The

princess hadn't said how long she'd stay. Perhaps she'd be leaving soon. *For the rest of my life, I'll celebrate that day as a holiday.*

"That would be delightful."

The other girl's tone sounded like she'd rather have her fingernails torn out than attend the play. Eliana stifled her impulse to wield her air magic to fill Derya's mouth with dust. Instead, Eliana fixed her faltering smile in place and pulled in a deep breath of the crisp air. "Wonderful. I'll arrange it." She pointed. "The statue on the right of the entrance depicts Kastellanos the Conqueror, for whom our royal house is named. My father is the thirty-fifth in his line."

"Mine is the ninety-first in his. What's that?" Derya pointed with her chin at the pillared building across the street.

Too bad your line didn't end at ninety. Stretching her lips into a bland expression, Eliana replied, "The Palace of Philosophers, where our learned men debate issues and current events. Would you like to observe?"

"Only if they include learned women in their debates." With a smug smile, Derya cast a sidelong glance at Eliana. "Oh, forgive me, I forgot. You have no educated women here."

Eliana put a hand to her mouth and coughed, hoping to cover her shock. While it was true few women in Ymittos received much education beyond simple reading and writing, this was not true of all. She'd enjoyed the benefit of tutors in most subjects the boys studied. How dare Derya include her in the ranks of the unlettered? "I think you may be misinformed on that point."

"I doubt it."

Eliana repressed a biting retort. Visiting princesses were every bit as tiresome as solving mathematical proofs, and much less interesting. She shot a hard look at the girl. A dimple dented Derya's smooth, gently tanned skin and her full lips were pulled into a grin. A stray beam of sunlight caressed her dark hair, illuminating its golden highlights.

How Eliana coveted those highlights, along with the jeweled lacing Derya used to belt her fine linen chemises. Her patterned leather boots inlaid with gemstones. And her tall, willowy build. But most of all, Eliana envied Derya's confidence, and her boldness to say what she thought even if it crossed the line into rudeness.

"I intend—" Eliana choked back her impulsive words. She couldn't let anyone know her plans for improving women's education once she became ruler. That might make her father question the wisdom of allowing her to inherit and prompt him to pass her over for one of her male cousins.

A tremor shook the ground, causing Eliana's horse to shy. Shouts froze passersby in place. Eliana stared in the direction of the noise, where a dusty plume rose into the frosty air. The princesses' guards drew closer, with two assuming positions beside the girls.

Pulling tighter on the reins, Eliana murmured to her mare. The bay tugged on the bit as if preparing to bolt. What was happening? The momentary shaking had not been the familiar trembling of an earthquake.

"Does this occur often?" Princess Derya asked. "We don't have such disruptions in Cinar."

Only when irritating visitors come to call. Eliana looked past Derya down a side street. "I think there's a problem with the canal repairs." She remembered vividly the last time there was an accident in the canal works. Scores of laborers had died. She'd never forget the desolation of the widows and fatherless children.

"What's it to us?"

The neutral expression Eliana had wrestled onto her face came close to cracking like an egg that had been squeezed too hard. While the canal works had mages to deal with accidents, she felt an obligation to aid her people, something that would no doubt elicit more scorn from Derya. *Let her sneer.* Eliana turned her horse. "I'm going to see what happened and offer to help."

"What can you possibly do?"

"I won't know until I get there." Without waiting for an answer, Eliana nudged her mount's sides with her heels and moved closer to her guard. "We're going to the work site. Lead on."

The man raised his eyebrows, but silently turned his horse.

"Excellent," Derya said. "Finally, something more stimulating than marble palaces."

Eliana ground her teeth. She wanted to like Derya, she really did. Neither of them had siblings, so both were destined to inherit their respective kingdoms. To be on good terms with the dominant empire in the western part of the continent of Ardebil would serve to maintain peace and stability. Everyone would benefit if she and Derya became friends. But Derya wasn't making it easy.

In a few moments, they reached the dig site. Crowds had gathered, some shouting, others wailing. Eliana guided her horse slowly through the throng, giving people time to move aside. When she neared the canal's edge, a mud-spattered foreman ran up to her.

"It's not safe, Highness. Please don't go any further."

"Can you tell me what happened?"

"The earthquake last week weakened the sides of the canal. Before we could finish the repairs, the rains came and eroded the earth around the supports. So we closed the dam's gates and drained the canal to continue the work. With the water pressure no longer holding up the stones, they collapsed." He grimaced. "Workers are trapped. I'm not sure how many."

"Can you get them out?"

"I don't know. When the canal sides fell, it weakened the supports. I fear the dam will collapse before we can reach the men. Half the workers are trying to shore up the dam. Others are working on the rescue."

"Have you sent word to my father?"

"Yes, Highness. But we don't have long to wait. Our mages are doing what they can, but their power isn't enough." The man shuddered. "At least it's not a sinkhole."

Eliana's throat clenched. Falling into a sinkhole was worse than drowning, indeed. Anyone sucked down into the dark, underground realm of Malkh never returned. Legend claimed that monsters who were half fish and half goat devoured them. Eliana wasn't sure she believed those tales, but she wasn't about to venture below to find out for herself.

"Can't we do something?" Derya asked.

"Us?" Eliana tensed in her saddle. Derya wanted to help?

"Yes, us. You've got air magic and I've got water."

This was true. Eliana tilted her head as she considered. At seventeen, neither she nor Derya were supposed to use their magic without supervision. It was a shocking idea.

And an intriguing one. As royals, they possessed more power than most mages. Using their magic could save many lives. Besides, the workers could die before other aid arrived. Eliana tossed her reins to the foreman. "We'll help." She jumped from her mount and looked up at Derya. "What are you waiting for?"

Derya grinned. "For you to quit being the perfect Ymittosian princess, I suppose."

Eliana wasn't sure what that meant, but insult or joke, she wasn't going to respond. "Then stay where you are." She turned to the foreman. "Where's the collapse?"

He pointed to a ladder. "You can see better from the level below."

Ignoring the protests of her guard, Eliana sprinted toward the ladder, Derya on her heels.

The two girls drew up to the canal's edge, breathless. The canal diggings loomed beneath them, an enormous ditch one hundred feet wide that stretched from the Bisaltes River to Lake Ptolemaida, many miles away.

Pausing only to hike up the skirts of her peplos and tuck a portion of its ornate hem into her belt, Eliana swung onto the ladder. Before beginning her descent, she gave a wink to her still-protesting guards.

Derya's tanned skin paled, and she stood wringing her hands. "We can't help from up here?"

Eliana repressed a grin. Derya was reluctant to descend the rickety ladder, clearly nervous about the height. *Too bad for her.* Eliana relished being in high places. It was the dark, enclosed spots that made her sweat.

"Wait, Your Highness." The foreman leaned over the edge. "You shouldn't —"

"Too late," Eliana called. She descended rapidly, reminded of her days climbing mountain cliffs with Evander. The familiar ache in her chest surfaced, the emptiness after Evander died. All because of her. She shoved her grief away. Now was not the time. She had to focus on saving the workers.

The ladder twitched, and she gripped the rough wood harder. A glance upwards told her that Derya was clambering down. Eliana smirked to see the girl's slow progress. Derya wasn't so condescending now.

Once she reached the bottom, Eliana jumped off the ladder onto the stone pavement of the narrow walkway lining the canal. The sides of the canal blocked the weak winter sun, leaving the air cold and damp. A few moments later, she was joined by a white-faced Derya, the sweating foreman, and a pair of guards. Eliana didn't give the men a chance to protest. "Show us the cave-in."

"Yes, Your Highness." The foreman moved to the edge of the walkway and pointed down.

Eliana gasped. Dozens of men were in the mud some fifty feet below, some half-submerged, others flailing to pull themselves from the swampy morass. To the left, the massive dam holding back the river water showed signs of a leak. A damp spot was seeping across the top. "Why is no one trying to rescue them?" she asked.

"Highness," the foreman said, "we had to stop. There's not much time before the dam gives way. It would be certain death to go down there." He gestured to a group of five men and women slumped on the walkway. A sixth lowered her hands and toppled to her knees. "Our water mages spent themselves trying to help the trapped men. They have nothing left."

"What do you think, Princess Derya?" Eliana said. "If you push water while I push air, will that keep the dam from breaking while they pull the men out?"

"Let's try." Derya flashed her a smile and Eliana wondered what had happened to the supercilious princess who sneered at everything and everyone. This version of Derya was almost likable.

No time to marvel about that now. Taking a deep breath, Eliana summoned her air magic, savoring the breathy coolness that filled her. Releasing the power, she blew a wind against the dam. She shuddered, feeling the weight of the water pressing against the earthen barrier. Beside her, Derya screwed up her face and waved a hand. The weight of the penned water against Eliana's air magic lessened.

Eliana jerked her chin at the foreman. "Tell them to hurry. I don't know how long we can hold it."

The foreman ran toward a group of workers huddled on the edge. "Go! Now!" were the only words of his shouted orders that reached Eliana's ears. Scores of men raced down the ladders and charged across the mud flat. Frantically, they dug out the trapped workers. Slowly, too slowly, they pulled most of the men from the mud.

When Eliana's toes began to tingle, she knew what it meant. Sure enough, a few minutes later, her feet went numb. The paralysis was a warning she wouldn't be able to use her magic much longer. She dropped to her knees. A moment later, even kneeling was too strenuous. She shifted and sat on the ground. *Better.*

Derya sagged against the wall and slid to sit next to Eliana. Sweat dripped down her tanned skin. "I can't do this much longer," she murmured.

"Me either. You can stop if you want to."

"Not a chance." Derya ground out the words.

Although Derya was annoying, Eliana had to admire her determination. Scanning the crater, Eliana pointed. "Only one left, on the far side."

Two men were digging out the last worker. They extracted him from the mud. One of his legs was bent in three places. Eliana guessed it would take at least a quarter of an hour for them to cross the flat carrying the wounded man.

"I don't have much left." Derya's head sagged forward, her chin on her chest.

Eliana couldn't move her legs or arms. Her power was running out. Every breath was an effort, every heartbeat sapped what little strength she possessed. She scanned the canal bed desperately and spotted a small boat. "I'm going to pull back, only a little, and for just a few moments. Can you push a bit harder?"

"I'll try." A trace of defiance laced the words.

Derya's response surprised Eliana. She didn't have to sacrifice herself like this, not for a people not her own. Eliana wasn't going to give up either, even though she couldn't feel anything below her knees and her hands and arms tingled. She licked her lips, tasting the salt from the sweat beading on her skin. She pulled a bit of her power from the dam. A crack formed and spread. "Just a little longer, Derya."

With her remaining strength, Eliana pushed her air magic at the rowboat and hurled it toward the three men as if it had been tossed by a mighty wind. It landed a few yards in front of them.

To her surprise, moving the boat had been easier than she expected. She turned her air magic back to the dam. The crack had widened, and water gushed through. She pushed with her air at the water, helping Derya to slow its rush.

The water spread over the floor of the crater. By this time, the men had climbed into the boat. The advancing water shoved against its side and lifted it over the waves. *Good. They had a chance.* Other men threw grappling hooks and reeled the boat toward shore. As soon as they reached it, Eliana said to Derya, "You can let go now."

But Derya remained fixed in place, her eyes wide and staring, one hand lifted. Eliana touched her arm.

Derya turned to face her, moving as if her muscles resisted with iron stiffness. Her eyelids flickered before she met Eliana's gaze. Sweat dripped from her brow. "Are they safe?" she gasped.

Eliana nodded. She felt a sudden surge of water against the dam when Derya stopped her magic, so she released her own magic in turn, halting the wind she blew against the dam. Her limp hands fell to her sides. The dam's wall cracked, and the river rushed through with a roar. Great chunks of stone collapsed under the torrents. Within moments, the water drowned the canal bed, covering it with surging currents.

Fighting to draw breath, Eliana tried to move her legs, but they were as lifeless as dead sticks and she couldn't raise her hands. She flicked her gaze to Derya, who didn't appear to be breathing. Eliana sagged against the rough stone.

A man bent over her. "Highness, it was good you were here."

She attempted to respond, but her tongue wouldn't move. Blackness overtook her and she knew no more.

2

Eliana stirred. Her head rested on something soft, not the cobbled pavement at the canal works. The earthy smell of burning walnut tickled her nose, pops and cracks indicated a fire blazing nearby. If only it wasn't so hard to open her eyes. Drowsiness tugged at her, but fierce hunger pangs stabbing her stomach made it difficult to lapse back into sleep. She let out a sigh.

"Eliana? Are you awake?" Her mother's voice was tense and strained.

"Yes." Eliana opened one eye.

"Oh, thank the Rider! I thought you'd never wake up." Eliana's mother stroked her daughter's forehead. The queen's black hair was bound in untidy braids, so unlike her normal elaborate arrangement. Her chestnut brown eyes were reddened and rimmed with dark circles, and her face lacked its usual makeup.

Eliana opened her other eye. "How long have I been asleep?"

"Since the day before yesterday," her father said.

Uh oh. In contrast to her mother's relieved tone, her father's voice was tight and angry. He sat in a chair near the foot of her bed, his chin clean-shaven, his chiton flawless white, and his deep blue himation draped evenly over his shoulders.

Eliana groped for something to say, anything to delay the inevitable lecture. "Where's Derya?"

"The Heir of Cinar is in her chamber, also sleeping off her irresponsible overuse of magic." Her father crossed his arms and glared at Eliana. "What got into you?"

"Many would have died had we not helped."

Her father's lips thinned into a harsh line. "True. But had you not held the dam as long as you did, not only the trapped workers but their rescuers would have drowned. You put them all—scores of men—in danger. Once again, your impulsiveness nearly caused a tragedy."

"But it didn't. We prevented one."

A muscle rippled in his jaw. "Not only did you risk the laborers, you jeopardized yourself and the Heir of Cinar. Can you imagine what her father would have done had she been injured? What could I have told him had she perished? Instead of forming an alliance, we could have had a war."

"And what if you had died?" her mother asked. "Ymittos would have lost its heir. Your cousin would inherit, and who knows if he would love our people the way you do?"

All true. Eliana bit her lip and looked at her hands. Her parents were right. She should have thought before acting. But how could she have ignored the men trapped in the mud? She couldn't allow them to be drowned in raging floodwaters.

A servant entered, carrying a tray. Eliana's mouth watered as the aroma of freshly baked bread tickled her nose. She struggled to sit upright. Even after two days, her limbs responded sluggishly, and her feet were still numb. "I'll take it here, please."

The king folded his arms across his chest. "If I didn't know how badly you need to eat right now, I'd make you wait. And don't think I haven't ruled out having you thrashed."

Her mother touched his arm. "Archelaos, she's a little old to be beaten with a slipper." She plumped a pillow and put it behind Eliana's head.

Eliana took a gulp of water. As the cool wetness soothed her dry tongue, strength returned to her limbs. She tore a piece off the sheet of flatbread and stuffed it in her mouth. A little food, a little more sleep, and she'd regain the ability to move down to her toes.

After gesturing for Eliana's mother to sit, her father pulled his own chair closer, studying his daughter as she ate. "What you did took a lot of power." His eyes raked over her face. "You haven't been practicing, have you?"

Though she wanted to pay attention to nothing but the bread in her hand, Eliana locked her gaze on her father's stone-cold eyes. "I know the rules," she said. "I can only study the theory of magic before I'm eighteen. And after that, only use it with a mage present."

"See that you remember," her father said through gritted teeth.

She nodded, trying to keep guilt from seeping onto her face.

"You're eighteen today," he said.

Eliana paused while chewing a mouthful of honey-drenched figs. Her birthday had finally arrived, the day she came of age, and she had nearly slept through it.

Her father's eyes bored into her own. "You need to behave like a responsible ruler. We don't need any more incidents or events like what happened to Evander."

Suddenly uninterested in eating, Eliana set down her bread. She swallowed a lump in her throat. Evander. Her third cousin, childhood friend, and intended husband.

His parents had died when he was four and he'd come to live with Eliana's family. She could never remember if one of his parents was her mother's first cousin, the other a second cousin of her father's, or perhaps the other way around.

In any case, he was sixth in line for the throne of Ymittos. Her parents raised the two of them with the understanding that one day, they'd wed. Evander would be king and she'd be queen.

What her parents didn't know was that she'd made a secret pact with Evander, a blood oath they swore to each other when they were ten. That Evander wouldn't be king alone, that she would rule with him as an equal. No sitting back and letting a man take over her birthright as the current king's only child.

But it all ended one hot summer day a year and a half ago. She and Evander climbed a mountain peak, challenging each other to go higher than they ever had before. They had no fear of falling. What person with air magic would? She jumped from a cliff, puffing the air below her, cushioning her fall almost as if she could fly.

With a whoop, Evander dove from the cliff. But a wounded eagle flew into him, breaking his concentration. And he plummeted to his death.

She blamed herself. She never should have coaxed him to climb so high or dared him to jump. Most of all, she'd been told over and over not to use her magic. A warning she'd laughed off every time she used her power.

In one heedless moment, she'd lost her best friend, future husband, and the only man she would ever love.

He'd been perfect. His olive skin was flawless, as was his silky onyx-colored hair. His dark, kind eyes were filled with humor and intelligence. By the time he died, he'd already passed the gangly stage and his muscular body was toned like a warrior's. No one would ever be able to compare.

"Eliana, pay attention," her father said.

She jerked her focus back to him. "Yes?"

"As I said, you're eighteen now. Time to stop playing games. Think of your future and the future of the realm. High time you were wed."

Ice pooled in her stomach. *No.* She'd been dreading this. *Not yet.*

"You know you're not capable of ruling by yourself," said her mother. "We want to know if you'll receive a suitor."

"What suitor?" Eliana narrowed her eyes and stuck her chin in the air. "If you're about to suggest the Duke of Orythraia again, forget it."

"I know he's a little older than you…" Her mother's voice trailed off.

Eliana pulled herself as upright as she could. She'd met the man on his last visit to court. "A little? He's fifty years old and his daughter was married before I was born. No."

"This is why you aren't suited to rule," her father said, his frown deepening. "You think only of yourself, not what's best for the country. Orythraia has the largest marble and silver mines in the country, as well as the only extensive forests. Ensuring their allegiance is paramount to maintaining our wealth and independence."

"I won't sacrifice myself to some elderly man who would likely use the marriage to put his oldest son on our throne."

Her father knitted his heavy eyebrows together. Eliana bit her lip to keep from pointing out that she was thinking of the realm with her objection. The pause in the conversation meant her father was considering her words. A small victory.

"I understand how you feel." Her mother patted her arm. "What about the oldest son of the Duke of Pefka?"

Eliana stared at the entwined leaves of the ceiling arabesques. Pefka was mostly islands. Its people harvested fish and pearls. The oldest son was about twenty. She'd heard some juicy gossip about him not long ago. "Isn't that the one who's on his fifth mistress in three months?"

Her mother shrugged. "It just means he hasn't found the right woman yet. Marrying you could change all that."

"And if I'm not the right woman, I'll be shackled to a philanderer. No, thank you."

"It would be best if you marry into one of the families that govern our provinces," her father said. "I had thought of trying to ally with one of the realms in the Cinarrian empire, but the emperor blocked all my efforts. Our best choice is to strengthen our internal ties."

"But who else is there?" Eliana's mother asked. "Nea Ionia? They have only daughters. Same with Faliro and Kalyvia. Those provinces are weak, anyway. Then there are the independent principalities. In Tavros, the king has only one son who isn't even walking yet. And Ethkarpia is ruled by a queen whose son married last year."

"That leaves only one other choice," her father said, his voice stern. "The fourth son of the Diodochi of Nafplio."

No. Everything inside her screamed no. She still wanted Evander. Wrapping her arms around herself, she shrank into her pillows. But she knew her duty was to sacrifice herself for the sake of her realm. That was the only way to atone for Evander's death. She was going to have to accept somebody.

The Diodochi of Nafplio was perhaps sixty. His first three sons were married, and his oldest grandson was already a proficient swordsman. She never heard much about this fourth son. "How old is he?"

"Oh, just a few years more than you," her father said. "And the match would almost be as good as marrying one of our stronger nobles. His mother is cousin to the Duke of Orythraia."

"Will you receive him?" Her mother's voice was pleading. "Allow him to come to court to meet you?"

As much as Eliana wanted to refuse, the princess in her knew she had to wed. No woman, especially a young one, would be allowed to rule alone. And an alliance with one of their stronger neighbors would ensure stability in the realm. "Do I need to decide right away?"

Her mother smiled. "No, my love. What say you to a betrothal by midsummer and a marriage the following year?"

Eliana chewed on the inside of her mouth. That would give her time, time to get to know this man, decide if she could love him, and convince him to agree to joint rule. If he didn't, she'd come up with some reason to reject him. She would rule as an equal, not a figurehead.

She nodded. "You may invite him."

Her parents beamed, clearly pleased with her compliance. If they knew her plans, they wouldn't be smiling. But that was a problem for another day.

3

———

The next day, Eliana stood in front of Derya's suite, shifting from one foot to the other. The intricate carving on the door was so lifelike, the dolphins seemed to leap from the waves while eagles soared overhead. *They had nothing to worry about.* She paused before knocking, biting her lip. After she'd led them into nearly magicking themselves to death, would Derya even want to see her?

Her maid, Alessia, fluttered at her side. "Maybe we should let her sleep. Come back later, after she's recovered."

That decided it. No taking the coward's way out. Eliana needed to know if her impulsive decision had injured Derya. No one would tell her anything, so she was going to find out for herself. She rapped on the door.

It swung open to reveal a maid wearing a pale-yellow chemise belted at the waist, her dark eyes wary. She stepped back and bowed her head. "Your Highness."

"I'm here to see Princess Derya," Eliana said.

"Come in, come in," called Derya. "What are you waiting for?"

Eliana swept past the maid, motioning to Alessia to follow her in, but to wait by the door.

The tall, wide windows of Derya's room faced southeast. Late morning sun flooded the chamber, the white stone framing the windows shining in contrast to the brilliant crimson, onyx, and white mosaic on the floor.

Derya sprawled on the window seat, her eyelids drooping lazily. She wore an emerald green chemise belted with a gold scarf, and her dark hair fell loose around her shoulders. Her bare feet rested on a cushion, and she held a ceramic bowl of winter berries in her lap. Raising a disdainful eyebrow, she said, "I was wondering when you'd show up."

Matching Derya's haughty glare, Eliana moved deeper into the room. "I would have come to inquire about you sooner, had I been able," she said. "My parents practically locked me in my room yesterday and only allowed me to get up today."

"Sounds like my ambassador, danisman, and the captain of my guard," Derya said, rolling her eyes. "When one ran out of breath, the next started with another lecture about irresponsibility or some such nonsense."

A smile tugged at Eliana's lips. "Just like my parents."

"Well, you're here now, and right on time." Derya waved a hand at the assorted dishes spread over a side table pulled within arm's reach. Eliana's mouth watered as she noted the dates, figs, dried fruit, cheese, and pile of flatbread.

Clearly, Derya's appetite was in full force, just as her own was.

"Care to join me?" Derya asked.

Eliana nodded and eased into a cushioned chair. "Thank you. I ate not long ago, but I'm starving again."

"Good. It's not just me." Derya stuffed a dried apricot into her mouth. She studied Eliana's face as she chewed. "Did you know the magic would paralyze you?"

"I heard something about it, but I wasn't sure. It never happened before." Eliana toyed with the end of her long braid. "I'm so sorry."

The other princess swung startled eyes toward Eliana. "For what?"

"I risked your life, asking you to use your magic like that."

Derya's mouth tightened, and she ripped her gaze away. Her throat bobbed as she reached for a fig.

"Are you alright?" Eliana asked. "I mean, you don't seem like you have any ill effects from the other day."

"No, not anymore. You?"

"No." Eliana wasn't sure what else to say. "Thank you for helping me."

"Of course." Derya paused, her face flushing. "I was surprised you asked."

"I was surprised you suggested it."

Derya stared at the fig in her hand. "You probably thought I was too self-centered to even want to help someone in need." She waved the fig at Eliana. "Oh, don't try to deny it." Her shoulders rose in a self-deprecating shrug. "I know I wasn't very nice, but you were just so courteous and proper. No matter what I said, you didn't drop the flawless princess facade. Perfectly polite, vapid, and dull."

Eliana blinked, her face heating. How impudent and rude! "You made fun of everything I said. I had no reason to come up with something more interesting."

"I kept hoping you'd be provoked into breaching proto-col." Derya chuckled. "The Rider knows I tried. It was fun watching you choke back whatever you were thinking. More than that, I wish you'd just blurted it out. That could have been entertaining." She twisted her mouth. "What was worse than finding you were insufferable was my father's insistence that I be friends with you. 'No matter what she's like,' he said, 'become her confidante.'"

"If it makes you feel better, I had the same orders. I didn't like it any more than you did."

Wearing a slight smile, Derya surveyed Eliana. "But you showed yourself to be a girl so concerned for people in danger she sped down a ladder, tromped through the mud, and ignored the spatters on her pure white peplos. A girl who was willing to sacrifice herself for others. That girl would be a worthy friend."

Surprise kept Eliana from answering immediately. There was more to Derya than the supercilious brat Eliana had longed to throttle. "And the girl who overcame her fear to climb down a shaky ladder and bravely used her magic to risk her own life for people with no claim on her, that's a girl I'd be proud to call a friend." Eliana allowed her lips to curl into a smirk. "As long as she quits the condescending act."

Derya laughed. "I will if you'll stop being the perfect princess."

In answer, Eliana picked up a date, tossed it in the air, and caught it in her mouth. Then she matched Derya's laugh. What a relief to be herself around someone. She hadn't had this since Evander died.

Eliana stretched her feet out and stifled a yawn. She was still so tired. But not so sleepy that she couldn't do a little fishing for information. "Why is it so important for me to be your friend?" she asked. "The empire is much larger than Ymittos."

"But you are the farthest west, and your land extends far into the ocean. You'll be the first point of attack if Cetus attempts to conquer the continent again."

Cetus. Of course. The evil sorcerer who'd challenged the Rider of the Ancient Skies over a thousand years earlier. The Rider sent the powerful mage Pirseus to defend the continent of Ardebil. After a battle that changed the landscape forever, Cetus's bid to subjugate the continent failed. The Rider banished Cetus to an underwater realm, far to the west. Rumors had reached Ymittos that Cetus had little by little subdued the western continent. But none of them had even hinted at an invasion of Ardebil.

"What makes you think he'd going to do that?" Eliana asked. "He barely survived the last defeat."

"And has had a millennium to plot his revenge."

No trace of joking or scorn showed on Derya's face. So, Eliana thought, the emperor feared Cetus could rise again. And that Ymittos would be his first target. "So, we are your buffer?"

Derya shrugged. "You could put it that way. My father wants to make sure you remain our allies and aren't tempted to ally with Cetus."

Narrowing her eyes, Eliana considered that. Her father hadn't mentioned anything about Cetus in all his lectures about Cinar. And why would Derya so openly share her father's intentions? She didn't want to challenge Derya, not when the girl was finally treating her with courtesy. Choosing her words carefully, she asked, "You're not trying to annex us into the empire?"

"If we did that, we'd be obligated to protect you against Cetus. Oh, if he were to attack you, we'd come to your defense. But more to keep the war on your lands, not ours."

"Hmmm." Eliana wasn't certain she liked that arrangement, but it was something to discuss another day, after she'd verified that what Derya said was true. "If you want to sacrifice Ymittos for your safety, we'll need something in return."

"I expect nothing less." Derya stretched her arms above her head and yawned. "They tell me I slept two days without waking up once."

"Same with me," Eliana said. She shivered. "Back in the canal, by the time we finished, I couldn't move my arms and legs and I could hardly breathe."

"Me, too. My last thought was how angry my father would be if I died."

Eliana tipped her head to the side. "Are you allowed to use your magic?"

Derya shook her head. "Only the basics. Once I'm eighteen, I can practice more advanced skills with an experienced mage until I'm deemed capable. Then I'll be able to do what I want."

So, women in Cinar were permitted to wield magic on their own. Eliana clenched her teeth and pressed her lips together. In Ymittos, women could never use magic without a male mage present to supervise.

"You know," Derya said, "there's something that puzzles me."

"Oh?"

"When we started and I felt the weight of the water against my magic, I was sure we'd fail. The weight of it was too much. But then later, even after I started losing the sensation in my toes, something changed. Like I was infused with more power than I ever dreamed I had."

Eliana widened her eyes. "Me, too. But I didn't have time to think about it. I wonder what happened?"

"It's very strange." Derya frowned. "Is there anyone around here who would tell us?"

"My parents certainly won't. All they'll say is that I shouldn't be pursing magic anyway."

The two girls studied each other. Eliana felt Derya had the same burning need to understand the sudden rush of magic as she did.

"Sometimes, when people want to know things, they ask their tutors," Alessia offered from her place by the door.

"Why are you here?" Derya stared at the maid.

"I'm sorry," said Eliana. "I'm not permitted to go anywhere in the palace without her."

"Good thing I'm fun to be around." Alessia tossed her long black braid over her shoulder.

Derya raised her eyebrows. "Your maid talks to you like that?"

"She's the daughter of a distant cousin. Or something." Eliana shrugged. "Anyway, she occasionally has good ideas."

Studying Derya's face, Eliana mused that perhaps she could trust her. After all, Derya had shared her father's strategy. Maybe Eliana could share one of her own secrets. "Do you want to visit my tutor with me?"

A smile spread across Derya's face. "I feel the need to improve my mind. A visit to a tutor is just the thing."

"Tomorrow, then."

"Why not today?"

"Well, in case you've forgotten, it's my birthday. We have a banquet to attend tonight. And my father, once he stopped lecturing me about my heedless ways, told me to meet with him this afternoon in his private office."

"What for, to give you gifts? A land grant? Another title?"

"I don't know. Could be any of them."

"That reminds me," Derya said. "I never asked you what you want for your birthday. Jewels? Silks? I bought an ample supply of both, knowing we'd be here for your big day."

Derya prattled on about the treasures she'd picked out for Eliana before she left Cinar, but Eliana wasn't listening.

What did she want? To choose her own husband, without considering the politics, perhaps. Or to be free to explore her magic. Or to have Evander back. A knot of emptiness throbbed in her chest. Somehow, Eliana was sure she wasn't going to get any of them.

4

An hour later, Eliana paused at the door to her father's private office, its gold plating embossed with the arms of Ymittos, an eagle surrounded by twelve arrows pointing outwards. The eagle stood for the power of the Ymittosian kings, the arrows for the reach of her family's influence that extended far beyond the borders of the kingdom. And that power and influence were wielded by her father, who'd curtly summoned her to his presence.

She smoothed her pristine white peplos and swallowed to moisten her dry tongue, her mouth tasting as if she'd been eating moldy flour. Surely, she wasn't in trouble. But the wrathful scowl on the king's face when he ordered her to appear before him at this hour foretold an unpleasant conversation.

No. She was reading too much into her father's grim looks. Perhaps Derya was right, and the king had prepared a gift for her.

With a jerk of her chin, she signaled to Alessia to wait outside. If her father was about to rebuke her, one fewer witness would be preferable. She nodded to the guard standing on the left of the entrance. He pushed the door open. Eliana swept in, a broad smile fixed on her face.

And froze.

Instead of a beaming father, or even an angry one, she was greeted by a man who looked as though he'd lost his best friend, his wife, and all his cattle. If possible, his three companions appeared even more depressed. Eliana's mother huddled near her husband, eyes red-rimmed, lips pressed together, dejected, and silent. The thin shoulders of her father's most trusted advisor, Keerios Bazyli, slumped and the corners of his mouth pointed to the floor. A scribe wearing a funereal expression sat at a table in the corner.

What had happened? Her father hadn't looked so defeated when the northern barbarians had invaded and plundered an entire province.

The king waved her to a seat. "Sit, child, we have news for you."

Eliana dropped into a chair. "It must be horrible. You all look so glum."

"First, we want to congratulate you on your birthday." Her father's lips twitched in a feeble smile.

The tension flowed out of Eliana as she expelled the breath she'd been holding. "Merciful winds, you had me frightened for a moment. I was expecting the worst, like war on the northern border or a massive earthquake."

"That those things did not happen is the one fortunate part." Her father's barely-there smile drooped into a frown.

"Then what?"

"Let your father talk, dear." Her mother's voice trembled and was raspy, as if she'd been crying.

Eliana examined her father's face, noticing how lined it was, how worn he looked. Was he ill? She wished he'd hurry up and spill the lentils already.

He crossed his arms on the table in front of him. "Eliana, you turn eighteen today."

She wanted to interrupt and say she was well aware of the date, but knew her objection would only slow him down. He'd tell her in his own way, whatever the horrific tidings were.

"Ninety-nine years ago, Cetus cursed the kingdom of Malkh."

A shudder passed through Eliana at the mention of the name. Cetus. The evil sorcerer who ruled under the sea. The enemy of the Rider of the Ancient Skies. "Cursed? Why would he do that when he destroyed them a millennium ago?"

"No," her father said. "The people of Malkh didn't die."

"But Cetus collapsed their land…"

Her father waved a hand at his scribe. The white-haired man brought a large, yellowed scroll and laid it on the table. The king unrolled it. "Here is Ymittos."

Eliana scrutinized the map of Ardebil, the continent to the east of the Thyellodic Ocean. Ymittos, a jagged peninsula shaped like the open jaws of a wolf, extended into the sea from Ardebil's western coast. Rocky cliffs and countless islands fringed the peninsula, with mountains edging the eastern border where Ymittos connected to the continent. East of the mountains were Ymittos' two neighbors, the Cinarrian empire that sprawled over the central portion of the continent, and tiny Nafplio. Several wide rivers flowed from the mountains to the sea. The Bisaltes River carved a gentle curve through the center of the country and emptied into the ocean at Ymittos' capital, Ptolemaida.

Instead of a continuous line, the northernmost of the major rivers was drawn by a series of short dashes. These, Eliana knew, marked the remnants of the Qvirila River, which once flowed through the bygone kingdom of Malkh.

"We don't know what happened," her father said, tracing his finger along the buried river. "But one thousand years ago, when Cetus mounted his challenge against the Rider of the Ancient Skies and the kings the Rider had established, he centered his invasion on Malkh." He tapped the map.

"When Cetus realized he was going to lose, he unleashed his power. The Qvirila River sank under the ground and every human nearby was pulled down with it. No one ever climbed out of the rubble, so it was presumed they all perished."

Her tutors had conveyed this history to Eliana numerous times. So why review it again today? "They didn't all die?"

"No," her father answered. "Many survived and built a kingdom deep underground. Somehow, they allied with the water fae. For centuries, our ancestors were unaware of this. But as our people resettled the land that had been Malkh, odd legends arose."

"You mean about the half-goat, half-fish people?" Eliana snorted. "Those fables can't be true."

Her father scowled. "Legends have a way of capturing kernels of truth."

"What does this have to do with me?" Eliana asked.

"You. Yes." Her father puffed out a breath, pursing his lips. "Well, it seems that sinking the Qvirila River drained Cetus of most of his power. He retreated to his underwater kingdom. The legendary warrior Pirseus pursued him. With the help of the Rider, Pirseus and his allies laid spells to bind Cetus from leaving his lair."

The king sighed. "But the spells didn't last. It took Cetus six centuries to regather his power and break free. He rebuilt his armies. Sailors brought tales of Cetus's forces attacking shipping. Rumors told of Cetus raiding the continent beyond the setting sun. Entire countries drowned under tidal waves and their inhabitants enslaved, either on land or far under the ocean depths. We all prayed Cetus would be content with conquering those lands and leave us in peace."

The princess frowned. Everyone lived in fear that Cetus would rise and resume his quest to enslave the entire world and drown the dry lands under hundreds of fathoms of water. Now that she thought about it, hoping the sorcerer would limit himself to one continent ignored Cetus's insatiable appetite to devour and destroy.

Eliana's father rubbed his forehead. "Cetus assumed he'd annihilated the inhabitants of Malkh and only discovered he was wrong a hundred years ago. So, he put a curse on them. He cast the prince of Malkh into an enchanted sleep. He can only be woken by a princess who will inherit the kingdom that controls what had been the territory of Malkh."

"I see." She really didn't. "So, um, what, is the prince still asleep?"

"Yes. Until you, no princess has stood to inherit."

Eliana's stomach clenched, forcing the air from her lungs. She slapped a hand to her mouth as her eyes flared wide. *Surely he's not saying what I think I heard.* The room blurred in a haze, and she had the sensation that the walls were spinning around her. The princess squeezed her eyes shut, then opened them to lock her gaze on her father. "*I* am the curse breaker?" Heat surged up her neck, burning her face, and she drew her eyebrows together. "Why am I just learning of this now?"

Her mother made a half-hearted shrug. "Because we didn't want it to be a burden. We'd hoped that someone else would break it."

"That seems like a foolish hope. Who else but me is heir to the kingdom?"

"Don't jump to conclusions before you hear the entire story," her father said.

"Then tell me," Eliana spat out.

He crossed his arms. "I'm not sure you are mature enough to handle it."

"Archelaos, please," Eliana's mother whispered. "We need to tell her everything."

5

———————

"Your Wisdom," Keerios Bazyli said, his deep voice smooth and placating. "I agree with Queen Vasiliki. The princess should know what lies ahead."

Her father's nostrils flared. "Very well. The curse can only be broken within fifteen days of the princess turning eighteen." He spit the words out as if they burned his tongue.

Fifteen days wasn't much time to break a century-old enchantment. "Or else what?" Eliana asked, indignation sharpening her tone.

The king's voice tightened. "Through dark spells woven into the curse, Cetus will conquer Malkh and enslave all who live there."

She looked from her father to her mother to Keerios Bazyli. "You mean the former lands of Malkh that are now part of our kingdom?"

"No, highness, the underground realm where the Malkhians live now," the keerios answered.

Eliana tapped her finger on the map where Malkh used to be. "Why does that concern us?"

"Because," Bazyli said, "the curse doesn't stop there. It also states that Ymittos will share in Malkh's fate. We've debated for decades, but the only meaning we can find is the obvious one."

Eliana glanced from Bazyli to her father, her eyebrows lifted.

The king nodded. "Yes, our realm would be destroyed, and our people enslaved."

Her lips parted, and she stared at her father, incredulous. They knew about this threat to Ymittos her whole life, yet didn't see fit to tell her, the heir and fated cursebreaker? "But—"

Her father cut her off. "Allow the keerios to finish."

Her jaw tightened and she pressed her lips together, limiting her outward reaction to a scowl.

Bazyli continued. "In the final line of the curse, Cetus says nothing will stop him from taking the rest. We believe that means he'll go after Cinar and all of Ardebil."

The princess jabbed a finger at the map. "So, if no one breaks the curse, Cetus will swoop in and conquer the entire continent? But we'd fight back. As would Cinar."

Bazyli shrugged. "Who knows what power evil sorcerers wield? Somehow, he must have infused the enchantment with a series of spells that would render us powerless to defeat him."

Unable to believe what she was hearing, Eliana leaned back in her chair, staring at the map. Her mouth filled with sour sand, and she swallowed hard. "This has got to be a hoax." The princess shook her head. "No. If Cetus can cast spells to enslave entire nations, why bother with a hundred-year-old curse?"

Bazyli traced a finger over the spiky coastline of Ymittos. "To magically enslave an entire nation, well, that demands the use of dark magic with tremendous force behind it. Cetus must have infused the curse with much of his power so that he could seize Malkh and Ymittos with one lethal, crushing blow. Perhaps he's toying with his prey, thinking he's grown so strong no one can oppose him. Or has he used the hundred years to accumulate power so that if his curse fails, he'll still be assured of victory?"

"It could be any or all of those," snapped the king. "The point is, my daughter has to shatter the curse or all of us, Ymittosians, Cinarrians, Tinaxians, whoever, will either die or become slaves in his underwater realm."

A sudden thought jerked Eliana's attention from the map. "What happens if someone does break the curse? Ymittos will remain free, right?"

Bazyli rested his hand over the gentle curve of the Bisaltes River, as if caressing Ymittos's heartland. "All we know for a certainty is that Cetus won't immediately enslave Ymittos and Malkh."

The king shifted in his seat, making the wood creak under him. "Without a doubt, Cetus won't give up his ambition to conquer everything under the sky and submerge the land under the sea. He'll invade Ardebil, starting with Ymittos and Malkh. And we presume he's used his time well. His last army was not only men but nightmare creations, twisted versions of predators of the deep. Who knows what horrors he'll unleash this time."

Eliana twisted her shaking fingers together. She did not want the burden of holding back Cetus's invasion. Lifting a curse with no inkling of how was impossible. This had to be some fantastic tale. She frowned at her father. "How do we know this is true?"

King Archelaos let out a long sigh. He raised a finger and gestured to the scribe. The man brought over a small, tattered scroll, placed it in front of Eliana, and carefully unrolled it.

"Shortly after the enchantment took hold, the king of the lower realm sent couriers to my great-grandfather, Eskander the Sixth," her father said. "Like you, Eskander didn't believe the story. More messengers came. He still didn't believe."

The king's shoulders drooped. "No one believed. My own

father told me the tale, showed me the scroll, and laughed. Just as Eskander had, we deemed it nonsense, an elaborate hoax dreamed up by madmen, especially because no one heard anything from the Malkhians for centuries. So, no one bothered to tell any of our neighbors about it. Why waste our breath repeating meaningless tripe?"

He rubbed his forehead. "Over the years, sailors brought tales of Cetus's growing army, and how one by one, the countries of the western continent were falling to his control. We told ourselves those wars were far away. That Cetus would never dare to set foot anywhere on the continent of Ardebil, not after the Rider of the Ancient Skies banished him." He shook his head and shrugged. "Besides, in every generation, there was a son to inherit. Even if we believed in the curse, we had no one to break it."

Eliana looked from the king's grim face to her mother's tear-streaked cheeks. "What made you believe it now?"

Her father let out a long breath. He looked at Eliana with what she thought was pity. "When you were born, a messenger came from Cetus, congratulating us. He offered to nullify the curse himself if we pledged you in marriage to him so he could have you as his queen. Naturally, we declined. And prayed fervently, desperately, for a son to inherit the kingdom. One never came."

Ice-cold fear seized Eliana's limbs. Silence swallowed the room, broken only by the crackling of the fire and her mother's sobs. Eliana's mind was a blizzard of conflicting thoughts. Why hadn't they bothered to verify if the curse was real? Why had no one thought to aid the western continent to repel Cetus's attacks? Why was she the one to break the curse? She could no more capture one idea any more than she could hold a snowflake in her hand. Any logic or reason melted in the face of the horrible truth.

"Perhaps, if I may suggest, we tell Princess Eliana the exact wording of the curse?" Bazyli asked.

Grateful for an end to the dreadful silence, Eliana sat bolt upright. "Yes, please. That would be helpful."

The scribe handed her a yellowed scroll with tattered edges. The letters were written in an odd script, upright characters with loops above or below. "I can't read this," she said.

"Of course not," the king replied. "That is Old Malkhian." He motioned to the scribe, who handed Eliana another scroll.

She dropped the first and unrolled the second. This, too, was penned in a script unfamiliar to her. A closer look made her realize it was Middle Ymittosian, the alphabet used a century ago. Slowly, she read the words aloud.

"Heir of Malkh, I curse you to sleep for a hundred years.

My spells already weave through your land, building in power until the century expires. Then Malkh will drown.

The fortunate among your people will perish beneath the waves. The unfortunate who survive will be my slaves under the sea. Their minds will be tools in my hands to be used whichever way I choose, shackled to my will and mine alone. The truly unfortunate will be my toys, taken apart and reformed, grafted with ferocious creatures of both sea and land, to become weapons of terror in my army.

Heir of Malkh, only one can save you: an unwed maid of eighteen years, heir to the realm that now rules your land. A day short of eighteen will not do, nor can she be more than a fortnight and one day past her eighteenth birthday. She alone must find you and she alone is able to wake you.

If either father or brother accompany her, she has no hope of success.

If she cannot brave the dangers of the dark or fails, her realm will share the fate of yours. As for the defeated cursebreaker, I have plans for her. Personal and intimate plans.

If no one wakes you within the hundred years, then the magic of my curse will release. Your kingdom and the one above will be mine.

And nothing will stop me from taking the rest."

Eliana's hands fell limply into her lap. Her shoulders sagged and her pulse throbbed in her ears. She stared, unseeing, unable to blink. *Personal and intimate plans*. Spots danced before her eyes and a knot formed in her gut. She cringed, pressing her fingers to her mouth to hold in a scream. After a long moment, she pulled in a shaky breath and turned to her mother. "This is a forgery, right?" She wrapped her arms around herself. "Tell me this isn't real."

Queen Vasiliki spoke gently. "The offer to wed you came with Cetus's seal, brought by an enchanted seagull with a woman's head. Once we saw that, we knew the threat about merging humans with beasts to create monsters was not empty words. Which meant the rest had to be true." Tears glistened in the corners of the queen's eyes, pity and grief overflowing to spill over her cheeks.

The quavering in Eliana's stomach turned into writhing, the sour taste in her mouth mixing with bitter bile. She clenched her shaking hands into fists and ground her teeth. "You knew about this my entire life and did nothing?" Eliana curled her lip.

"No, of course not." The king glared at her. "What do you take us for? After we received that message, I sent an expedition to the rift where the old Qvirila River had flowed. They built a tower and ventured down."

"What good would that do?" Eliana rubbed the back of her sweating neck and sniffed.

"We wanted to ask the Malkhians what they knew." The king sighed. "None of those who descended came back."

"Merciful winds! That's all you did?" Eliana spit out.

Her father scowled. "No. Just listen, will you?" He closed his eyes briefly, the wrinkles that framed his mouth deepening as if the weight of the threats tugged at his skin. "Our most talented and powerful mages were part of the expedition. They verified that dark spells had been cast over Malkh, dark spells that were unlike any power they'd ever encountered before. No one had any idea how to break those spells. Since then, they've been scouring our archives for counterspells. To no avail."

"I prayed, I begged the Rider for someone else," Queen Vasiliki said. "Anyone, anything to save my girl from this doom. He didn't answer." She let out a sobbing breath. "You have to break the curse."

Icy fear chased angry heat through Eliana's limbs, draining her strength. It all seemed hopeless. "But how?"

Her father spoke gently. "We don't know. You'll have to find the prince and then figure it out."

Down into Malkh? Into the dark with the savage water fae, their teeth like knives? Where monsters prowled, half goat and half fish? Her stomach twisted and her palms dampened. Her heart thumped like the hoofbeats of a galloping horse fleeing a fearsome beast. Every instinct screamed at her to run away. "No."

Her father's eyebrows shot up. "No?"

"No. I'm not going." Sweat trickled down the back of her neck.

An old memory made her breath hitch. Her cousin Ormolai had lured Eliana into the lower wine cellar on the guise of exploring the castle's subterranean levels for secret passages. She descended a rickety ladder, thinking he would be right behind. Instead, Ormolai taunted her, saying she'd never find her way out. His mocking laugh drowned out her pleas as he slammed the trap door shut.

At first, she thought he'd relent after a few minutes. But when the chill damp of the cellar made her toes grow numb, she realized he'd abandoned her. She screamed for her parents, for Evander, her guards, until she lost her voice. Then she wandered in the dark, dragging her fingers along the rough stone on the side of the corridor, fighting her urge to sob. Her stomach writhed at the memory of the danger she'd faced down before Evander and her guard Dimitris found her. Ormolai, to her relief, had been banished for his stunt. But she never could banish her fear of the dark. Just imagining underground spaces made her heart pound and her palms sweat. "No."

"If you don't," her father said, "Cetus will destroy Ymittos and enslave all our people." He gave her a stern look. "Eliana, you need to think about your duty."

"I have." Eliana jerked her chin up and leaned toward the king. "If this is a magical curse, then it will take magic to break it. You've not let me learn to use my magic, so what good will I be?" She crossed her arms and lifted her chin. No, she was not going on some fruitless quest. "And besides, I only have air and light magic. A wielder of stone and water would do much better underground."

"Light magic would be useful in the dark," Bazyli put in.

She glared at him. "How will I figure out how to break the curse if no one else knows? Journeying there impulsively without a specific plan seems unwise to me."

Her mother, at least, caught her rebuke. "This is different."

Eliana tightened her arms around her ribs. "Nothing you say will persuade me to reconsider."

Her father leaned back in his chair, resting his head against the carved frame. "If you are so set against it, we could find someone else to make the attempt."

"What do you mean?" Eliana frowned. "Are you planning to get rid of me and have another daughter?"

"Certainly not. There's no time, anyway. The hundred years will end in two months." A muscle twitched in the king's jaw. "We could place ourselves under the protection of the emperor."

Eliana gasped. "What, give up our independence?"

"It would mean you wouldn't have to be the cursebreaker." Her father gripped the armrests of his chair, his knuckles whitening.

A glimmer of hope, like a single firefly on a mountain,

sparked within her. She wouldn't be forced into the dark. There was a way out. She wouldn't be doomed to endure life as Cetus's plaything. *But.* "No, but Princess Derya would." Eliana studied her father's face. "Was this why you insisted I become friends with Derya? Not so I would have an ally when we both ruled, but so I would serve an overlord who would regard me favorably."

Heaviness descended on her, a weight that shattered her illusions of her father. She'd honored him as a just sovereign. Now he proved himself to be as cunning as a bandit chief. He knew that her sense of honor would prevent her from slipping out of her duty. She sucked in her cheeks and bit down on them. She was the goat being readied for sacrifice. And like the priests who readied the animal, her parents were giving no thought to what the sacrifice had to say about the matter.

The queen covered Eliana's hand with her own. "This is a decision that bears thinking over. We do have a little time."

"Do you think I should go?"

"I do. Cetus must be thwarted. Do not underestimate him." Her mother looked into Eliana's eyes, her own dark eyes filled with gentle pleading. "Please, give it some thought."

Eliana stared back at her. "I'll think about it." *But I'm not changing my mind.*

Her father relaxed his grip on his chair's armrests. "I'll give you to the end of the week. Just swear on your word you won't tell the Princess of Cinar. Not yet." He took a deep breath. "But remember. The fate of Ymittos rests on you."

6

"If you'll excuse me." Eliana pulled in a shaky breath, tore her gaze from her mother's tear-stained face, and pretended she didn't hear the king's demand for her to stay. She had to be alone with her thoughts.

When the princess burst out of the king's office, she startled the two guards and Alessia. She jerked her head at her maid in a silent command for the girl to follow. Without waiting to see if she understood, Eliana sprinted down the marble corridor and bounded up the wide staircase. Her footsteps echoed like the beats of a warning drum.

Panting, she burst through the doors of the library and sped to an alcove screened by a towering bookshelf filled with ancient scrolls and pottery. She flung herself onto a divan and buried her face in her hands.

"Highness, what happened?" Alessia asked through her gasps for air.

"Find a book and read it." Eliana spoke harshly, more harshly than she intended. But she couldn't make any sense of the turmoil within. And until she could, she wasn't going to talk to anyone.

The scraping of a chair over the tiled floor suggested that

for once, Alessia followed orders without questions. Eliana scrubbed a hand over her face and leaned into the cushions. What had happened?

Her parents had known about this curse and never told her. Eliana's hands curled into fists, fingernails digging into the flesh of her palms. She wanted to throw something. *Merciful winds, how could they have hidden such a monstrous fate from me?* Yes, they were being protective. An icy shudder ripped through her core, cramping her stomach. No wonder they didn't want to burden her. *Personal and intimate plans.* That knowledge would have been a blight, indeed.

Had he known, Evander would have stormed Cetus's lair, even though that was the path to certain death. She would have become even more reckless, jumping from every cliff she could find, wondering if splattering herself on sharp rocks would be better than life as Cetus's slave, kept for his private amusement.

While her parents shielded her from the truth, giving her a happy childhood free of the shadow of curses and doom, they dumped a dangerous task on her, giving her little time to prepare. She pounded her fist on her thigh. They should have encouraged her to explore her magical abilities.

A sleet storm of thoughts assaulted her mind. The curse must be why her parents had fostered her relationship with Evander. Now that he was gone, they were pushing her into an early betrothal for the same reason. So that she'd have someone committed to her, someone determined to protect her and ensure she returned from Malkh.

Bile burned the back of her throat, and she curled her lips into a snarl. Before she agreed to anything, she needed to know what her father had offered this fourth son of the Diodochi of Nafplio to entice him to venture into the perilous underground realm. Her heart skipped a beat. Had the king promised to name him the ruler of Ymittos if he helped break the curse? No. Her father would never do that.

Or would he? Her mouth filled with the bitter taste of unripe olives, denial warring against a stinging hint of betrayal.

She repressed the urge to grab a vase and fling it into the fire. All this speculation would have to wait for tomorrow, when she'd tackle her tutor first, then her father. In the meantime, she had a birthday banquet to attend.

EARLY THE NEXT MORNING, Eliana strode through chilly marble corridors and bolted up a narrow flight of stairs. Her mind teemed with the revelations from the day before, thoughts of curses, monsters and underground realms that clouded any joy she would have found in her birthday. Throughout the banquet, she'd moved as if in a fog, barely able to taste the lavish food or respond to well-wishers. That she'd had to pretend she was delighted by the jugglers, dancers, and musicians made it even more insufferable.

"Raging waters! What's the rush?" Derya called from halfway down the staircase.

Eliana peered over her shoulder. "We don't have much time." She hadn't told Derya about the curse and wasn't sure she would. But at least she could get some answers about magic. Answers she needed more now than ever. "Hurry."

Derya huffed her way up the steps. "If you say so, Highness. But I don't understand what's going on. Yesterday, everyone looked like they were preparing for the plague, not a birthday banquet. You certainly didn't seem enthused about it. Now you're running as if you're chasing the moon."

Alessia staggered up and stood a few steps below, panting. "I've never known you to be so eager for lessons before."

Ignoring their comments, Eliana led them to a sunny room on the southeast side of the palace, one with a commanding view of the city's temples, theaters, and markets below. In the distance, the winter sun twinkled on the ocean's waves.

She motioned for Alessia to sit by the door and advanced toward the room's sole occupant.

A man in his early forties sat at a table covered with scrolls, maps, and reeds. White strands mingled in his wavy ebony hair and a black band held it away from his face. Jagged scars ran from his eyes to his chin, marring his olive skin. A crutch was propped next to his table.

When Eliana approached, he smiled broadly, the skin around his eyes crinkling. "Highness. I didn't expect you today."

Just seeing her tutor lightened her mood. "Keerios Corban, how could I shirk my time with you?"

The keerios snorted. "Quite easily. I haven't seen much of you since your royal visitor arrived. I assumed you were still recovering from your last outing with Princess Derya. Or that the pair of you had turned to less taxing diversions."

How much had he heard about the day at the canal? She chose to respond to his first statement. "I apologize for that. Quite remiss of me." Eliana turned to Derya. "Princess Derya, my tutor, Corban."

"Your Highness, I am honored." He moved as if to stand, but Derya gestured for him to remain seated.

"Keerios Corban, the honor is mine."

"So, I am blessed with two princesses as students. What subject shall we delve into today?" He waved the girls to the stools in front of his table. "History? Mathematics? Or have your interests turned to canal engineering?" He raised his eyebrows.

"You heard." Eliana's face warmed, and she dropped her eyes. He probably thought her an impulsive simpleton.

"How could I not? Everyone was talking about it." He didn't seem to be angry, but his lips compressed into a thin line.

Eliana squirmed in her seat, well familiar with his disapproving expression. "I had to do something. Princess Derya was gracious enough to help."

"That was a foolish but heroic and impressive use of magic."

"Please." Eliana raised her hand. "My parents lectured me for an hour."

Derya leaned forward. "While we were performing our foolish magic, as you say, we both felt a sudden increase in the power. More than either of us knew we had."

Corban stiffened and blinked a few times, but remained silent.

"I never knew a surge of power like that was possible," Eliana said. "What was that?"

Corban raised his bushy eyebrows. "You realize I have not been commissioned to teach such matters. Your parents would be most displeased."

Eliana flicked her gaze from him to Derya. He was right to hesitate. She'd sworn to never let anyone other than Alessia in on the secret about their magic lessons, lessons that went beyond theory into actual practice.

"They'd be more displeased if I accidentally hurt myself," Eliana said. "As would Derya's. How can we control the magic if we don't know why it surges so powerfully?"

Eyes locked on Eliana's, Corban spoke in a low voice. "You do know I risk myself every time I discuss this with you."

She reached across the table to grasp his scarred hand. "I do. And I appreciate it. More than you know."

"I hope so." Corban pulled his hand out of hers and held up a finger. "First, you must understand the cost of magic." He gave them a wry smile. "I believe you both have first-hand knowledge of that."

"You mean the paralysis?" Eliana asked.

"Yes. As you use your power, it drains your strength. The first sign is losing the feeling in your toes. Am I right?"

Eliana and Derya exchanged looks. "Yes, we both felt that," Eliana said.

"As you use more magic, the paralysis spreads. The danger is that it can reach your lungs, leaving you unable to breathe. Or it could stop your heart."

Derya nodded soberly. "So that's why I was gasping for air when I passed out."

"Which is what saved your life. You stopped using the magic, so your strength had a chance to replenish, and the paralysis receded. In both your cases, it took nearly two days. But imagine you're in a battle. You burn out your power and fall, paralyzed and unconscious. What would your enemy do then?"

"Cut off my head, I suppose," said Derya.

"Right. So, you need to understand your limits."

"But how do we do that?" Eliana asked.

"Through practice." Corban let out a slow breath. "Which is why I've risked my life to teach you. I don't want you experimenting on your own, only to end up burning yourself out."

Eliana winced. She'd need to be careful not to expose him.

Corban crossed his arms on the table. "Are we clear on why you shouldn't use your magic without an experienced mage by your side? It's so you don't push beyond the limits of your power." He rested his eyes on Eliana. "Do you understand?"

She nodded.

"Good. Now, Eliana, what can you do with your air magic?"

"I can make a wind blow, so strong it moves heavy objects. And—" her breath hitched, "make a puff of air to break my fall." She hadn't tried that since the day Evander died. Why, oh why, did she ever think exploring the limits of that particular ability was a good idea?

"Good," Corban said. "And what does your light magic do?"

Derya's eyes snapped wide. "You have light magic?"

"I do. All I can do with it is to create illumination."

"You have two powers." Derya twisted her mouth into a pout. "I've only got water."

"Water is a powerful magic," Corban said. "What do you know about using it?"

"I can create waves, and using them, push water away from myself." She tipped her head to the side and frowned. "But water mages can do so much more. I've seen them pull water from the ground, freeze, purify, or muddy it. And some use it to induce vomiting."

Eliana laughed. "That could be useful."

"It could indeed," Corban said. "Suppose you ingested poison. The power of water magic could be the only thing that keeps you alive."

"Keerios Corban, this is very interesting." Derya spoke respectfully, but an insistent tone crept into her voice. "However, it doesn't answer our question. Why did we both have a surge of power?"

"And why can mages do so many things with the same magic?" Eliana asked. "I've heard that air magic can heat or cool the air or create something like ropes with it. And light magic can create a mist. Why can't I do those things?"

"Many would say women aren't capable of using the magic in any but the simplest ways," Corban answered.

"Because no one will teach them," Eliana said.

"Because overuse of magic, so they say, can kill an unborn child." Corban sighed. "Or interfere with the ability to conceive. That's why most women are barred from using magic until they've passed the age of bearing children."

Derya frowned. "I've never heard that. Women aren't restricted from magic in Cinar once they come of age."

Corban lifted an eyebrow. "Perhaps women's bodies are different here."

From his sarcastic tone, Eliana guessed he didn't agree

with the restrictions on women. She bit her lip. "If women in Cinar can use magic, why not here?"

"Many also believe that women are too emotional to use their power."

Eliana scowled. "Why is that? Do emotions play a part in one's ability to control the magic?"

"Well," Corban said, "I suppose fear could prevent you from thinking rationally about what you're doing, causing you to go too far and paralyze yourself."

"That could happen to anyone," Derya said.

"True. But magic is hard to control. You know that yourselves."

The two princesses exchanged a long look.

"That sudden rush of magic was so strong," Derya said. "I began to think we could save them all, and I didn't want to quit." She shook her head. "I'm not sure I could have pulled back."

"Same here. Please, Corban, tell us." Eliana opened her eyes wide, pleading with him. "What was that extra power?"

Corban bent his head and stared at the table. Eliana's heart sank. He was going to refuse to answer.

After several long minutes, he sighed. "You put me in a hard position. There is much I think you both need to know because you possess strong powers." He rubbed a hand over his brow. "I've argued with your father many times, telling him you need this knowledge, and not just because you will rule one day. He expressly ordered me not to tell you, not until he decided the time was right."

Eliana sagged on her stool. She'd be forty before her father relented.

"But you taught me some before, and let me practice a little," she said.

"And how did that turn out for you? For Evander?"

His words hit her like she'd been dunked in an icy lake. He was right. She'd abused her power and Evander died.

"Your father was furious. He questioned everyone, including me, as to how you could wield such complex air magic. Ultimately, he concluded that Evander himself had taught you."

Which was the truth. She'd shared every lesson with Evander. Whether history, mathematics, rhetoric, archery, or fencing, they'd learned everything together. And the only lessons Eliana was excluded from—magic—Evander made sure he taught her all he knew.

Corban's shoulders drooped. "While you were sleeping off the results of your last escapade, the king interrogated us all again. Me, most of all. This time, no one could insinuate that Evander had anything to do with it." He shot a look at Derya. "Since you have water magic, no one believed you'd taught Eliana anything about air magic. The king issued a decree. Anyone found teaching more than the basic theory of magic to his daughter would be imprisoned for twenty years, then banished. Unless that person died in prison first."

With a shiver, Eliana realized how risky their questions were for Corban. If it weren't for the curse, she'd seek answers elsewhere. But the fortnight would pass all too soon, and she had no time to find another source. If Corban refused her, they'd all be doomed. She to the worst fate of all.

7

———

Eliana's chin drooped as she crossed her arms, gripping her elbows until she winced from the pain. Just when she thought Corban was going to give her some answers, he'd pulled back.

She clamped her jaw tight, repressing the pleading words that begged to leap from her mouth while she scrutinized her tutor's face. She knew that look of resolve, the tight lips and steady gaze. But did his tapping fingers betray a trace of indecision?

"Keerios Corban," Eliana said slowly, "I understand your reluctance. But you have always taught me that knowledge holds as much strength as any physical skill. And as a woman, I must gain all the knowledge I can. Otherwise, how can I hope to overcome the perils of ruling?"

His eyes flickered and he gazed down. She pressed her advantage. "I know going against my father's orders is unthinkable. But you've told me that when confronted with a problem, I should think the unthinkable. This is one of those times."

The keerios picked up a quill and toyed with it, a tiny

smile on his face. "That's an interesting way of twisting an academic principle of discovery and invention."

She knew him well enough to remain silent, to give him the time he needed to reach his decision.

After a long moment, during which Eliana thought her heart would thump its way out of her chest, he dropped the quill. "I will not have you face your destiny unprepared." His gaze clamped onto hers. "You can never tell anyone how you gained this knowledge. Am I clear?"

Eliana restrained herself from grinning and bouncing in her chair. She nodded soberly. "I promise."

Turning his eyes to Derya, Corban raised his eyebrows. "Princess Derya?"

Derya placed her right fist over her heart, the first two fingers extended. "You have my word as a Cinarrian."

Corban tipped his head back and stared at the ceiling. "Rider forgive me for disobeying my lord." He rubbed his hands together. "But time is short, and you need to be proficient in wielding your powers."

His reference to time sent a shiver down Eliana's spine. Fifteen days, and they'd be at Cetus's mercy. Unless she ventured into the dark world of Malkh. She forced her attention back to her tutor.

"You do realize," Corban said, his eyes flicking from one princess to the other, "that you displayed not just an impressive amount of power, but at a level very few have attained."

"How can that be?" Eliana asked. "Women have less power than men."

Derya snorted. "Is that what they told you?"

"Unfortunately," Corban said, "someone has misled Princess Eliana. Since our laws don't permit women in Ymittos to develop their powers, it only follows that they don't explore the limits of what they can do."

Eliana's skin tingled. She must have more power than she suspected. But why had this been kept from her?

A grin erupted on Derya's face. "Imagine what we could do if we tried."

Corban waved a finger at her. "Magic is not a toy, Highness."

The smile slid away, replaced by a sheepish expression.

The tutor continued. "It's not surprising that you two possess so much power. To begin with, you're both royal. How do you think your ancestors came to rule in the first place?"

"They had the most magic?" Eliana replied.

"Exactly. You both have deep natural reserves of power." He fixed a glowering stare on Eliana. "Which is another reason your actions at the canal diggings were foolish. Imagine, if you will, the ruler of a smaller country has ambitions. Then he learns of a princess with extraordinary powers. He might decide it's worth kidnapping her and taking her as his bride in the hopes his offspring will inherit the magic."

Eliana gulped. She never dreamed of that possibility. Could that be one reason Cetus had *plans* for her? Derya's eyes were wide, and her olive skin turned pale.

"Don't look so stricken," Corban said. "King Archelaos made sure all the foreign ambassadors and envoys knew there were many water and air mages involved in the rescue. Hopefully, that will be enough to cast doubt on the fantastical tale of two young girls preventing a dam break with their magic. As far as what really occurred the other day," he squared his shoulders and folded his hands on the table, "explain what happened right before your power surged. Every little detail, no matter how insignificant."

"We'd saved all but the last three men." Eliana tipped her head to the side, picturing the scene. "I spotted a tiny boat and thought if I could push it to the men, they could climb in. Then we could let the water flow. I was losing the feeling in my legs, and knew we had to hurry."

"That's right," Derya said. "By then, every breath was a struggle."

"I pulled some of my air magic from the dam and hurled it at the boat. Moving it was easier than I thought." She flipped her palms up and twitched her shoulders in half a shrug. "I had no idea I controlled that much power."

Corban held up a hand. "Stop. What precisely did you do when you pulled your power back from the dam to move the boat? What did you feel? See? Sense?"

Eliana scrunched up her face. "Nothing." She nibbled her lower lip as she struggled to remember. "I was sweating. I remember because I licked my lips and tasted salt."

"Hm. And you, Highness?"

Derya stared at him. "Eliana pulled her magic back. I thought the effort of holding the water by myself would kill me. Everything went misty, and I felt faint. I must have bitten my lip because the pain jerked me back awake."

His eyebrows raised, Corban shifted in his seat. "Did you draw blood when you bit yourself?"

"Yes. But what does that have to do with anything?"

"Blood, like sweat, contains salt."

Eliana exchanged a confused glance with Derya.

Corban smiled. "Salt is one of the nine amplifiers of magical power."

"Amplifiers?" Eliana's jaw slackened.

"Some call them modifiers, others say extenders," Corban explained. "The words don't matter."

Derya jerked upright. "You can strengthen your power?"

"Yes," Corban answered. "A small taste of an amplifier will magnify your power, and in some cases, focus the magic. This enables you to use the magic to do things you couldn't otherwise do."

"So, the salt made me more powerful?" Eliana asked.

"It enabled you to move more air with a greater force than you could normally, yes."

"And my water?" Derya asked.

"Salt intensifies the action of waves," Corban said. "It

allowed you to push the water more forcefully, creating bigger waves in the opposite direction. Which had the effect of lessening the pressure on the dam."

"What about my light magic?" Eliana asked.

"Salt will intensify or focus whatever light you have created."

Eliana's heart sped up. If she could amplify her powers, she'd be better equipped to face the dangers of Malkh. She rested a quizzical gaze on her tutor's face. "Why didn't you tell me this before?"

"Wasn't it enough that I allowed you to practice, even when it was forbidden?" He shook his head. "I knew that if I didn't, Evander would teach you all he was learning. I thought it was far better for me to educate you in the proper way to use your power than to correct sloppy habits he might pass on to you."

Guilt swamped Eliana at the mention of Evander. He'd given in to her constant teasing and pleading about magic. And ended up dead because of it.

Corban looked at Derya. "You didn't know these things because in Cinar, they only share this knowledge with those over eighteen, when they presume people are mature enough to handle the increased power."

Derya nodded. "Keerios Corban, you mentioned amplifiers. Does that mean things other than salt can amplify powers?"

"Yes."

"And these other amplifiers modify the magic so you can do more than simple manipulation of the element?"

"Yes."

Eliana grimaced, trying to pull a question from her jumbled thoughts. Derya didn't appear to have that problem.

"Which amplifier do water mages use to induce vomiting?" she asked.

"If there's one bit of knowledge that should be kept from

you, that's it." Eliana chuckled, imagining Derya causing unwelcome guests to suddenly become ill. "Keerios Corban, I only tasted a trace of salt. How much is necessary?"

"As you discovered, only a small amount. Just enough to create the taste in your mouth. Too much, and the amplifier might not work."

"Do you have any salt?" Eliana asked. "I want to practice."

Corban closed his eyes and shook his head. He sighed and turned troubled eyes on Eliana. "Highness, I beseech you, don't experiment. If your father found out…"

Eliana's chest squeezed tight around her heart. Corban had opened a new world for her and now was begging her not to enter it. But he had a good reason. She couldn't risk his life for her curiosity.

"I understand," she said.

Derya leaned forward. "That is ridiculous. We can learn to control our magic. The risks are worth it."

She had a point, but it would be better to err on the side of caution, Eliana decided, at least until her parents calmed down. She resolved to do what she always did. Sacrifice a little and find the middle ground between what her parents wanted and what she needed. As the heir, she lived a life of compromise. *May as well get some more practice.* "I'm willing to wait a bit," she said. *But not for long. I've got a sorcerer to defeat.*

"Thank you, Princess Eliana." Corban let out a long sigh. "And while the risks of learning are great, the other risks you'll be facing are greater still."

What did he mean by that? Was he referring to the dangers any ruler faced, or did he know about the curse? His expression was inscrutable. She'd have to ask him later when they were alone. If anyone would tell her the full story, it would be him. "I'll make sure my parents understand that since I am now eighteen, I will study the theory of magic so I know how it works. All in the name of being prepared to rule. That will take care of one risk."

She ignored the curl of Derya's lip.

"Theory?" the other princess asked. "You'll be content with that?"

Corban gave Eliana an approving nod. "Very sensible of you, Highness." He dug through a stack of books. "Here." He handed her a worn, slim volume. "This covers the basics of how to augment the magic with different tastes."

Eliana stared at him. "You're going to let us read that?"

"Why, yes. It's better than having you experiment with every animal, vegetable, and mineral you can think of." He scowled at them. "Be sure you pay attention to the limits of what you can control. I don't want to hear about any clandestine practice sessions getting out of hand." He gestured to his face and withered leg. "The consequences can be permanent."

Eliana sucked in a breath. He was right. She'd have to be very careful.

"If you value me at all," Corban continued, "you will not let anyone see you with that book." He bit his lip. "And for the love of the Rider, never tell anyone that I even hinted that amplifiers, once mastered, could be combined into powerful spells. That's very tricky magic for only the most skilled and experienced mages." He curved his mouth into a wry smile. "If we are found out, I hope this doesn't cause too much trouble for you. And that you'll visit me in the dungeon."

Running her fingers over the worn cover of the book, Eliana could hardly believe she now had a path to learning what she wanted to know. Corban had as much as given her permission to experiment on her own while making it appear he'd forbidden it. And his references to spells were intriguing. Was that how Cetus laid his curse? Whatever the answer to that question, she'd have to make sure Corban's actions didn't consign him to a sunless, damp cell in the dungeons.

With a grunt, Corban stood and reached for his crutch. "I feel the need for some refreshment," he said. "So, I'll leave you to read for half an hour. Then we'll turn our attention to the history of Nafplio. Agreed?"

While Eliana had hoped to have the afternoon to study the book, this was better than nothing. She nodded as she watched her tutor limp across the room and out of the door before she opened the book. "Let's review air magic first," she said. She gently turned the pages and then read aloud: "Intensifying the power must be done with extreme caution."

"The writers must think we are fools," Derya said. "Everyone knows that."

Eliana snorted. "Except, perhaps, us?" She feigned a guilty look. "Only minute amounts of an intensifying taste should be used. If these items are eaten during a meal, the mouth should be thoroughly rinsed to avoid triggering the effects."

"I suppose that's so you don't blow someone over accidentally if you get into an argument at dinner." Derya snickered. "Think of the diplomatic incident that could cause."

"But that explains it, don't you see? Why, after every meal, and even after every course, we all rinse our mouths out." Eliana grinned. "State dinners could become a lot more interesting if we got rid of that custom." She ran her finger down the page, continuing to read aloud: "Wielders of air magic can dirty the air. A tiny sip of beer will intensify the effects."

"As fun as drinking the beer would be, I don't understand why you'd make the air dirty," Derya said. "Tell me what it does for water magic."

Flipping the pages to the water section, Eliana read, "Only minute amounts —"

"Yes, yes, we know that part."

"It muddies the water."

"Why would anyone want to do that?"

"Perhaps to hide something you've hidden under the surface?" Eliana shrugged. "I can't think of much use for that. Cleaning would be better."

"I agree," Derya said. "How would you do it?"

Eliana flipped a few more pages. "Vinegar. Works the same for both air and water."

After studying the nine ways to amplify air magic, they perused the sections on light, water, stone, metal, and wood magic. Then Eliana handed the book to Derya. "Quiz me."

Derya nodded. "How does salt affect stone magic?"

"You can sharpen stone."

"Right. What about light?"

"Salt intensifies light. That could be useful in a dark place." The thought made Eliana shiver. Fortunately, she wasn't going to venture into a dark place, like an underground realm, anytime soon. Or was she? Wrenching her attention from the terror that twisted her bowels, she returned to the task at hand. "Metal magic. What does salt do to it?"

The two girls huddled over the book for the next half hour, quizzing each other on the amplifiers, their uses, and potential hazards.

"Your tutor should be back soon, don't you think?" asked Derya.

"Maybe. Ask me again. I have to know this." Eliana ran a hand through her hair, leaned close to Derya, and spoke softly. "Maybe it's time we started practicing."

Derya's mouth dropped open. "What? Something has happened. You're tense and edgy and obsessed with memorizing this book. And now you're suddenly eager to risk a little practice. What's got into you?"

Eliana let her gaze fall. The burden of her knowledge ate at her like acid etching its way into granite. She wanted to confide in Derya, but her father had ordered her to keep the curse a secret. Her chest tightened and a vein in her head throbbed. The king kept secrets from her, so why should she feel bound to keep his? Heat surged across her face. She was angry, furious even, that her parents had kept the knowledge of the curse from her for so long.

But should she tell Derya? As much as she wanted a confidante, telling Derya was a political act, not merely a personal one. Eliana's decision would determine who would rule Ymittos, and Derya could hardly be called a disinterested party. Although maybe that gave her a right to the knowledge.

Sucking in a deep breath, Eliana let it out slowly. "Yesterday morning, my father summoned me to his private office." She fixed her eyes on Derya's face. "Then he and my mother told me about the Curse of Malkh."

"Malkh? You mean the land Cetus destroyed?"

"There's a bit more to it than that, I'm afraid." She started slowly, explaining what she'd learned about the Malkhian survivors and Cetus's curse. By the time she reached the end, the words tumbled from her lips like boulders rolling down a slope. When she finished speaking, she slumped, drained by the recitation and relieved to have told someone. "So, I have fifteen days to break the curse, or Cetus will destroy both Ymittos and Malkh, and enslave all our people. And I—" Her voice broke and she buried her face in her hands.

Derya pulled Eliana into her arms. "You will not end up a slave of that monster. You can't." She tightened her grip and stroked Eliana's hair. "What are you going to do?"

Eliana eased away from Derya. "If I don't break the curse, my people will be dead, enslaved or worse." A tear slid down her cheek. "But I don't know how. I feel like I'm doomed before I start. There's no hope for me." She met Derya's gaze. "And we assume Cinar will be next."

Derya's eyes looked twice their normal size, all trace of mirth or merriment vanishing like ice under a summer sun, replaced by understanding and dismay. "This is why you need the magic, to break the curse."

Eliana nodded solemnly. "Or if I don't break it, to do what I can to fight off Cetus." She wiped the tears from her face. "Will you help me?"

"Study or fight? Either way, I will. You have my word." Derya pressed her hand against her chest, the first two fingers outstretched in the Cinarrian salute. "To the death."

8

Eliana fidgeted, shifting her weight from side to side as she waited on the white marble steps of the palace, flanked by her parents. Dark gray clouds striped the afternoon sky. Their smoky writhing mirrored the princess's inner turmoil.

After a third gust of bone-chilling wind, Eliana stamped her feet, trying to coax some warmth into them. Her new suitor, the one chosen by her parents, was due to arrive at any moment. Only three days had passed since she agreed to meet him. That told her the negotiations had started months ago, without her knowledge, and that her father had sent a bird summoning the dochan as soon as she acquiesced. She balled her hands into fists. Never again would her parents make agreements on her behalf.

Waiting for her suitor to arrive was a waste of time. The minute he learned she was fated to break the underground prince's curse, this Dochan of Nafplio would suddenly remember he had pressing family business elsewhere. Besides, she had more important matters to deal with than flirtations and an arranged marriage.

The icy wind fluttered Eliana's cloak, and she pulled it

tight around herself. *Maybe I can use the time productively.* Eliana considered her air magic. Had she tasted something peppery, perhaps she could augment her magic to heat the air. Would she have enough power to warm the whole courtyard? She repressed a chuckle, thinking what her father would say if she tried it.

If only she could return to her experiments. Now, there was nothing she could do but wait. The day before, scouts spotted the entourage from Nafplio on the road from the east. One hundred horsemen and ten baggage wagons were rumbling toward the capital. Most likely bearing ostentatious gifts, Eliana thought. *I don't want them. I want to hear Evander's laugh.* A stab of grief stung her eyes.

She gulped down her pain and stared straight ahead. Earlier that morning, a messenger conveyed word that the Nafplians would arrive by the third hour after noon. Eliana's mother, of course, insisted that they be waiting outside a quarter of an hour earlier.

The castle's clock had chimed three times long ago. As the minutes plodded past slower than a weary ewe, Eliana's impatience turned to nerves. What if he doesn't want this marriage and has only come because his father commanded him to?

Gripping her hands together under her cloak, Eliana tried to stop them from shaking, and failed. At least the queen had permitted her to wear gloves until the dochan arrived. It would never do to greet him with covered hands.

So many silly rules. If only Derya had been invited to stand with her while she waited. But her mother had refused, saying, "The Heir of Cinar isn't interested in our domestic affairs."

Eliana had smirked at that. The Heir of Cinar was almost as interested as Eliana herself. Not only was Derya duty-bound to report to her father about any alliance Ymittos made through marriage, she filled every break they took from poring over the magic book with wild speculations about what

Eliana's suitor would be like. Eliana hoped Derya's predictions of a frog-faced, ill-tempered man weren't anywhere near the truth.

But it was clear Eliana's mother didn't want any competition for the suitor's attention, at least when he first arrived. So Derya would obtain her initial glimpse of the Dochan Istvan, the fourth son of the Diodochi of Nafplio, from one of the castle balconies.

Eliana reviewed what she knew of Nafplio, a small realm the size of a dukedom populated with fiercely independent, proud people. So much that they scorned the title of duke and insisted on using their own: diodochi for the ruler, dochan for his sons.

Cheers floated on the frosty air. He must have entered the town gates. Istvan. Eliana rolled the name around in her mouth. Istvan. It didn't make her feel warm inside like Evander's name had.

Stop. Evander was dead. He would not be back. *I'll have to make do with the living.* She yanked the gloves from her suddenly sweaty hands and rubbed her damp palms on her cloak.

Long minutes dragged by. Eliana couldn't feel her feet by the time the courtyard's tall iron gates swung open. A dark-haired man astride an immense chestnut stallion rode through, followed by his standard bearer. The same wind that fluttered the flag of Nafplio, a twelve-pointed, gold star on a scarlet field, tugged at her cloak and chilled her bones. The man rode through the courtyard while one hundred horsemen lined up in rows behind their dochan, their horses' hooves clattering on the stone pavement.

Heart pounding with anticipation, Eliana took her first look at the dochan. He wore a heavy cloak as black as his shining onyx hair. The cloak was open, revealing the traditional Nafplian jacket with vertical bands of embroidery across the chest. The jacket was cut to reveal the high-necked shirt underneath, also embellished with embroidery under the thin band that served as a collar. Knee-high black leather boots covered the lower part of his legs. Eliana let her gaze travel to his face. Smooth olive skin over a powerful jaw, a clean-shaven, jutting chin. An imperious nose flanked by dark eyes that barely contained their fierceness. His black hair was braided back from his brow, as if for battle.

Istvan swung off his horse with a smooth motion and his boots thumped onto the cobblestones. Only then did Eliana notice how tall he was, standing a head taller than her father. But instead of a gangly youth, he was solidly filled out. Her breath caught. Istvan was a grown man in his mid-twenties, not a youth who'd seen only a summer or two more than she had.

The dochan bounded toward the steps and bowed to her father. "Your Wisdom. I wish you many years of health." He reached for her mother's hand and kissed it. "Your Wisdom. Many years of health."

Then he turned to Eliana, his deep-set eyes seeking her own. After holding her gaze for a moment, he swept his eyes to her feet and back. A smile covered his face, erasing a few years from his appearance. He stared at her as if mesmerized. "Princess Eliana. At last." He breathed the words as if he was a starving man who'd found a loaf of bread fresh from the oven.

He reached for her hand and slowly raised her numb fingers to his full lips. Their warmth startled her, and tingles spread to her icy toes. He stared into her eyes. After a few heartbeats, he dropped her hand, letting her fingers slide through his as if reluctant to release them.

Eliana let out the breath she hadn't realized she'd been holding.

The queen smiled. "Shall we go in? The wind is picking up and I'm sure you're all cold." She took Istvan's arm and led him up the stairs and into the palace. Eliana followed, escorted by her father, who pulled her close.

"What do you think?" he asked.

What did she think? Istvan was older than expected. But now was not the time to confront her father on that point. "He's handsome."

Her father squeezed her arm. "That's a good start."

A heartbeat after Eliana entered the palace, Alessia whisked her away to her chamber. Eliana put up no resistance. Her thoughts were so confused she wasn't sure if she could form a coherent reply to anything the dochan said. Far better to not humiliate herself by blurting out her tumbled, conflicting thoughts. The dochan was handsome. He was much older. *Could I like him? Would he like me?*

She stood stiffly in the center of her room, wishing she could crawl under the bed and stay there. Normally, Eliana enjoyed dressing for a state dinner or a court celebration. But somehow this felt different. As if she were on display. Or being prepared for sacrifice.

Which, if she was honest with herself, was exactly the case. She always knew she'd have to marry someone suitable. Regardless of her personal feelings. And if the one she loved left her to go to the realm of the dead, then she'd have to accept another.

The princess stuck her chin out. At least Istvan was giving her something else to think about than curses and monsters and dark, underground realms. Maybe this Istvan wouldn't be so bad. He couldn't possibly be worse than Cetus. She'd give him a chance. But she wouldn't hesitate to reject him if he failed to measure up to Evander. She dropped her cloak on a chair and motioned to Alessia to prepare her bath.

After a long, hot soak, which thawed Eliana's feet and hands but did nothing to settle her fluttering stomach, Alessia helped her to dress and arrange her jewelry. Eliana sat at her dressing table and stared at her wide eyes in the mirror. *Stop looking like a startled deer.* "You can do my hair now." Alessia unbound Eliana's braids and began to brush them out.

The door flew open and Derya rushed in. "So, what did you think?"

Why did everyone want to know that? "Well, he's certainly not frog-faced," Eliana answered. "He's rather good-looking."

"In an artificial sort of way, if you ask me."

"Why do you say that?"

"Because she's got eyes in her head and a brain that sits behind them," Alessia chimed in.

"Hush, you," Eliana said. She surveyed Derya's attire. The princess had belted her sage green gown with a sash crusted with diamonds, onyx, and blue topaz. The dress shimmered in the light and set off the gold tints in her dark brown hair. Eliana sighed. Somehow, Derya always looked sophisticated beyond her seventeen years.

Derya raised an eyebrow and nodded at Eliana's attire. "What's with the dress?"

Eliana smiled. She'd chosen a midnight blue gown. Her parents would have preferred a lighter, more festive hue if she didn't select the customary white. But the dark blue made a dramatic contrast with her coral and pearl jewelry. And no one else would wear any color like it. If her mother desired her to stand out, stand out she would. On her own terms.

"I wanted something different, that's all." Eliana shrugged. "What about you? I love the fabric of your dress. Where did you get it?"

"Oh, the first vizier of Pasargadae sent it to my father as a gift. He got it from Tinaxia."

"Really?" Tinaxia's fine silks rarely made it farther west than Pasargadae. The vizier had given the emperor a costly gift indeed.

Derya chattered about silks, gems, and exotic fruits from distant lands as Alessia arranged Eliana's hair in complicated braids. With an effort of will, Eliana managed to sit without fidgeting. Her heart pattered out an uneven rhythm and her limbs tingled as if scores of ants crawled over her skin.

Alessia finished and stepped back. Eliana surveyed her reflection in a polished bronze mirror, admiring the placement of pearls in the knot on the top of her head and the cascading braids that hung behind. She nodded. "Thank you."

And with that, the time had come. She stood and offered an arm to Derya before nerves froze her to her chair. "Shall we?"

Moments later, the two princesses reached the gold-inlaid doors to the state dining hall. A footman in a white tunic with a deep blue hem swung the door wide. The herald standing just inside bowed to Eliana. Too soon, he announced, "Her Highness, the Princess Eliana."

Eliana placed a hand on her racing heart and inclined her head in a brief nod. Holding her chin high, she strode into the room, heading for the seat on her father's left. Dimly she heard the herald announce, "Princess Derya, Heir of Cinar."

Istvan stood behind the chair to the left of her own seat. Her mother was already sitting across the table, having given up her customary place on the king's right to Derya. Another move on the queen's part to make sure Istvan didn't give any attention to Derya.

Tables were scattered around the room for the rest of the nobility and the other guests. Eliana noted nearly everyone wore white or pastels. Even Derya, for once, wore a soft shade. Eliana had been right to choose a dark color.

She sat and allowed the footman to push in her seat. Istvan slid into his place next to her.

"Dochan Istvan, please tell us," her father said. "How is your father's health?"

"He is well, thank you. Although he does not seem as hale as you."

The king smiled. "My daughter keeps me young."

"Beautiful girls have a way of doing that," Istvan replied. He turned to Eliana. "How did you know midnight blue is my favorite color?"

Eliana bit her lip. She hadn't known. "Is that why you're wearing it yourself?" She tipped her head toward his white jacket with its blue-black embroidery.

"Of course." He leaned toward her and whispered, "I'm delighted we think alike, even on such a small matter."

Before she could reply, the queen asked, "Your brothers are all well?"

Istvan straightened in his seat. "Yes, and their wives. The oldest has just had his second son, much to my father's delight. The succession is well and truly secured."

Pretending to turn her attention to the food on her plate, Eliana studied Istvan out of the corner of her eye. He had little chance of inheriting the throne of Nafplio. Did that mean he had designs on her kingdom? He didn't seem regretful that his brother and then nephew would inherit, but his expression didn't reveal much. His countenance lacked the openness of Evander's. Perhaps that was due to the formal circumstances.

She continued her surreptitious observations of the dochan. While they both had olive skin and dark hair, Evander's hair had curled in exuberant ringlets, while Istvan's was straight and sleek. Now, close up, she noted he had a few auburn strands in his hair. She found them strangely fascinating.

Her eyes trailed lower to Istvan's bulging shoulders and arms. Evander had been wiry and agile. This one was solid muscle and exuded strength. She wasn't sure she liked that. Istvan brought back no echo of Evander, and she felt none of the joy she'd felt near him.

In its place were those beguiling tingles she'd felt in her fingers when Istvan had pressed them to his lips, and the tantalizing thought of experiencing them again.

"Isn't that right, my dear?"

Eliana jerked her head up. "I'm sorry, Papa. What did you ask me?"

"I said that we were all hoping for a wedding in the next year. Isn't that right?"

Her years of court training helped keep her brow smooth and a faint smile on her lips. What was the rush? She'd barely exchanged two sentences with the man. She flicked her eyes to Derya. That one would elope with a goatherd if someone tried to force her into an objectionable marriage.

But there was another way. "Papa," she said gently. "I don't want to rush anyone into marrying me. It's best to give Dochan Istvan a chance to know me before he makes his choice. I wouldn't want him to make a mistake."

"So very considerate," Istvan said. "Know that your kindness intrigues me even more than the tales of your beauty and wit."

Derya coughed. Eliana shot a glare at her. Derya rolled her eyes.

Eliana wrinkled her nose at the other girl and frowned. Surely, Derya understood the royal game of flattery. What else was the dochan supposed to say in this first public meeting?

Turning to Istvan, she beamed at him. "Thank you. You are very kind. Please tell me about your travels here. What do you think of Ymittos?"

Out of the corner of her eye, she caught a glimpse of her mother's approving smile.

9

———

Over the next two days, Eliana barely had a moment's respite from a rotating medley of feasts and plays, attendance at philosophers' debates, and on one sunny afternoon, a short ride into the countryside. Her parents were relentless, demanding that she make up her mind not only about whether to accept Istvan but regarding breaking the curse as well. The weight of the decisions bore down on her, dampening her enjoyment of anything.

While Istvan didn't have Evander's buoyant spirit, Eliana had to admit he was good company. He'd listened to her analyze the plots of plays, helped her solve mathematical equations, and spoke with her in Cinarrian, chuckling amiably when she mocked his accent as even worse than her own.

On the second afternoon, Eliana curled up by the fire in a small solarium, sheltered from the blustery winds outside by tall windows, the clouds and chill offset by scarlet and gold mats on the floor and intricate tapestries on the wall. With her feet tucked under her, she leaned against the back of her chair, making slow, precise stitches as she embroidered the decorative hem on a peplos. Alessia sat a few yards away, intent on her own sewing.

A breath of fresh air tickled Eliana's nose, and a shadow fell over her work. She jerked her chin up.

Istvan's smile flickered. "I'm sorry. Did I startle you?" He eased himself into the chair on the opposite side of the fire.

She glanced out the window at the spiraling snowflakes. "Too windy for a ride?"

He nodded. "Not only that, there's ice on the road. I don't want to risk injuring my horses." He held up the book in his hand. "Would you like me to read to you while you work?"

"That's thoughtful of you. What do you suggest?"

"A collection of poems by Narcyz Jiri."

Eliana raised her eyebrows. Jiri was one of Ymittos's most revered poets. She dipped her chin in a nod. "Please. Does it have "The Epic of Vilppu"? That's my favorite."

Istvan thumbed through the pages. "Yes, here." He began to read the epic story of a young goatherd who'd saved Ymittos from an invasion hundreds of years ago.

His deep voice rumbled as he read and Eliana sewed steadily, the cadence of his words caressing her ears. She completed embroidering a leaf and tied off her thread. After scooting to the edge of her chair, she dug through her work-basket, seeking a skein of gold thread.

Silence in the room made her look up. Istvan was watching her intently. "Are you tired of reading?" she asked.

"No. I was just curious."

"About what?"

"How do you decide which colors to use?"

She stared at him. His eyes didn't flicker, and he met her gaze steadily. She pursed her lips. "You really want to know?"

"Why, yes." His eyes shifted the tiniest bit, like the flutter of a gnat's wing.

Eliana scoffed. "I find that hard to believe."

He laughed. "No, I suppose I don't."

"I'd be surprised if you did." She pulled a strand of thread from the skein and slid it through her needle's eye. "Please go on. You read so well; I was lost in the story."

Bending her head over her work, Eliana's lips twitched into a smile. It was kind of Istvan to at least inquire about her embroidery. Evander never pretended to be interested. Maybe he wasn't as perfect as she remembered him.

She peered at Istvan from under her eyelashes. Somehow, when she was near him, her memories of Evander's visage faded. At the same time, her curiosity about the man beside her sharpened. When he'd kissed her hand when they first met, his lips were warm and soft. What would they feel like against hers? Her face warmed, and she stabbed her needle into the fabric.

Barely listening as he read, she followed her own more compelling thoughts. Istvan, while older than she'd expected, was kind, considerate, and treated her like an equal. He made an effort to please, to listen, and to understand. All attractive qualities, she had to admit.

And not to be overlooked, he barely gave any other young woman a second glance. Even Derya's elegant flirting and higher rank had failed to attract even cursory attention from him. Alessia, as hard as she tried, had been unable to uncover even a whisper of him speaking with, let alone dallying with, any of the maids.

Istvan read to the bottom of the page, his expressive inflection bringing to life the story of the hero who rode a dolphin to slay a monstrous octopus. Eliana shivered. How bold Vilppu had been to plunge beneath the sea. She allowed her work to lie in her lap as Istvan read of Vilppu standing eye to eye with the beast, his sword raised in his mighty arm. Would Istvan be as valiant to slay Cetus for her? Just as Vilppu was about to deliver the killing blow, Derya arrived, accompanied by a page.

Eliana huffed. *Merciful winds.* Why did she have to show up now?

"There you are," Derya said. "Istvan, the king sent this boy to look for you."

A flicker of annoyance hardened the dochan's eyes. "Why?" he asked.

The page bowed. "Dochan Istvan, King Archelaos would like you to wait upon him in his workroom."

Istvan snapped the book shut. "Then I'd best not keep him waiting." He stood up and tipped his head to Eliana. "Thank you for allowing me to join you, even if only for a short time." His dark eyes held hers for a moment. He glanced at Derya and dipped his chin. "Princess." In a moment, he was gone.

"There, you can thank me," Derya said.

Eliana slid her eyes over the other girl's smirking face. "For what?"

"I rescued you from that oily goat."

"From what?" Irritation sharpened Eliana's voice.

Derya flounced into the chair Istvan had vacated. "Your suitor. He's like a goat with oiled skin. Causes trouble but never gets caught."

"What makes you say that?"

"I have a feeling." Derya leaned forward. "His smile hides a false heart."

Eliana snorted. "What gave you that idea?"

"He lied to you. Midnight blue is his favorite color, and I love to converse with fools." Derya scoffed. "Midnight blue and white are the colors of Ymittos, so what better way to gain favor with the king but to wear his colors?"

Raising her chin, Eliana glared at Derya. "I'll have you know I've spent quite a bit of time with him and he's not what you think."

"You like him?" Derya's voice was high and incredulous.

"Why shouldn't I?" Eliana asked.

"He's not for you," put in Alessia.

Eliana scowled at her maid. "Why not?"

"Don't you think it odd," Derya answered, "that someone

so much older than you would be so, I don't know, deferential to you?" She shook her head. "Something's not right about him."

Heat prickled the back of Eliana's neck and her jaw tightened. What was wrong with those two? Alessia loved to be contrary, but this was more than her usual joking. Derya was probably jealous. If she wasn't, why was her assessment of Istvan so harsh?

The Heir of Cinar, of all people, should know better. Princesses can't be picky.

Seeking to calm herself, Eliana slowly exhaled. Istvan's biggest flaw was his age, seven years more than her own. But that wasn't as bad as the other suitors her parents had proposed. Her father, when questioned, had said he wanted her to give Istvan a chance. He hadn't told her about the dochan's age because he feared a seven-year difference might put her off. Her father had been wrong to lie, but at least with Istvan, he wasn't forcing someone twice her age on her. And deep down she had to admit that tall, strapping Istvan would be a reassuring escort into Malkh if she attempted to break the curse. No, marrying Istvan deserved serious consideration, no matter what Derya and Alessia thought. Eliana entertained little hope that she could find better.

THE NEXT MORNING, Eliana and Derya were descending the palace steps under a clear winter sky when Istvan caught up with them. "Where are you off to?" he asked.

Eliana smiled. "Aren't you supposed to be hunting with my father?"

He leaned toward her with a conspiratorial look. "My favorite horse has inexplicably gone lame."

Her heart picked up its pace, moving from a comfortable trot to a rapid canter. "So, I'm second to your horse?"

"Never. I didn't want to hinder your father, so I pleaded to be excused. Truth be told, I was hoping to find you." He took a step back. "Unless you don't wish to be burdened with my company."

She tipped her head to the side and trained her eyes on his. "Oh, I'd be delighted to be burdened." A glance at Derya's pursed lips told her the other girl was not pleased.

A groom arrived, leading Eliana's bay mare. She gestured to the animal as she kept her gaze meshed with Istvan's. "We're off to the canal diggings. They're going to reopen the dam, and I promised to attend."

A shadow flittered over his face. "Might I accompany you?"

Eliana peered over his shoulder at Derya, who was emphatically shaking her head.

"Would you take offense if I said no?" Eliana laid a hand on his arm. "They didn't want to make this a formal event, and only invited the princess and me because we —"

"Rescued so many of the workers." He nodded. "Of course, I quite understand. Will you be free afterward?"

He looked so hopeful she hated to refuse. "We promised to visit the wounded this afternoon."

"Would you accept my attendance then?"

This surprised her. Most men shunned anything to do with the ill or infirm. Any mention of sickness turned their olive skin into the color of oats. "Are you sure?"

"If it's important for you, then it's important for me." Tiny wrinkles formed around his eyes.

His smile set her heart to thumping and her face felt hot. He couldn't have offered a better gift. "It's settled then," she said. "I look forward to it."

That afternoon, Istvan met Eliana in the courtyard, where she waited for the grooms to bring the horses for her, a quartet of guards, a pair of pages, and a herald. Derya had begged off, saying she had a long-overdue letter to write to her father.

Eliana greeted Istvan with a broad smile. "It's a lovely day. Maybe we could go riding later."

Istvan frowned. "I'm afraid your father has requested my presence and made it clear he felt it was my duty to attend."

Her spirits drooped like sails without a wind. "Well, then you must."

"Yes, to live up to your example. Your commitment to duty is the mark of a fine ruler. It's an unusual and lovely quality."

His compliment warmed the place within her that had been chilled by her disappointment. She appreciated his wording, his praise untainted by patronizing comments about her age.

He pressed a small oilskin bag into her hand. "In place of my attendance, would you accept this?"

"What is it?"

"Artemisia."

Gripping the tiny pouch, she brought her other hand up to clasp his. Artemisia was the rarest of the healing herbs. Even tiny amounts were worth much gold. "Thank you. Where did you get it?"

"A Tinaxian trader sold it to my father." He squeezed her hand. "I've been told it amplifies the use of tamarisk bark and terebinth leaf poultices in easing pain."

"This is very generous of you."

"Nothing is too much for your people." He bent his neck and gazed into her eyes. "People, I hope, to whom I will belong one day."

Her heart sped up and her fingers tingled where he pressed them. She had so many questions for him. Perhaps this was as good a time as any. Whatever was holding up the grooms, she hoped it would delay them a little longer.

She pulled him to a quiet corner of the courtyard. "Istvan, I want to ask you something."

"Anything."

Her stomach twitched, and she wasn't sure she could find the courage.

"Ask me what?" His voice was gentle and patient, with no hint of condescension.

Swallowing her nervousness, she blurted out the question she'd been longing to ask. "What do you want in a wife?"

He blinked, then his face broke into a grin. "I didn't expect that."

His surprise emboldened her. "The bluntness, or the question?"

"Both. But I'm glad you asked. I know your people say a man should rule his home and only a king can rule a country. But I don't need another servant. I need a partner, someone who can be a friend, not just the mother of my children and the one who makes sure my meals are prepared to my liking."

Her breath caught in her throat. This was better than she'd hoped. "And if the woman you marry inherits a kingdom?"

"It would hardly be fair if I took over and didn't permit her any say in how her people were ruled. I would allow, no, expect her to rule. I would simply be her consort."

"You'd willingly settle for that?"

He jerked back, his eyes narrowed. After a pause, he smiled. "As the fourth son, I've long known my chance of ruling anything is small. Serving as consort to a woman I admire and love is the best I can hope for." He leaned toward her with a wry grin. "My brothers are eager for me to wed you, so I won't foment a rebellion in Nafplio."

"And what about you? Would you rather lead a rebellion?"

"What, and plunge Nafplio into civil war?"

"Of course not. I wasn't thinking of that." Did he know about the curse? She couldn't allow him to commit himself if he didn't. "Istvan, there's something you should know…" Eliana couldn't bring herself to meet his eye.

"Eliana, if you're talking about the curse, I know all about it. Your father told me yesterday."

She raised her eyes to his, pursing her lips in confusion. "And you're still here?"

Istvan studied his feet for a heartbeat before looking into her eyes. "What I'd heard of you made me think marrying you would give me at least a tolerable existence. Since I've met you, I've allowed myself to hope for happiness and joy." He ran a finger along her jaw. "I hope you've started to feel the same. All I ask is that you offer me a chance to win your heart."

For a moment, she swayed toward him. Then the whinny of a horse reminded her where they were. She stiffened. "But the curse—"

He smiled. "I have no doubt that with my help you'll be able to break it." He glanced over his shoulder at the approaching grooms. "And since I am some years older than you, I hope you will look to me for guidance." He winked. "Or at least pretend to."

Eliana studied his face. His request was reasonable. He probably wasn't as impulsive as she was, so he might provide some balance. And his skill with a sword would be helpful in Malkh.

He picked up her hand and held it between his large, strong palms, warming her chilled fingers. Briefly, he held her hand to his lips. Heat shot through her veins down to her toes.

Her parents had chosen well. If marrying Istvan was an act of self-sacrifice, she'd make it willingly. She wouldn't find anyone better if she searched high and low, although a part of her whispered that perhaps she should wait, take some more time. She suppressed that idea. After what she'd done to Evander, she wasn't worthy of a marriage of love. Perhaps in time, their mutual respect would grow into something more. It was the most she could hope for, and more than she deserved.

Istvan caressed her hand and stroked a finger against her

wrist, tracing a meandering line up her arm. Even through her clothing, his touch left a tingling sensation, making her breath hitch.

"Istvan." She had trouble getting past his name. "Istvan."

"Yes?"

"If you were to ask my father for permission to offer a betrothal, I wouldn't be against it."

His lips twitched. "But would you be for it?" He slid his hand up her arm and caressed her shoulder.

Eliana's cheeks burned and she let her eyelids droop. "I think you could convince me."

10

A few hours later, Eliana sat stiffly beside Istvan, shredding a pastry drenched in honey. Istvan had wasted no time informing the king of their chat in the courtyard. Over dinner, King Archelaos had announced the betrothal, and then plunged into a conversation with Istvan about the curse and how Istvan would accompany Eliana on her quest.

While she was glad he'd be with her, Eliana seethed, every word that fell from his lips fueling her irritation. No one had bothered to inform her about Istvan going with her, let alone ask her, although it only made sense. And the idea did hold a certain appeal. She wouldn't be lost by herself in the dark.

But they all appeared to have forgotten that she hadn't consented to venture into the underground realm.

Never had a banquet been so tedious, a feast that was supposed to celebrate her official betrothal to Istvan. Instead, the elaborate foods, the roasted venison, the towers of fruit, or the complex pastries could not tempt her writhing stomach. Everything tasted like sand. The dancers, singers, and poets seemed shallow and frivolous, out of place like jesters at a funeral. What need did she have for their well wishes and congratulations, when she could easily end up dead in the darkness of Malkh?

Most annoying of all, the festivities had cut short her practice session with Derya. They'd started with salt, since they had some experience with that amplifier. It took only minutes for Eliana to figure out how much salt she needed to intensify her light.

Then they tried pepper, exploring how it affected their magic. After two attempts, Derya mastered boiling water, while Eliana couldn't heat either air or light. A quick check in the book told them that most mages could only manipulate one element and use one or two amplifiers. That she could manipulate both air and light was a mark of an unusually powerful mage.

Eliana took that as consolation for not being able to use pepper. She was about to move onto citrus when their maids summoned them to dress for the banquet. Reluctantly, they hid the book and agreed to meet the next day.

And now here she was, bored at the celebration of her own betrothal, chafing to return to her magical studies.

"Don't you agree, Eliana?" Istvan asked.

Preoccupied with her thoughts, she hadn't heard his question. "Agree to what?"

"Leaving for Malkh in two days."

She eyed him. He'd given her pretty words about serving as her consort, but now he and her father were making all the decisions. That was going to have to stop.

"Perhaps…" *No.* No *perhaps.* She locked her gaze on his as she continued. "We can discuss this tomorrow. They say it will be fine in the morning. Let's go on an early ride. Shall we meet soon after dawn?"

His eyes narrowed, then relaxed. "As you say."

Her father frowned. *Fine.* Let him be annoyed and let Istvan be unsure of her intent. The decision to break the curse was hers, and hers alone. She nodded. "Wonderful. I'm looking forward to it."

ELIANA WOKE in the dim stillness of dawn. Rosy light crept over the tiled floor, warming the chill that took over after the fire burned down to coals.

Staccato knocking at her door brought her fully awake. She listened as Alessia hissed at the knocker.

"We didn't call for a rooster. Who dares disturb the princess's rest?"

A male voice rumbled. Alessia murmured a reply. The door shut with a click.

Alessia sidled up to the bed carrying a tray with a teapot, bread, honey, dates, and oranges. "Highness, your breakfast is here."

"Already?" *Oh.* She was meeting Istvan this morning. What kind of fool was she to plan an early ride after a banquet? With a sigh, Eliana tugged her quilts around herself. "I'll stay here until you bank up the fire." She watched Alessia lay the wood and coax it into flames, idly wondering why there were no fire mages. That was something to ask Corban.

Wincing in the cold, Eliana bounded from the bed. "Quick, Alessia, my riding clothes."

An hour later, she met Istvan in the courtyard. This time the grooms had the horses ready and their guards were mounted, five of his and five of hers.

Istvan extended a hand and helped her onto her horse. "How did you sleep?"

"Quite well, thank you." She forced herself to smile to cover her lie. She'd seethed long into the night, rehearsing what she'd say to him. First, they needed to get away from the palace so she could talk to him without being overheard or interrupted.

He swung into the saddle. "Shall we ride in the mountains today?"

"No, I thought we'd go along the shore." On the wide sandy beach, she and Istvan could ride well ahead of the guards, beyond the reach of their ears. That would be as close to a private chat as she could hope for. "The wind has dropped, so it should be pleasant."

"Lead on."

They followed a pair of guards through the quiet city streets, few people out in the frosty hour just after dawn. The rising sun cast long shadows over the marble palaces, turning their white walls pale blue. Eliana and Istvan chatted about the banquet, the dancers, and the unseasonably cold weather until they exited the gates of the city and reached the open shore.

Eliana tipped back her head and inhaled the crisp air. She'd always loved the sea air, the smell of salt and fish and life. The vast reach of the ocean gave her a glimmer of freedom. The hiss of the surf created an impression of peace that seeped into her apprehension about the difficult talk she was about to have with Istvan. She hoped he'd be reasonable, and not argue. She hated arguments. Especially in public. Her cheeks heated as she imagined what the guards would think if the dochan shouted at her.

Istvan surveyed the wide beach. "I'm surprised this wasn't built up."

"The water's too shallow for a port and the land is subject to flooding." She looked out to the placid sea, seeking strength to begin. She roved her eyes over the clear blue water near the shore that darkened further out.

Except for one spot. "Istvan, what's that?"

He put a hand over his eyes. "It looks like a small boat."

"A very flat, small boat." She squinted. "More like a raft." A short mast stood up from the boat, its sail limp and lifeless in the still air. "Is there anyone on it?"

"I think so. But he's lying down."

She frowned. The raft was fifty or more yards from shore. Without the west wind, the craft would soon be driven south by the currents, where it would be forced against the jagged cliffs. No one would survive the treacherous thrashing waves. "We need to help," she said.

"But how?" Istvan looked back at the city. "Should I send a guard to hire a boat?"

"No. That will take too long." Eliana reached inside for her air magic. It wouldn't take much, just a puff or two, to drive that little boat to shore. She waved a hand, gesturing toward herself.

The gentle wind blew her hood from her head. The boat moved toward the shore.

"What are you doing, Eliana?"

Glancing at his scowling face, she shrugged. "Helping." She pulled a little more with her magic. The raft approached the breakers, rising and falling with the waves. "Captain," she said to one of her guards. "Could you help?"

"Yes, Highness." The captain leaped from his horse. "You two, come with me."

Two others joined him to run into the surf. They were drenched to the waist before they seized the raft and dragged it onto the shore.

Eliana dismounted and dashed over. The sole occupant of the raft was a gray-haired man garbed in what had been rich clothing that was now tattered and grimy, the white of his tunic smudged, the gilt trim on the hem faded, his heavy green cloak damp and salt stained. Several days' growth of beard darkened his chin and lower part of his face. Fiery crimson sunburn covered his nose and cheeks, and his lips were cracked. He moaned.

Istvan joined her, his face tight and angry. "What is wrong with you?" He ground the words out through clenched jaws.

She ignored him and addressed the guards. "Do any of you have water?"

One man sprinted to the horses and returned with a waterskin. The captain held it to the stranger's lips.

The man drank greedily, sucking the water down as if he'd been wandering in a desert for days. After he drained the waterskin, he let it fall into his lap. "Thank you," he croaked. "Thank you." He scanned the faces around him and settled his gaze on Istvan. "Where am I?"

"Ymittos, just south of the capital," Istvan answered. "Who are you, and where are you from?"

"I must see the king."

"Why?" asked Eliana.

The man looked at her as if deciding whether to answer.

She lifted her chin but spoke gently. "I am the Princess Eliana. Who might you be?"

"Duke Abelardo, from the Western Islands." His throat bobbed. "Highness, your father needs to know. Cetus has invaded."

Merciful winds. An icy hand gripped Eliana's heart. "You do need to see my father." She turned to her guards. "Captain, will you and a few men escort the duke to the palace?"

The princess watched as her guards assisted the duke to a horse. They set off at a slow pace toward the city, a guard walking alongside the duke to steady him in place. As Eliana approached her horse, Istvan gripped her arm.

She stared at him. "Yes?"

"Come walk with me." His voice was taut, as if suppressing anger.

Perplexed, Eliana glanced at him. What was causing that scowl?

They strolled several yards along the shore, leaving their remaining guards near the raft. "How could you?" he said.

"How could I what?"

"Use your magic."

"I was offering aid to someone in need. What's wrong with that?"

"Because magic is not something you should use for years and years. If at all."

"What do you mean?" She stiffened her spine and bit out the words. "I used it just last week to rescue scores of workmen."

"From what I hear, you were rather immobile for a time afterward."

That was putting it politely, she had to admit. "It was a small price to pay to save many lives. My people were spared a tragedy because I acted."

"And you nearly got yourself and Princess Derya killed."

He didn't need to know that it was as much Derya's idea as her own. "So?" she said. "We both take our obligations to our respective peoples seriously. And if using magic will help them, then we should use it."

"But your role is to rule, not be the savior."

"It's not?" She curled her lip and snorted. "What do you call having to break a hundred-year-old curse? Besides, if we'd studied magic, if we'd been allowed to learn how to control it and intensify it, we wouldn't have been in any danger."

His face darkened. "What do you know about intensifying magic?"

Mentally, she kicked herself. She shouldn't have let that drop. While she was old enough to study the theory, she needed to keep the advanced knowledge Corban had shared a secret. "Only that there is a way to intensify magic powers safely."

"Not so safely. Some light mages have gone blind experimenting with amplifiers."

She blinked, forcing herself to keep her jaw from dropping. Blind? Maybe she shouldn't have skipped the "Warnings, Cautions, and Other Points of Vital Concern" chapter in the magic text.

Istvan took advantage of her silence. "Those are dangerous waters, not for little girls."

"If I'm a little girl," she said, squaring her shoulders and narrowing her eyes, "you have no business marrying me."

Only the blinking of his eyelids showed his surprise. The long, dark eyelashes that shaded his seductive brown eyes—brown like the shell of a chestnut—distracted her from her indignation and made her almost regret her fury.

He hung his head. "I apologize."

His words came out stiffly, as if he was unused to admitting fault. Or did he not mean what he was saying?

"You are a grown woman," Istvan continued, "and have the right to choose how you spend your time. But as your future husband…" He tipped his head to the side and smiled. "I feel so protective of you and have an interest in your health. We both have a duty to further the line."

She took a step away from him. "Is that all I am to you? A source of heirs?"

"Of course not. But you were the one who brought up duty. Anyway, along with the joys of children, I've always hoped to have a clever and valiant wife. You are that and more." He paused, shackling her gaze with his own. "You know that using magic can ruin a woman's health and destroy her ability to have a child. That is most likely why your parents didn't want you to explore your powers at all. There's time for that later once you've secured the succession with a few heirs." He leaned toward her, his eyes wide and beseeching.

He was persuasive. She might have believed him if she didn't know that using magic had nothing to do with her ability to conceive.

"But what about the curse, if I decide to break it? Won't I need magic for that?"

Istvan pressed his lips into a thin line and pulled his eyebrows together. After a few moments, he sighed. "That's a fair point. But often these magical curses are broken by some means other than magical powers."

Yes, that was true. The Rider knew she'd read more than a few tales and legends of heroes who broke curses without relying on magic. A sudden thought made her lean toward Istvan. "You know, you never told me. What magic do you have?"

Reaching for her hand, he stroked her palm and wrist with one gentle finger. Feelings other than anger and defiance fought for her attention so fiercely she could barely concentrate on what he was saying. "Since you're the curse breaker, my magic won't help you. Let's hope magic won't be needed." He squeezed her fingers. "Besides, I have every confidence you'll be able to do what's necessary."

She wanted to believe him. The idea of pitting her magic against whatever evil spells Cetus had laid terrified her. Istvan could be right, but there was no way to know. It was better to be prepared. She wanted to share with him what Corban had taught her, that she wasn't risking her fertility by exploring her magic. But some instinct restrained her tongue. After all, Istvan had kept a secret from her, one he'd shared with her father. "When did you decide to accompany me to Malkh? And why didn't you tell me?"

He blinked and stiffened. "Your father begged me not to."

"Why?"

"The marriage. He didn't want you to agree to it just so you'd have my help in breaking the curse."

"Fine." She lifted her chin. "But as you said, I am a grown woman. And heir to the throne. I will not be shuffled to the side and allow others to make decisions for me." She raked her gaze over his face. "I need to know that your loyalty is to me, not my father."

Answering her piercing stare with his own, he leaned forward. "Can you make me a promise in return? To not use your magic without guidance?"

Why couldn't he understand? She had to master as much magic as she could to ward off Cetus or any other invader. She rubbed her mouth. *In a way, Corban is guiding me in my magical studies.* For now, she'd keep that to herself. Just until she was sure Istvan wouldn't tell her father. She had to protect her tutor. "Very well. No magic without guidance."

"Thank you." His white teeth gleamed as his lips parted, his smile spreading across his face and up to his eyes. "And I won't make any more decisions without you." He squeezed her hand again. "Eliana, know that I'll always do what is right for you. May my arm be torn from my shoulder if I am lying."

She matched his smile with one of her own. If this conversation was any indication, they'd be able to work out whatever problems rose between them. She'd have a long and happy future with Istvan. Assuming, of course, Cetus didn't destroy them first. They'd wasted enough time on their personal differences. She let out a long breath and tucked a hand under his arm. "What do you think? Has Cetus really invaded the Western Islands?"

He rested his fingers over hers. "Let's find out, shall we?"

11

———

The morning sun shone through the palace's windows as Eliana and Istvan followed a footman through long, drafty corridors. White marble columns stood like silent sentries over the intricate black and rust colored mosaic floors. Eliana pressed her lips together to restrain her impatience at the footman's slow pace. Or was she grateful for the delay? Bile crept up her throat. Duke Abelardo's tidings meant war was imminent. And everyone would expect her to embrace a fate she was dreading.

At last, they arrived at the massive doors to the king's council chamber. The footman swung the doors wide, and Eliana strode into the vast room, its molded ceiling supported by twenty-foot columns, their capitals carved into leaves and flowers. The king occupied the head of a long, polished oak table. Her mother sat to his right, leaving Eliana's empty seat to his left. The archon of Ptolemaida and the seven members of her father's boule filled eight of the remaining seats. The duke's news must have seriously alarmed her father for him to have summoned his principal advisors. The duke himself was seated at the foot of the table, sipping a cup of steaming tea.

"Good morning, Father," Eliana said as she walked to her

seat. "This seems to be an important meeting." She eased into her chair. Istvan stalked to a place near the duke and sat down heavily.

The king sighed. "We are all here." He gestured to the rescued man. "My lords, this is Duke Abelardo, from the Western Islands. He arrived this morning with news. I thought you should hear it."

The duke cradled the delicate porcelain teacup in his weather-beaten hands. "A month ago, Your Wisdom, a fishing boat limped into one of our harbors." His throat bobbed. "It came from Lanzarote, carrying the few survivors of Cetus's invasion."

Eliana gasped, and hers was not the only shocked reaction. Several of the boule members cursed. Lanzarote was one of the largest of the Western Islands.

The duke gulped his tea. "The refugees told of atrocities committed by Cetus's army. The monsters tore the limbs off their captives, bit the heads off children. Some prisoners were fed to the sharks." Hands shaking, he placed the teacup on the table. "Women were dragged to the water's edge. Their screams lasted for hours, until one by one, they faded into whimpers." He shuddered. "Those who escaped hid in the marshes. While Cetus's soldiers were busy setting fire to the main port, the survivors of the massacre traveled overland to a tiny fishing village. They set sail on the only boat left."

A weight settled on Eliana's chest. She leaned against the table, dismay souring her stomach. No longer could she deny that Cetus was rising.

"It took them a fortnight to reach Coelleira," Duke Abelardo continued, "battling storms the entire way."

Eliana gulped. Cetus's legendary power over storms and sea was formidable. A sea voyage from Lanzarote to the main island of Coelleira should only have taken two or three days.

"King Saturno sent several birds to you," the Duke said. "When no reply came, he feared they had gone astray."

"As I told you," Eliana's father said. "We received no word from the Western Islands."

Abelardo rubbed his forehead and nodded. "So, King Saturno sent me and a small crew." He closed his eyes briefly. "The journey nearly cost me my life. I've never seen such storms. Cetus clearly didn't want us to reach you. Two weeks ago, our ship went aground on your northern coast. The five of us who escaped drowning clung to pieces of the ship. No matter how hard we paddled, we couldn't escape the currents that kept us from shore. One by one, the others slipped away."

"Thank the Rider you didn't perish," Eliana's father said.

The duke smiled weakly. He turned his weary blue eyes to Eliana before looking around at his listeners. "King Saturno wants to warn you. Now that Cetus is on the move, we know he won't be content with the Western Islands."

Eliana shivered.

"In the past few months, we've captured some of Cetus's spies." The duke's face hardened. "Even when tortured, they revealed little. Other than Malkh is the key to taking Ymittos." He picked up his teacup. "We're not sure if that means they intend to invade right away or not."

Eliana opened her mouth, but a pointed glance from her father silenced her. King Archelaos studied the duke's face. "Do you have any idea why Cetus attacked your lands now?"

Abelardo shook his head. "None. It's been centuries since anyone had heard of Cetus, other than shreds of news about his conquests on the western continent. We dared to hope he'd given up here in the east." He let out a long sigh. "It seems we were mistaken."

"Indeed," Eliana's father said.

Heavy silence filled the room, much like the quieting of birds and the stilling of the air before a thunderstorm.

Eliana's heartbeat throbbed in her throat. Cetus had nearly destroyed the continent a millennium ago. He was coming after them again.

The queen murmured her name. Eliana looked into her mother's pinched, pale face and saw the question in her eyes, the same question radiating from her father's stern countenance.

"Lord Abelardo," the king said, "We are in your debt for this news." He nodded to Keerios Bazyli. "Could you see him to a room? And provide anything else he needs?" He cast his glance over his other advisors. "I need information on our readiness for war. The status of our army and navy, our food supplies, and defenses. Return in an hour with your reports."

Chairs scraped over the tile. The duke, the boule members, and the archon stood, murmuring "Yes, Your Wisdom."

After they left, the silence grew more oppressive. Sweat dampened Eliana's neck.

"I can only speculate, Eliana," her father said, "but it seems to me Cetus is using Lanzarote to move his armies. After he conquers the rest of the Western Islands, he'll strike Ardebil through Malkh and Ymittos. Breaking the curse will thwart that plan. He'll lose the magic infused in the enchantment, forcing him to retreat for a generation or two. Or at least until we muster a defense for the inevitable invasion. Are you willing to do your part?"

Eliana's breath came in ragged gasps, as if she'd been fleeing an enemy. She folded her trembling hands on her lap. "I might be more willing had you prepared me for it. You denied me my best weapon by keeping me from my magic."

Her father's face reddened, and a vein pulsed on the side of his temple. "Is that how you see it? Foolish girl. You see only what you don't have and ignore what you do."

She frowned. "What are —"

The king cut her off with a jerk of his hand. "Did you never wonder why we carefully educated you not only in history and military strategy, but in all the myths and legends of the world, making sure you'd read even the most obscure stories of magical curses and how to break them?"

"No —"

"Or ask yourself why, of all the noble-born girls in the kingdom, you were the only one taught hunting and archery? And how to live off the land? Did you never wonder why you trained in fencing and swordsmanship beside Evander?" He glared at her. "We wanted to give you every advantage we could without clouding your childhood with this burden."

Her jaw fell slack.

"Do you still not understand why we raised Evander with you, nurturing a strong bond between you, to give you an ally you could trust with your life?" He sucked in a deep breath. "And all you worry about is the magic," he scoffed. "We knew Evander shared his lessons with you. And we didn't stop him. We knew forbidding you to use your magic would limit how often you'd use it, so you'd have less chance of hurting yourself." His crimson face turned purple. "And you dare say we didn't prepare you. If you'd paid any attention to your lessons at all, you'd know that most magical curses have a non-magical solution." He was nearly shouting. "We tried to give you every weapon imaginable—weapons that would most likely be more useful than magic."

Eliana sat as if turned to stone, barely able to breathe. What her father said was true. They had tried, in a way, to prepare her for this quest. But they should have told her long ago, so the news wouldn't have pierced her like an arrow to the liver, sapping her will and courage under the debilitating shock. She glanced from the king's flaring nostrils and flinty eyes to her mother's trembling lips. "You expect me to go."

"Yes," her father said. "These are the tides through which we move. It's the only way to thwart Cetus's plan and keep Ymittos an independent kingdom."

But to venture underground, to the dark realm of Malkh, to face the beasts that lurked there? She shuddered. Sweat beaded on her forehead just thinking of wandering in lightless caverns and her hands shook with trepidation. She did not want to die alone in the inky blackness.

Istvan rose from his place near the end of the table and moved to sit beside her. "Eliana, you are the best suited to break the curse."

She stared at him. He was right. Her parents had done much to prepare her. Derya never learned swordplay. And she hadn't studied much beyond Cinarrian literature.

Eliana's mouth went dry and her limbs went weak. She couldn't possibly go to Malkh. She wrapped her arms around herself. And if the curse wasn't broken…That was a thought too horrible to even consider.

"I don't understand why you hesitate," Istvan said. "You were so quick to help the canal workers, even at risk to yourself. You didn't let a little thing like fear keep you from your duty."

Lifting her head, she fixed her eyes on his. She detected no sign of a taunt in his expression. He was right. It was her duty to break the curse.

"Besides," Istvan said. "I'll be with you to protect and defend you from all dangers. Whatever comes our way, I will stay with you until you succeed."

"Should they wed before they go?" Eliana's mother asked. "It's really not proper for them to travel together, unmarried."

Her father shook his head. "No, the curse is very specific. The unwed daughter of the king, who is to inherit the kingdom."

Eliana bit her lip. "If I agree, when would I need to leave?"

The tension lines between her father's eyes relaxed slightly. "In the morning. It will take all of today to prepare. You'll need an armed escort. What do you think? Should two taxarchias be enough?"

Two taxarchias would be forty soldiers. She nibbled the inside of her cheek. Would forty be sufficient?

Istvan straightened his spine and addressed King Archelaos. "If I may, I propose that the escort be half my men, half yours. Ten should accompany the princess and me, while the other thirty guard the rift where we descend to Malkh. They can send word back to you of our progress, or come to our aid if necessary."

"Fair enough," the king said. "Eliana, would you like any person in particular to accompany you?"

Her mother cut in. "Her maid. I'll not have my daughter alone with all those men."

Eliana's tense chest relaxed. Alessia would be a welcome companion. "If I go, I'd also like to bring Dimitris, assuming he's willing." One of her guards since she was seven years old, Dimitris had taught her to hunt and shoot. Between him and Istvan, she'd be well protected.

"Very well," her father said. "Anyone else?"

Eliana didn't hesitate. "The Heir of Cinar."

Istvan narrowed his eyes. "Why her?"

Eliana set her jaw. "If I fail, she could try."

"But that would mean…" Her mother's words trailed off.

"You'd hand the kingdom over to Cinar?" her father asked.

"Well, only if I died." Eliana pressed her lips together, not wanting to reveal how his words stung. As always, her father cared more for the kingdom than her. "It would be you handing the kingdom over."

"If I may," said Istvan. "Perhaps this talk of failure is hasty. I have every confidence that Eliana will succeed. Maybe the Heir of Cinar could wait here, in the unlikely event she would be needed as a cursebreaker."

The king rubbed a hand over his chin. "Yes, it would be prudent to avoid endangering the emperor's heir unnecessarily. But Eliana has a point. We'll have to think about this." He turned to his daughter. "So, this means you'll go?"

Eliana tipped her chin up. "I haven't decided." Her bowels writhed, while she considered how her parents assumed she'd eagerly embrace this wild quest simply because they wanted her to.

Her father exhaled slowly. "You have until noon tomorrow. If you refuse, we'll have to let the Heir of Cinar know of the obligation you saddled her with in exchange for handing over our kingdom." He gestured to the door. "You may go."

"I'll see you at noon, then." Eliana stood and strode from the room, holding her chin high and her back straight. She wasn't sure what her father planned to discuss with Istvan in her absence. She'd find out soon enough. In the meantime, she needed to visit Corban. But first, she had another stop to make.

12

When Eliana burst from the council room, five guards snapped to attention. The sixth dropped Alessia's hand and jumped back, his face turning a mottled fuchsia.

Alessia spun, smoothing her hair back from her flushed cheeks. "What happened?"

"Come with me." Eliana curled her lip. "If you can tear yourself away." She scurried down the corridor. Alessia followed, her footsteps tapping a frantic rhythm that mocked Eliana's efforts to contain her panic.

Eliana raced through the marble corridors and dashed up the wide, curving staircase, ignoring Alessia's pleas for her to slow down, stopping only when she reached Derya's door. A pair of soldiers wearing Cinar's black and turquoise guarded the chamber's entrance. They bowed impassively, not revealing what they thought about the arrival of the panting and sweaty Princess of Ymittos.

With a curt nod, Eliana acknowledged them. "Is the princess here?"

The older guard nodded. "Yes, Highness." He rapped on the door.

Derya's maid peeked out. "What do you want—" Her face reddened, and she dipped into a low curtsy. "My apologies, Highness."

"No matter," Eliana said. "Is the princess awake?"

"Yes, but—"

Bolting past the maid, Eliana found Derya sprawled on the massive bed, thick quilts pulled up to her chin. With a few quick steps and a short bound, Eliana landed on the bed next to her, jostling the other girl.

"What brings you here so early?" Derya asked. "Surely you have your own bed to lounge in."

"Stop, Derya. I need you to listen."

Derya sat up, her large eyes doubling in size. "What is it?"

In a few concise sentences, Eliana told her of the tidings brought by Duke Abelardo. She searched the other princess's countenance as she spoke, her heart constricting as Derya's complexion blanched.

"Such awful news, Eliana," she said softly. "What are you going to do?"

Eliana's spine melted, and she flopped face-first onto the quilts. The damp of her sweat chilled her skin, and the cold seeped throughout her body, turning her toes to ice and freezing the marrow in her bones. She longed to burrow under the covers and never come out. It was one thing to know deep down what she would do. It was another to utter the words out loud.

"I know this is terrible for you." Derya stroked her hair. "I wish I could make it go away."

Eliana rolled over and stared up at the white bed hangings. "That's the worst of it. You can."

"I can?" Derya tipped her head to the side.

"But I won't let you do it."

"Do what?"

"It seems," Eliana said, attempting a nonchalant tone, "if we hand Ymittos over to Cinar, then you, as the one destined to rule the land that used to be Malkh, would be the curse-breaker."

Derya's complexion, which had been a pale olive color, now turned gray.

"Oh, don't worry," Eliana said. "I won't burden you. This is my duty, my curse to break." Bitterness oozed into her tone. She took a deep breath and raised her chin, forcing herself to speak more decisively. "If I am called to sacrifice for my people, then sacrifice I will. Even if a monster in Malkh eats me. Or Cetus carries out his personal—" Her breath caught and her voice failed.

For a long moment, Derya held her gaze. "Thank you. Although I wouldn't blame you if you did fob it off on me." She pursed her lips. "Do you want me to come with you?"

Warmth like the first breath of spring that melts lingering snow coursed through Eliana's veins. She grabbed Derya's hand. "I would love nothing more. But I hate to drag you into danger."

"And what will you be doing? Going to the theater?" Derya asked. "Consider this. If you fail, I'll try. Since I'm three weeks younger than you, I'd have some time to get ready."

"That's true." Eliana gnawed on her lower lip. "Perhaps you shouldn't come with me. Let's see what happens before you venture into Malkh."

"What, sit on my hands, waiting for you to return?"

"That's what Istvan suggested."

"Oh, he did, did he? Then it's not a good idea."

Eliana frowned. "I don't understand why you don't like him."

Derya shook her head. "He's too perfect, don't you think?"

"No. He's not perfect. But I think I could love him. And he seems to want to do right by me. Isn't that as much as a princess can expect?"

The other princess grimaced. Her shoulders drooped, and she exchanged a resigned look with Eliana. Derya, it seemed, understood as well as Eliana did that marriage for them was a political contract first. Everything else was secondary.

"Anyway," Derya said, "just as you have a duty to break this curse, I have a duty to my father and empire. I must get word to him as soon as I can. And just in case Cetus—or someone else—intercepts my birds, I need to go myself."

"Are you sure?"

"I wouldn't believe this if I read about it in a message, no matter who sent it. Better I tell my father myself to make sure he understands. He needs to be prepared for any possibility."

"But what if—"

Derya gripped Eliana's shoulder. "Your father will send birds to me, as will our ambassador. And I swear to you, even if I can't break the curse, if the worst happens, I will avenge your death."

Eliana shuddered. Derya had uttered the word she'd been trying to ignore. She could die in Malkh, in the dark, alone…

She blew out a long breath, feeling as if she was standing on the edge of a precipice, nerving herself to jump, hoping her air magic would save her. But nothing could rescue her. If she went to Malkh, she'd be going to her death. Or worse.

"Then it's settled," she said. "I'll go as soon as possible, and you'll be ready if—" Her words stuck in her dry mouth. "The worst happens." Heart pounding, she continued, speaking quickly to blurt the words out before she changed her mind. "Derya, I think we should send word to your father now, before anyone tells me not to. Quick, get dressed."

Sliding from the bed, Derya hurried to her bathing room. "Raging waters, you can be pushy when you want to be."

Fifteen minutes later, the two girls, tailed by their maids and a quartet of guards, raced up the steps of the palace's south tower. At the top, they were greeted by a cold wind and the sour scent of bird droppings. Hundreds of small gray birds perched in rows, heads tucked under their wings, their ruffled feathers making them resemble tiny, ash-colored pillows.

Derya led Eliana to the far corner. "Here are my pigeons." She pulled a tiny scroll from her pocket, where she had scrawled a hasty summary of events for her father. She smiled at Eliana. "Don't worry, I encoded the message. Only he will be able to read it." She frowned. "But it will take days for the bird to reach him."

"Maybe not," Eliana said. "I have an idea." As she watched Derya affix the scroll to the pigeon's spindly leg, Eliana pushed down her fear. Once they sent the message to the emperor, she'd be committed. "Let the bird go." Eliana licked her lips, tasting the salty sweat produced by her run up the steps.

As soon as Derya tossed the pigeon out the window, it spread its wings and banked, heading east to Cinar.

Eliana readied her magic. She waited for the bird to soar before pushing her air magic. The gust caught the bird under its outstretched wings and shot it through the sky. In a moment, the pigeon had disappeared.

"How did you know to do that?" Derya looked at her with wide eyes.

"I didn't." Eliana shrugged. "But I thought it was worth a try." She winced. "Perhaps you should send a second bird, just in case I wounded that one."

13

Swirling snow obscured the road, the white flakes spinning in the frigid wind. Eliana hunched her shoulders, tugging her cloak tighter. It did no good. Snowflakes caked her eyelashes, and the scarf over her nose and mouth was damp from her breath and the snow that it melted. She didn't know which was worse: the icy wind that stung her face, or the wet scarf that chapped her lips.

Derya rode at her side, a fur-lined hood pulled over her head. Snow covered her shoulders and her brown leather gloves were sooty black. Eliana flexed her frozen fingers inside her own gloves, darkened by melting snow.

Over all objections, Derya had insisted on setting out immediately for Cinar. She pointed out that her shortest route was the one Eliana would take to the rift. They could all travel together that far. After Eliana and her companions descended into the underworld, Derya would proceed through Nafplio on her way home.

Eliana was grateful to have Derya's company for the beginning of her journey, but silently plodding over icy roads into a cutting wind with all conversation stifled by the effort to keep warm wasn't how she'd envisioned this trip. She'd wanted to talk with the other princess, to discuss possible ways to break the curse. And to sneak peeks at the book of magic. But three days on the road in a winter storm shattered her hope like pouring cold water on heated glass.

Only at night, when they huddled in Eliana's tent with Alessia and Derya's maid Rasheda, could they exchange more than a few words. To Eliana's amazement, Derya brushed aside protocol and suggested they share to save the weary guards from having to put up two royal tents. Eliana agreed, understanding this was Derya's way of creating time with her so they could study magic amplifiers.

But after a long day of travel, they were too cold and exhausted to do more than eat their meager supper of dried meat, figs, cheese, and tea before rolling up in furs and succumbing to their fatigue. The best Eliana could do was recite to herself what she'd learned from the book and consider Corban's final warnings to her. *Think the unthinkable. Look for non-magical solutions first. Don't overuse the magic. What works for one mage might not work for another.* All good advice, but it did little to boost her wavering confidence. Or lessen her conviction that she'd die in the inky gloom of Malkh.

Istvan led their entourage at a measured pace. He was wise, Eliana thought, to be wary of a horse slipping on the icy roads. The dochan kept his standard bearer and armorer close to his side, along with two of his most trusted warriors. From time to time, one of them rode ahead, seeking the advance party Istvan had dispatched, a group of four men tasked with scouting for wolves, bandits, and a suitable place to camp each night.

Nearly every hour, Istvan would ride along the line of their entourage, passing the first half of his men to reach Eliana, Derya, and their maids. After ensuring Eliana and her companions were able to continue without taking a rest, he'd ride on, past Eliana's two taxarchias, consisting of forty of Ymittos's finest soldiers, and Derya's retinue of nearly two hundred that followed. The rest of Istvan's soldiers served as a rearguard.

Miserable and cold as she was, Eliana didn't begrudge their sluggish pace. Whenever she thought of descending into Malkh, her chest tightened and she had to fight for every breath. The idea of delving deep underground into the tunnels that snaked their way underneath hundreds of feet of rock and clay, far beneath the sunlit slopes and meadows of the land she loved, made her hands shake and sweat. Would she be able to breathe in those closed-in caverns? What if she got trapped in the dark and couldn't find a way out? If she had to embark on a dangerous adventure, why couldn't it have been to high mountain peaks where there was warm light and fresh air?

To distract herself, she reviewed the warnings and advice from the magic book. If amplifiers were overused, air mages could lose their sense of smell and light mages could go blind. She hadn't noticed losing her sight that day by the canal, but then again, she thought everything had gone black because she was losing consciousness.

Although according to the magic book, the loss of a sense was temporary. *Usually.* Water mages, what happened to them? Eliana shrunk into her cloak to shield her face from a blast of stinging sleet. *Deaf. Water mages might go deaf.* Had Derya lost her hearing when they rescued the canal workers? She'd never said.

Tugging her scarf from her mouth, Eliana brushed away a layer of frosty crystals that had formed from her breath. With fumbling, stiff fingers, she re-wrapped the scarf around the lower part of her face, trying to put the least damp place against her skin.

What happened to stone mages who overused amplifiers? She couldn't remember. No matter how fatigued she was that night, she'd study the magic text. Whoever had written the book had a sense of humor, titling it, *Magic for Those Who Dare.*

The Rider knew there were enough warnings on its pages to scare off all but the most determined.

Eliana wiggled her toes, wincing at the cold's biting sting. She continued her silent recitation. Wine removed impurities from metal, wood, and stone. Was it wine that made air magic produce gusty winds? Or was that beer?

The relentless wind cut through her cloak like a spear. She gasped and tugged her hood lower over her face. Too bad she couldn't use pepper as an amplifier. One taste, and she'd be able to warm the surrounding air.

Or maybe not. In this bitter cold, it would be easy to overuse the magic. Besides, Istvan would be vexed. She huffed. *When I'm queen, we'll end this foolishness of women not practicing magic.*

Her mind wandered to schemes for establishing a school for women mages. She had just settled on the number of students she'd accept each year when the mellow sound of Istvan's horn interrupted her daydream. Her mouth went dry as she pulled on the reins, stopping her horse.

"Sounds like we've run into trouble," Derya said.

A dark cleft marred the valley below, a long canyon that stretched beyond their vision, nearly splitting Ymittos into two uneven parts. Eliana pointed. "No. We're here." She gripped her saddle to fight the feeling that she was falling into a tomb.

Derya brushed snow from her face. "Lucky you. No more traveling in this wind, once you're below. Maybe you'll have dry feet for a change."

That was one way to look at it. But Derya didn't have to wander in airless dark tunnels closed in by unyielding rock.

Istvan rode toward them, his chestnut stallion's breath forming long plumes in the frigid air. A few days' growth of beard darkened the dochan's chin, the black hairs flecked with snowflakes.

"Our scouts have made it to the rift, Eliana," he said. "We'll arrive there in less than an hour." He turned to Derya.

"Highness, will you camp here for the night, or continue? Several hours of daylight remain."

"I would like to consult with the captain of my guard." Derya gave him a frosty look.

Eliana leaned toward her. "If it makes any difference, we're going into the rift now."

"Now, Eliana?" Istvan scowled at her.

"Yes, now. There's no sense in staying in all this snow to just get colder and wetter."

"It's damp below."

"But out of the wind."

He shook his head. "We are all tired and hungry, too fatigued to climb down safely. Better to descend tomorrow when we're fresh. Besides, the scouts have already set up your tent."

"Well, in that case," Derya said, "I'll leave in the morning." She winked at Eliana.

A shadow crossed Istvan's face. Then he nodded. "I will let your escort know, Princess."

Part of Eliana wanted to delay descending into the dark as long as she could. Another part longed to get on with it, to face her fear rather than imagining what terrors lurked below. Her parents had advised her to trust Istvan's judgment. She had no reason to argue other than her own terror.

Derya clicked to her horse, urging it into a walk. "Are you coming? Or will you sit there until you turn into a snowdrift?"

Eliana touched her heels to her mare's sides. At least she'd have one more night with Derya's bracing company, and to glean any final advice from the book.

When they reached the rift, Eliana dismounted. She gave her horse a lingering pat and rested her forehead against the animal's withers. "Thank you." This was the last day she'd ride Filos, her dependable yet spirited mare. Would she ever see her again?

With a sigh, she handed her reins to a groom and trudged

after Derya through knee-deep snow. When she reached the area trampled by Istvan's men, she stamped her feet. Her effort neither knocked the snow from her boots nor warmed her numb toes.

Four of Istvan's men were hastily erecting Eliana's tent. Derya's eyes narrowed. "I thought they'd already put it up."

"I did, too." Eliana snaked an arm through Derya's, huddling close for warmth. "It seems Istvan didn't want you to stay."

"He hates me."

"That's a bit dramatic, don't you think? Perhaps he knows you make fun of him, and he doesn't like it."

"Do you really want to marry a man who can't stand a little teasing?"

That was a good question. Evander had been the first one to laugh at himself. That quality made him easy to be around. Not to mention, he'd been as quick to pull a prank as Derya.

"It's ready for you, Highness," a soldier called.

"Thank you!" Eliana darted for the entrance, Derya close behind her. Inside, they shucked off their sodden cloaks and dropped them on the wooden floor. They knelt near the brazier, extending their chilled hands to the warming flames. *Rider bless the soldier who started the fire.* A few moments later, Alessia and Derya's maid entered, followed by their luggage.

Within a few moments, all four of them had changed into dry clothing. Eliana sat by the brazier, rubbing her chapped fingers. Her toes prickled and stung as if she'd walked barefoot over a patch of nettles. Derya was massaging her own white toes, wincing as they turned scarlet.

The burning in Eliana's feet was subsiding when a soldier brought water, a teapot, and cups. Alessia knelt by the fire and began to brew tea.

Rasheda, Derya's maid, drew near. "Kiral, if I may..."

Derya glanced up. "What is it?"

"A messenger arrived for Dochan Istvan. From Nafplio."

"So?"

"The message said, 'They're all gone.' That made the dochan grin."

"Who's all gone?"

"It didn't say."

"Whatever it's about," Eliana said, "it probably has nothing to do with us. Most likely it was about bandits or pirates or something like that."

"Right," said Derya. "Anyway, we've got more important things to do tonight than worry about the affairs of minor dochandoms."

Eliana nodded. She dug the book from her pack and handed it to Derya. Then she pulled a fur blanket around her shoulders. "Start with air."

Derya tugged her own blanket close before flipping the pages. "How does the taste of dates amplify air magic?"

"Dates. They chill or condense the air."

"Right. And berries?"

"Berries. Scent the air, to drug anyone who smells it?"

"No, that's bitter herbs. Berries push air away. How about the taste of vinegar?"

"Makes you think of Istvan?" Alessia said.

Eliana burst into giggles. Then she felt ashamed. She shouldn't laugh at her betrothed, but Alessia's comment was funny.

Before she could answer, Istvan pushed into the tent, scowling. Derya buried the book under her blanket.

"Istvan!" Eliana's heart thumped, and she forced a smile to her face. She gestured to the teapot. "Would you care for some tea?"

"No, I would not." He snapped the words like a whip. "I wouldn't want to sour your fun." He curled a lip in Alessia's direction. "Are you sure you need this maid? Give me one reason to not send her back."

"Oh, Istvan, why be so upset over a silly joke? We're all

cold and tired." Honestly, he could have a better sense of humor.

"A courier is leaving in an hour to inform your father we've made it here. I think your maid should go with him."

How odd that he'd interfere with her choice of servants. "Please sit and have some tea. They'll be bringing food shortly. You can dine with us if you wish." Eliana gave him a shy smile.

To her relief, he sat down, the tightness in his face relaxing. "Food sounds like something we all need."

"I hope they hurry," Derya said. "I'm so tired I might fall asleep before they get here."

Istvan gave Eliana a piercing stare, as if attempting to read her thoughts. "Why were you discussing the use of vinegar with air magic? You promised me you wouldn't practice without proper supervision."

That wasn't exactly how Eliana remembered their conversation. She took a breath and spoke in her best diplomatic voice. "We were speculating, not practicing."

He studied her face. "Oh." His shoulders slumped. "I would be grateful for some tea."

Eliana poured him a cup. As she handed it to him, she caught a glimpse of Derya. The other princess pointed her chin toward Alessia, whose head was bowed so low her chin touched her chest.

Derya's meaning was clear. Queens and princesses always chose the members of their own household. Even in this circumstance, it was Eliana's choice, not Istvan's, whether her maid stayed or went. It was a small matter, but it rankled. Especially since most of the men chosen to accompany them into Malkh were Istvan's retainers. Originally, Istvan had told her father he would select five of his own men and five of Eliana's.

But somewhere along the road, Istvan decided he wanted men he knew well and could trust. Not that the king's men weren't trustworthy, he'd assured her. But in a dangerous situation, Istvan wanted to surround himself with warriors he'd served alongside and trained to follow his lead.

Eliana understood his reasoning. If he was the one tasked with fighting off enemies, he needed men used to fighting together as a unit. But somehow, she felt uneasy. She'd managed to negotiate with Istvan to allow one of her retainers, Dimitris, to accompany them in place of one of the Nafplians. And Alessia was coming with her, whether Istvan liked it or not. Knowing she'd have Dimitris and Alessia eased the knot of terror in her stomach. Without them, she didn't know if she could go on. But antagonizing Istvan, the one who was to protect her from the perils of Malkh, was not a good idea.

As Istvan poured himself more tea, Eliana studied him, noting with a flash of irritation that he hadn't offered any to Derya or herself. She motioned for Alessia to fill the teacups.

Compressing her lips, Eliana resolved to make a few things clear to Istvan. Right away. She opened her mouth, then closed it. Her parents had warned her about being impulsive. She was tired and not at her best. Istvan was probably as chilled and worn out as she was. Perhaps he hadn't meant to treat her like a child. She'd give him the benefit of the doubt, at least for a few moments.

She accepted a cup of steaming tea and wrapped her aching fingers around it, moaning in relief as warmth seeped into her icy bones. After a few sips, she collected her thoughts enough to confront her betrothed.

"Dochan Istvan," she began, hoping to gain some dignity from her formal language. "Alessia meant no harm. And surely you understand. I cannot send her back. My mother insisted that I have a maid. You yourself said time was of the essence. We can't wait for a replacement to come." She smiled sweetly. "Oh, look, here's our supper now." She waved the soldier in, pointing to a spot where the platter of food could be set. Their meal was only dried meat, dates, figs, and bread, but it would do.

"Thank you," she said to the soldier, who bowed and left the tent. Leaning toward Istvan, she asked, "Which do you prefer? The dates? Or the figs? I'm partial to dates, myself." She picked one up and bit into it.

Letting the sweet taste roll over her tongue, she gave into a sudden impulse. She pushed on her power, ever so slightly. A chill filled the tent, then almost immediately fled. So, she could use dates as an amplifier. *Excellent.*

Istvan gave her a sharp look. She met his gaze blandly, then gestured to the platter. "I think this is dried goat. Would you like some?"

Internally, she berated herself. Of course, he knew that dates would amplify her ability to cool the air. She'd have to be more careful around him, at least until she convinced him to stop objecting to her use of magic. She couldn't afford ill feelings between them as they delved into the treacherous underworld. Battling monsters and breaking a curse were perils enough.

14

———————

Eliana peeked out of the tent at the gray wintry sky. Ash-colored clouds rolled in twisting stripes, driven by a bitter wind. The weak winter sun, even at noon, could barely pierce the gloom. At least the snow stopped. Eliana ducked back inside. The foul weather which had delayed Derya's departure almost made Eliana long to descend into the rift. Anything to escape the frigid gusts that intensified her shaking, the trembling that came only partially from the cold.

Derya's soldiers had loaded their wagons, and her retinue was mounted. This was it. Derya was leaving. Eliana clenched her jaw. She yearned to beg the princess to stay with her. But she would not allow fear to reduce her to pathetic groveling.

The Heir of Cinar tugged on one glove as she met Eliana's gaze.

"I'll miss you," Eliana said.

"I'll miss you." Derya pulled her into a hug. She whispered into Eliana's ear. "Be careful. There's something about Istvan I don't trust. Use your magic if you want to, if you need to." She stepped back and tapped Eliana's chin. "And make sure you invite me to the wedding. I'll never forgive you if I don't dance at your marriage feast."

"Don't count on it," Alessia said. "We only invite civilized people."

Eliana laughed. "Rest assured, you'll be invited. And I'll line up all the young and charming nobles of the land for you. Who wouldn't fancy a dance with the Heir of Cinar?"

The grin slid from Derya's face and she frowned at Alessia. "If you don't mind, I want a word with the princess."

Alessia pouted, but Eliana raised her eyebrows and jerked her chin. "Please go see if Istvan has everything ready for the descent." She wasn't entirely successful in keeping a tremor from her voice.

With narrowed eyes, Derya watched Alessia leave the tent. "Listen, don't talk." She shoved a small pouch into Eliana's hand. "Your tutor gave me this. He said to give it to you at the last moment, and for you not to tell anyone you have it."

Eliana's fingers curled over the soft leather sack. Its contents clinked faintly. "What is it?"

"Can't you guess?" Derya let out a huff and put her lips next to Eliana's ear. "Corban said you won't be able to use all the amplifiers, but he gave you little bits of each kind."

Tears stung Eliana's eyes. *Corban. May the Rider bless him for a thousand generations.* "Thank you, Derya. So much." She tied the pouch to the belt of her inner tunic, then arranged her outer tunic to cover it.

Derya grabbed her hand again and pressed a long, thin object into it. "This is from me. Don't let anyone know you have it. And don't hesitate to use it."

The sheathed dagger bore the arms of Cinar on its gem-encrusted hilt, fashioned from scores of tiny chips of turquoise, lapis lazuli, and diamond. Eliana handed it back to Derya. "Thank you, but I don't need it. I have a sword."

"It never hurts to have a weapon no one else knows

about." Derya slid the dagger into Eliana's boot. "Now, you're ready."

"I suppose." The bread Eliana had eaten turned to rock in her stomach and her knees refused to stop shaking. "Derya, thank you." She dug in the bag that hung from her shoulder. "Here." She thrust the magic book at Derya. "You take it."

"No, you need it more." Derya pushed it back.

"I doubt there'll be much light to read by, even if I find the time," Eliana said. "And it might be useful to you." *If I fail.*

Derya took the book and bowed low. "I am in your debt. And will be even more once you've broken this curse." She swung her cloak around her shoulders. "Let's show them what steel spines we little girls have, shall we?"

With a snort, Eliana strapped her sword to her back. She was putting on her cloak when Istvan strode into the tent. "Are you ready?" he asked.

"Yes." *As ready as I'll ever be.*

Istvan approached Derya and extended a hand. "May I?" he asked.

"Why, thank you." After flashing a smirk at Eliana, Derya put her hand in his. She allowed him to lead her out of the tent to her mare. Amused, Eliana followed and stood nearby as he helped Derya onto her mount.

With a puzzled frown on her face, Derya asked him, "You have nothing for me?"

"What do you mean?"

"Our route will take us through Nafplio. Do you not want to send messages to your father?"

"Thank you for the offer," Istvan tipped his head to her, "but I sent a courier yesterday. I wanted to make sure my family was ready to receive you."

Blinking tears from her eyes, Eliana remembered when Derya arrived in Ymittos. Back then, she couldn't wait for the other princess to depart. Now that she was leaving, Eliana felt she was losing part of her soul. She fixed a smile on her face and raised a hand in farewell.

Fastening her eyes on Eliana, Derya placed her right fist over her heart, the first two fingers extended. She clicked to her horse and her entourage moved off to the south.

Eliana watched her go, her stock of courage contracting as Derya's retreating figure grew smaller.

Istvan put his hand on Eliana's shoulder. "Shall we?"

She looked at him, unable to coax her lips into a smile. "I suppose it's time. Which men are coming with us?"

He pointed at the ten men he'd selected. "I chose the most experienced climbers."

Scanning the group, Eliana frowned. "I thought Dimitris was coming. He's the one I know the best."

"Which is why I thought he should inform your parents about our progress."

"Anyone can do that." She turned to face him. "I want him to come."

"We shouldn't have more than two who don't know how to climb," he said. "Does this mean you will send your maid back?"

She narrowed her eyes. Why was he still fighting her over Alessia and Dimitris? Was he just trying to do what he thought best? "No. We've discussed this. Alessia comes, as does Dimitris. You choose the other nine. Once we're at the bottom, it won't matter who can climb and who can't." She stifled a huff. Why was he so stubborn? "Please. It would mean a lot to me." She gave him an innocent smile. "Going into the rift, into Malkh, is frightening. Surely you understand why I want the man who has been my guard since I was seven."

A shadow traveled across his face and deep creases formed between his eyes.

"It's only because I know you can't be at my side every moment," she hastened to add.

His expression lightened. "Of course." He strode to his waiting men. After a brief conversation, one of them joined the others who stood outside the largest of the tents. Earlier, they'd agreed that twenty-five men would remain at the rift, while five would return to Ptolemaida with word of their progress. Every day five would journey to Ptolemaida, and another five would take their places at the rift, rotating every day until Eliana and Istvan returned from Malkh. *If we do...*

Istvan rejoined Eliana. "That's settled. Are you ready?"

She nodded, her mouth gone dry. She couldn't put it off any longer.

She followed Istvan to the wide rift, a thousand foot deep slash in the earth gaping one hundred yards or more from side to side. An elaborate tower jutted above the closer edge. Constructed of tree branches lashed together with vines, Eliana's father built it shortly after she was born, when he realized his daughter would likely be called upon to break the curse. Eliana shivered. "That's what we'll climb down?"

"No reason why we shouldn't," Istvan said. "It will be easier than scaling down the cliffs."

Palms sweating, she inched closer to get a better look.

Two men looped ropes around their waists, below the packs on their backs. Both had swords strapped to their backs. They each tied one end of their rope to the uppermost beam of the tower. After tugging on the ropes to verify the knots would hold, they stepped onto the wood frame.

The first man reached down with one leg, testing for a secure foothold. Gradually, he descended a few feet. After his head was lower than the edge of the rift, he shouted, "My lord, the vines make good steps. If it's like this the whole way down, the climb won't be too difficult."

The second man began the descent and Istvan sent four more men after them. "Dimitris," he said, "you go next. Then me, then you, Eliana, one of my men, then your maid. Then the last two."

She'd rather venture down into the dark alongside Dimitris. But Istvan was right to split them up, leaving more experienced climbers in between. She nodded. "I'm ready." Her heart thumped erratically.

Dimitris was already standing on the ledge by the tower, a rope tied around his waist. He gave Eliana a wave and stepped onto the frame. She gripped her hands together.

Istvan moved into position, tying the rope around himself. "Use your hands and feet to climb," he said. "The tether is only in case you slip and fall. And keep your gloves on. There are some nasty thorns."

Eliana gulped. Just one more danger to be afraid of. She bit her lip hard. *I will not whimper.*

Picking up a rope, he held it in front of Eliana. "May I?" At her nod, he tied it around her waist, tugging the knot. "That's not too tight?"

Reluctant to trust her voice, she shook her head. He bound the other end of her rope to the tower's crossbeam and turned to his remaining two men. "Make sure you verify the princess is secure before you allow her to begin. I hold you responsible for her life."

"On our honor," they replied as one.

He gave them a curt nod. "Don't rush," he said to Eliana. "It will probably take two hours to get to the bottom, so rest if you need to." He flashed a reassuring smile and swung onto the platform.

Eliana fiddled with the fastenings of her cloak and watched him descend, waiting until she could only see the top of his head. She clenched her jaw, willing her breathing to remain steady, begging her pounding heart to slow, her break-fast to stay in her writhing stomach. Now it was her turn. There was no going back.

15

Eliana's throat tightened, and her heart skipped a beat. She clenched her jaw and straightened her shoulders. She would not show fear, not in front of Istvan's men. It was better that Dimitris had descended already. She might have shamed herself by clinging to him. Or wetting herself.

One of Istvan's soldiers, a man with bushy eyebrows and kind gray eyes, asked her if she was ready. She forced a smile and bobbed her head, unable to get a word out of her dry mouth.

He pointed. "See those branches? They'll hold your weight with no problem. The vines will make good handholds. You won't even need the rope."

She stepped to the edge of the rift, tipped her chin back, and sucked the clean morning air into her lungs. How long would it be before she breathed fresh air again? Or stood on the towering heights of a mountain?

Her attire suited a climb: leggings under two tunics. She'd already tied up her cloak so that it hung no lower than her knees. Her clothing wouldn't impede her. The only obstacle was the terror that drained the strength from her limbs and the resolve from her will.

Weak-kneed, she peered into the darkness. *Don't be silly.* There was no need to fear falling. She'd jumped from higher cliffs than this one and used her air magic to reach the ground safely. An impulse made her yearn to cast off the rope and jump. *But no.* Accidents, she thought with a wince, do happen. Her cramping stomach flung a splash of bile into her throat. And what would she discover at the bottom, lurking in the dark? She was in no hurry to find out.

With another deep breath, she grasped the vines and stepped onto one of their horizontal branches. Then she forced her left foot to join her right. One step done. How many hundreds to go?

"Eliana, how goes it?" Istvan's voice floated up to her.

"I'm fine, thank you. This isn't too bad." *Yet.* While she could still see the sky, she'd be calm. When they were crammed between the rock walls of the rift or crawling through lightless underground tunnels—that was when fear would dissolve her into a sobbing mess.

Eight ropes hung next to her, the tethers that supported the others who had descended before her. The ropes shifted back and forth gently with the motion of the climbers. She tugged on her line. All secure. Nothing to worry about.

As she climbed, crackling brown leaves brushed her skin, leaves that were the crumbling remnants of the previous summer. Had these vines born any fruit? They didn't look like the vines in her father's vineyards. *A glass of wine wouldn't be a bad idea right now.*

She grasped a vine and yanked her hand back. *Merciful winds.* A thorn had nearly pierced her leather glove. Istvan hadn't been joking about the spiky prickles. She'd have to choose what she touched more carefully.

Foot by foot, she descended. The light shifted as the sun

rose higher, casting the southern face of the rocky walls into shadow and illuminating the northern side.

Contrary to her expectations, the walls of the rift weren't sheer rock. Hundreds of fissures carved by centuries of rainfall descended in twisting vertical patterns. Dark green and rusty-colored moss softened the contours of rocks and withered vines trailed over outcroppings like an elderly giant's thinning hair. The faint smell of damp leaves in a forest after a rain rose to tickle her nose.

Eliana glanced down. Istvan and his men were climbing more rapidly than she was. She could barely see the top of the dochan's head, his iron helmet disappearing into the gloom, only glimmering now and then when it caught the weak sunlight.

Resolutely, she extended her foot and stepped down. One of the ropes near her jerked and bobbed. A man shouted. "Dimitris fell!"

Her breath hitched and her stomach dropped. No. She couldn't lose him. She summoned her air magic and pulled. Gusts of wind raced upwards from the bottom of the rift, bringing the smells of damp decay, roasting meat, and smoke. She drew on her power. The air rushed past her, blowing her hair around her face.

Istvan's roar ascended from the darkness. "Eliana, stop! Do you want to alert the Malkhians we are here?"

No, she didn't. But that wasn't as important to her as Dimitris. She pulled harder, hoping she could save him from any injury.

Indistinct shouts echoed up through the rift. Then Istvan's voice: "Eliana, stop. He's at the bottom. Unharmed."

She released her power. Dark spots danced before her eyes. She clung to the vines, panting.

The soldier who'd been climbing above her reached her side. "Princess, are you well?"

"Yes, yes," she said. "I just need a moment." She raised

her waterskin to her lips and took a long gulp. Already she was feeling stronger. She wiggled her toes. They were cold, but not paralyzed like on the day Derya and she rescued the canal workers.

After another swallow of water, she wiped her mouth with the back of her hand. "I'm ready to go on now."

Twenty feet down, she caught up with Istvan. "Is Dimitris all right?" she asked.

The dochan scowled at her. "He seems to have survived."

"Then why are you angry?"

He didn't answer immediately. When he spoke, his tone was icy. "Eliana, they told me you were impulsive. I didn't realize that meant dangerously so."

"What are you talking about?" she snapped. "Dimitris would have died had I not done something."

"Yes, and you could have hurt yourself. Must I remind you that you, of all people, need to survive this climb? You are the one who must break the curse. Without you, we're all doomed."

That was true. "I was in no danger—"

"Only because Dimitris was close enough to the bottom that you didn't have to use your magic for very long."

Eliana shrugged. "So, no harm done." Why was he making such a fuss?

"Except for that wind you created. I doubt the Malkhians failed to notice all that dust flying around. The last thing we want to do is announce our presence while we are separated, with some of our men on the ground and others still climbing down."

"Well, it couldn't be helped. Besides, once we meet them, we can explain."

He frowned. "If they let us. They might not want a powerful mage to enter their realm."

"Or they might not want to offend the powerful mage." She glared at him, unwilling to admit that a small part of her thought he was right. She'd acted impulsively to save Dimitris. And in doing so, she might have doomed the rest of them.

But something was bothering her. They'd assured her no one could fall because of the ropes attached to the structure at the top. What happened? She knew what Derya would say. That Istvan was behind it. She rejected that thought. Istvan, as superior as he tried to be, wasn't a killer.

More shouts from below drew her attention. From the few words she understood, it seemed the Malkhians had found them.

16

Heart thumping in her throat, Eliana continued to descend. The air cooled, drying the sweat on her face. She climbed as fast as she could, worry for Dimitris overshadowing her fear. And she was curious to see the Malkhians' appearance. She didn't put much credence in tales of half-goat, half-fish monsters. But something about them must have spawned those rumors.

Raised voices grew louder as she clambered down. The rock walls spread out, widening the rift as if wanting to distance themselves from the tower. Eliana noted the tower's supports were thicker at the bottom, which she supposed provided strength and stability to the structure. Thirteen people descending had shaken it so little the dead leaves on the vines barely ruffled.

A thump from below jerked her attention downward. Istvan had jumped to the ground. Her eyes found Dimitris, who stood nearby, watching her. He gave her a reassuring smile and bowed his head in thanks. Relief flooded her, and she grinned in return. At least her guard was unharmed.

A company of tall, regal men stood in a semicircle surrounding the tower, both ends of their arc on the banks of a wide river. All held drawn swords. They wore goatskin cloaks, leather leggings, sand-colored tunics, and shoes made of strips of leather plaited in complicated patterns. The hems of their tunics were decorated with tiny gems of brilliant colors that flashed in the dim light. Every face bore a menacing scowl.

Eliana's heart sank. Was she going to have to fight her way to the cursed prince? With a deep breath, she stepped off the tower and stood next to Istvan. She raised her hand in greeting. "Many years of health to you. We have traveled from Ymittos—"

"We know where you're from, overworlder," a wiry man snarled. "And you're not welcome."

Eliana tilted her head. The man's speech, while heavily accented, was an understandable form of Middle Ymittosian. That was one less complication she'd have to contend with.

By this time, Alessia had reached the rift's floor. She sidled up to Eliana. "Not the friendliest sort, is he?" she muttered.

Istvan spread his hands wide. "We want—"

"We don't care what you want."

A tall man with sloping shoulders pushed to the front. "We're not giving back the cattle, if that's what you're after."

"What cattle?" Eliana asked. "That's not why we're here." She wished she could just announce her mission. Surely the Malkhians would welcome the one who came to break the curse on their prince.

The wiry man scratched his thick black beard. "If you don't want the cattle, why are you here?"

The second snarled, "Why else would they be here?"

"Who knows?" the bearded man answered. "But if they think they can take our cattle with a handful of ropes, they're bigger fools than I thought."

A tall woman with deep-set blue eyes, a confident jaw, and a sheathed sword hanging from her hip pushed through the semi-circle. Like the men, she wore a goatskin cloak. A sand-colored tunic reached below her knees, and leggings of a similar shade covered her legs. Her clothing was decorated lavishly with gems and crystals of many colors, with midnight blue, black, and turquoise dominating. Her black hair hung in thick braids on either side of her face, a few white hairs glinting in the dim light. Eliana squinted. It looked like the woman had three slanting, parallel scars on both sides of her neck.

The woman stared down her long nose at the assembled men. "I don't know why they're here. But here they are. All guests come from the Rider, you know. The least we can do is provide them with food. It's on our honor as Chorokhese."

Eliana's heart thumped once, twice, three times. Then the bearded man shoved his sword into the sheath at his hip. "As you say, Tavkatseen." The others followed his lead.

The woman grinned at Eliana and held out a hand. "Come with me, my sunshine."

Tipping her head to the side, Eliana assessed the woman. She seemed sincere in her offer of hospitality. But who were the Chorokhese? That must be a clan or family name.

"Don't do it," Istvan murmured into her ear.

She shook him off. "Why not? They're offering refreshment. It's not like they're demanding that we leave our weapons behind." She put her hand in the woman's. "May I ask your name?"

"Shirdona. And you?"

"Xanthia." Eliana didn't like using her middle name, but that's what she'd agreed to do. Just until they knew the Malkhians wouldn't kill them on the spot.

Shirdona squeezed Eliana's hand, released it, and led them down a path that followed the river upstream. Eliana squinted in the pale blue light that came from tiny round objects attached to the canyon walls. She wondered what light magic—or whose magic—was their source. If she could catch up with Shirdona, she'd ask. But Shirdona walked with a quick, graceful saunter that forced Eliana to trot to keep up.

Turning to her right, Shirdona led them into a narrow cave with a low ceiling. Eliana's pulse quickened. They were going underground. Hundreds of feet of rock and clay could fall on her and crush her. She'd never see the sun again. She pressed icy fingers against her mouth.

A small hand slipped under her arm. "We're alright," Alessia whispered.

Her maid's reassurance gave Eliana enough strength to refrain from losing her composure. She let out a slow, controlled breath and placed her fingers over Alessia's. "I hope so."

They turned a corner, and she blinked in the sudden illumination. The tunnel had opened into an enormous cavern, as bright as if hundreds of torches burned.

Eliana tipped her head back. The gloom above her obscured the cavern's roof. A single shaft of sunlight pierced the darkness, but Eliana knew that couldn't be the only light source. Then she noticed that instead of torches, much of the radiance came from the same small glowing spheres she'd seen already, spheres that emitted a steady, pale blue light.

Near the center of the cavern, an immense bonfire blazed, its flames leaping high. Sparks spiraled upward, their tiny red glows winking out as they rose toward an opening to the sky.

The rock walls glittered, reflecting the dancing flames of the fire. Eliana couldn't tell if the walls were damp, made of crystals, or both. A few stalagmites jutted from the cavern's floor, their tops lopped off to make what looked like tiny tables.

Shirdona smiled, her white teeth gleaming like newly fallen snow. "Welcome to Qala Kambada."

Behind the bonfire rose a four-sided tower. Eliana counted six stories before the shadows blocked her sight. On either side of the tower were two long, low stone structures. Perhaps twenty feet long, they looked like cattle troughs carved from the cavern's rock. Holes were bored through the sides, flush with the ground. Instead of water, a stone table filled much of the open space and was covered with platters of food. The sides, Eliana realized, were stone benches. Shirdona gestured to Eliana and Alessia to join her at one of the tables. Istvan made a move to follow, but Shirdona wagged a finger at him.

"What are you thinking, trying to sit with the women?" she said. "Put your belly button where it belongs and sit with the men. We have beer today, so you should enjoy yourself."

Eliana repressed a smile, seeing Istvan's confounded face. He was torn, she was sure, between wanting to protect her and not offending their hosts. "Go on," she said. "There's no need to worry."

"Just be careful what you say," he muttered before stalking over to the men's table, followed by his warriors.

Shirdona sat at the head of the women's table, with Eliana on her right. The tavkatseen sent Alessia to a spot near the foot. The maid's frown told Eliana she didn't care for that.

A young woman approached Eliana with a basin. "Water for our guests," Shirdona said. The young woman poured the water over Eliana's hands and offered her a towel. Then she moved on to Alessia.

Lifting a loaf of bread and a tiny dish, Shirdona held them up, then placed them before Eliana. "Bread and salt for our guests. Welcome."

Eliana tipped her head. "On behalf of all of us, I thank you."

When Shirdona clapped her hands, five young girls appeared, all with the same impudent grin as Shirdona, bearing pitchers of beer. Shirdona jerked her chin at the girls. "My daughters." She filled a tankard for Eliana, who sipped it politely.

"This is excellent beer," she said. "Where do you get the grain?"

The table erupted into laughter. One of Shirdona's daughters smirked. "Same place we get our beef."

To cover her confusion, Eliana took another sip, savoring the taste of the hops. Why were beef and beer so amusing?

Shirdona cut a chunk of meat and placed it on a dagger. She stood up. Everyone went silent, even the men surrounding the cask of beer.

She raised the dagger, balancing the beef on its tip. "To the Rider of the Ancient Skies, we give thanks."

The assembled company murmured the same phrase.

"We welcome our guests from the upper lands."

Everyone repeated her words, sending echoes through the cavern as if hundreds of warriors had gathered for the feast.

Shirdona resumed her seat and slid the meat from her dagger onto Eliana's plate. Within a few moments, the woman had piled it high with beef kebobs, roasted mushrooms and potatoes, and small round cakes filled with honey.

Eliana speared a chunk of meat with her fork and put it in her mouth. A mix of spices exploded in her mouth, hot and sweet and pungent, creating an exotic flavor. Her eyes widened. The beef was as tender as if it was from a newborn calf.

"Eat," Shirdona said, adding more meat to her plate.

"Thank you. This is delicious." Eliana took a gulp of beer. The girl seated next to her topped off her mug. Eliana pursed her lips. If she wasn't careful, she'd wind up under the table, which was not behavior that would impress their hosts. Or, judging from the way they were all guzzling their drinks, perhaps it might.

The feasting and drinking and dancing lasted through the morning, the afternoon and into the evening. The Malkhians seemed to have no end of zest for a party. Eliana noticed some of them rested their heads on the table, letting their eyes close. After a short nap, they'd rejoin the festivities. The princess rested her elbows on the table, propping her head up. Her nerves and the climb into Malkh had fatigued her. But she didn't dare imitate the sleepers. Weariness pulled on her eyelids, her eyelashes feeling heavier than lead pipes.

It must have been approaching midnight when Shirdona turned her attention from dancing, carousing, and feasting to Eliana. She plied the girl with questions about the people of Ymittos, how they lived, and what they ate.

Eliana didn't see any reason to refuse to reply, and was far too sleepy to try to dissemble. After answering Shirdona, she posed a query of her own. "Legends say Malkh is populated with people who are half goat, half fish."

Shirdona spit a mouthful of beer, spraying it over her plate. "What?"

"We were told that those who lived here were half goat, half fish."

Shirdona roared with laughter and beat her fork on the table. The women seated nearby turned their faces toward their tavkatseen.

When Shirdona's mirth faded enough for her to speak, she said, "You thought we were half goat and half fish?" She burst into more gales of laughter, joined by the other women.

Eliana sat stiff-backed, a rigid smile frozen on her face. She was only repeating what everyone knew. Why was the woman laughing at her?

At last, Shirdona composed herself. "I suppose I shouldn't laugh at a guest. But what else could I do?" She took a long swallow of beer. "Tell me, why do you think that?"

Not willing to provoke more mocking, Eliana hesitated. "After Malkh sank below the surface, word was everyone perished. Then we heard tales of creatures who were half goat, half fish."

Shirdona smirked. "You've got it all wrong. To begin with, Malkh is no more."

17

"What do you mean, Malkh is no more?" Eliana put her fork down with a thump. "If you aren't Malkhians, who are you?" *And if there is no Malkh, why am I here?*

Someone on the other side of the cavern started playing a harp, accompanied by a flute, bells, and a tambourine. A pair of men picked up rubber mallets and hit the tops and sides of the broken-off stalagmites, creating deep, rumbling tones. About twelve of the younger men jumped to their feet and began an intricate circle dance. The jeweled hems of the men's clothes twinkled in the flickering flames of the fire.

"A thousand years ago," Shirdona said, "our people occupied the upper lands, next to your kingdom."

"Yes." Eliana forced herself to speak patiently. Everyone knew that.

"Queen Dzovinar of the water fae offended Kharan-Khuag. No one knows exactly how. He stormed from his underwater lair, vowing to destroy all the water fae and the humans who were friendly to them. Some of our ancestors tried to make amends, but it was hopeless. Kharan-Khuag unleashed his power and caused a flood that set off a cataclysm. The Qvirila River and its tributaries were buried under the earth, and the surrounding land collapsed. Only by using all their combined magic did anyone survive, humans or water fae." She sighed. "That was when we decided to let Kharan-Khuag think he'd succeeded in killing us all. Malkh died, and we rebuilt our nation as Chorokha."

Eliana stared into the distance, the moving shapes of the dancers blurring. "I don't know who Kharan-Khuag is. Could he be the one we call Cetus?"

Shirdona nodded. "The name means 'Insatiable Greed' in our language."

Cetus must possess fearsome power if he could bury rivers and cleave canyons. Eliana's dinner turned into a boulder in her stomach. If Cetus lived up to the Chorokhese name for him, no land was safe from his ambition.

The dance's tempo increased. Drumbeats echoed off the rocks, creating a complex, wild rhythm of their own. The flute's soaring tones made her long to dance, to lose herself in the throbbing beat and shake off the sense of being trapped and constrained.

More men joined the dance, leaping onto the shoulders of the first twelve, forming a two-story ring that circled and bobbed. Now and then, an onlooker handed a dancer a tankard of beer, accompanied by shouts, laughter, and the occasional jesting curse.

Another group was having some kind of competition. A small, three-legged table was set with food and drink. The dancers had to perform on top of the table without disturbing the layout of the food or spilling a drop of beer. A young woman whose black hair was braided into a complicated knot and with coins strung across her forehead leaped onto the table. Rising onto her toes, she pranced among the beer mugs and plates. The long ends of her sand-colored tunic waved, the gems of the wide border of its hem sparkling. The beer didn't shift. Nor did a single coin move out of place.

"Ho! Istvan! I challenge you."

Eliana jerked her head to find the speaker. A tall man with a grizzled beard pointed at the tiny table and the dancing woman. With a scowl, Istvan slowly rose from his seat. The princess wanted to see how well he could dance on his toes, but her curiosity to hear Shirdona's story won out. Eliana turned back to the tavkatseen. "Please go on."

"Over the centuries, our peoples mingled. The human side gives us the physical strength and agility to climb like goats. Which is a useful skill when raiding the cattle of our neighbors, no?" She grinned at Eliana.

"Whose cattle are you talking about?"

"Yours, of course. Where do you think the meat you're eating or the beer you're drinking comes from? We have no pastures or fields down here."

Anger whipped through Eliana's chest. She waved a hand at the laden table. "This is all stolen?"

"Well, appropriated from the people who stole our lands."

Eliana forced her words through a clenched jaw. "But you abandoned them."

"Not through any choice of our own. We intend to repossess our realm someday, when the Rider defeats Kharan-Khuag."

After one thousand years, they want to reclaim their old lands? Eliana wasn't about to cede any territory to these cattle thieves. She opened her mouth to say so. Then, stifling her impulse to argue, she dropped her hands limply into her lap. This argument had to wait until she broke the curse. She studied Shirdona's face. Being part fae would explain the limber build of these people. "What does your fae heritage give you?"

Shirdona tapped the side of her neck. The lines Eliana had thought were scars flared open and shut. Now she noticed that all the Chorokhese had similar slits. "The water fae gave us the ability to breathe underwater. In some ways, we are half goat and half fish. But not really."

"But why does everyone think that?"

"We spread that rumor for two reasons. First, so that anyone living on the surface wouldn't come exploring and discover us." She took a long swallow of beer. "And second, we hoped that if the only word about the survivors of Malkh were fables of fabulous monsters, Kharan-Khuag would think he had succeeded in destroying us. We managed to keep ourselves concealed from him for about nine hundred years."

"Why didn't he hear about your raids on my people?"

"If he did, it wouldn't matter," Shirdona said. "There are raiders and bandits everywhere."

Eliana rubbed a hand over her mouth. That was true, and Ymittos had its share of thieves. Shirdona's news explained the stories of vanishing cattle, casks of beer, and barrels of freshly milled flour that circulated throughout the rural areas.

Fascinated horror drew her attention back to Cetus's part in the tale. "So, he thought you were all dead for nine centuries. That would mean about one hundred years ago, Cetus, or Kharan-Khuag, as you call him, learned you'd survived."

Shirdona nodded. "He was so enraged he cursed our tagavlon. You would call him our prince."

"But why not kill you all immediately?"

"A little bloodthirsty, are we, princess?" She snorted. "Because he wanted to toy with us, to make us live knowing our doom. He especially relished watching our tagavoi die of a broken heart, unable to save his cursed son."

Shivers ran up and down Eliana's spine. There seemed to be no limit to Cetus's cruelty. What would he do to her if he knew she was seeking to break the curse? Now she wished Istvan had brought more soldiers.

"If our tagavlon isn't awakened soon, Kharan-Khuag will take over our land and enslave us all." The woman shuddered.

"Do you fathom what that means? We'll all be compelled to do his bidding, no matter how evil or repugnant. He'll make us do far worse than dig in his mines or fight in his wars." Shirdona sighed and her face twisted. "I don't understand why those weak-livered, ox-footed Ymittosians don't send their princess. If Kharan-Khuag takes our land, he won't stop there. Ymittos will be next. Are they that stupid? Is the princess a coward? Or feeble-minded?"

"I'm not feeble-minded—"

Shirdona's mouth curled in a smirk.

Eliana huffed and clamped her jaw shut. She could no sooner retract her words than collect sparks that rose from a campfire. She straightened her spine and took a deep breath. "I am the Princess Eliana, come to break the curse on your prince."

"Of course you are." Shirdona let out a guffaw. She seized her mug and drained it. "What other girl would climb down here, accompanied by a handful of armed guards?" She snorted. "Who else would brave the monsters in the dark?"

"You knew all along? Why didn't you say so?"

"Obviously, you had your own game to play. I just wanted to see where you were going with it. But you should have told us from the beginning." Shirdona tipped her head toward the dancing men. "Some of those young hotheads were eager to skewer you as you came down the tower. And the ones that didn't like that idea thought you'd make excellent target practice."

"You would kill people just like that?" Eliana asked.

"We don't take kindly to people coming onto our territory. They might want to steal our supplies, you know."

Eliana shook her head and glanced at Istvan. He stood on his toes on the tiny table, surrounded by mugs of beer filled to the brim. He shuffled a step and lost his balance. With athletic grace, he jumped off to land on his feet. A smiling girl with a headband of gold coins offered him a mug of beer, the froth overflowing. Eliana was glad he was occupied, but there was a flirtatious gleam in the girl's eye and Istvan seemed rather entertained. Should she interrupt him, or was it better to continue her conversation with Shirdona without his opposition?

While Eliana was still collecting her thoughts, Shirdona drew her eyebrows together. "Are you sure you're the princess? I don't know much about her, but her name isn't Xanthia."

"Xanthia is one of my names. Eliana Xanthia Vasiliki Kastellanos."

"Any Ymittosian would know that." Shirdona crossed her arms. "Tell me something only the princess would know."

"If only the princess knew it, then how would you know she was telling the truth?" Eliana asked.

Shirdona's face creased into a reluctant smile. "True. Then tell me, Your Highness, why did you conceal who you are?"

Eliana hesitated. She'd promised Istvan not to reveal her true identity or anything else to the Malkhians—or the Chorokhese, if that's what they called themselves—until it was clear they wanted the curse broken. But Shirdona already knew why she'd come to Malkh. While her instincts prompted her to trust the tavkatseen, she couldn't be sure.

The princess decided an aggressive move was in order. Sitting up straight and lifting her chin, she imitated her mother's most imperious tone. "Why all the questions? Do you want the curse broken or not?"

The tavkatseen tipped her head to the side. "Some do, some don't."

"What do you mean?" Eliana asked. More importantly, to which group did Shirdona and her relatives belong?

"Some of our people like ruling themselves, not answering to any leader. It's been this way for decades, since the old tagavoi died. They're mostly from the stronger clans, the ones who live upstream, farthest from the sea." She pointed with her chin. "Us here, and those downstream, we want the curse broken. We're the first ones who Kharan-Khuag's monsters will destroy."

"How can we tell who's on what side?" Eliana asked.

"You don't. Not until they try to help you. Or kill you."

Eliana's face froze. Shirdona's cackling didn't give her any clue about the woman's intentions. While thinking of how to respond, Eliana let her gaze roam over the dancing crowd. Istvan was receiving what looked like a dancing lesson from the girl who'd offered him beer. The Chorokhese girl gazed up into his eyes, stroking his arm as she lifted it, fluidly moving it over his head. Eliana scowled. Istvan needed to break off his dalliance and get his attention back to their situation.

"Don't worry, my sunshine," Shirdona said, still chuckling. "I'm not about to kill you. I want that curse broken. Our only hope against Kharan-Khuag is to unite, and our tagavlon is the only one all our clans would rally around. I suppose you want to know where he is."

"I do."

"Then let's you and I talk, and that handsome one who seems to think he's in charge." She walked over to Istvan, shoving her way between him and the simpering girl. "You. I want a word with you." Without waiting for him to reply, she swaggered to a bench at the base of the tower and sat on it as if it were a throne.

Eliana followed her and perched on the far end of the bench. Istvan strode to join them and stood with his legs apart and arms crossed. "What's all this about?"

"Who wants to know?" asked Shirdona.

Istvan glared. "I am Dochan Istvan Atreus, son of the Diodochi of Nafplio."

"Nafplio? Never heard of it. Well, Istvan, the princess tells me you're here to break the curse."

A muscle twitched in Istvan's jaw and his nostrils flared. He was displeased, either because Shirdona had ignored his title, or Eliana told Shirdona their mission. He flicked a sharp glance at the princess before shooting Shirdona a bland smile. "So, she informed you. What do you think?" He slid his hand to rest on the pommel of his sword.

Shirdona scoffed. "There's no need to panic like an eel on a hook. Us around here? We want the tagavlon woken up."

A crease formed between Istvan's eyebrows. "Does that mean some don't want the curse broken?"

"I already told the princess about them. But they're not important. It's Kharan-Khuag—Cetus, as you call him—that you should be worried about. He's getting ready to invade."

"We know that." Istvan's voice was tight.

"I don't think you do. Ever since he learned we're alive, he's sent his monsters, mutant water fae and worse, to harass us and learn about our defenses. When these monsters capture someone, they cut off their hands and feet and leave them for the vishapions to feast on. Or they carve threats into their flesh, threats about what they'll do to us and our children once they rule Chorokha. We know that dying in battle against Kharan-Khuag's forces would be a far easier death. The same fate waits for your people if you fail to break the curse. If you succeed, well, no one thinks Kharan-Khuag will give up. But at least we won't be mindless slaves and can prepare for the invasion, whenever it comes. Unless you decide that you'd rather kill yourselves before you are overrun."

18

With every word, the food in Eliana's stomach felt heavier and the burden she bore dragged on her shoulders. If she failed, Kharan-Khuag would seize Chorokha and invade Ymittos. His army of monsters would ravage her unprepared people. Not to mention his plans for her. She shuddered. Her tongue was dry and lifeless, and she struggled to pose the all-important question.

"Where is your prince?"

"Our tagavlon? I could tell you, but you'll never locate him without a guide."

"Why not?"

Shirdona tipped her head toward the flowing water. "If the tagavlon was near the river, you'd have no problem. But his parents laid him in the family tower. To reach him, you'll have to traverse a labyrinth of tunnels. Only someone who has walked them for many years can find the surest route."

"Can't you draw us a map?" Istvan asked.

Eliana frowned. Why didn't Istvan want a guide? Did he not trust Shirdona? To be fair, they had just met her. The woman could be telling them anything while planning to lose them far underground. Eliana shivered. Deep underground, under all the rock and clay… She shook herself. *No.* She wouldn't let herself think about suffocating in a collapsed tunnel.

"A map, he wants." Shirdona chuckled. "Good luck with that. Just as the river changes where the stones lie, so we move the rock and alter the pathways. That way we give the mushrooms a rest, and keep the bagalas, vishapions, and other beasts at bay."

Why would mushrooms need to rest? Eliana didn't know what bagalas and vishapions were, but exploring the underworld was sounding less appealing by the minute. "What are those?" she asked.

"Big monsters. Hungry ones," Shirdona said. "Now, do you want a guide or not? I'll be delighted to lead you."

Istvan wrinkled his brow. "Why would you be willing to guide us through dark tunnels past ferocious beasts? What will you demand in return?"

Shirdona shook her head. "Oh, I have a reason or two. But you're not much for thinking, are you? The tagavlon is likely to reward whoever helps the cursebreaker. May as well be me."

"Can we trust you?" Istvan fixed his dark eyes on her.

"What else are you going to do?" Shirdona asked.

"I think Istvan and I need to discuss your offer." Eliana stood up. "Do you mind?"

"Talk all you want." Shirdona waved a lazy hand. "You won't find anyone better."

Eliana walked a short distance away, Istvan on her heels. "Istvan—"

"How dare you."

"What?"

"I'm leading this expedition. You don't make the decisions." Deep creases formed between his eyebrows and a vein pulsed in his temple.

Her body tensed, and she bared her teeth in a snarl.

"Since I'm the one doing the curse-breaking, my opinion matters. And as your future wife, I would think that goes without saying." She crossed her arms and tightened her jaw.

He traded glares with her. After a few heartbeats, he sighed and the muscles around his eyes relaxed. "I see your point."

She put a hand on his biceps. "We don't know what lurks in these tunnels or how to find the prince. If Shirdona wants a reward from him, she'll make sure we succeed."

Istvan pursed his lips. "So she says. I just don't think we should trust the first person who offers to help."

"But do we have time to look for another? We only had fifteen days to break the curse, and we've used up nine."

"If this Shirdona can't find the prince, we could end up losing more time."

Eliana pulled in a long breath. "That's true," she said slowly. "What if we ask her a few questions, like how she knows the prince's location? That might help us decide."

He frowned. "She could lie."

"She could. But let's try." She darted back to Shirdona before Istvan could stop her.

"Well, what's it to be?" Shirdona asked.

"We have some questions." Eliana offered her most gracious smile. "Do you know where the prince is?"

Shirdona snickered. "Everyone down here knows that, my sunshine. Each year on the anniversary of his cursing, we make a pilgrimage to his tower and ask the Rider of the Ancient Skies to send a cursebreaker."

Istvan scoffed. "Then anyone could show us the way. Why do we need you?"

"They could *show* you. But keep you safe in that maze? That's another matter." Shirdona's gaze homed in on Eliana's eyes. "I'm the only one around with sufficient forces to protect you on the way. If you don't want to work with me, fine. The closest alternative is a day or so east. Assuming nothing eats you, or one of those who prefers things as they are, doesn't find you first."

Eliana watched Shirdona's face carefully as the woman spoke. Flickering torchlight made it difficult to tell, but she seemed sincere.

But Istvan was scowling. "Travel east? Is that in the prince's direction, or no?"

"He's an ox-footed dancer," Shirdona said, "but he's got a brain behind his eyes."

Eliana stiffened, hoping Istvan would refrain from responding to the taunt.

Shirdona didn't seem to think she'd said anything at all insulting. She shook her head, dark braids lashing her shoulders. "The tagavlon lies east of here, but the safest route is through a tunnel that leads west. That is, if you want to avoid the bagalas and a few other hungry beasts. If you prefer another guide, you'll waste time going east, then more coming back." She narrowed her eyes. "And just in case the tagavlon doesn't give me a reward, you'll have to pay me as well."

"How much?" Istvan asked.

"Fifty head of cattle, fifty casks of beer, and fifty barrels of flour. Payable on demand."

Eliana thought that was a small price to pay to thwart Cetus's invasion plans. She looked up at Istvan. "I think we've found a guide."

"Are you sure about this?" he asked.

"We need to find the prince. She can get us there."

His gaze hardened, and she wavered. She didn't want to cross him. While she coveted his approval, she was also sure she was right.

Tugging on his arm, she led him a few feet away from Shirdona. With a fleeting glance back at the woman, whose smirk was visible even in the dusky light, Eliana stood on her tiptoes and whispered into Istvan's ear. "Listen. Let's just try with her and see how it goes. And have all our people nose around. Maybe they can learn how much of what she says is true."

He rubbed the side of his face. "And find someone else, if she proves untrustworthy?"

"Something like that. But we came here to act, not wait."

"I don't like this, but we have no other choice." He hardened his jaw. "Just be alert for any hint of deception."

With a grim nod, she returned to Shirdona, whose smirk had widened into a toothy grin, her teeth reflecting the pale blue light. "If you're willing," Eliana said, "we'd like for you to take us to the prince. When can we leave?"

"So, you agree to my terms?" Shirdona asked.

"No," said Istvan. "Fifty head of cattle, fine. No beer or flour."

Eliana stared at him. "What are you doing?" she asked.

"Negotiating," Istvan replied without taking his eyes from Shirdona's face.

Shirdona chuckled. "Twenty casks of beer and thirty of flour."

"Ten of each." Istvan crossed his arms.

"Fine, ten of each," Shirdona said. "Plus, twelve bottles of wine."

"Take it." Eliana elbowed him. "My father will pay."

He nodded.

"Good," Shirdona said. "Now swear. Blood oath."

Eliana extended her hands toward Shirdona, palms up. "I, Eliana Kastellanos of Ymittos, give you my word, that on the lives of my father and mother and the honor of my people, I will pay you what you demand in return for safely guiding us to your prince."

Istvan jerked his eyebrows together in a puzzled glance at Eliana. He turned to Shirdona and held up his right arm, his hand extended over his head. "I, Istvan Atreus of Nafplio, give you my word on the lives of my father and brothers. We will pay you fifty head of cattle, ten casks of wine, and ten barrels of beer, along with twelve bottles of wine."

Shirdona nodded. "May all your forged steel turn brittle and break if you fail to keep your word. And the blood in your veins turn to bile." She crooked her finger, summoning one of her daughters, who brought a full tankard of beer. Shirdona dropped a pebble into it. "We each drink three times." She took a sip and handed the tankard to Istvan. He sipped, then handed it to Eliana.

When all had drunk three times, Shirdona drained the dregs and smacked her lips.

"Are you satisfied?" Istvan asked flatly.

A grin split Shirdona's face. "Oh yes. You've just sealed a sacred oath. Break it on pain of death." She handed the tankard to her daughter. "Princess, where are your cattle?"

"I don't have any," Eliana said.

"Well, my sunshine, how will you pay me?"

"You'll get your reward after we break the curse," Istvan said. Eliana nodded in agreement.

"Oh, no," Shirdona said. "The deal was I take you to our tagavlon. What if you die trying to break the curse? Will I still get paid? No. My terms are payable on demand. I'm demanding now."

Eliana stared at her for a long moment, unsure how to respond. Shirdona was demanding the impossible. Sweat prickled the back of Eliana's neck. She looked into Istvan's angry, narrowed eyes.

He rested his hand on the hilt of his sword. "Just how do you expect us to get the cattle and beer?"

"The way we do. You'll have to take them." Her eyes lit up and her face brightened. "And I'll tell you what. We'll help you."

"We can't steal from my people," Eliana said, indignation sharpening her tone.

"It's only borrowing. After you break the curse, you can

pay for what you took. If you fail, well, those farmers will have bigger problems."

"Why don't I simply buy the things? I could send word to my father…"

Shirdona glared at her. "It's dishonorable to refuse to go on a cattle raid. If you refuse now, how will my men know you are worthy of aid, worthy for us to risk our lives for you?" She spat. "Does a blood oath mean nothing to you?"

Eliana's shoulders slumped. Stealing from her own people was wrong. But Shirdona was her best hope to break the curse, unless the woman had been lying. She didn't like this, not one bit. It was a violation of her people's trust. But much worse could happen if she failed in her quest. And they'd sworn a blood oath. She looked at Istvan. "We should do it."

His arms were crossed, and a glower had overtaken his face like a thundercloud obscures the sun. Long minutes passed while shivers ran up and down Eliana's back.

Istvan let out a sigh. "We will go on your cattle raid. But we take no more than what we promised you. No damage to the farms, fields, or fences. And if I sense even a whiff of a hint that you are putting either me or the princess in danger, I will kill you all."

19

Eliana pulled in deep, slow breaths, struggling to remain calm. Shirdona had seemed friendly, but there was a hint of iron behind her words that suggested she would not easily be cowed. Or take kindly to threats.

The woman stared at Istvan, her eyes glinting like a wild beast's in the darkness. Then she chuckled. "Bluster all you want, boy. I'm not afraid of you. You needn't worry. Of course, we don't damage the farms. How else would they raise grain for us next year?" She snorted. "Not much for thinking ahead, are you?"

Before Istvan managed to speak through his sputtering, Eliana squeezed his arm. "Later," she whispered. "We'll deal with her later. First, we break the curse."

He grasped her hand and intertwined his fingers with hers. "You're right. It's good one of us can think ahead."

Eliana wasn't sure if his tone was sarcastic or hurt. "It's better if she underestimates you."

"Right again." He squeezed her hand. "So, Shirdona, what are we waiting for? Are your men too drunk to joust with cows?"

Shirdona tossed her head and pushed into the center of the circling dancers. "I need thirty for a raid. Who will it be?"

The upper circle of dancers leaped to the ground. The revelers began shouting and waving their arms in the air, arguing over whose turn it was, as if a cattle raid was the height of entertainment.

"At this rate, we'll be here until summer," Istvan muttered to Eliana.

She seized his elbow. "We'd better explain to the others what we're doing."

"I'll inform my men." He removed his arm from her grasp and strode over to the table where his soldiers were still sampling Shirdona's beer.

Eliana gulped. She wasn't sure how Alessia and Dimitris would react. Disapproval was the best she could hope for. She caught Dimitris's eye and motioned with her head for him to join her. Alessia was already moving in her direction.

When they reached her side, she pulled them around the corner of the tower. In a few words, she explained the deal she'd reluctantly made with Shirdona.

Dimitris scowled. "This is bad, Highness, very bad."

"I know. But we didn't think there was time to find another alternative." She looked up into his angry eyes, pleading with her gaze for him to understand.

"It's not all bad," Alessia said.

"What?" Both Eliana and Dimitris asked.

"Well, if the princess breaks the curse, she can compensate the farmers. The prince might even want to pay. And since she now knows who's responsible for the raiding in this part of the country, she'll be able to do something to stop it in the future."

Dimitris rubbed his chin. "Yes, I suppose that's true." He sighed. "As Shirdona says, if you fail, we'll all have bigger problems. Fine. But, Highness, you're not going anywhere without me."

The shouting by the fire ceased. Eliana peeked around the tower. Thirty of Shirdona's followers, mostly men but with a handful of women, were donning leather masks, some shaped like goat's heads, others like fish. Istvan and his eight men all held masks.

Eliana walked over to them. "Are you goats or fish?"

Istvan held up a fistful of masks. "Some of each." He handed Eliana three masks. "We left fish for you."

She passed masks to Dimitris and Alessia. "I suppose this means we're going now?"

"Apparently." Istvan rolled his eyes. "They tell me they like to raid at night."

"Princess!" Shirdona yelled. "Let's go!"

The raiding party followed Shirdona back through the tunnel to the river, which the woman said had been the Qvirila River before the cataclysm. They walked upstream a short distance before turning into another tunnel, then another. Shirdona hadn't exaggerated when she said the underworld was a maze. The walls of the tunnels all looked the same, jagged rock lit by feeble dots of light and an occasional sunbeam that shone through a broken spot in the rock above.

As Eliana grew accustomed to the tunnel's dim light, she noticed the colors of the rocks. Some were pale yellow crystal. Stalactites of rusty red and streaky white hung from the roof. In some places, they'd formed pillars when they met stalagmites that grew from the floor. The dripping water, Shirdona told her, was laden with minerals. Over centuries, the drips left deposits that created the fantastic structures. She pointed out what looked like a throne for a giant and a group of round formations that resembled the tops of leafy trees.

The tunnels' odor varied from damp to damper, sometimes with a puff of fresher air. In other spots, the smell of rot and decay stung Eliana's nose. And everywhere, as a counterpoint to the tramp of feet, was the steady dripping of water from the roof and walls.

They walked for nearly an hour through the winding tunnels, which were at times so narrow only two could walk abreast. Then they passed through a cavern that could hold hundreds. Eliana struggled to breathe the dank air as the rock above seemed to press down on her. One good thing about this cattle raid was the chance to inhale the fresh air above. Or would that make it worse, knowing she'd have to descend into this dark world again? She wasn't sure she'd be able to force herself to make the descent a second time.

To banish her anxiety, she studied the tiny glowing points dotting the walls of the caverns. Squinting, she realized the blue light that allowed them to see their way came from mushrooms. Interesting that the Chorokhese cultivated such plants to use light magic.

She quickened her steps to catch up with Shirdona. "May I ask you something?"

"Ask away, my sunshine," Shirdona replied.

"How does your light magic make the mushrooms glow?"

"Oh, that's not magic," Shirdona said. "They grow that way."

Eliana stared at the glowing spheres, amazed that a fungus could give off light naturally. "Would light magic make them brighter?"

"It could. But we need to be careful how we use magic."

"Oh, you don't want to paralyze yourselves?"

"That's the least of our worries. No, we decided long ago to limit our magic to emergencies. It's not hard to detect its use. We knew Kharan-Khuag would search for magic users in case any Malkhians had survived. All of us have water magic to some extent, thanks to our water fae ancestors. Some of us have bits of the other magics. As I said, we don't use it much. We've found other ways to survive. Like the mushrooms that give light."

"Or raiding cattle and grain." That the Chorokhese shamelessly raided her people grated on Eliana like sand in her boot.

"Exactly."

"But how do you move the cattle down here without magic?"

Shirdona snickered. "Watch and learn. Mind your step."

The woman leaped over a narrow stream flowing through the tunnel from a side passage. She turned into the side tunnel and rounded a sharp corner. The passage ended in an open area, a small cavern the size of a large crypt. A beam of silvery light illuminated the open space, light cast by the full moon overhead shining through the tiny piece of sky visible from the bottom of a thousand-foot shaft. Water trickled across the floor in two rivulets that merged and flowed toward the stream they'd just crossed. Moonlight glinted on the shiny, slick floor.

"This was once a pond," Shirdona waved at the walls of the shaft. "It was drained in the cataclysm. Since then, we dug under it to open it to the sky."

The area was barely sufficient for the raiding party to crowd into. Two wooden platforms large enough to hold five cows each stood on either side of the shaft. The tops of the platforms were just over Eliana's knees.

Alessia murmured into Eliana's ear. "Do they force the cows to jump down? That would save time not having to kill them."

"Shh. What are they doing?"

Eight of Shirdona's people, four men and four women, mounted one platform. Another, a woman with large hands and long fingers, knelt between the platform and the wall of the shaft. She gripped what looked like a wheel affixed to the wall. With a grunt, she turned it.

Gurgles and hisses filled the air, followed by the sound of rushing water. The platform lurched and began to rise.

Shirdona jumped onto the other platform, a coil of rope slung over one shoulder. Seven of her people joined her, all carrying coils of rope over their shoulders, bows in their hands, quivers and swords slung at their hips.

"Princess, you and Istvan can join me," Shirdona said. "Alessia can stay below and help with the cows."

Eliana and Alessia exchanged puzzled looks. "Seems I get the easy job," Alessia said.

"Hope you enjoy it," Eliana replied. She yawned, weariness threatening to overcome the jitters that had been keeping her alert. "How long do you think this will take?"

"Sleepy, are you, my sunshine? Then drink this." Shirdona thrust a metal flask at Eliana.

"What is it?"

"Something to help you through the night."

"Don't drink it," Istvan said.

Another order. Eliana scowled. She was tired of him telling her what to do. She snatched the flask from Shirdona, tipped her head back, and drank.

"That's enough, my sunshine. You don't want to stay awake for a week."

Eliana handed the flask back and wiped her mouth. "Thank you. But I don't feel any less tired."

"Just wait for it."

Dimitris pushed his way forward. "I go with the princess."

"No, you stay below," Istvan said.

"It doesn't matter," Shirdona said. "Let him come."

With a shrug, Istvan hopped onto the platform. He extended a hand to Eliana and helped her up. Dimitris clambered up behind her. A man turned the valve. Accompanied by the babbling of water, the platform lurched and rose.

Eliana swayed with the motion of the platform. "How is this happening?"

Shirdona chuckled. "We carved reservoirs in the rock.

They're fed by streams from above and collect rainwater. We use it."

"I saw someone turn a wheel."

"Exactly. That valve lets the water flow into a pipe under the platform. As the pipe fills, it lifts the platform."

"How do you get down?" Istvan asked.

"We reverse the valve and the water flows back into the reservoir. What we don't need, we allow to spill out. It joins that stream we crossed and eventually makes its way to the river."

That was one way to get things done without magic. Eliana tucked that thought away. Maybe she wouldn't need her power to break the curse after all.

As they ascended, the air cooled from that of a damp autumn day after a heavy rain to a clear, frosty winter night. Eliana sucked in the bracing air, savoring the crisp sting in her nose.

At the top, she jumped off, her boots thudding on the snowy ground. She turned her face up to beam at the carpet of stars overhead and grinned. She'd wondered if she'd ever see them again.

Eliana shuffled a few steps to allow others to leave the platform and surveyed the snow-covered landscape. A few outbuildings clustered around a larger structure. She twirled, startled by a creaking noise behind her.

Four of Shirdona's men were pulling metal brackets from the walls of the shaft. Wheels were attached to the ends of the brackets. The men looped their ropes over the wheels and tied one end to a clamp on each corner of the platform. One made the sound of a hooting owl, and the four dropped the other ends of their ropes into the shaft.

Shirdona pointed at the wheels. "Those pulleys help the crew below steady the platform as it goes up and down. Wouldn't do to have a nervous cow shift its weight and topple the whole contraption, would it?" She pointed at the mask in Eliana's hand. "Put it on."

The fish mask was made of a surprisingly soft material that didn't chafe Eliana's skin as she tugged it on. The mask clung to her face and didn't impede either her breathing or sight. It all reminded the princess of pageants and plays. But this was no staged entertainment. Someone could easily end up dead.

Beside her, Istvan was fumbling with a goat mask while Dimitris had his fish mask securely in place.

"Goats with me," Shirdona said. "Fish follow Kuan."

"No," said Istvan. "I stay with the princess."

Eliana put a hand on his arm and stood on her tiptoes to whisper through gritted teeth into his ear. "Let's not waste time arguing. Dimitris will be with me."

"I can't help but think this is an elaborate plot to separate us so she can kill us."

"She could have done that many times over already. Besides, we swore on our honor."

"What's wrong?" Shirdona asked. "Has the mighty dochan lost his manhood and fears jousting with a few kegs of beer?"

"We'll discuss this later," Istvan growled to Eliana. He swung his face toward Shirdona. "No, I was just wondering if your men were all talk. Will they be able to face down cattle, or will they run from the newborn calves?"

Shirdona chuckled. "We'll see, won't we? This way." She strode into the darkness, Istvan and four men behind her.

The eight from the first platform split into two groups of two men and two women each. One group stood near the platform they'd used to ascend, waiting as if for the market to open. The others trotted after Shirdona's group.

That left Eliana, Dimitris, the man named Kuan, and one other. Kuan whispered as he handed around lumps of salt.

"They'll get the beer, flour, and wine. We go to the cowsheds and start rounding up the cattle."

"Just the four of us to get fifty cows?" Dimitris asked.

"Others are coming up. They'll help. For now, we take fifty and lead them this way, slowly. Once the other supplies are down below, then we move faster."

Eliana didn't see how this would possibly work but held her tongue. They'd obviously done this before.

Moving with cautious stealth, the group headed toward the cowshed. Eliana watched Kuan approach the door, and with a wave of his hand, cause it to slide open. Another mage was muttering an incantation. An air mage, Eliana realized, casting a spell to muffle the sound, probably using wine as an amplifier. That was a trick she needed to learn.

She followed Kuan into the cowshed, greeted by the warmth of dozens of cows, the pungent odor of manure mixed with the scent of musty hay. Kuan approached the nearest cow, offered it a lump of salt to lick, tugged its ear, and led it out the door.

How hard could this be? Squaring her shoulders, Eliana inched toward a cow, giving its lashing tail a wide berth. "Easy, now," she murmured. With an effort, she steadied her shaking hand and extended the salt to the animal.

It raised its head and sniffed. With a snort, it swiped its tongue over the salt, swathing Eliana's glove with saliva.

Her heart pounded. *What if it won't follow me?* She took a step back. The cow moved with her, keeping its mouth near the salt, ceaselessly licking. Eliana turned and led it out of cowshed and across the snowy field to the shaft.

Once there, one of Shirdona's goat-masked followers herded the animal onto the platform. Eliana filled her lungs with the crisp night air. She'd done it. This was more gratifying than memorizing Ymittosian military victories or reciting the works of ancient poets. The thrill almost rivaled the exhilaration she'd felt the first time she jumped from a cliff, her heart racing, the feeling of being ten feet tall, invincible. She stood to the side as Dimitris guided a cow onto the platform. When five animals were in place, Shirdona's people below began to lower it.

"Why aren't they making any noise?" Eliana asked.

"The salt is laced with something that calms them," Kuan replied. "As long as we don't startle them, they'll stay quiet. Let's go for more."

A whooshing sound made her look up. A barrel was flying through the air. Eliana gasped as it swooped down. The four shadowy figures near the shaft's edge held up their hands. The barrel slowed and settled into place on the second platform.

"What was that?" Eliana asked.

Kuan chuckled. "Our wood and air mages move the barrels. It's a lot faster that way."

"But I thought you didn't use magic."

"That's just below. Up here, it's safe. Kharan-Khuag knows your people use magic. He has no way to know it's us."

Two more barrels soared out of the dark and took places next to the first.

"Let's go, princess," Kuan said. "Time to get more cows."

By the time they returned with another four cows, the other platform was loaded with ten casks of flour. The twelve bottles of wine were there as well, held in ingenious wire carriers. Whether they were sent by a metal mage or someone had carried them, Eliana didn't know. Either way, she found it amazing how seamlessly Shirdona's people worked together.

Shirdona rode up on a dark horse, a grin on her face. Istvan and several others wearing goat masks trudged after her, all leading cows. Five barrels of beer were already lined up by the edge of the shaft. A sixth flew over and settled into place.

"Any trouble?" Kuan asked.

"Nope," Shirdona said. "The guard was asleep. We gave

him something to make him sleep more soundly." She rubbed her hands together. "Princess, you and your two attendants can come with us. We've got more cattle to round up."

Istvan bristled. He clearly did not like being called an attendant.

Eliana didn't bother to placate him. She sighed. Didn't he see Shirdona was being deliberately provocative?

And she had a more pressing concern, one that soured the taste in her mouth. While Eliana hated the idea of stealing from her own people, there was a certain thrill to this night-time raid. She should not be enjoying this. Part of her felt horrible, but her sense of adventure tingled, her heart raced, and she could hardly keep from running back to the cowshed. Derya would have found all this great fun, too. With a huff, she trudged after Shirdona. They had forty more cows to steal. Maybe her guilt would fade when the novelty wore off. This raid was going to take all night.

When the eight who'd been moving the beer and flour finished their task and joined them in the fields, Eliana realized her assessment was wrong. All eight were riding horses they'd taken from the barn. One of them nudged Eliana with his toe. "We can't let you have all the fun. This is the best part."

She frowned at the man. "No one said anything about stealing horses."

The man laughed. "No one is. We're just borrowing them until we collect the cattle."

Worried he wasn't being truthful, Eliana's wild feeling of excitement soured like milk left under the summer sun. *Never again will I steal as much as an olive.* She followed Dimitris into the darkness, Istvan at her side.

Sidling up to an animal, she offered it the salt lick, its rough tongue wetly scraping her glove. She tugged on its ear, and it followed her out of the shed.

A shadow appeared out of the darkness. "What are you doing?" a reedy voice asked. "That's my cow."

She froze, unable to see the speaker in the dark. The starlight gave little light, and a stray cloud obscured the moon. Maybe she could explain to him and offer to buy the cow.

Before she could collect her thoughts, shouts from other parts of the field seized her attention. Shirdona's men weren't bothering to be quiet. They were riding in circles around a dozen or more cows, guiding them toward the shaft.

Other men were running toward them. The shadows made it seem like they bore flaming spears instead of simple torches.

The clash of steel nearby caused her to jerk her head around. She'd forgotten about the young farmer who'd accosted her about the cow. Dimitris and he were exchanging blows.

Istvan drew his sword. She clutched his arm. "Don't kill him."

"But we can't let him stop us."

"I know. Just wait a moment."

He scowled at her, but stepped back.

Dimitris swung at the youth, who stumbled. That was her chance. She pulled on her air magic and sent a gust of wind at him. The youth fell over backward.

Lunging forward, Dimitris hit the farmer on the head. He fell to the ground and lay still. "He'll wake up with a headache," Dimitris said, "but he'll be fine."

"Then let's grab a few cows and go," Istvan said.

They each led a cow toward the shaft. Eliana blinked. Why had the air gone murky? Was that more work of Shirdona's air mages?

A shadow appeared out of the foggy air. Shirdona. "There you are. I thought we'd lost you."

"Do you have all the cows?" Istvan asked, his tone harsh and impatient.

"With your three, that brings us to forty-seven. You can go down with them. We're just about done."

Eliana led her cow to the platform. She took a careful step from the damp ground up to the wood. Then she blinked. The sudden revelation made her catch her breath. This shaft was one of the sinkholes that dotted Ymittos. No wonder legends had sprung up about them, how anyone who fell into a sinkhole would be killed by monsters. The inhabitants below might not be half fish and half goat, but they wouldn't allow anyone who stumbled into their realm to leave.

The yells and sounds of clashing steel grew fainter as the platform lowered, replaced by the dripping of water and a few snorts from the cows. "Won't they see where you're taking their animals?" Eliana asked.

"Nope," Shirdona said. "I sent a group to lure them to the woods nearby. They'll lose them there, then circle back. Meanwhile, our water mages will wash away our footprints, and the air mages will dry the soil and dust the area with snow. No one will know we were here."

After tucking into a spot on the platform, Eliana was stroking the nose of a cow when wails cut through the shouts and clanging of swords. The keening sounded like several women and a few children mourning the loss of their cows and flour and beer, and the hours of hard labor that went into them. Or worse, had one of their men been killed? Eliana hung her head, a thickness forming in her throat. How could she ever have enjoyed this nighttime raid, even for a heartbeat? Her shame was barely a pebble compared to the mountain she should be feeling.

"We sacrificed our morals to enrich a skilled bunch of thieves," Dimitris murmured in her ear. "I hope it's worth it in the end."

If this cattle raid helped her break the curse, then it had to be worth it. Eliana leaned her head on her guard's shoulder and vowed she'd pay the farmers back seven times over. Icy dread ran up her spine. Breaking the curse was proving to be costly in ways she'd never imagined. And she had no idea what other compromises she might have to make. What else would she sacrifice to save her people—and herself—from Cetus's evil plans?

20

T he platform settled on the stone floor of the shaft with a hard thump. Eliana grabbed a cow's back to keep her balance. She sagged against the shuffling animal, relief weakening her knees. They'd survived the cattle raid. The princess sucked in a deep breath, wrinkling her nose at the underground smell, thick and stifling after the brisk, fresh air of the world above. *Now, we'll find out if Shirdona will deliver on her word.*

Two of Shirdona's men herded the cattle off the platform and into the dark tunnel. Shirdona motioned to Eliana. "This way, my sunshine."

She followed, Istvan and Dimitris close behind her. Other than those operating the lift, most of Shirdona's warriors had already left the shaft, leading the cattle. The clopping of hundreds of hooves echoed through the tunnels.

"That was the simple part," Shirdona said.

"What do you mean?" Eliana asked.

"We're not the only ones who like beef," the woman answered. "The bagalas and vishapions do too. Keep your ears open and be ready to fight." She drew her sword and stalked past the men in front of them.

Eliana glanced over her shoulder. They walked at the tail end of the line, with only two of Shirdona's warriors behind them. "Istvan, where are Alessia and your men?"

He frowned. "I've been wondering that myself. I'll go look. Will you be alright?"

"Yes, of course," she answered, clutching Dimitris's arm. "Wild beasts would attack the cows first, right?"

Dimitris glanced over his shoulder. "The rest of Shirdona's people, the ones who are erasing our tracks above, will catch up. We'll be fine."

Istvan gave Eliana a curt nod. "Be careful." He strode up the line, pushing past tramping people and plodding cattle until Eliana could no longer see him in the dusky light.

"I hope the others come soon," she said.

"Me too," said Dimitris.

They walked without speaking. The pounding of the cows' hooves mingled with the people's thudding footfalls, drowning out the trickling stream and water dripping from the stalactites. She wasn't sure what sound would warn her of danger. Would it be a beast's furious roar? A clanging sword? Or a man's shriek as a monster dragged him to its lair?

And those were the new perils. She peered up at the roof of the tunnel and strained her ears, listening, dreading the rumble of a cave-in.

A muffled gasp behind her made her whirl. A pair of immense men held Shirdona's two soldiers by their necks. The strangers slit the throats of their captives and let the bodies crash to the ground.

"Ware!" shouted Dimitris as he pulled his sword. "Enemies!"

One man sprang toward him, a raised dagger in one hand and a battleaxe in the other. The second, a burly man with red curling hair, advanced on Eliana. "Don't bother putting up a fight, little fish," he said.

In lieu of a reply, she drew her sword. Indistinctly, she

spotted several men massing on the heels of the first two. One kicked the corpse of Shirdona's fallen soldier to the side. Shouts echoed through the tunnel, telling her that Shirdona's men were also battling attackers.

Eliana snorted. *How ironic.* The stolen cows and supplies were likely to exchange hands again, the robbers turning into victims.

That would be far better than ending up dead in a heap. She shuffled back a step, putting more space between herself and her adversaries. At least the cavern was narrow. No more than three attackers could push through at once. She stood shoulder to shoulder with Dimitris, who pointed his sword at the advancing men.

"You should turn around now," said Dimitris.

"Why? Does Shirdona's fish think he can fight?" The man lunged for Eliana, swinging his axe toward her neck.

She ducked and swung low, slicing his thigh. Blood stained his gray trousers. The princess recoiled. Never, in all her practice, had she wounded someone that badly. She winced as the man roared in pain. *But it was either him or me.*

The man bellowed and reeled backward as his red-haired comrade charged Dimitris. Clanging steel echoed through the tunnel like a cartload of pots and pans flung down a chimney.

Parrying her opponent's stroke, Eliana leaped to avoid another blow. He missed her, but sliced into Dimitris's sword arm. Her retainer shouted and dropped his weapon. His opponent kicked it away. He slashed the back of Dimitris' leg. With a shout, Dimitris toppled to the ground.

Now she faced the two of them. At least it was only two. What had happened to the fighters she'd spotted in the tunnel behind them? She stood over Dimitris, panting. Her hair tumbled from its knot and she shoved it from her eyes.

"Oh, look, Shirdona's using little girls to fight her battles."

Eliana snarled. *Little girl, he thinks?* She darted forward. With a slash, she hacked off the hand of the red-haired man.

He howled, seizing the stump of his arm. His partner jumped into the fray and knocked Eliana's sword from her grasp. She scrambled back, stooping to pull Derya's dagger from her boot.

Before she could extract it, the man shoved Eliana against the tunnel's wall and raised his ax over Eliana's head. "How many cattle do you have?"

She opened her mouth to answer when a sword crashed into the man's skull. He staggered backwards. With a quick stroke, Shirdona lopped off his head.

A fountain of blood sprayed into the air, and scarlet rain dampened Eliana's hair. The man's body toppled to the ground, blood still gushing from the stump of his neck. Eliana gasped and gagged on the blood that spewed into her open mouth.

Shirdona whirled and faced down the redhead. After a flurry of parries, she sliced his calf. When he tumbled to the ground, she ran him through, piercing his heart. He died with a final gurgling moan.

Panting, Shirdona peered down the tunnel toward the shaft where they'd brought down the cattle. The clanging of swords reverberated. "I think my warriors will finish them off," she said. "Are you injured?"

"No, but Dimitris is," Eliana answered, gagging on a mouthful of the headless man's blood. She took a gulp of water, swished it from side to side, and spit it out. "I'm sorry," she added. "They killed two of your men."

"That makes eight we lost." Shirdona let out a long breath and grimaced. "And six cows. But not to worry, your Istvan is fine."

"Who are they?" Eliana asked.

"The Saumarota family." Shirdona wiped her sword on the olive-green tunic of the headless corpse. "The upstream clan." She spat. "They're in the camp who'd rather not have the tagavlon woken." She scoffed. "And they think they're too good to do their own cattle raiding. Instead, they come after us once we've taken all the risks. Daughters of pigs and sons of donkeys, that's what they are."

Eliana knelt by Dimitris. Blood flowed from his wounded arm, forming a crimson puddle. She pulled the pieces of his slashed sleeve apart and winced. A long slash severed the muscle halfway to the bone. She ripped his ruined sleeve and bunched it up. "Can you press that on the wound?"

He grunted.

She tore a strip of cloth from her tunic and bound it around his arm. Then she turned to his leg. The gash barely went below the skin and was already clotting. She bandaged it as best she could and helped him to his feet. "Can you walk?"

He mumbled a few syllables she took as a yes.

Eight goat-masked people bolted up to Shirdona. Eliana recognized them as those who'd remained behind to erase tracks after the raid. "Tavkatseen, are you well?" one asked.

"We just fought off some Saumarota. You?"

"There's seven of them that won't bother us anymore." He pointed with his sword into the tunnel. "They didn't as much as nick any of us."

Shirdona gestured with her chin at her two dead followers. "Bring them," she told her warriors. "Come along, my sunshine."

Eliana complied, with Dimitris leaning on her shoulder. Shirdona had tricked them into going on the cattle raid. Did she want to get them killed, as Istvan said? But Shirdona saved her. Could she trust the woman or not? Her life, and the survival of her kingdom, depended on her making the right choice.

Huddling with her thoughts, Eliana paid little attention to the man who took his place at her side. He slid an arm around her waist.

She gasped and jerked away. Clutching Dimitris with one

arm, she shoved at the stranger with the other. "What are you doing?" she shouted.

The man stepped back and raised his hands. "Eliana, it's me."

"Istvan." She put a hand on her racing heart. "I'm sorry. You startled me." She adjusted her grip on Dimitris, staggering under his bulk.

Moving to the wounded man's opposite side, Istvan put an arm around his shoulders, relieving Eliana of some of his weight. "I didn't mean to scare you," he said. "Are you alright?"

"I'm fine, uninjured at least. You?"

"The same." He paused. "Dimitris?"

"Leg and arm wounds," Dimitris grunted.

"Hmm. Hope it's not serious. I found my men and your maid. They're unharmed. Eliana, what do you mean, 'uninjured at least?'"

Relief for Alessia turned her knees to water and she staggered. Recovering her balance, she tightened her grasp on Dimitris, pulling him close. "This whole thing has me unsettled. First, we steal cattle and food from our own people."

Istvan huffed. "We only did because we were duped into it."

"Might want to think a little more before making deals, no?" Dimitris asked.

"You're right," Eliana said. "And Shirdona's men didn't seem to have too many scruples about killing those who got in their way."

"You noticed that, too?" Istvan asked. "It was a game to them."

"You seemed to be enjoying yourself." She tamped down her own lingering guilt.

He sighed. "I admit, there was a certain excitement to the adventure. But Eliana, I swear to you, killing or wounding anyone isn't my idea of fun."

She wanted to believe him and had no reason to think he was lying. "And being attacked was certainly not fun," she said. "We barely managed to fight the Saumarotas off." She shuddered, recalling the man who nearly killed her. A few more seconds, and she would have been the one lying headless on the ground.

"Are you wondering if Shirdona can make good on her promises?" Istvan asked.

"That occurred to me, yes." She squinted at the rocky floor, as if the answers she needed were chiseled into the stone.

"Perhaps we should think this through," Istvan suggested. "She doesn't seem to be trustworthy."

"But what is our alternative?" Only a few days remained to break the curse. If she didn't find the prince in time, would Derya be able to try? Or would Kharan-Khuag consider Eliana a failed cursebreaker, mount his invasion and carry her off for whatever his deviant plans involved? She shuffled closer to Dimitris, hoping the warmth of his presence would melt the icy terror that gripped her heart.

"The other family, the Saumarotas," Istvan said. "They're skilled fighters. Maybe we should try them."

"But they don't want the prince back," Eliana said. "They'd as soon kill us as help us."

"That's what Shirdona says. How do we know that's true?"

Eliana nibbled her lip. He made a valid point. How did they know what to believe?

"How do you know anything is the truth?" Shirdona asked.

Eliana jumped. Where had the woman come from? She moved through the darkness as stealthy as a cat.

"Kindly explain that to us, if you would," Istvan said.

"You're miffed about the visit from the Saumarotas?" Shirdona snorted. "I didn't lie about them. They don't want to restore the tagavlon. They believe since they're the largest clan, they should claim the throne."

"If that's true, why haven't they claimed it already?" Istvan asked.

Shirdona cocked her head to the side. "You do ask good questions. It's because the royal family, the Alagatas, are the most powerful mages in Chorokha. Even the cursed tagavlon, may the Rider have mercy on him. Those who long for his restoration want his magic as a defense against Kharan-Khuag. If you don't believe me, you can ask one of the other families. That is, if you can spare the time to visit them."

"How far away is the nearest one?" Eliana asked.

"Four days."

Eliana pursed her lips. Shirdona had told them that before, so perhaps it was the truth. "But why trick us into a cattle raid?"

"Trick you? Oh, no, my sunshine. We made a bargain. You need help finding the tagavlon. I want to be paid for my time and didn't know if you could be trusted. I also needed proof you were worthy of being helped."

"And are we?"

"You're at least brave enough for a little raiding. You'll need more courage than that before you're done. But yes, I think you're worthy."

"Tavkatseen, we've reached the first vault." One of Shirdona's soldiers beckoned to her.

Shirdona nodded. "We'll talk later." She strode off, following the woman who'd called her.

"Now, what do you think?" Eliana asked.

Istvan didn't hesitate. "We should try with someone else."

Eliana rubbed her eyes. "We already paid Shirdona. Another family might demand more."

"Or less."

"True. But Shirdona saved my life just now. I'd rather not

make a hasty decision, and I think she'll follow through on her word."

"You have no reason to believe that."

"Other than she risked herself to save me? And that we don't have time to go searching for another guide?"

"So, you want to stay with her?"

"For now." Eliana hesitated. "But Istvan, I think you're right. We should learn what we can about these other families. At the first chance, Dimitris and Alessia should ask around."

Dimitris nodded. "We might get people talking more easily than you two."

"Fine." Istvan's tone rasped with irritation. "We'll stay with Shirdona. And maybe, for once, we'll get some use out of that annoying maid of yours."

21

Eliana's shoulder ached where Dimitris leaned against it. They'd trudged for hours through the maze of twisting musty tunnels and her toes throbbed and her legs cramped. She was ready to give Shirdona half the cows in Ymittos if the woman call a halt long enough to her aching feet.

From time to time, they reached gated rooms off the tunnels that Shirdona called vaults. Her men would roll a few barrels of beer or flour inside. Then they'd herd a dozen or so cows into the vaults, which Eliana understood to be storerooms and abattoirs.

During one of those pauses, Eliana seized the chance to rinse her head under a waterfall, washing the blood of battle from her face and hair. She gazed longingly at the cold water, wanting to soak her sore feet. But she was afraid that once she eased her boots from her swollen toes, she'd never get them back on again.

Istvan stood nearby, muttering about cattle and fools. Eliana choked back a curt reply. *Let him stew.* She had her own worries to cope with and no desire to provoke an argument.

Silently, she took her place next to him when they set out again.

Just as a blister was forming on Eliana's heel, she noticed dust motes swirling in a beam of light. Tipping her head, she spotted a small opening far above her, letting in early morning sunlight. It was no wonder her legs were protesting. They'd been stealing cattle and walking all night. With a start, she realized she wasn't craving sleep. Whatever Shirdona had given her to drink had a powerful effect. She'd been right to ignore Istvan's warning.

When they reached a cavern, Eliana let her gaze roam over its rocky walls, wondering if the shadowed crevices hid unseen threats. She shook herself. *We're a large, heavily armed party. There's no reason to fear.*

Unless… She cast her gaze upwards. *No. Don't even think it.* The caverns had lasted for centuries. There was no cause to imagine they'd collapse.

Unless Cetus knows we're here and tries to stop us.

Her mouth went dry. *It doesn't matter what Cetus knows. I still have to find the prince. Or tagavlon, or whatever they call him.*

Dimitris stumbled, and she gripped his leather-clad arm to steady him.

"I'm fine," he said before she could ask. "Where do you think we're going? I thought Shirdona's tower was the other direction."

Eliana frowned. How would he know that? She'd completely lost track of which way they were headed hours ago.

He nudged her. "The angle of the light. Means we're headed west."

"Good thing one of us knows."

The cavern on Eliana's left widened. A four-sided tower stood in the recess. Eliana ran her eyes over it. They'd passed other wide spots where towers stood. Some were only three stories, while the tops of others disappeared into the darkness, the way Shirdona's had.

She nudged Alessia, who was walking on her other side. "What do you think? The tall towers belong to more wealthy or powerful families?"

"Or the other ones are just lazy?" Alessia snickered.

They rounded a bend and came to another wide spot. Instead of a lofty tower, a tumbled ruin stood by the entrance to the adjoining tunnel.

Eliana stopped walking and gawked. "Merciful winds, what happened here?"

Shirdona's warrior Kuan answered. "Every so often, Kharan-Khuag sends karcharias."

"What's a karcharia?" Alessia asked.

Eliana wasn't sure she wanted to hear his response.

"Men with shark's heads," Kuan answered with a shudder. "They swim up the river so we don't know they're coming. They kill by biting your neck and draining your blood."

Hot sweat added to the dampness on Eliana's face. Men with shark's heads. Who were those unfortunates who Cetus enchanted to wear the head of a shark? She glanced at the warriors walking before her. Is that how some of them will end up? *Or many of my people?* Her breath came faster, gasps that verged on sobs.

"But don't worry, princess." The man looked at her with concern. "They've never attacked a raiding party. Usually, they wait until we've butchered the meat and shared it out, then they pounce. They destroy a tower, kidnap the residents, and steal the beef. Can you believe that? Pilfering our meat? That's despicable."

Eliana didn't dare look at Alessia. If she started to laugh, she'd end up in hysterics. She overlooked the irony of a cattle thief objecting to someone robbing him and returned to what she thought was far more terrifying. "What happens to the people they kidnap?"

"We don't know. They end up as food for the karcharias, maybe, or slaves. The girls? The rumor is Kharan-Khuag keeps a large harem. Over a thousand, the last we heard. If you can believe anything a karcharia says."

A harem of stolen women. Eliana shuddered and scowled. One thousand more reasons to defeat the evil monster. *I won't be taken by him. I won't.*

After a few more turns through narrow tunnels, Eliana shivered. They'd been descending for some time, and the air was danker and colder. They passed another tower. Dark rings circled its walls at intervals, like someone had painted it. "Why paint the tower?" she asked.

Kuan shook his head. "Those are water marks from flooding."

She swallowed hard. "It floods down here?"

"Of course, in the spring. Why do you think we build towers? When the river swells after the rains, we move to the higher floors."

"Why don't you just live in tunnels higher up?" Alessia asked. "Seems like it would be less work, and you wouldn't have to worry about floods."

"No, not unless a stream found its way into your tunnel." Kuan shook his head. "Did I forget to tell you about the snakes and centipedes that live in those tunnels? Or the stinging worms that crave heat? We'd spend all our time fighting them off. No, the higher passages are only for emergencies. And even then, we think long and hard about using them."

"Are there spiders and snakes and worms throughout the cavern?" Eliana thought she'd kept her voice neutral, as if she wasn't terribly interested in the answer.

Kuan chuckled. "Don't worry, Highness. Not everywhere. They don't like the blue mushrooms. As long as you stay out of the less traveled tunnels, you stand a good chance of avoiding them."

A faint whine flew past Eliana's ear. The man slapped his neck and cursed. "Of course, these flying midges love the damp, and they're everywhere. At least you had the sense to come in winter when most of them aren't out. In summer, you can sometimes hardly see through the clouds of them."

Prickling down her neck made Eliana decide she'd had enough of this talk about tiny creatures that crept and crawled. She directed the conversation to what seemed like a safer topic. "How high do the floods go?"

"This far back from the ocean, rarely more than the second story of a tower. If the water rises higher, someone might employ a spot of water magic to hold it back. The people who live closer to the sea have more problems, as you can imagine."

"If you can use water magic to hold back the flood waters, why don't you use it all the time?"

Kuan stopped and stared at Eliana. "You don't understand. For centuries, avoiding our magic was all that kept up the deception that no one lived here. I don't know how Kharan-Khuag saw through it, but he did. We still use the magic as little as possible, hoping he thinks we have next to no power. That way, if you fail to break the curse and he enslaves us, he won't know what magical strength we have. Will it be enough to mount a rebellion?" He shrugged. "Only the Rider knows. But taking Kharan-Khuag by surprise will be our only chance."

Eliana pondered his words as Shirdona led them into a dimly lit side tunnel. The princess couldn't tell if the light in the tunnel came from the glowing mushrooms or some other source. "Be careful," Shirdona said. "Don't slip and fall. You'd be sorry."

Keeping her eyes on the ground, Eliana realized the reason for Shirdona's warning. Rocks jutted up from the cave floor. In spots, pillars rose higher than Eliana's head, columns that guarded the dark entrances to side passages. In other places, narrow crevices split the path in jagged cracks. It would be easy to twist an ankle.

A bellowing roar burst through the caverns. It echoed and Eliana couldn't tell if it was one or one hundred beasts. Their twelve remaining cows lowed, fear and alarm evident in their frantic calls.

Shirdona's warriors shouted. The only word Eliana understood was "vishapion," which had been described to her as a beast with the head of a boar, massive, curled tusks, clawed feet, and a spiked tail. Her heart pounded and the weariness in her legs vanished.

"My sunshine, let's go." Shirdona grabbed Eliana's arm and pulled her away from the roaring. "I'll protect the princess," she yelled.

A second roar erupted in front of them. Shirdona drew her sword. "Get ready to fight, my sunshine."

Eliana pulled her own blade. "Alessia, you and Dimitris stand against the wall."

"You should, too," Istvan said.

She bared her teeth at him. Another roar filled the cavern. Sucking in a breath, she charged toward Shirdona, who was battling the eight-foot-tall vishapion.

The beast flung back its boar-like head and roared again, revealing two rows of jagged teeth. It shook its long tusks and lashed its spiked tail at Shirdona.

The woman leaped backward. Eliana slashed at the tail. When her sword hit the beast's mud-brown scales, a jolt ran up her arm as if she had struck a stone. Her blow didn't even leave a scratch.

"No, my sunshine," Shirdona shouted. "You can't penetrate the scales. Go for the throat or the belly."

Eliana gulped. That would mean getting closer to those fearsome jaws.

Shirdona waved her sword at the beast, shouting curses.

The beast locked its tiny eyes on the woman and stalked toward her.

Istvan darted past Shirdona and drove his sword deep into the vishapion's gullet. The beast howled. Blood the color of bear scat and smelling of rotted meat gushed from the wound and spattered Istvan's face.

Dashing to Istvan's side, Shirdona sliced the monster's throat. A shower of brown blood rained on her. The vishapion gurgled and crashed to the stone floor.

Open-mouthed, Eliana stared. Istvan had been brave to approach the monster like that, darting under its jaws. And he'd been fast. She'd barely begun to plan her next move when he'd launched into motion. She tipped her head to the side and the corners of her mouth crept upwards. Her tight shoulders relaxed. *Thank the Rider Istvan is here.*

"Quick." Shirdona hacked at the beast's throat. "Need to make sure."

Joining her, Istvan delivered a few fierce blows. When only a single ligament attached the monster's head to its body, he paused. "Is that enough?"

"Yes," Shirdona said. She wiped her face on her sleeve. "Well done. I didn't know you had it in you." After a quick glance over her shoulder, she nodded. "That's one down."

"Shouldn't we stay and help the others?" Eliana asked.

"No," Shirdona said. "The vishapions hunt in packs of three. It's best to go now, while they are distracted. My people will take care of the other two."

Eliana pulled her eyebrows together. "But—"

"But nothing. Would you rather be eaten or find the tagavlon? Come with me. What else are you going to do?"

A warrior ran up. "Tavkatseen, are you well?"

She pointed at the dead vishapion with her bloodstained sword. "Well enough. You?"

"We killed one. Another is prowling ahead."

Shirdona nodded. "You know what to do. I'll take the

princess. Guard her maid and Dimitris. One of the Saumarotas, may his sword turn to rust, wounded him. Once you've
taken care of the vishapions, come after us."

"We're not leaving the princess," Dimitris said.

"You'll just slow us down," Shirdona retorted. "This is our
best chance of getting past the vishapions."

"She's right," Istvan said. "Besides, you and Alessia have
something else to do."

Eliana chewed her lower lip. She didn't want to be separated from Dimitris and Alessia. But if success in finding the
prince meant they needed to travel quickly, then it would be
wiser to leave them behind. And this could give them a chance
to learn about the other Chorokhese families. "I'm not
sure…"

"This is not the time to cling childishly to your maid or
servant." Istvan wiped his sword on the scales of the vishapion. "You need to face reality. "

How dare he speak to her like that? She scowled, even
though he had a point. "Very well. Dimitris, we'll meet you
once we've found the prince."

He opened his mouth, but Shirdona cut him off. "What
else are you going to do?" She pointed at one of her warriors.
"You, watch out for these two." She jerked her chin at Eliana.
"My sunshine, let's go." She turned and strode along the cave
as confidently as if it were a smooth, paved path in bright
sunlight.

Before Shirdona was lost in shadow, Eliana hurried to
catch up with her, Istvan a few paces behind. "Shirdona,
there's something I'd like you to help me with."

"Oh, that might cost you extra." She chuckled.

"It's nothing new. I was wondering, have you heard how
I'm supposed to break the curse?"

"You don't know?"

"No." Istvan would be irked Eliana had revealed this
information, but she didn't see how concealing it would help.

Everyone would find out when they reached the prince and saw that she didn't know what to do, anyway. Better to try to figure it out now.

Shirdona hummed a few bars of a lively tune. Eliana recognized it from the dancing the night before.

The princess had given up expecting an answer when suddenly Shirdona spoke. "You know, I never did hear how you were supposed to do it."

"Really?" Eliana's heart sank. This was an impossible quest. Why had she even bothered? Weariness surged through her muscles. Her head drooped and her feet dragged.

"Well, I've heard nothing certain. Lots of rumors, of course. Seems every clan has a different story."

"Could you tell me? Anything might be of help."

"One bunch says you need to gather pike mushrooms under a full moon, roast them with the haunch of a goat, and rest three mushroom caps on the prince's lips."

"Where would I get those mushrooms?"

Shirdona shook her head. "They grow up high, in places where forests grow near the edges of the rift. But that won't do you any good."

"Why—. Oh." Eliana let her chin drop to her chest. The next full moon was two weeks away. She had less time than that to break the curse.

"But don't worry. I wouldn't believe anything those Saumarotas say. The Khatavians think you need to braid a lock of your hair into the prince's hair, cut the locks off, and burn them in a fire with bitter herbs."

"Which herbs, exactly?"

"That's the thing. Some think chamomile, others rue. A few say milk thistle or marrubium. I've even heard wormwood. If it were me, I'd try them all."

Thanks to Corban, she had chamomile, rue, and marrubium. They'd have to do. A glimmer of hope ignited in her soul. "Any other ideas?"

"The most outrageous was that the princess had to drive a dagger into her own heart and let three drops of blood fall into his mouth."

Eliana gasped. "But then I'd die."

"Sacrificing yourself for the good of our realm, yours, and maybe the entire continent."

Self-sacrifice in the name of duty was something she'd been brought up to value. But killing herself was a bit much. Her shoulders slumped and she let out a long sigh. "Which of the three do you think is right?"

Shirdona shrugged. "I haven't a clue. My best guess is none of them. But I could be wrong."

None of this was reassuring to Eliana. She was still trying to figure out her next question when shrieks and clanging from behind made her whirl around.

"No, quick, this way." Shirdona grabbed her wrist and yanked her into a narrow passage to the side. Istvan grabbed Eliana's other hand and pulled in the opposite direction.

"No, you fool," Shirdona said. "That noise means more Saumarotas have come. We have to get away."

Istvan took a step toward the sound of fighting. "Shouldn't we help fight them off?"

"Do whatever you want," Shirdona said. "I'm taking the princess to the tagavlon. Let those idiots try to get past my men. And let your men show just how useful they are." She pulled Eliana after her.

Eliana looked over her shoulder at Istvan. "Are you coming?"

"If there are more enemies around, we should return to our men."

Shirdona put her hands on her hips and huffed. "And I'm telling you, your best chance is to move while they're busy. You can find your survivors later." She spat out the words, her lip curling. "My warriors will make sure they don't get eaten by roaming monsters."

The princess glanced from one to the other as the shouts and shrieks of the battle grew louder. Banging metal echoed like hundreds of blacksmiths forging swords. All that racket was sure to attract more enemies or more beasts. "We might as well head for the prince. That's what our people would expect us to do." She raised her chin to look at Istvan. "What do you think?"

He scowled and rubbed his scruff-covered jaw. "I don't like this, but I can't argue with you. So be it."

"Then it's settled. Shirdona, which way from here?"

The woman darted into a small side tunnel. Eliana gulped and followed. As terrifying as the dark passage was, it was a relief to be doing something other than cowering in a cave, waiting for a monster to eat her. The roars of beasts and clanging of weapons faded. While she'd escaped those threats, the dark quiet that surrounded her seemed to hold a brooding menace, all the greater for being silent.

22

Eliana ducked as she followed Shirdona into a narrow, low-ceilinged tunnel. The only light came from the celery-green glow of the mushrooms growing on the walls and low ceiling of the passage, light that cast an eerie, sickly shade on the faces of her companions. She choked on the damp air. The stony, dank walls seemed to shift toward her as if to crush her between them.

"Don't touch the walls, the floor, the rocks. Nothing," Shirdona said.

"Why not?" Istvan asked.

"Do you not see the green mushrooms? This is where poison centipedes and stinging worms feed. In this light, you won't know you've touched one until it's too late."

Istvan scoffed. "And we don't want that to happen because?"

Hardly believing her ears, Eliana stared at him. He blinked and looked away as if the tunnel's walls had suddenly become fascinating.

"Has it snowed on your brain?" Shirdona's voice was mocking, which Eliana thought Istvan deserved for asking such a foolish question. "The poison will burn your fingers off, including the bone. The stinging worms burrow into your skin and feast on your muscles. There's no way to get rid of them other than cutting off the limb." She snickered. "But of course, if that's your idea of fun…"

Eliana shuddered and stumbled. Her breath caught in her throat as her arms flailed, one hand scraping the rough floor.

Istvan grabbed her shoulders, steadying Eliana and pulling her upright.

She shook off his hands. "I'm fine."

"Are you sure?"

"We've been walking all night. I'm a little tired, that's all." Exhausted and overwhelmed was more accurate, but she wasn't about to confess.

"Be careful, my sunshine." Shirdona turned abruptly and eased herself through a narrow opening.

Grasping Eliana's cloak, Istvan drew her close, pressing his mouth to her ear. "How much longer are we going to follow her?"

"Until we find the prince?"

"Why? She doesn't seem like she knows what she's doing. Shouldn't she have prepared better for the vishapions?"

Eliana sighed. "Let's give it another hour, shall we?"

The pale green shadows accented Istvan's jutting chin as he huffed through his nose and nodded.

Careful not to touch the rock walls, Eliana inched her way between them. At least the opposite side was well lit, with several shafts of light radiating from an opening high above. Whether they were sinkholes that had formed over the centuries or the remnants of ancient springs, she couldn't tell. But she was grateful for the light.

She took a few tentative steps before she noticed that the floor she walked on wasn't uneven rock. Instead, it was paved with stones that were perfectly fitted in diagonal patterns, each one the same size. Were they drawing near to the tower of the ruler of the Chorokhese?

With a wave to get Istvan's attention, Eliana pointed to the ground. He glanced at the pavement, then back at her with raised eyebrows. He nodded and gave her a small smile.

Good. He thinks we're close, too.

Several ruined towers lined the sides of the cavern, their tumbledown walls and crumbling facades creating a desolate, forsaken air.

"What happened to the people?" Eliana asked.

"I suppose no one wanted to live near a cursed tagavlon," Shirdona said without turning around. "They left. What else could they do?"

Eliana had no answer to that. Judging by his silence, neither did Istvan.

Glancing from side to side, Shirdona walked a little farther, then turned and shrugged her pack from her shoulders. "It's all quiet now, and we're past the place where the worms and centipedes hide. We should take a minute to have something to eat. Can't have the princess fainting on us just when we need her the most."

Although Shirdona's words made sense, Eliana's tense stomach didn't feel like it would welcome food. Nonetheless, she lowered herself to a flat, broken rock that looked the remnant of a stalagmite. The wall behind her was smooth and shiny, formed of rusty red, white, and pale yellow bands stacked one over the other, a testament to the different minerals that comprised the rock. Rows of delicate pillars lined the sides of the cavern, illuminated by glowing blue mushrooms.

Shirdona handed around dried beef and pickled mushrooms. Istvan, Eliana noted, ate heartily. She couldn't do more than swallow some water and choke down a mushroom. The thought of swallowing the dried meat made her stomach churn.

Just as they had resumed walking, a roar echoed through the cave. Shirdona cursed.

"What is it?" Eliana asked. Her heart galloped as if trying to escape from her constricting ribs.

Istvan drew his sword and shoved her behind him. "Does it matter?"

"Well, yes," Eliana said.

"It's another vishapion." Shirdona scanned the cavern.

"Seems like we're running into a lot of them," Istvan said. "Isn't it your job to make sure we don't?"

"What do you think the cattle were for?" Shirdona asked. "They were the bait. My men knew the vishapions would go for the cows, making it easier for us to get past them." She shook her head. "Usually, they roam in packs of three. Let's hope the Rider is merciful, and this one is a loner." Another roar reverberated through the cavern. "We'll have to run for it."

Without waiting for a reply, she sprinted deeper into the chamber. Eliana gave Istvan a wide-eyed glance and darted after Shirdona. Istvan's footsteps pounded the stone floor as he ran behind her.

The roaring grew louder. The clicking of claws on rock added a counterpoint to the beast's harsh cries.

"My sunshine, you can manipulate air, right?"

"I thought you didn't use magic down here."

"We don't, except in emergencies. What would you call this?"

Eliana brushed a stray strand of hair from her eyes with a shaking hand. What good would her air be against a vishapion? She nibbled her lower lip. There was one thing she could try. "Do you have any beer?"

Istvan snorted. "You want to drink now?"

The princess ignored him and took the flask Shirdona held out to her. She sucked in a sip of beer and swished it around in her mouth. Would this work? She'd never tried beer as an amplifier before and wasn't sure she could harness its power.

With a deep breath, she summoned her air magic, reveling as it thrummed in her veins. She let it out gradually, allowing the air from her lungs to mix with the taste of hops on her tongue.

Her eyes widened as a brown mist spread throughout the cavern. The mist thickened until it was as dense as fog on a spring morning, obscuring any object more than a few feet away. The roars of the beast grew muffled, as if a heavy blanket had draped itself over Eliana's head.

A calloused hand grabbed hers. "Great job, my sunshine," Shirdona said. "Let's go." She pulled Eliana after her. "And be quiet about it."

Eliana scurried after the woman. Istvan followed, muttering something about wanting to check on his men. She had sympathy for him as she wondered about Dimitris and Alessia. But somehow, she felt Shirdona was right. They had to find the prince first.

Shirdona darted through the cavern, jumping over crevasses and skirting stalagmites and pillars, twisting through the maze of ruins. *She must see in the dark like a cat.* Eliana stumbled after the woman, trying to follow closely to avoid tripping. *How does she know where we're going?* Eliana had lost all sense of direction. Without Shirdona, she'd never survive Chorokha.

Mentally, she scolded herself. That wasn't true. To escape, all she needed was to find a sinkhole or rift and use her air magic to lift herself out. But that wouldn't break the curse. *Or free me from Cetus's personal and intimate plans.* An icy hand twisted her stomach at the thought.

"Quick, now," Shirdona said. "That mist won't hold it up long. Once the monster loses our scent, it'll most likely come here."

"Where exactly is here?" Istvan asked.

"Here." Shirdona waved a hand, pointing to where hundreds of glowing mushrooms illuminated a neighboring cavern. In the center stood a seven-story tower shining in a narrow sunbeam. Shirdona pointed with her chin. "Qala Bisen. The tagavlon is in there."

23

Eliana wrapped her trembling arms around herself and took a step back. Her muscles tensed and she stared, wide-eyed at the structure dominating the cavern. Now that they'd finally found the prince's tower, her feet were as reluctant to approach as if it were a roaring dragon.

She studied the tower's exterior. The lower three stories were stone and the upper four were wood. Intricate carvings of the Rider of the Ancient Skies flanked the double door, which was painted a blue so dark it appeared nearly black. Large, unshuttered windows ringed each level. "Has anyone lived here since the prince was cursed?"

Shirdona shook her head. "The tagavoi and tagavli—his parents—did until they died sixty years ago."

"Then what's in there?" Eliana asked. "Other than the prince?"

"No one's been in there since we carried the old tagavoi out. You won't know until you go in."

Eliana chewed on the inside of her cheek until she tasted blood. That tower could be a vishapion's lair. Or teem with stinging worms.

"Go on." Shirdona nudged her. "What else are you going to do?"

"You're right," Eliana said. She clenched her fists, set her jaw, and darted for the tower. This was no time for cowardice.

"Wait, Eliana," Istvan said. "Allow me—"

"Don't you get in her way," Shirdona said. "You'll only mess up what's meant to be."

"I'll do as I please," Istvan retorted.

Eliana let them argue. She didn't want to hesitate for a heartbeat, lest her shaky determination crumbled like a sand-castle under a wave. The sooner she broke the curse, the better.

She sprinted to the entrance. Sucking in a shaky breath, she laid her hand on the bronze handle, turned, and pushed. The door swung inward soundlessly, as if someone had oiled the hinges that morning.

Gulping down the sour taste in her mouth, she drew her sword and stepped inside.

The interior was plain. Barren stone walls surrounded a flagstone floor. Perhaps it once served as a storeroom, but now it was empty and cold, like a mausoleum waiting to receive the dead.

Glancing around, Eliana saw no threats in the dim still-ness. The echoes of her footsteps suggested she was alone, the silence so thick she was certain no living thing lurked in the shadows. She returned her sword to its scabbard and headed for the stairs.

Istvan burst through the door. "Eliana—"

"Are you coming?" She scurried up the worn stone steps. Her feet slid on the slick surfaces and she slowed her pace. Better to go slowly than use the banister for support. In the dim light, she couldn't see if the carved railing hid spiders or worms or some other unknown threat. Her neck prickled as if something was crawling under her clothing. She jostled her shoulders and continued her climb, Istvan close behind her.

The second level held massive fireplaces, wood tables, and a collection of metal cookware. "This must have been the kitchen," Eliana said.

Istvan shrugged. "Does it matter?"

"I suppose not." She picked her way through the silent room, full of items that once saw daily use. Now they lay where they'd been abandoned decades ago, undisturbed by anything but a thin layer of dust.

She led the way up the stairs. The third level was a single large room with two thrones on one side. Huge tapestries hung on the walls, the crimson, emerald, and cobalt shades still vibrant, glints of gold threads shining in the light of the mushrooms that grew from the ceiling. Eliana shivered, wondering about the magic that preserved everything as if it had been made just the day before. A mosaic covered the floor in an intricate geometric pattern of deep blue, turquoise, and sea green tiles, with accents of scarlet.

The weak light from the sunbeam lit the space enough to offset the blue glimmer of the mushrooms, giving the shadows a purple cast. Eliana didn't want to peer into those shadows too closely. She mounted the stairs, hoping for more light above.

The fourth, fifth, and sixth floors contained bedrooms, sitting and dining areas, and a library. The books' pages were metal sheets wrapped in oiled cloth. Eliana ran a finger over the icy surface of a large volume. How clever, she thought, to use metal. Paper would fall apart in this damp environment.

Her heartbeat quickened. The prince was just above. With a deep breath and a clench of her jaw, Eliana ascended to the seventh level.

Floor-to-ceiling windows on all sides admitted a single ray of sunlight along with the bluish glow of the mushrooms. Hanging draperies were pulled back from the windows, midnight blue alternating with turquoise and the green of the sea. The floor repeated the mosaic of the lower levels. In the center, on a platform raised three steps above the floor, was an enormous bed. A young man lay motionless on it.

The princess stared at the sleeping prince, her feet rooted to the floor. Prickles ran up and down her spine, and her mouth went dry. Heavy breathing told Eliana Istvan had joined her. She turned her eyes to meet his. "Now what?" she asked.

He approached the bed. "I don't know." Stalking like a jungle cat approaching its prey, he circled the platform.

Eliana shuffled to the head of the bed, each step an effort as if her feet were reluctant to separate from the floor. She wasn't sure if she was more curious or afraid to finally see what this cursed prince looked like.

He lay motionless, so still that had it not been for the gentle rise and fall of his chest, she would've thought he was dead. His clothing was similar to that of Shirdona's men—a sand-colored, knee-length tunic and leggings. But the hem and neck of the prince's tunic were embroidered with silver thread and crusted with tiny gemstones in place of the crystals that decorated the others' clothing.

The prince—or tagavlon, as Shirdona called him—had the dark hair of his people, but with auburn highlights. Long black eyelashes rested on his cheeks. She wondered if his eyes were dark or if he'd inherited some other color from his water fae ancestors, along with the three parallel slits on both sides of his neck.

His face was pale olive, his features regular. Eliana noted his firm jaw, a narrow upper lip over a full one, and straight nose. Rumors that the Malkhians had been the most beautiful people in the world were justified in the prince's case. She felt oddly attracted to him, as if she knew him, or wanted to know him. A sense of something familiar, but different. She raised a hand to stroke his long, curling hair.

"Eliana."

She jerked her hand back, startled by Istvan's voice. "What is it?"

"Come see." He stood at the foot of the bed.

Her eyes widened when she saw what he was pointing at.

A large bronze plaque was affixed to the foot of the bed. A message was carved in three languages: Ymittosian, Cinarrian, and the vile tongue of Cetus's realm, Magor-Missabibian.

While she could read the first two, the third was nothing more to her than harsh, jagged characters. "Can you read all three?" she asked Istvan. "Do they say the same thing?"

Istvan shook his head. "I don't know those languages."

She frowned. "But it's Ymittosian, Cinarrian and Magor-Missabibian. Surely you can read the first two."

"I can. But the message isn't written in any of them. I've never seen such a script."

Her stomach fluttered. Why couldn't he read the inscription when it was so plain to her? "But I tell you I recognize the script. Do you think that only the cursebreaker can read it?"

He nodded. "You might be right. That would explain why Shirdona didn't know how to break the spell."

"Yes." She turned her attention to the carved words.

Here lies the cursed tagavlon of Malkh,
Who only a kiss can wake.
She who breaks the curse must be the unwed heir of Ymittos.

Her kiss will wake him, but the curse will linger. To fully break the enchantment, the tagavlon and cursebreaker must remain alone together for three full days, as measured by the time of the Ymittosians, binding them in marriage.

If she ever leaves him, a far more terrible curse will descend on the peoples of Ymittos and Malkh.

And if she fails or abandons her Malkhian husband, she will belong to me.

"That's it? A kiss?" Istvan said.

"In Ymittos, to stay alone with a man for three days means you are married. Cetus must have known that." Eliana shuddered. Acrid bile filled her mouth, and her breathing grew ragged. She didn't know what was worse, marrying a stranger, or living underground deprived of sunlight and open air. Suddenly, Istvan was more appealing than he'd been since the first day she met him.

Her knees wobbled, and she clutched his arm. "What am I to do?"

He pursed his lips. "I think you have to kiss him."

"And agree to this forced marriage? Merciful winds, I'm betrothed to you. I don't want to back out of that. All the papers were signed. That would bring horrible shame on both our peoples."

Istvan snorted. "That's what's important to you? The shame?" He flapped a hand in dismissal. "Besides, no one will ever find out."

"What are you talking about?"

"Only you and I will know the truth. You kiss the prince and break the curse."

"But then I'll be bound to him." Didn't Istvan understand what that meant?

"Not forever."

She frowned. "What do you mean?"

"I mean, you wake him up and stay here for three days."

"But after that, I can't leave. Or something worse will happen. We'll probably all end up enslaved to Cetus. Or dead. Not to mention what he'll do to me." Her voice wavered, and she choked back a sob.

"Not if we kill the prince."

She gasped and stared at him. "Kill him?"

"That's the only way. If he dies, he will have left you. You'll be free."

Eliana surveyed the sleeping prince. Istvan might be right. "But to leave me alone with him for three days. What if he—"

"Use your magic to fight him off. Oh, I know you shouldn't be using it. I also know you've been practicing. So, do what you have to do to survive three days. Then I'll help you put an end to him and we can go home."

It *was* a solution. But a cold and bloodthirsty one. And dishonorable. Not to mention Istvan didn't seem troubled by the possibility that if the prince forced himself on her, she might not be able to fend him off. Three days was a long time to go without sleep, repelling unwanted advances. And if she over-used her magic, she could end up unconscious and paralyzed. At the mercy of the prince.

Twisting her hands together until they ached, Eliana gave Istvan a sidelong glance. She'd never seen this cold, calculating side of him before. Or had it been there, and she hadn't noticed?

To wed someone intending to have him killed was wrong, that was clear. The prince had done nothing to hurt her. His only fault was letting Cetus curse him in the first place. And he probably couldn't have prevented it.

"I don't like this. I lose either way. Stuck here with the prince." She shuddered. Marrying one of the Chorokhese, however handsome, was as appealing as wedding a rotting fish. "Or having you win me through murder." *Or ending up Cetus's slave.*

Istvan scowled. "Saving the lives of the people of two nations through ending one life hardly merits being called murder."

"It doesn't bother you I would break our betrothal and bind myself to another?"

"Since I'm sure you don't love him, no."

"And you're not at all concerned about what he might do to me?"

"Since I intend to kill him, no. The only difference is how

painfully he dies." He shrugged. "I thought you were committed to sacrificing yourself for your people. Three days in exchange for freedom from a curse and conquest doesn't seem like an onerous sacrifice to me.

"But I'm the one making the sacrifice."

"If you think the notion of you with another for three days is something I take lightly, then you're wrong. And no matter what happens with the prince—" his face darkened— "I fully intend to marry you in the end."

Eliana took a step back, studying Istvan's stony face. How did he feel? He had so calmly and quickly proposed his solution, as if it were as obvious as warming water before using it to wash.

His plan was a simple answer to their problem. But Istvan's willingness to kill the prince without trying to find any other solution was callous and cruel. She shivered. Would that ruthlessness ever be turned against her?

She froze, unable to even blink. It already had. Istvan was willing to place her at great risk. While she knew the whole venture of breaking the curse entailed danger, Istvan had insisted from the start that he'd protect her.

Now, he wanted to gamble her safety without a qualm. Should she go along with his proposal? He was right, three days was a small sacrifice to make to save both realms. Compared to the enslavement of two nations, what was the death of one man? And it would rescue her from whatever horrors Cetus conjured up for her. A niggling doubt quivered in her stomach. Should she seek another way?

The steely glint in Istvan's eyes made Eliana blurt out her wild desire. "I want to go home." *Back to my life before the prince's curse became my own.*

"What?" At Istvan's shout, Eliana jumped.

"You can't," he growled through his teeth.

"I mean, I need my parents." She jerked her chin up. Something was wrong and she wasn't about to let Istvan force her into a rash decision. "There's time to send a bird and ask what they think." She narrowed her eyes. "I want their opinion about what to do."

"My counsel isn't good enough for you?" He shook his head, twisting his lips into a sneer.

"Both you and my parents have told me repeatedly not to make impulsive decisions without guidance. I've heard your advice. After I hear from my parents, I'll decide. Now that I know what to do to break the curse, things will be easier. And I can ask my father to send some cattle for Shirdona to ensure she helps us again."

"Speaking of Shirdona, where is she?" Istvan asked.

Eliana hurried to the windows and glanced down into the cavern. Shirdona wasn't standing where they'd left her. Eliana ran to each of the other windows. A quick look out of each one confirmed the woman had left the cave. Eliana's jaw slackened in dismay. Their guide had abandoned them.

24

"We need to find Shirdona, now," Istvan said. He charged down the stairs, his footsteps thumping harder than Eliana's racing heart.

For once, Eliana completely agreed with him. Without Shirdona, they'd never find the rest of their party. Eliana forced her stiff muscles into motion and sprinted after him.

She caught up with him in the first-floor storeroom. He stood at the tower's door, studying the empty, silent cavern. Cold, musty air poured in through the opening, tickling Eliana's nose. She sneezed.

With a sigh, Istvan yanked a cloth from his pocket and wiped his sweating face. A scrap of paper fluttered to the ground, but he didn't seem to notice. He drew his sword, the metal blade scraping the edges of the scabbard. "I'm going to scout around. Wait here." Without looking at her, he strode into the cavern.

Eliana let him go. She desperately craved a few moments of peace to think. On impulse, she picked up the parchment that Istvan had dropped. It bore the seal of Nafplio. News from his family, no doubt. She tucked it into her pocket and scurried after him, not wanting to lose him in the dim tunnels.

As he moved through the cavern, his back was straight and stiff, like the mast of a ship holding sails. And he held the rudder, determining the course. Maybe Istvan needed to be in control. But she would not let him dictate to her. Not now, not for the rest of their lives.

The flickering light of the lone sunbeam mirrored her shifting thoughts. She had to break the curse to save her people. She didn't think her army could withstand Cetus. Would Cinar and other realms support Ymittos if they knew she could have stopped Cetus but refused?

But to break the curse was to breach her promise, to violate her honor. She was betrothed to Istvan. Maybe she didn't feel the romantic love she'd felt for Evander. But it was time to move on, to grow up, to face the reality of what was and not cling to her dreams.

Besides, Istvan could be winsome, although she hadn't seen much of that lately. She had to believe he could be reasoned with. His dictatorial side was only coming out because of their perilous situation. Once she broke the curse, his earlier charm and courtesy would return. She was sure of it.

But she and Istvan would only have a life together if he killed the cursed prince. Otherwise, her betrothal contract would be annulled. That would create all kinds of political complications. Would the Nafplians forgive that offense to their dochan and their realm? Or would that drive them to ally with Cetus? And she wasn't sure she wanted to marry a man who would kill another in cold blood.

Maybe Istvan and the prince could duel for her. That would at least make things fair. But if things went badly, she could easily end up with no husband. *This is too complicated.* She rubbed her throbbing forehead, longing for someone, anyone, who could help her sort through the decision.

Eliana massaged her stiff neck and scowled. Who was she fooling? Her honor meant nothing, compared to what would happen if she failed as cursebreaker. Three days with the cursed prince, or a lifetime with Istvan, either would be far better than one minute as Cetus's slave. Her scruples, her morals, her fears were of no consequence. The only escape was waking up the prince.

A raucous laugh rang out, echoing faintly among the stalactites. Eliana screwed up her face. Where had she heard that voice before?

A moment later, she spotted Istvan returning, his sword now sheathed. Shirdona sauntered next to him, leading a crowd of men. Alessia trailed behind Istvan, Dimitris limping beside her.

"There you are!" Shirdona's voice held triumph. "We found you."

Eliana gasped with relief. Stifling the impulse to run, she walked with a measured pace to meet the woman. She craned her neck to peer past Shirdona. It appeared that most of Shirdona's and all Istvan's men had survived the battle with the vishapions. *At least this day hasn't been a complete disaster.*

With a scowl, Istvan waved a hand at Shirdona. "She says she went to find the others."

"I needed to make certain they'd killed all the beasts. Which they had." The woman twitched her shoulders. "What else would I do?"

Istvan snarled and said, "But you left us with the prince."

"I did." Shirdona's eyebrows drew together. "Where is he? Why didn't you wake him up?"

Eliana hesitated. Shirdona would not take kindly to Istvan's plan to kill the tagavlon. The princess explained the curse-breaking instructions, omitting any mention of Istvan's intentions. "I don't think I can legally end my betrothal without my parents' consent. I need their advice."

Even as the words fell from her lips, she winced, hearing how weak her reasoning was. Her father would tell her to break the curse, no matter what. But luring the cursed prince to his death would be as bad as killing him herself.

"You can't." Both Istvan and Shirdona voiced their opposition at the same time.

Eliana glanced from one scowling face to the other. "Why not?"

"Do I have to spell it out for you?" Istvan asked. "We've used ten days of the fifteen you had. It will take at least a day to return to the rift. A day to send a bird and receive a reply makes thirteen. Another day to return here. That leaves only one day, when three are required to break the curse. You're short two days. And that's assuming your parents give you an answer immediately."

His tone was condescending, sending fiery heat across Eliana's cheeks, but she couldn't argue with his logic.

Istvan threw his hands in the air. "How are you going to explain all this in a message tied to a bird? Besides, you came here to break the curse. I'm sure your parents would agree that's what you must do."

Eliana glued her eyes on Istvan's face. After a long moment, she turned to Shirdona. "What do you think?"

"You'll waste a lot of time seeking advice. And you'll give the Saumarotas an opportunity to barricade the tagavlon's tower so you can't get to it. Now that they know you've come, they'll be watching."

The woman had a point. If the other family kept her from waking the prince, the curse would remain in effect, with all its horrible consequences. Eliana thought for a moment. "I need to talk to Dimitris."

"You could do that," Shirdona said.

"If you want to behave like a child," Istvan added. "For someone who wants to rule a country, you're wavering over a simple decision like a dithering fool." He scoffed. "Little girls who don't know their duty have no business ruling."

Eliana gasped, stunned by his words. "You're the one who told me to not make hasty decisions. What happened to that?"

"You can't recognize sound advice when you receive it. Have you never heard that too many opinions sink the boat?" He sneered. "You talk about mutual respect in a marriage. It seems that only goes one way. Your way. You cling to your pride rather than offer the least sliver of consideration to me."

Now she'd done it. *I hit him in his weak spot.* Maybe the time had come to sacrifice her principles.

He took a step closer, looming over her. "We came here to break the curse. And when we've completely broken it, you and I will return to Ymittos."

Her instincts screamed at her that Istvan was wrong, that killing the cursed prince wasn't the way.

She glimpsed Dimitris's frown and the almost imperceptible shake of his head. What was he trying to tell her?

While she was still collecting her jumbled thoughts, Istvan continued in a softer tone. "I'll always do what's best for you, Eliana. You need to believe that."

But could she? He didn't seem to understand her need to resist impulsively grabbing the first solution that presented itself. Or the importance of preserving her integrity and not sacrificing innocent people. All Istvan cared about was being in control. "Thank you, Istvan." She swallowed the sour taste in her mouth. Time. She needed time. "Shirdona, do you have any food? We're all tired and hungry and cranky."

The woman laughed. "Yes, you certainly are. We have some provisions. The Alagata family was gracious enough to share with the cursebreaker and her attendants. They're setting up camp in the next cavern. Come and see."

Istvan stiffened. He didn't appreciate being lumped in with the underlings, but Eliana was too annoyed to appease him. She took a few quick steps to catch up with Shirdona.

They passed from the prince's cavern into the next one,

where the intricate mosaic of the floor was now stained with vishapion blood.

A score of Chorokhese was scurrying about, lighting fires, brewing tea, and arranging mats on the ground. Some looked familiar, probably Shirdona's people. The others, Eliana thought, had to be the Alagatas.

"Shirdona," Eliana said, "If I wanted to get word to my parents, is there another way? A quicker way to the surface, perhaps?"

"The Alagatas are planning a cattle raid. You can go up with them."

"You want to help cattle thieves?" Istvan's sarcasm was thick and caustic.

Eliana suppressed her annoyance. "Why not? If I break the curse as you seem to want me to do, I'm destined to rule these people alongside their prince. Shouldn't I join in their raids?" Although if Istvan's plan prevailed, she wouldn't be ruling with the prince of Chorokha for more than a few days.

Istvan's nostrils flared, and his face reddened. Eliana had to clench her jaw to keep a grin from curving her lips.

He gave her a curt nod. "Yes, you should learn their barbaric ways. You already fit in quite well."

Keeping her chin high, Eliana froze her expression into one of bland boredom. She wasn't about to let him see how deeply his barb stung.

Shirdona pointed to a narrow waterfall that splashed into a small pool. "Istvan, you and your men can fill your water skins there."

With a muttered curse, he strode off.

"Come to think of it," Eliana said, "I am thirsty."

"Better to wait for the tea," Shirdona answered. "I only suggested the water because I thought you wanted to be free of him for a moment."

That was true, but Eliana wasn't about to admit it. "Thank you for your kindness."

The woman's usual smirk vanished. "If you're going to break the curse, you need to act. At any point, the Saumarotas might try to stop you. Or another vishapion could roam by." She nodded to Dimitris. "Maybe you can talk some sense into her." She turned away.

Eliana watched her go. "I didn't tell you the entire story." She plucked Alessia's sleeve and motioned for Dimitris to move closer. In a few terse sentences, she told them of her dilemma and Istvan's solution.

Alessia snorted. "He's a cold-hearted mongrel, that's what I say. I knew there was a reason I never liked him." She folded her arms over her chest.

That wasn't helpful. Eliana huffed and sought Dimitris's gaze.

He shook his head, a mournful look on his face. "This is hard. If you honor your betrothal, you doom Ymittos and Chorokha to slavery under Cetus. If you wake the prince, you give both peoples a chance to fight back, if that's what they choose. Under the circumstances, I don't think anyone would condemn you if you chose the Tagavlon of Chorokha over the Dochan of Nafplio."

"You already know Istvan is as slippery as an eel," Alessia said, nudging Eliana. "And not as good-tempered."

Dimitris sighed. "Worse than that. If Istvan's so quick to propose killing the tagavlon simply because he's an impediment, wouldn't he adopt a similar strategy in other circumstances? For instance, suppose his wife fails to produce an heir?"

Eliana gulped. Istvan certainly enjoyed getting his own way. And he didn't seem to have many scruples about how to get it. Would he really kill her? He'd already proven he would destroy someone who interfered with his plans.

Why had she bound herself to him? The answer came to her, swift as an eagle. She had taken the first acceptable suitor, telling herself that it was one more sacrifice she needed to make for Ymittos, another effort to atone for Evander's death. Far too often she grabbed at a solution only to bitterly regret it. Her hunger to ease her guilt over Evander blinded her to jump at any chance to sacrifice for her people. And now Istvan had used that drive to convince her that another kind of sacrifice was in order. That she spend three days with a stranger, this Chorokhese prince, binding herself to him. All the while knowing that Istvan would kill him.

Sour bile filled her mouth. What was she becoming that she would even consider Istvan's plan? No. She would not be a party to murder. Sacrifice for others shouldn't demand a betrayal of what she knew to be right and true.

If she woke the prince, then, as Dimitris pointed out, the people could choose if they wanted to fight Cetus or succumb to slavery. And the prince himself, shouldn't he have a say in what happened to him?

A sudden thought came to her, and she stared at the cavern's ceiling, her mind awhirl. In all the stories she'd read about curses, the enchanted person knew how to break it. So, her best choice could very well be to ask the prince and to work with him to free both their realms from Cetus's threats.

With a start, she realized she no longer cared about keeping her betrothal intact. Defeating Cetus was of far greater consequence. If breaking the curse meant binding herself to the prince, so be it. A weight lifted from her chest for the space of a thought.

Then it crashed down on her again. She'd free herself from Istvan only to be tethered to another. Would the cursed prince—or the tagavlon, as she better get used to calling him, barbarian that he was, be a superior husband than Istvan? She'd have to face that problem when it arose. The question was, how to get back to the tower undetected by Istvan? She didn't want him anywhere around until she could warn the tagavlon about the dochan's murderous intentions.

The bustle of the Alagata family mixing with Shirdona's

people gave Eliana an idea. "Dimitris. Alessia. Don't let anyone know I've gone."

Dimitris gave her an approving nod.

Alessia wrinkled her forehead. "Where are you going?"

"To break the curse."

25

____

"What should we tell Istvan if he wonders where you are?" Alessia asked.

Eliana glanced at Istvan and his men standing around the waterfall, splashing water on their faces and drinking deeply. "Distract him. It should be easy enough with all these people milling around. I only need enough time to wake the tagavlon and warn him about Istvan."

"Will half an hour be sufficient?" Dimitris asked.

"To do what?" Shirdona asked.

"What?" Eliana jumped back and whirled. Where had the woman come from?

"My sunshine, I hope you're planning on breaking the curse. Time is running out."

"I know that. But I was consulting with Dimitris."

"Not Istvan?" Shirdona chuckled and raised her eyebrows.

Eliana stiffened. *If Shirdona knew Istvan's plans, would she turn on us?*

"He told you what to do, right?" Shirdona looked into Eliana's face. "And you weren't pleased with what he had to say."

"Not exactly…" *You would be even less pleased.*

Shirdona shook her head like a disappointed tutor. "When were you going to tell me, my sunshine?"

"Tell you what?" Eliana's mind spun like she was caught in a whirlpool, unable to keep up with Shirdona's nimble mind.

"That your Istvan is planning to kill our tagavlon." When Eliana gasped, Shirdona held up a hand. "Istvan's men aren't very discreet."

Eliana gaped at her.

"Oh, don't look so shocked, my sunshine. It was obvious."

"Obvious how?" Was the woman a mind reader?

"To break the curse, you'd have to marry the tagavlon. Your betrothed, of course, would have an objection or two to that idea. But being a man of lofty ambition, he'd use the situation to his benefit. It made sense that he'd wait for you to fully break the spell. Then he'd do whatever it took to reclaim his bride."

Heat rose to Eliana's face. "You knew I'd have to stay with the tagavlon for three days."

"The old tagavoi didn't keep it a secret."

"But you said you didn't know." She spit the bitter accusation from her mouth as if the words burned her tongue.

"I lied." Shirdona answered nonchalantly. "What was the point of telling you in advance? It might have scared you off. I knew you'd find out soon enough. But you still had to break the curse. What else would you do?"

"Come up with a plan, at least." Was Shirdona trying to help her or not? From Shirdona's indifferent demeanor, Eliana couldn't tell.

"And your Istvan would still want to kill our tagavlon." Shirdona scoffed. "This way, you can wake the tagavlon and warn him."

Eliana lifted her hands with the palms facing up. "That's what I intend to do."

"Good, my sunshine. What are you waiting for?"

"I don't want Istvan to stop me."

"Oh, he won't." Shirdona smirked. "At least, not right away." She jerked her chin toward the throng of men gathered around the waterfall.

Several of Istvan's men clutched their stomachs and darted for the shadows of a side cavern. Laughs and jeers from the Alagatas and Shirdona's family chased them, their mirth echoing in the cave like the cries of mockingbirds.

"What's going on?" Alessia asked.

"That's what I want to know." Puzzled, Eliana watched Istvan sprint for the darkness.

Shirdona shrugged. "Too bad your Istvan and his men drank from a pool where orange mushrooms grow. Every fool knows to drink only from pools where blue or green mushrooms grow, or to boil the water first."

"But you directed him to that water." Eliana frowned. Was this Shirdona's way of helping?

The woman cackled. "If you'd like to see a line of bare butts, go on over. Or if you have other places to be…"

So Istvan and his men all had some kind of bowel flux. "Will they be alright?"

"Oh, they're all young and healthy. It'll stop in a few hours. But they won't be eager to do any jousting for a day or two." She tipped her head to the side. "I'll tell him even though you're a little girl, you know which water is safe." Her last words were sarcastic, and Eliana realized Shirdona hadn't liked Istvan's slur any more than she had.

Waving her hands at Eliana like she was shooing a fly, Shirdona asked, "Don't you have a curse to break?"

Eliana straightened her spine. She did, if she could remember which passage would take her to the tagavlon. "Which way do I go?"

Shirdona pointed at a tunnel. "Back the way you came.

The tagavlon's tower is in the next cavern. It's not far, and you should have no trouble getting there. Now, get going."

Alessia squeezed the princess's hand. "I'll tell Istvan you were sick, but that it wasn't too bad and you're sleeping it off. Go. Dimitris and I will be fine."

"Thank you, I think," Eliana answered. In the distance, she heard Istvan yelling for someone to bring him clean breeches.

"Go," Alessia said. "We'll deal with him."

With one last look at Alessia's nodding head, Dimitris' worried frown, and Shirdona's sardonic grin, Eliana darted into the tunnel. The pale green mushrooms gave her just enough light, so she could find her footing and avoid sliding into a crevasse.

She hoped the raucous laughter of Shirdona's people was sufficient to lure any predators roaming the tunnels. Although the most dangerous predator, Istvan, was behind her. Eliana allowed a smile to curve her lips. While she didn't want him to be deathly ill, she wasn't sorry his bowels were taking over his life.

But had she put Alessia and Dimitris in danger? Eliana winced, thinking of what Istvan would do to them if he learned they'd helped her slip away. He'd never liked either of her servants and would find it hard to believe they didn't know where she had gone.

No time for that now. The princess scurried over the mosaic tile, slowing her pace as she approached the tagavlon's tower. She peered from the mouth of the tunnel, listening. No one was about.

Eliana clenched her fists, took a deep breath, and darted for the tower's door. No hail of arrows, shouts, or clanging of swords. No roaring beasts. Just the silence of Qala Bisen and the steady drip of water, a constant sound in Chorokha.

Squaring her shoulders, she mounted the stairs. The silent rooms felt like they guarded ominous secrets. The hair on the back of her neck rose. The shadows shifted as she walked past them, disturbing their silent watch. During her previous foray into the tower, Istvan's presence had distracted her from its brooding, eerie ambiance.

Not wanting to linger, she raced past the throne room and up the steps. The quiet chambers were oversized graves, waiting to snare her for all eternity. Her heart sped up, and not just because of the climb.

When she reached the seventh level, she was panting and sweaty. *So here I am, to break a curse. To encounter the one to whom I must bind myself.*

The state of her clothes made Eliana let out a huff. She'd dressed in her finest to meet Istvan. Now, she wore a filthy tunic and leggings, and sturdy boots rather than elegant sandals. Her unwashed hair was twisted in simple braids, unadorned by any jewelry. This was not the way a princess met her future consort.

She circled the bier and read the instructions again. Kiss the tagavlon, stay alone with him for three days, then be bound to him forever. There was no alternative. *I sacrifice myself or condemn at least two kingdoms to death and destruction at Cetus's hand. And myself to far worse.*

Forcing in a breath, she shook herself. Maybe the tagavlon had another idea. He must. After all, since he was the one cursed, he had to know how to break it. The only way to find out was to wake him.

Eliana straightened her spine. *Then do it.* She strode to the head of the platform, climbed the three steps, and gazed at the prince. He was handsome. Would he be kind? She studied his features. Was that stubbornness she read in his powerful jaw? His lips were bent in a whisper of a smile. Maybe he'd be fun. With his eyes closed, she couldn't tell if he was intelligent or dull, open or reserved.

She chewed her lower lip while she studied his clothing. His tunic looked fresh, as if the linen had been woven that day. The silver and gold threads of the embroidery around his collar and cuffs glinted in the dim light, bright against the dark blue fabric of the hems. Sand-colored trousers were tucked into tall boots, the leather still bearing a newly polished gleam. Even his chin appeared as smooth as if he'd shaved that morning.

If only she could have washed her face. Maybe the tagavlon would be so grateful for being woken up, he wouldn't notice her bedraggled state.

No more delays, Eliana admonished herself. She swallowed hard, sucked in a breath, and leaned over the prince. Gently, she pressed her lips to his.

What had she expected? An explosion like fireworks, perhaps? Him opening his eyes and looking at her with love? A burst of sunlight illuminating the room?

None of that happened. Instead, her lips tingled, and heat surged to her toes. She pulled her head away from the prince's face. He lay motionless, not even a flicker of an eyelid to suggest he was rousing from the enchanted sleep. Maybe she should try again.

She laid a hand on his cheek, closed her eyes, held her breath, and moved her face close to his. Two powerful hands pushed against her shoulders, shoving her back. She staggered and stumbled backwards down the steps. Her arms flailed as she caught her balance.

"No! Go away!"

The prince's deep voice was raspy from disuse. But there was no mistaking the urgency in his tone.

Eliana stared at him, wide-eyed. "Why? I came to break the curse."

He sat up and rubbed a hand over his eyes. She took a step toward him.

"Stay back!" he yelled.

She froze in place, blinking. "I don't understand."

"Of course, you don't." He glared at her with large, dark

blue eyes. "Keep your distance. Better yet, leave." He pointed at the stairs. "Return to your kingdom." He wagged his finger at her like a master reproving a careless student. "Never come back."

"Never come back? I can't do that." Eliana shook her head. "The spell hasn't been broken. I must remain with you for three days."

"Oh, do you now? And I suppose you think that will wed you to me. Or else a horrible doom will descend on both your realm and mine."

"Right." At least he knew that much. "Why are you sending me away? Don't you want the curse broken?"

"The girl wonders if I'd rather lie in an enchanted sleep until I rot," he said to the ceiling. "What's your name?"

"Eliana."

"Eliana, heir to Ymittos, I imagine. Do the Kastellanos still rule?" When she nodded, he pursed his lips. "Well, Eliana Kastellanos, you need to leave before I kill you."

None of this made sense to Eliana. Why would he want to kill her? Had his long sleep stolen his sanity? "Will you at least tell me your name? I'd like to know who to curse as I'm dying."

He gave her a wry smile. "Adakizh Bonvarnon Alagata Bisen, at your service." He swung his legs over the side of the bed and twisted to sit facing away from her. He rested his forearms on his knees and bent over, speaking to the floor. "You have to go."

"But the curse—"

"You don't consider marrying someone you barely know a curse?"

"That's the common fate of princesses, in case you haven't noticed." Exasperation sharped her tone.

He slid off the bed and stood up, moving as if his muscles were stiff from long disuse. He swayed, holding out his hands as if his legs were unsure how to support his weight. "True. But your people would consider us barbarians."

Eliana pursed her lips, considering her response. "In some ways, you are."

"Then you shouldn't want to bind yourself to me. Go home. Now." He spun around sharply to face her, shouting the last words.

She flinched but didn't move. "The only way to break the curse on both our kingdoms is for me to be with you for three days." she asked.

"Look, I don't know you." He tipped his head to the side and studied her face. "You're clearly brave, willing to sacrifice for your people, and pretty, in a disheveled sort of way. But none of that matters. Leave me."

"Why? Is it because Istvan wants to kill you?"

"Istvan? Who's that? Some Ymittosian noble?" He narrowed his eyes. "Your brother? No, couldn't be. Your betrothed?"

"He—"

"I can tell from your face he is. So. You spend three days with me, which means we are married, according to both your traditions and mine. Once the curse is broken, this Istvan will kill me."

Eliana winced. "Yes, that was his idea. He reasoned if you died, I wouldn't have left you, so the enchantment would be lifted. How did you know?"

"An educated guess." Adakizh crossed his arms. "Kharan-Khuag didn't just drop the curse on me. That would have been too merciful. Instead, he gave me three days to decide. Surrender Chorokha or be cursed."

Her eyes flared wide and a gasp escaped her lips. "You chose to be cursed?"

"Of course. Oh, it wasn't a simple decision. My parents, our whole family, we cried and argued for days. We thought of every possible outcome. Would Kharan-Khuag invade before the curse was broken? Would no princess be valiant or noble enough to try? Being woken from the curse and killed three days later was a very real possibility. But in the end, we chose freedom. Even if it was only for one hundred years."

He'd sacrificed himself so his people could live free, even knowing there was scant hope for him. Eliana could find no words.

Adakizh raised an eyebrow. "What's your plan? That Istvan and you would rule my kingdom, no doubt."

"Merciful winds, of course not." At least, she didn't want to. She'd never considered whether Istvan entertained ambitions regarding Chorokha.

Clenching his hands on his elbows so hard his knuckles whitened, Adakizh took a step closer to Eliana. "Why did you tell me about Istvan?"

"To warn you. And ask if you knew a different way to break the curse."

"Which one?"

Her jaw slackened. "What do you mean?"

"You broke part of the first curse. There is a second curse."

"Two curses?" Eliana expelled a long breath, feeling all hope depart with the air from her lungs. How much worse could this get?

"Two. The second one states that after I'm freed of the enchanted sleep, I have to kill the person who awakened me."

"Kill me? No. You're mistaken." Her mouth went dry and she crossed her arms.

He smiled sadly. "I wish I was. But if I don't, Kharan-Khuag will seize my kingdom." He glared at her. "There's no way out for us. If you don't spend three days with me, the first curse holds. Kharan-Khuag will take over Chorokha, enslave my people and yours. And if I don't kill you within those three days, Kharan-Khuag will invade and enslave everyone in my realm—and yours." Adakizh's voice wavered. "He promised to save an especially grisly death for me."

Her shoulders drooped. "Not to mention what he plans for me."

"For you?"

The words caught in her throat and her voice shook. "Personal and intimate plans, he called them."

He stared at her for a long moment. "Then killing you might be a kindness."

She took a step back and held up her hands. "Don't kill me. I can enlist my father to liberate your kingdom."

He snorted. "Wouldn't that be lovely? Do you really think your father's army can defeat Kharan-Khuag? You forget, Ymittos will already be magically enslaved. I'll still be dead." He shuddered. "And you, worse than dead." He grimaced and rubbed his forehead. "The curse compels me to want to kill you." One of his hands stretched toward Eliana. He screwed up his face, struggling, and shoved his hand in his pocket. "I'm fighting it with all I have, but it's hard. That's why you need to go." His voice rose to a command. "Leave, before I can't stop myself."

"But surely there's another way."

"Why are you here? You still have time."

Eliana squeezed her eyebrows together. "Time for what?"

Adakizh rolled his eyes. "I'm a bit weak from having been asleep for so long. But I feel my strength returning as we speak. In a few moments, I'll be able to snap your neck as easily as a chicken's."

Eliana shuddered and sidled toward the door, her heart thumping erratically. "I have to save my people."

"And I should save mine. But I'm not about to lose my soul to do it. I'd rather give you a chance to live. Go back to Ymittos and spread the word. Even better, flee as far as you can, alerting everyone you meet. At least the continent will have some warning of Kharan-Khuag's invasion, and you'll delay your own enslavement. It's all hopeless, probably, but better than nothing."

"I still think——"

"Would you go?" He roared the words at her and vaulted over the bed.

She let out a startled squeak, whirled, and fled down the stairs.

26

Derya huddled on her mare, tugging the sable-lined hood of her cloak over her face. Even though they'd traveled steadily ever since Eliana descended into the rift that morning, Derya and her entourage had made little progress on their way to Nafplio. Blowing snow obscured the road, slowing their pace to that of a horse plowing a rocky field. A gust of wind sliced through her heavy cloak, chilling her like she'd been doused in icy water. At least Eliana was safe from the squalls and sleet.

Derya glanced back at the wagons trundling over the bumpy road. The princess was tempted to join her maids inside them for a respite from the cutting wind, but that was not fitting for the future ruler of the Cinarrian Empire. No, she'd brave the elements like the soldiers under her command. There were plenty who believed a woman wasn't strong enough to rule the vast empire. She had to use every opportunity to prove them wrong.

Her entourage stretched in a serpentine line following the stone road, the vivid turquoise and black of Cinar's colors bright in the weak winter sun, a stark contrast to the snow-covered fields. Two hundred people made up her escort of soldiers, courtiers, servants, smiths, and healers. Derya shook her head. To think Eliana had descended to Malkh with only ten warriors, her maid, and Istvan.

The thought of Eliana's betrothed made Derya scowl. She didn't like him. Why, she wasn't sure. At least she didn't have to marry the man. Maybe it would turn out well for Eliana. Derya hoped so. If not, she'd have to content herself with insulting Istvan every time they met, but subtly, so he couldn't take public offense.

She squinted through the falling snow, grateful the driving sleet had let up. Now, only small, soft flakes drifted in the wind.

A horse came alongside hers. She looked into the weathered face of Chiliarch Bahadir. Sleet crusted his heavy dark eyebrows, and his eyes were bloodshot and weary. "Chiliarch, how goes it?"

"Kiral Derya, since the sleet has stopped, we should reach the southern pass in another day or so. Assuming the weather doesn't take an ugly turn."

"A blizzard would be most inconvenient." She gave the chiliarch what she hoped was an encouraging smile. "I trust no one else has fallen ill?"

"Yes, thank the Rider. Only five cases of grippe and one sprained ankle. We have plenty of room in the wagons for them."

"Good." She nodded. "I hope Nafplio's weather is truly as mild as they claim. We'll all be grateful to leave this ice behind."

"Taking this route was a wise move, Kiral. That last snowfall most likely blocked the northern passes."

She pursed her lips. "Exactly how much longer to the pass?"

"Hard to say in this weather, with the days so short. In summer, I'd say late tomorrow. If the weather turns, could be two or three more days. The scouts tell me there's a town—

Glyfadu, they call it—just south of here. I believe we should stop for the night and hope the sleet is gone for good."

Derya turned to her right to face the woman who served as advisor, companion and chaperone, Danisman Safiye. "What do you think? We'd planned to reach Zografou today."

"That's true, Kiral." The fur scarf wrapped around the woman's face muffled her voice. "But we're all worn out. Fires, hot food, and shelter from the wind are what we need so we don't all fall ill."

"Or slip on the ice," the chiliarch added. "Tired horses aren't as sure-footed."

"All right. Send scouts ahead to secure lodgings for as many as possible and food for all. I know I'll be glad to feel my toes again." Derya huddled back into her furs. "And send word to Zografou that we won't be there until tomorrow."

A gust of wind blew a handful of snowflakes into Derya's face, their icy crystals pricking her frozen cheeks like knives wielded by tiny warriors. No need to second guess herself, she thought. Better to proceed at the pace of weary oxen than court disaster.

Half an hour's ride brought them to a bend in the road and the outskirts of Glyfadu. A score of two- and three-story houses huddled around a paved square surrounded by ramshackle cottages and huts. While weather-beaten, the wood structures looked sturdy. Derya noted that smoke rose from the chimneys. Wherever they found shelter, it would certainly be warmer than outside.

The scouts had done their work well. The inn's six rooms could accommodate twenty people, Chiliarch Bahadir told her. "That would be you, your danisman, your maids—"

"No, chiliarch," Derya said. "Put the five with grippe in two of the rooms, along with a servant to tend them in the night. Give two rooms to the oldest six of my advisors and healers. The other two are for you and whoever of your men you choose."

The chiliarch's eyes widened, and he opened his mouth, blinking rapidly. "Kiral——"

"After a few hours sitting by a fire and eating something hot, I'll be happy to sleep in my tent. The braziers keep it warm enough. My maids can join me there, as can Danisman Safiye, if she'd care to. Let's allow the ill, the aged, and those who worked the hardest today—and I include you in that number—to sleep indoors. That is my word." She gave him the Cinarrian salute, her right fist over her heart, the first two fingers extended, and raised her eyebrows.

After staring at her for a heartbeat as if turned to ice, the chiliarch relaxed his shoulders and returned the salute. "Yes, Kiral. And thank you." He turned his mount and rode to the field where his officers were supervising the raising of tents for the soldiers.

Danisman Safiye leaned over to Derya. "That was well done, Kiral. Surprising, but well done."

"How could I sleep by a fire indoors when most of my people are housed in tents on the hard ground?" She shook her head. "My tent has a wood floor and braziers. I'll be comfortable enough."

"In that case, I'll be happy to join you."

"I'd be honored. Now, shall we see what this inn offers in the way of food?"

Derya swung from the saddle and handed the reins to a waiting groom. She waited for Danisman Safiye to dismount, then trod gingerly across the icy cobblestones to the inn. Its large front windows gleamed with flickering light. Derya slid her arm through Safiye's.

Chiliarch Bahadir joined them just as they reached the entrance. "If I may, Kiral Derya, I'd like to suggest we wait for a few of your personal guard before going in. The scouts mumbled something about a rough crowd."

"Rough could be entertaining," Derya said. "Do they know who we are?"

"Of course, they do," the chiliarch said. "An entourage this big, flying the royal banner of Cinar? I'm sure every hamlet, goatherd, and field mouse around know we're here."

A note of worry had crept into the chiliarch's voice that Derya didn't understand. As she pondered the cause of it, five of her personal guard strode up. "Are we all here?" Derya asked.

"Yes, Kiral," answered the chiliarch. Two guards pushed open the door, letting out a gust of warm air, a tantalizing scent of roasting meat, and the sounds of clanking tankards and coarse laughter. They held the door open so Derya, Bahadir, and Safiye could enter.

Derya stepped into the room and moaned as the warm air met her frozen nose. Her toes and fingers stung as the warmth returned. She flexed her hands a few times and looked around.

Only then did she notice that the room had gone silent. Not a respectful silence, or a curious one, but one brimming with resentment and sullen anger. No wonder the scouts had thought something was amiss. Bahadir wasn't just indulging his usual paranoia. The skin on the back of her neck prickled.

She probed the room with her gaze. It was longer than wide, the wood floor worn and scuffed. Immense fireplaces stood at either end, large enough for a tall man to stand inside. Over the crackling flames of the fires hung huge black pots. Derya hoped they contained stew. And that they had more in the kitchen. She'd content herself with bread and tea if there wasn't enough for her soldiers.

Iron chandeliers dangled from the ceiling, their candles giving weak light that flickered with every draft. Plumes of smoke from the fires circled the candlesticks like serpents coiling to strike.

Narrow tables filled the center of the room, the benches occupied by men in dirty, threadbare tunics and leggings, leather cloaks slung on their shoulders. They wore their long black hair loose, not braided like the Ymittosians of the capital or her own soldiers. She let her eyes pass over a few faces. Derya wondered what was fueling the resentment. Was there simmering hatred underneath? For a moment, she thought of leaving the town.

No. The sun was approaching the horizon. It would be folly to press on to Zografou in the dark. She straightened her spine and strode to the wiry innkeeper, the chiliarch and her advisor a pace behind her.

Derya looked him in the eye, trying not to stare at his pointed teeth. She hadn't realized forest fae still lived in Ymittos. "Greetings. I trust you and your household are well."

He scowled. "You got coin to pay for all your hangers-on?"

Bahadir stepped to Derya's side. "The Princess of Cinar can most certainly compensate you fairly for providing food and drink for her people."

"Depends on what you call fair. Supplies from Nafplio were interrupted. Now they're back at twice the price. You'll have to pay the going rate."

Was that true? Or was this innkeeper just trying to earn a few extra coins? That would be something for Bahadir to investigate before they paid the bill. Derya nodded. "Very well. Now, would you be so kind as to serve us some of that stew I smell, and have enough for two hundred sent to my camp?"

The man grunted. "Do they want beer while they're waiting? Stew for that many will take a while."

That was probably true, Derya thought. Preparing stew for her entourage most likely meant butchering another ram.

"Send tea to the camp," Bahadir said. "Quick as you can. Tea, not beer. I'll send some men to help."

Bahadir was right. No need for the soldiers to get drunk. And if this innkeeper was one of the fae, drinking his beer might prove to be disastrous. Derya hoped the man's offer was prompted by nothing more than a desire for profit.

The innkeeper grunted and jerked his chin at an empty table near the larger fireplace. Derya took that to mean he wanted them to sit there. She gave him a confident smile she didn't quite feel and walked to the fire.

The heat hit her face in a wave, stinging the raw spots left by the sleet. Derya pulled off her gloves, shoved them into a pocket, and held her aching hands toward the flames.

"Kiral."

"Yes, Chiliarch Bahadir?"

"I don't like this."

"Neither do I. I would much prefer an inn with a view of the seaside, where we could watch the sun dance on the waves. If that's not possible, then to be served by a smiling widow who loves to feed people."

"It's not just the inn or the innkeeper. It reminds me of how I felt at the end of our war with Catalagzi, after they surrendered. They looked at us the same way. At every opportunity, someone tried to stick a knife between our ribs."

"But we're still in Ymittos. They're our ally."

"Maybe the king is. But in this remote border town, populated with forest fae and who knows who else? I'm not so sure."

She huddled in her cloak and nibbled her lip, trying to remember the history. As Cinar expanded, many fled, including most of the water and forest fae. If these people were the descendants of refugees who made new homes in Ymittos, that could explain the resentment.

The thump of bowls on the table behind them made Derya turn. A smile crossed her face. "Stew!"

Bahadir put a hand on her arm. "Let someone else taste it first."

Derya squirmed as she watched her food taster sniff the stew, then take a tiny spoonful. He rolled it around in his mouth, then swallowed. She hated having a food taster. What if the poor soul died eating something meant to kill her?

The man nodded. "Kiral Derya, it's fine." He motioned with his chin toward the fireplace. "We watched them ladle the stew out of the common pot and bring it over."

"Thank you," Derya said. She slid onto the bench and pulled a bowl toward herself. She took a spoonful and grimaced. The meat was an ancient mutton, its musty taste of grass and soil uncut by any spices. She chewed the tough morsel until she could swallow it. "Thank the Rider, it's hot."

The food taster laughed. "That's about all you can say for it."

She consumed her stew in silence, wishing the inn had brewed hot kahve instead of weak herbal tea. She needed alertness rather than relaxation. The chiliarch was right. The restless crowd, mostly men, had the gaunt look of the malnourished. Was this their only warm meal of the day? Or perhaps it was their only meal.

A group by the fire sang a lively tune in one of the rural Ymittosian dialects. Derya pursed her lips. From the few words she understood, she deduced the song was either about the pursuit of a village wanton or a rebellion against the local lord. Neither topic made her curious enough to ask for a translation of the lyrics.

After every line, the singers shouted and raised tiny glasses to down a clear liquid Bahadir told her was distilled with anise seed. "Very strong," the chiliarch added.

Most of the inn's patrons, however, huddled on the benches, clutching their bowls and glowering in Derya's direction. A fight broke out over a loaf of flatbread. The innkeeper and a huge hulking man wearing a bloodstained apron tossed the fighters into the street.

Her eyes roaming the crowd, Derya reflected that in midwinter, people would ration their food carefully to ensure it lasted until summer. But these people looked like they'd been surviving on short rations for years. Their hilly land might not be very fertile. Or was there a different reason for their apparent poverty?

Another fight broke out, this one, thankfully, limited to words. But it was also over bread. Derya wondered if the combatants wanted the food for themselves or their families. Men with hungry children would take risks they might not otherwise. Which could lead them to fight. Or worse. The supplies on one of her wagons were enough for this village to eat better through the winter than they did during harvest season.

A strong smell of sweat and goat pulled Derya's attention to her left. A man in a mud-spattered tunic stood nearby, his brown eyes hard, his protruding jaw set in a challenge. "You. Lady."

Bahadir rose slowly and put his hand on his sword. "The Princess is occupied."

"Looks like she's done eating to me." The man spat on the chiliarch's boots and bared his pointed teeth.

Derya sat up straight and lifted her chin, hiding her trembling hands in her lap. "I'm sorry, I'm too tired to sing tonight for boshers like you."

The man flinched at her use of the vulgar slang. Repressing a grin, she continued in the same bored tone. "Perhaps your wife would give us a tune?"

His jaw dropped. He opened and closed his mouth a few times.

"Chiliarch," Derya said, "would you find our friend here a seat somewhere else?"

"With pleasure, Kiral Derya." He gripped the arm of the man, whose mouth was still flapping, and escorted him back to his friends.

Danisman Safiye nudged Derya with her elbow. "May I suggest, Kiral, that we take our leave?"

"Yes. I don't like the feel of this room." Animosity oozed

from the inn's patrons. *Better to avoid a fight if we can.* She watched the chiliarch return. "Has everyone eaten, Chiliarch? If they have, I think we should be on our way."

He leaned over the table. "And not a moment too soon. Some of these men are talking about dueling with my soldiers. Others, I'm afraid, want to wrestle with you."

27

The hair rose on the nape of Derya's neck. She met Chiliarch Bahadir's eyes. "Then perhaps we should depart." She stood up slowly, keeping her face impassive, ignoring the bawdy shouts of the carousing men.

Her back straight and her chin high, Derya marched out of the noisy inn accompanied by Safiye and Bahadir. A few paces into the yard, she halted, filling her lungs with fresh, icy air.

The chiliarch stopped next to her. "Kiral, this is not a good situation."

"No, it's not. But we're here for the night." She tipped her head back and surveyed the sky. "No stars. I hope that means warmer weather, not more snow."

"Too true. Kiral, you and the danisman should retire. I'll inform the kentarchs."

"As you please, chiliarch. Is everyone settled in the inn?"

"Yes. And I've posted guards. They'll bed down on the floors of the rooms when not on watch."

"You think of everything," Derya said. "Thank you, chiliarch."

The three walked over the snow, followed by Derya's

guards, their boots crunching with each step. Derya's breath made long plumes of steam that formed crystals of ice on the scarf wrapped over her chin.

When they reached the field where their entourage had camped, Derya noted the chiliarch had arranged the tents as if expecting an attack in the night. The horses were tethered to one side, with the wagons nearby. Derya's tent was next, surrounded by the tents of the other officials and soldiers. Several patrols circled the entire camp, all heavily armed for battle. "Is this necessary?" she asked.

The chiliarch shrugged. "Let's hope not."

Derya nodded. "Good night, Chiliarch. May the Rider give you a quiet night, if such a thing is possible in that inn."

When she heard him draw breath, she raised a hand. "No, Chiliarch. You need to be fresh in the morning. Your soldiers can protect us." She held his gaze until he dipped his chin.

"Yes, Kiral." With a salute, he strode back to the inn.

"Shall we?" Derya said to her danisman.

Safiye rubbed her gloved hands together. "If you don't mind. I'm not sure if I'll be able to sleep, but at least to be out of the wind…"

They made their way along a path tramped into the snow to Derya's tent, its white sides and top gleaming in the light of the campfires. The black and turquoise banner of Cinar flew overhead.

Derya pushed aside the door flap and went in, gasping in relief at the warm air that caressed her icy cheeks.

Four braziers burned brightly, giving the room at least an illusion of warmth. Mats covered the wood floor and Derya's bed had been assembled, the sheets, pillows, and fur blankets arranged as neatly as if her maids in the palace had placed them. A faint odor of mutton told Derya stew had been brought earlier. *Good.* Her maids had eaten.

Five bedrolls were spread near the braziers, three already

occupied by Derya's maids. The fourth was still fully dressed and seated by a brazier.

"I suppose you drew lots, and you were the unlucky loser who had to wait up for me?" Derya asked.

The maid flushed. "No, Kiral, I…"

Derya laughed. "Don't worry, Rasheda. Is there any hot water?"

Rasheda scurried to bring a basin and ewer. Derya used the chamber pot and washed her face and hands. With a few quick motions, she shrugged off her outer garments and crawled into the warm embrace of the furs.

The hushed voices of Safiye and Rasheda as they made preparations for bed were soothing after the rasping shouts in the inn. Her maid and advisor settled down for the night, and the only sounds were the crackling flames in the braziers and the tramp of sentries. Derya drifted into an uneasy sleep.

A thump jolted her from slumber. She opened her eyes, staring into the dark. It must be late, she thought. The brazier had burned down to glowing red coals.

She raised her head, straining to listen. All was silent, so quiet she could hear the even breathing of her danisman and maids.

A faint clank from outside scratched through the silence. The sentries, perhaps. She sank back into her pillows and drowsed in their warm embrace.

A draft of icy air jerked her eyes toward the tent's opening. Someone was coming in. Derya slid her hand under her pillow, seeking her dagger. Nothing. Had it fallen to the floor as she slept?

A figure crept into the tent. Whoever it was had barely disturbed the flap. Had Derya not been awake, she wouldn't have noticed the cold draft. She squinted. Who would the sentries have allowed to enter her tent? Was it Bahadir bringing bad news? Derya's heart sped up.

The figure approached her bedside. She propped herself up on one elbow. "Chiliarch—"

In a swift move, the man clamped a calloused hand over her mouth. "Lady," he growled in her ear. "You come now."

He had a strange accent, but she couldn't place it.

"No noise. Or they die."

That must mean her maids. Her heart burst into a gallop. She had to free herself. But how?

Her first instinct was to bite the hand covering her lips. Its massive size and rough callouses made her think that would do no more than annoy her kidnapper. If only she had her dagger.

"Get up." He shook her arm and pressed his hand harder against her mouth. She could taste the sweat on his palm.

Sweat. Salt. And was that a little pepper, too? The man must be a sloppy eater who neglected to wipe his hands. That would work to her advantage. All she needed was some water.

As the man yanked her to her feet, she cast her mind around the room. The ewer stood not far off, hopefully still full of the water she'd washed in. She nudged the man's leg with her foot and mumbled, "I need shoes."

When he tilted his head to look down, she reached for the water with her mind. Her magic felt its cool wetness, and she used the amplifying effect of the pepper to heat it. Then she drew the water upwards. With a quick push, she flung the steaming water into her assailant's face.

He yelped and let go of her. He pressed his hands against his eyes. Derya dove for her pillows, searching for her dagger.

Danisman Safiye's shriek broke through the kidnapper's curses. "What's going on?" she yelled.

By this time, the four maids were awake and screaming. The man shouted curses at Derya, insulting her, the emperor and all her ancestors. He grabbed her roughly around the waist. She kicked and thrashed, still seeking her blade. Where had it gotten to?

Cold steel against her neck stilled her. "Come. Now." The thug hauled her from the bed. "You. Be quiet or she dies."

Derya's face heated. Fear and anger warred with frustration. How dare this brute threaten her maids? She needed a weapon, but had used all the water. If she had her dagger, she could end this. And what was the man's elusive accent?

The maids' screams subsided into whimpers. The danisman sat motionless, her silhouette erect like a pine tree.

Surely someone heard all this racket. Where are my guards?

The attacker clutched Derya's arm with fingers as hard and cold as a blacksmith's vise and pulled her toward the door. He stumbled over something that clattered.

The chamber pot. Derya dragged her feet as the man tugged her arm, hoping her assailant had knocked the lid off the pot. She licked her lips. Not much of the salt and pepper taste remained. Would it be enough? She reached with her mind to the contents of the chamber pot and used the pepper to heat it, wrinkling her nose at the acrid smell. And hurled the steaming urine into the eyes of her attacker.

The man released her with a bellow of agony and dropped to his knees, his hands clawing at his eyes. Derya stepped back, rubbing her arm where her assailant had grasped it. His beefy hand and iron grip most likely left a bruise. That erased any drop of pity she might have felt for the wailing, cursing man. The acrid liquid must have stung the burns the boiling water had made.

The tent flap flew open and Kentarch Sezgin, Bahadir's second in command, charged inside, sword drawn. "Kiral—"

Finally. Thank the Rider. Relief made her hand shake as she pointed at the writhing man sprawled on the floor. "He tried to kidnap me." She straightened her shoulders. "Where are my sentries?"

Three more soldiers burst into the tent. The kentarch gave them curt orders to bind and remove the prisoner.

"If you're feeling merciful, allow him to wash his face,"

Derya said to the soldiers. She turned to the kentarch. "Tell me what happened."

"Kiral Derya, please forgive us." His tawny eyes were wide and his deep voice shook. "From what I could find out, at least ten men crept into camp. They drugged the sentries and killed most of them." Sezgin took a deep breath. "They poisoned the men during the midnight watch, but didn't realize we vary the length of our watches. Thank the Rider they chose the middle of the shortest watch. Only about ten minutes passed between the time the attackers entered our camp and the time the new sentries reported for duty. They discovered the poisoned men and alerted me at once. We killed all the intruders we found and are searching the camp. I sent word to the chiliarch."

"Have him come to me before he questions the prisoner." She paused, not sure she wanted to know the answer to her next question. "The sentries outside my tent?"

Sezgin shook his head. "Dead, I'm afraid."

Derya closed her eyes and let her head sag forward. Those four valiant young men. Zeno. Enayat. Symeon. Cemil. They'd politely wished her a quiet night just a few hours ago. Now they'd gone to the eternal realm. The thump that woke her must have been one of them falling to the ground, dead or dying.

With thanks, she dismissed the kentarch. Turning to her maids, she said, "Since we are up, could someone light the brazier and a few candles? And shall we get some fresh water?" Better to put them to work than have them rehashing the night's terrors. That was a conversation Derya would rather have in the light of day.

She returned to her bed. A quick search revealed her dagger had fallen to the floor. *Maybe I should strap it to my wrist.* She retreated under the furs, running her fingers over the turquoise inlay on the hilt of her weapon.

Danisman Safiye sat next to her. "Kiral, are you unharmed?"

"Not physically." She let out a sigh.

"Should I make you a tonic? Or some soothing tea?"

The tent flap fluttered, admitting Chiliarch Bahadir. "Kiral Derya, are you unharmed?"

Derya's lips twitched. Amusing, that they would frame the question in the same way. "Yes, chiliarch, just troubled. How could this happen? Who attacked us?"

The chiliarch shook his head. He took a few steps to stand in front of Derya. "I don't know."

"Did you kill the intruders?"

"We have nine bodies, Kiral. They have no money or letters or anything to identify them. If they were wearing tan or white, I'd have thought they were Ymittosian peasants. But they're wearing nothing but black."

"Are they Ymittosian nobles?"

"We suspect not, Kiral. Not all of them have raven hair or dark eyes. Their skin tones are mixed as well, resembling—"

"Cinarrians." Derya swallowed hard, wrapping her arms around her stomach and the rock that had settled in it. "Were we attacked by our own people?"

Bahadir's shoulders slumped. "That's possible, Kiral. But they could have been from any number of nations."

Derya ran a finger along the hilt of her dagger. "The man spoke a few words in Ymittosian with an odd accent." She pressed her lips together and frowned. "Maybe Euxinian?"

"Kiral, if I may," Rasheda said. "He sounded Issedonian to me. Something about the way he drew out the vowel when he said 'die.'"

"That's possible," Danisman Safiye said. "Although, I think he sounded more like an Terremarian mercenary." She grimaced. "But a few of his curses were definitely Nafplian."

The tent flap opened to admit Farooq, Bahadir's other

kentarch. "Kiral Derya, Chiliarch Bahadir, I beg your pardon."

"Yes, kentarch, what is it?" Bahadir asked.

"The prisoner. He had some of the poison used on the sentries hidden on his person."

"Don't tell me he drugged his guards and got away." A note of menace laced Bahadir's tone.

"No, not that," Farooq said quickly. "He used it on himself. He's dead."

A heavy silence filled the tent, broken by Derya. "Well, then, we won't be able to pursue our linguistic analysis of his accent. Or get any other information out of him." She huffed. "Was he so shamed by what I'd done that he couldn't live? Or was he under orders to not be taken alive?"

"Kiral," Bahadir said slowly. "What did you do?"

"I used my magic to heat the water in the ewer and threw it in his face. While he was distracted, I searched for this." She held up her dagger.

"But he recovered enough to grab you," Safiye said.

Rasheda giggled. "So the Kiral heated the contents of the chamber pot and tossed it in his eyes."

Bahadir jerked his head back. "You didn't."

Derya gave him an innocent look. "You've always said a good soldier uses every weapon at hand."

The chiliarch's lips twitched. "True. That was quick thinking, Kiral." He rubbed a hand over his chin. "But it is neither here nor there. We need to decide what to do now. I suggest leaving at first light. The only question is to where."

Derya looked at her danisman. "Your thoughts?"

"We agree your attacker had a southern accent, and is possibly Nafplian. Would it be prudent to avoid Nafplio? Perhaps we should turn north and return home that way."

The muscles in Bahadir's jaw pulsed, making the three irregular scars on his cheek move in a jerky dance. "Going north would be more direct, but would lead us into foul weather. We'd be forced to go slower and be more vulnerable to attack."

Both of them made good points, which didn't make the decision any easier for Derya. "The problem is not knowing who was behind that attack. It was clearly well planned."

"And possibly expensive, if they were hired mercenaries," Safiye said. "Do you think Pasargadae is making a move?"

Derya pursed her lips. Pasargadae was a rival empire that for centuries had nibbled at Cinar's eastern frontier. "That's possible."

"Ten or more mercenaries would be costly," Bahadir said. "And Pasargadae could easily afford them. But that's not my chief worry right now. We don't know if we killed all those involved, or if others are prowling about."

Derya let the dagger slip through her fingers into her lap. She hadn't considered the possibility of more enemies lurking along their route. "My primary concern," she said, "is informing my father about the events in Ymittos and Princess Eliana's mission in Malkh." She pulled in a deep breath. "And the fact there is someone so dissatisfied with the rule of Cinar that they would attempt to kidnap the heir." She couldn't bring herself to speak more directly, to voice the idea that she was the target. Using her title created a distance and helped her speak as if panic wasn't twisting her bowels. "We need to know who."

"Then, Kiral," said Bahadir, "I think we should continue to Nafplio. We can consult your father's ambassador there and have him send a bird or two to the emperor."

"And while we're at it," Safiye put in, "we can find out if Nafplio knows of any unrest in Cinar's southern vassal states."

"A day or so in the court of the Princess of Ymittos' betrothed could be informative," Derya said. "And give our ill and wounded a little time to recover."

Safiye smiled. "I think your maids and I can ferret out the latest gossip. We might learn something useful."

"If we continue to Nafplio," Derya said slowly, "we'll need to be ready for more unwanted attention."

"Is that what you call an attempted kidnapping?" Bahadir gave her an approving smile. "You're right, Kiral. We'll double the patrols and move as quickly as we can. If we're attacked again, we might have to abandon the wagons."

After holding his eyes for a moment, Derya nodded. "It would be rather ironic to end up someone else's possession because I couldn't part with my own."

She dismissed Bahadir and the kentarch with a salute and clenched her jaw. Euxine, Issedonnes, Terramare. Just a few of Cinar's vassal states that were always seething with rebellion, usually fomented by their small fae populations. Every few decades, those states boiled over into brutal wars. And every time, Cinar asserted control. Derya gripped her dagger. Cinar's empire and Cinar's heir would not be cowed by midnight kidnappers. Or anyone else.

28

Eliana sped down the steps of the prince's tower, the sour taste of fear flooding her mouth. In the pale light, the shadows on the steps looked like slanted boards, making her footing uncertain. She bounded onto the mosaic floor of the sixth level and skidded on its slippery surface. Flailing her arms to prevent a fall, she sprinted past the dusty metal books of the silent library.

Thudding from the stairwell told her the prince was right behind her. She bolted down to the fifth floor and around the long dining table. She'd just reached the fourth floor sitting room when she heard a crash, followed by a muffled curse. Adakizh must have tripped and fallen.

If only he would hurt himself, Eliana thought. Not badly, just enough so she could get away. She glanced over her shoulder and tripped over her own feet.

A cry escaped her throat as she tumbled to the floor. Pain shot through her elbow. With a moan, she staggered to her feet.

"Are you hurt?" Adakizh yelled down the stairs.

"I'm fine, are you?"

"Yes, yes. Run."

She sprinted three steps to the stairs that led to the throne room on the level below. Her breath came in pants and heaves and her muscles ached. When she reached the tower's first floor, she burst through the door and into the cavern.

Pressing a hand against a stitch in her side, she scurried to the left, toward the tunnel that would take her back to Shirdona and Dimitris. She knew she could trust them to help her, if she could outrun the prince that long.

As she dashed through the cavern, she strained to listen for the prince who was driven to kill her. Scuffling from behind told her she hadn't lost him.

Eliana charged around a corner and halted. A waterfall flowed down a rock wall in front of her, glowing faintly blue in the mushrooms' light. Bilious panic burned her throat. This wasn't the correct tunnel. She needed the one with green mushrooms.

Voices from the passage to her right made her freeze. Were they friends or enemies? Stepping silently through puddles, she cautiously peeked around a corner.

And let out a sob of relief. Istvan and a handful of his men clustered in a space where four tunnels met. A few clumps of Shirdona's people stood nearby. She bolted to Istvan's side, grateful for the protection he would provide.

Istvan seized her by the shoulders. "Where have you been?"

Eliana shuffled a step back. "Here."

"Alessia said you were ill." He jerked his chin at her maid, who was approaching with more of Shirdona's men.

Eliana raised her chin. "It's true. I wasn't feeling all that well. But not like what you were dealing with." She repressed a grin. Mocking Istvan's illness wouldn't do much to placate him.

"How did you avoid the flux?" Istvan asked.

"I waited for the tea." She shook her head. "That's not important. I have to tell you something."

He narrowed his eyes. "What?"

His suspicion made her hesitate. How to tell him without revealing she knew some of his schemes?

The echoes of rapid footsteps pounding the stony floor and splashing through the puddles made Eliana whirl. Adakizh sprinted around the bend in the tunnel. He slid to a halt. His eyes darted over Eliana, Istvan, and the soldiers. Without a word, he spun on his heel and darted into the darkness.

"Who was that?" Istvan asked.

"The prince."

"What? You woke him? Without telling me?"

She quivered at his angry tone but looked him in the eye. "Well, when everyone took ill, I realized we couldn't afford any delays. So I returned to the prince and woke him up."

"But you're not dead!" He blurted the words. His eyes flared, and he snapped his jaw shut, compressing his lips into a thin line.

"Dead?" she asked, frowning. "Why would I be dead?"

Istvan slid an arm around her shoulders. "Come talk with me in private."

His touch would have set her heart pounding a few days ago. Now her pulse sped up, but not for the same reason. If it surprised him she'd survived waking the prince, then he must have known about the second curse. Why hadn't he told her about it?

When she pulled away, he added, "Please. And quickly. I don't know how much time I have before the flux returns."

Eliana allowed him to lead her through the groups of warriors to a narrow alcove. She wasn't sure what he wanted to say, but it was bound to be a mix of lies and truth. It would be no simple task to sort out which was which.

Rather than wait for him to collect his thoughts, Eliana decided to make a bold move. "Why are you surprised that I'm still alive?" she asked.

He recoiled and stared at her for a few long moments. "Well, breaking the curse could have involved a counterspell dangerous to the cursebreaker."

"It *could* have? Why would you even think such a thing?"

"Someone had to think through all the possibilities."

A stab of remorse pierced her chest. She had read of curses being turned on the curse breaker, but never considered what that could mean for her. Eliana narrowed her eyes and directed her anger at Istvan instead of herself. "And you didn't think to mention it to me?"

"I didn't want to alarm you."

"So, you let me walk into that tower unprepared."

"If you recall, I wanted to be nearby. I never intended for you to go there alone."

No, he probably didn't. But protecting her wasn't his only reason. She crossed her arms and drilled her gaze into his. "That doesn't explain why you expected me to be dead."

Shirdona peered around Istvan's shoulder. "Are you going to tell her, or should I?"

Istvan glared at the woman's mocking face. "We are having a private conversation. This is none of your concern."

"You're talking about my tagavlon. It is my concern." Shirdona met Istvan's steely gaze with a granite-hard stare.

When Istvan looked down, Shirdona continued. "My sunshine, I caught wind of a vague rumor the tagavlon would try to kill whoever broke the curse. It seems your betrothed heard the same tale. I didn't believe it, so saw no reason to bother telling you."

"But if you knew, why did you send me there?"

"Well, my sunshine, I wanted the curse broken. Your life is your problem."

Eliana gasped, and her heart dropped. No wonder Shirdona had insisted on being paid upfront. The woman had sent her to break the spell, unconcerned whether she survived or not. The princess opened her mouth to retort but couldn't find the words.

Shirdona gave Eliana a mocking bow. "Now that it seems you've broken part of the curse, we can have a party." She waved a finger in Eliana's face. "You best get back to Qala Bisen. Your work isn't done for three more days." She strode off, calling to her followers to break open a barrel of beer.

Outrage still had Eliana sputtering when Istvan broke into her thoughts. "Don't bother about her. She can't be trusted."

He's right about that.

Istvan leaned closer to her, his breath warm and damp against her ear. "Now, do you understand? I have to kill him so you can live. Or if he kills you, your death must be avenged."

"But I don't want him murdered." Adakizh was rather kind when he stopped yelling at her to flee before he killed her, and handsome. It wasn't his fault Cetus put a second curse on him.

What she wanted was to figure out what Istvan was up to. "I need to understand. You were willing to risk me being slain by the prince. After all, I had to be alone with him when I broke the curse. What would you have done had he attacked me?"

"Charged into that tower to defend you, of course."

Something about his oily tone made Eliana doubt his words. "You would have let him kill me. Three days were more than enough time for a vigorous man to overpower me. And you couldn't come to my aid during those days, because the curse wouldn't have been completely broken."

"I knew you'd been practicing your magic." Istvan gave her a gentle smile. "I had every confidence you'd be able to hold him off."

That was flattering and possibly true. But did Istvan believe it? She chewed on the inside of her cheek, trying to sort her confused thoughts.

"Eliana, we both know that our responsibility—our destiny—as royals means we must sacrifice for our people. To put ourselves in danger, if need be, to defend our lands. A little risk, a little discomfort, all mean nothing compared to the glory of defending our subjects, the dwellers of our realms. You showed me your valiant heart, clever mind, and clear sense of duty. I knew that you would do the honorable thing, no matter what."

His words eased some of the sting caused by Shirdona's callous betrayal. She wanted to believe him. And he was right about sacrifice for the people. Eliana supposed she could work with Istvan to keep the prince at bay for three days. Then they could find a way out of this mess. Or, since she'd left the tower, did that mean she'd already failed?

Istvan was still talking about the glory she'd win if she broke the curse. "Then we'll kill the barbarian prince and merge our three realms: Nafplio, Ymittos and Chorokha."

But Eliana didn't want to rule the Chorokhese. *Let them have their own dark realm.* A few stolen cattle were a minor inconvenience. Perhaps she could devise a way to trade with the underworlders. But since they enjoyed the raids so much, she sensed they would find it difficult to give them up.

"We'd have a glorious reign, you and I." Istvan waved his arm in the air. "Our fame would go far and wide."

Not if Cetus had anything to do with it. Istvan didn't seem to consider that.

"Are you going to babble like fishwives all day?" Shirdona said. "Our tagavlon is awake and if the Saumarotas find out, they'll try to kill him themselves, curse or no curse. We've got to find him first." She darted into the darkness, shouting orders to her followers.

"I have somewhere I have to be," Istvan said. He jerked away from Eliana and trotted toward the necessary ditch.

Eliana gripped Alessia's arm. "Fetch Dimitris. Quickly."

With a nod, the maid slipped into the crowd of milling warriors.

Pursing her lips, Eliana considered Istvan's behavior. In Ymittos, he'd been nothing but polite and attentive. Except when he was complimentary and flirtatious. Her face heated thinking about the things he'd whispered to her and the way they excited her senses.

Now she saw another side of him. Ambition, in itself, could be a virtue. But when it inspired one to be conniving and deceptive, that was a different matter. Perhaps Istvan was desperate and willing to do anything to deal with the present crisis. Or was this the real man who he'd covered up while courting her?

She wanted her mother more than ever.

After a few anxious minutes, Alessia reappeared at her side, alone.

"Where's Dimitris?" Eliana asked.

"I don't know."

"I ordered you to find him." Eliana tugged at the collar of her tunic. Why couldn't Alessia do as she was told? And why did she look so upset?

"He's not important."

Eliana narrowed her eyes. "What are you talking about?"

"Listen." Alessia glanced over her shoulder, then stepped close to Eliana. "Since I hadn't seen Dimitris for a while, I wondered if he'd taken ill. So I went by the necessary ditch. Some of Istvan's men were using it, so I stayed in the shadows."

"What, watching them?"

"No. I thought whatever the Nafplians had to say might be worth overhearing."

"What would they be talking about other than being sick?"

"Some were complaining. Then Istvan said they'd recover soon and needed to look to the future. Then he made a joke about how even incapacitated by a flux, it was easy to conquer a kingdom."

"What does that mean?"

"He said all you have to do is kill the king and steal the princess."

Pulsing anxiety throbbed in Eliana's temple. "What are you talking about?"

"It wasn't clear at first. The more they talked, the more I understood." Alessia's voice quavered. "I'm so sorry. The reason Istvan doesn't want you to contact your parents is that they are dead."

29

Eliana's chest tightened, and she struggled to pull air into her lungs. The ground tipped and swayed as if she were adrift in a rowboat on a rough sea. She leaned against the damp, slimy wall. "Dead? They can't be."

Alessia's head drooped. "The troops Istvan left poisoned them."

Sagging against the rock wall, Eliana pressed her forehead against its cold dampness. The water trickling over the stone blended with the tears on her cheeks. Her parents, dead by poison? She squeezed her eyes shut, but she couldn't dismiss the images from her mind—her gentle mother retching in agony, her stalwart father convulsing in pain.

"You're mistaken." Eliana's face grew rigid. She stepped back from the wall and shook her head. "That's impossible." Her parents couldn't be gone. Surely Istvan wasn't that ruthless.

"His men were talking about it. Jesting about who would be the steward of Nafplio once you two settled in Ymittos."

A sudden thought left Eliana queasy. "He planned to kill the tagavlon even before we came here."

"Yes." Alessia nodded grimly. "They were boasting about

the honors Istvan had promised them. This one will be governor of New Ionia, another will be foreign minister, a third, overlord of Chorokha. They have it all worked out."

The princess's head spun. Cold exploded through her body and her knees buckled.

Alessia slid an arm around Eliana's waist, supporting the limp princess. "You're now the queen. When you go back, you can get justice for your parents."

Eliana clenched her fists. Oh, she'd track down the assassins and make them pay. But Istvan—. He wouldn't allow that, not if he was involved. He'd bribe or murder anyone who supported her as the rightful ruler until there was no opposition left and he was the sole power in Ymittos. *Rider, help me.*

Raucous cheers echoed in the tunnel, sounds of joy that mocked Eliana's sorrow. She jerked her head to see what was causing the commotion. Istvan, declaring himself king of Ymittos?

A man built like a bear raised a mug of beer in a green-gloved hand, the white froth spilling over to splash his face. "May your raids be successful and the cattle you bring home fat." He guzzled the beer and flung the tankard against the wall, the metal clattering on the stone. With a wave of his arm and a bellowed farewell, he led a group of five armed men out of the cavern.

Shirdona lifted her mug to him, grinning at a towering man with a crooked nose and a two-headed axe in his hand.

Eliana watched, grateful the woman who'd played so many tricks was busy with her own schemes. She'd deal with Shirdona later. But for now, Eliana needed a few minutes alone to make sense of what she'd learned. "Alessia, go find Dimitris. At once." She gave her maid a little push and waved her hand as if she was shooing away a fly.

Alessia gave her a startled look before vanishing into the crowd of laughing and drinking Chorokhese.

Hunching her shoulders, Eliana ran her hands up and

down her sleeves. She refused to believe her parents were dead. And on Istvan's orders. It was unthinkable.

She pressed her icy fingers to her trembling lips. How could she find out the truth? Asking Istvan directly, she thought, would get her nowhere. If he hadn't ordered her parents killed, he'd be justifiably insulted. And if he had? A shiver ran down her spine. Her core turned hard, like a packed snowdrift. She wrapped her arms around herself, gripping the sides of her tunic.

The crackle of paper under her fingers made her widen her eyes. She'd forgotten the paper Istvan dropped in Adakizh's tower. She yanked it from her pocket and held it near one of the glowing blue mushrooms.

The missive was written in Nafplian and addressed to Istvan. The initial greetings were easy to translate. She struggled over the next part because of the writer's sloppy penmanship. Word by word, she picked out the meaning.

The death of your last rival dampened our winter festival, but I rejoice, anticipating the start of your reign.

Eliana labored through the rest of the message, her heart rate increasing with each sentence. If Istvan was the sovereign of Nafplio, that meant his father, brother, and his brother's four sons were dead. Not to mention Istvan's other two brothers and their children.

How could they all have died at the same time? When Istvan arrived in Ymittos, he said his oldest brother was in good health, his four nephews all thriving. Just a few days ago, he'd talked about sending messages to his parents.

She shuddered. Istvan had lied. To her, to her parents, to everyone. One reason they'd chosen him as her consort was that he didn't have a realm of his own to rule, so he wouldn't have divided interests. What other falsehoods had he told?

Sweat beaded on her forehead. He'd seemed so sincere when he wooed her, saying he loved her and wanted her to rule, that he'd be content to be her consort. Her face heated to remember how her heart raced when he'd touched her cheek, how her fingers tingled when he'd caressed them. How proud she'd felt when people told her they made a handsome couple. How she'd loved his regal bearing and hearty laugh. And how he'd made her forget the pain and loneliness of Evander's death.

Maybe he did love her. Maybe he'd lied because he feared her parents wouldn't let him marry her and he'd lose her. She grasped that thought, but like a handful of sand, it slipped away.

More likely, he'd deceived them all.

Betrayal speared her heart. He'd pretended to want her, but it was her kingdom he lusted for. And her parents? Why would they push her to marry an older man if they expected her to rule alongside him? They'd been humoring her.

Her stomach hardened. In the process of doing what they thought was best, her parents had deceived her. And allowed themselves to be hoodwinked by a conniving scoundrel, all while criticizing her for questioning their decision.

Were they still alive? Eliana let out a sob, wishing she could believe they were. But in the face of Istvan's lies, she had to consider that her parents were no more. The ice in her veins turned to lava, fiery rage burning to seek retribution against the man who'd dared plot to take her kingdom and kill its king. She clenched her jaw. *Think, Eliana. You have to learn the truth. And if need be, avenge your parents' death.*

She was still trying to figure out how to worm a confession out of Istvan when he stumbled over to her.

"I still don't understand how you escaped this flux," he said, petulance sharpening his inflection.

Adopting a casual tone, she said, "Just lucky, I suppose. Are you feeling any better?"

"I think it's slowing down."

"And your men?"

"I suppose they'll survive."

Did that mean he hadn't bothered to inquire about his soldiers, who must be suffering as much as he was, or that he didn't care? She bit her lip to repress her scorn. His only loyalty was to himself.

He saved her from having to make further polite inquiries. "Where were we? Oh, yes, reigning over both Ymittos and Chorokha."

Eliana struggled to speak calmly to conceal her inner distress. "Why would we want to rule Chorokha?" Did he notice the tremor in her voice? She took a slow, steadying breath. "It's dark. And damp. The best things they have are the ones they've stolen from us." She didn't have to force indignation into her tone.

With disdain, Istvan stared down at her. "For one thing, if we rule Chorokha, we can charge them for the cattle and grain and beer. Maybe establish trade. Baked goods and textiles. We could make them pay through the nose."

Willing herself to ignore his pedantic manner, Eliana swallowed hard. "I can see why they would want our goods. What do they have that we don't?"

"Oh, I'm sure they have something. Like these glowing mushrooms. Our miners could use them. Or anyone who works in the dark."

She tightened her jaw. *He must think I'm a fool. Our light mages have an arsenal of spells to conjure up bright light. We don't need these feeble mushrooms.*

Istvan kept talking. "But that's not the most important part. If Ymittos and Chorokha ally, we can mount a unified defense against invasion from the sea."

Eliana had to concede that was true. If the two kingdoms worked together, they might have a chance to repel Cetus and his monsters and save both kingdoms from that horrible threat.

And she didn't want to die at the hand of a cursed prince. She looked into Istvan's eyes, trying to read his intentions.

Would she make it out of Chorokha alive? The dim blue light made irregular shadows on his features, turning his soft smile into a leer, giving his firm chin a jagged point. There was nothing in his visage that gave her any insight into his thoughts.

All she knew was that she had to save her people from Cetus. If working with Istvan was her best chance, avenging her parents would have to wait. Maybe killing Adakizh was the only way to thwart Cetus's evil plan.

Doubt quivered within her. She could sacrifice herself for her kingdom, but not if it meant binding herself to the man who'd ordered the deaths of her parents. That thought caused her stomach to lurch. "Istvan, you said we'd be ruling both Ymittos and Chorokha. That won't happen for quite a while."

"Why not? The barbarian prince will be dead in three days."

"Surely my parents will live for many years to come."

She kept her expression bland while scrutinizing his eyes. His smile didn't falter, but his face froze like the stone formations around them. He blinked a few times before answering. "Oh, of course. Many years. And you're right, we shouldn't get ahead of ourselves. You haven't broken the curse completely. The barbarian prince still lives." He touched her cheek with one finger. "If you die breaking the curse, I will avenge you. And songs will be sung in praise of your exploits at every holiday and every wedding. Your death would be the most glorious sacrifice you could make for your people."

When he mentioned wedding songs in her honor, the awful realization struck her. This wasn't just spur-of-the-moment talk. He'd thought about her demise. Not merely as a possibility, but as a likely outcome. Which meant the idea of him ruling Ymittos—without her—was uppermost in his mind.

Eliana clenched her jaw, inwardly cringing at the way

she'd fallen for Istvan's lies and flattery. That she'd seriously considered marrying him. That she ever found him attractive.

Now, she'd sooner embrace a vishapion.

"Let's hope I'm not called to make the ultimate sacrifice," she said, twisting her mouth into what she hoped resembled a trusting smile.

But Eliana couldn't deny the truth. Istvan intended to rule Ymittos. Which meant her parents were most likely dead. Istvan hadn't come to Ymittos to marry her. He'd come to steal her kingdom.

As he chattered something about the merger of three kingdoms, his tone became more animated than Eliana had ever heard it. She sucked in a breath. He'd made that slip earlier, and she hadn't noticed. Ymittos and Chorokha were two. He must have been counting his homeland as the third kingdom. The note in her pocket confirmed her suspicions. His schemes also included seizing Nafplio.

Istvan moved closer. "So you see, Eliana, you need to return to the prince's tower. He'll probably go there as well. I'll wait outside. Once you've survived the three days, I'll take care of the barbarian. Then you'll be mine."

No, I will not. Skin crawling, she took a step away from him.

With a grimace, Istvan clapped a hand to his abdomen. "I'll be back," he said, then turned and fled toward the necessary trench.

Eliana snorted. *At least there's that.* In all her daydreams of handsome suitors vying for her favor or of her own heroic exploits, a case of the flux never seemed to find its way into the story. But there it was.

She released a slow breath. Should she wait for Alessia to return, hopefully with Dimitris? Or should she seize the chance to get away from Istvan long enough to come up with a plan?

Bands of tension circled her head like a heavy, constricting crown. Her forehead throbbed, and she winced to hear the shouts of Shirdona's followers at their rowdy celebration. Just a few minutes of quiet. That's all she needed. She was tired, so tired. She'd been up all night and now most of this day. The drink Shirdona had given her had worn off hours before. A few moments alone to rest her aching head, sort through this tangle, and decide what to do—that was what she needed most.

Slipping a hand into her bag, Eliana fumbled through the tiny pouches and bottles until she found the hops. Hoping it was close enough to the taste of beer to serve as an amplifier, she slid one grain into her mouth.

As the sour taste spread over her tongue, she mustered her air magic and created a dark cloud in the air. Masked by the mist she'd summoned, she slipped away into the dark, silent tunnel.

30

Eliana sprinted through the passage, splashing through puddles and leaping over rocks as if a gang of blood-thirsty bandits were in hot pursuit. Her one thought was to put as much distance as she could between herself and Istvan. Then find Adakizh. But he could be anywhere in this maze of tunnels. All she could do was return to his tower and hope he was there. Or that the curse would attract him to her like a corpse draws flies.

Goosebumps rose on her arms. Adakizh might be lurking in the dark, waiting to pounce. Every drip of water could mask his stealthy approach. Why, oh why, couldn't the prince have been cursed on a mountain peak? Swinging from a rope on the heights of a cliff would be less terrifying than creeping through these confining subterranean passages. At least on a mountain, she could see where she was going. Down here, every tunnel looked the same. After two turns, she had no idea how to retrace her steps.

A faint cracking sound behind her made her heart skip a beat. Was that a cave-in about to happen? She slowed her pace and struggled to listen over the rasp of her panting breaths.

The noise sharpened into a series of metallic clinks, like the tapping of a nail against stone. Her mouth went dry as she peered over her shoulder into the gloom.

A roar sent her leaping ahead, screaming. She charged down the tunnel. The clicking and howling pursued her. She whirled to see a massive head resembling a boar's, its wide-open jaws revealing two rows of sword-like teeth. *No. Not a vishapion*. Nearly unable to breathe, she scrambled backwards.

Menacing curved claws protruded from each foot. The vishapion's long, spiked tail lashed from side to side, its mud-brown scales broken by jagged scars.

The animal roared, its rage and lust for her blood resounding in every echo. Eliana knew she couldn't outrun the vishapion. Would the beast kill her quickly, or toy with her like a cat plays with a mouse? A whimper escaped her lips.

Her first instinct was to draw her sword, but she stopped herself from yanking it from its scabbard. She wasn't skilled enough to defeat the vishapion alone.

But perhaps she could distract it. Eliana sucked in a deep breath and readied her light magic, concentrating on her power. She hurled the magic toward the beast in one massive burst of light aimed at the black beady eyes over its snarling maw.

Squeezing her eyelids closed against the sudden brightness, she heard the beast wail, a high-pitched shriek that sounded more like pain than aggression. Even before her eyes adjusted to the renewed dimness, she heard the clicking of the beast's toenails as it retreated.

With a shaky hand, Eliana rubbed the sweat from her forehead and expelled a long sigh of relief. Now, where was the prince's tower? From what she remembered, the mushrooms near it glowed celery green, not blue like the ones lighting her current path. She studied the walls. The rock here was dark blue, almost black, a hue she didn't remember seeing anywhere else.

She peeked over her shoulder. Going back would lead her right to the beast. Forward then.

The next side tunnel contained shining pillars that looked familiar. Or maybe not. Should she try it? She stood, gnawing on her lower lip. Abruptly, she strode into the tunnel. *Better to explore an unknown passage than stand still and wait for something to eat me.*

Less than a minute later, the floor seemed to tip beneath Eliana's feet. Her breath became labored as if she was climbing a steep hill. Ripples formed in the air and pain shot through her skull. What had Shirdona—or was it Istvan—said about poisonous underground gases? Invisible death?

Her eyes burned and watered. If only she hadn't used so much of her magic. She was still weary from her encounter with the vishapion. With all the strength she had left, she summoned a wisp of her air magic and puffed it down the passage. Then she staggered back to the main tunnel.

As she gulped for breath, the pain in her head eased from stabbing to a dull ache. The floor no longer rocked, but her dizziness lingered.

Eliana ran both hands over her hair. She was in no condition to pursue anyone, let alone a prince determined to kill her. She needed a place to recover.

Exhausted, she tottered along the main tunnel, seeking an alcove where she could hide. After trotting for what felt like hours, she found a niche and sank into it. In the dim light, she hoped any passersby wouldn't notice her crouching in the shadows.

She sank down onto the cold, damp stone. Wrapping her arms around her shins, she laid her head on her knees. What was she doing? She'd lost herself in this underground maze.

And she was tired, so tired. She tried to account for the hours. They'd descended into the rift, met Shirdona, went on a moonlight cattle raid, found the cursed tagavlon—was that the next morning? Since then, she'd been running back and forth. Her dry mouth begged for water, her aching head for sleep.

Light pierced the gloom from a small opening far above, a single feeble ray of the winter sun. From the angle, she guessed it was either early morning or late afternoon. She'd been in constant motion for almost two days. No wonder she was so confused. Eliana closed her eyes and let slumber pull a dark curtain over her troubled thoughts.

Jumbled images of vishapions and worms invaded her dreams. Istvan mounted a goat with razor-sharp tusks and the teeth of a shark. He rode up the stairs of Adakizh's tower as he debated with someone about the price he could fetch for her.

With a jerk, she opened her eyes. There were people, Chorokhese, by the sound of their speech, standing in front of her niche, haggling over the price they could demand for her.

How long had she been asleep? The trace of sunlight had vanished. It must be evening, then. Her stiff neck told her she'd slept, but the fogginess in her brain revealed that whatever time had passed, it wasn't nearly enough.

Who were these people who wanted to sell her? She had a bad feeling they were Saumarotas, or others who didn't want the curse broken. The five she could see in the blue mushroom's glow wore sand-colored tunics and leggings, like Shirdona's people, along with goatskin cloaks. But they spoke with a clipped accent, unlike the drawl of Shirdona's family.

Closing her eyelids, she held herself still, hoping no one noticed she'd woken.

"Kharan-Khuag will give us many cattle and casks of beer for her."

"Since when does he have beer?" Another person cursed in a woman's high-pitched voice. Probably a woman. "Better to try with their tagavlon."

Was she talking about Adakizh? *They'd sell me to him?* She clamped her lips together. She believed Adakizh when he said he didn't want to kill her. Had he resorted to bounty hunters to do away with her?

"What would that Ymittosian prince pay?" the first one asked.

Did he mean Istvan? Eliana's eyes flared in surprise before she could stop them.

"Could we play them against each other?"

"Kharan-Khuag and the Ymittosian?"

"Yeah. Sell her to the highest bidder."

"That might work. They both want her kingdom. Using her would be easier than fighting for it. That should be worth a lifetime's supply of cattle. And bread. And beer."

"Then let's grab her and go before anyone comes looking for her."

Metal clanged on the rock above Eliana's head. "Princess, it's time to go."

She considered ignoring the man, then thought better of it. Straightening her spine, Eliana imitated the tone of her haughtiest courtiers. "Go where?"

"To my home. Wouldn't you like to be my guest for the evening?"

"No, thank you."

A few men laughed. One with a bushy black beard smirked. "Too good for us, are you?"

Eliana shrugged. "I don't even know who you are."

The stockiest of the men leaned toward her. "Dymek Saumarota. Don't you forget it." He clanged the hilt of his sword on the rock. "And you don't have a choice."

That's what you think. Eliana reached for her magic, and to her relief, the brief rest had restored much of her power. Light and air should be enough. She rose slowly and peeked out of the niche. Her would-be kidnappers all stood to her right. Out of the corner of her eye, she spotted two tunnels to the left. The smaller one would provide a place to hide. If she could get that far. She readied her magic.

"If you want to be hospitable, shouldn't you allow your guest the choice?" She tried to speak lightly and was proud of herself when her voice didn't quaver.

"What makes you think you're really a guest?"

"If I'm not a guest, what am I? Your jailer?" She pooled her magic, savoring the warmth of the light and the breathy quality of the air as the power built within her.

The man snorted, sending a spray of spittle. "You got that backward. Now let's get moving."

"I don't think so." She let out a burst of light, followed by a blast of air.

The woman shrieked. The men yelled. All of them staggered backwards. Three lost their balance and tumbled to the ground in a heap.

Eliana vaulted over their tangled flailing limbs and darted for the smaller tunnel. She scurried along it, hoping it didn't lead to the lairs of vishapions or other creatures of the dark.

Foul curses and heavy footsteps followed her. She rounded a corner and came to a fork. She sent up a mist, obscuring the dim light of the mushrooms. Then she plunged into the passage on the left and ran for all she had.

The clamor of pursuit grew faint. Eliana jumped over a small stream and paused to listen. The only noise was her panting breath and the trickle of water down the walls of the cavern.

Where was she? Under the glow of the blue mushrooms, she noticed the walls were as smooth as polished marble. She'd never been in this tunnel before, she was sure of it.

She followed the course of the stream, thinking it might lead to the river. Her breath came faster and her heart thumped louder. Panic rose in her throat, threatening to choke her. She was lost in an underground maze, friendless and alone, trapped in the dark, never to find her way out.

A dark filled with enemies. Ferocious vishapions, poison

gas, and people who wanted to sell her. She clenched her sweaty hands. *Think, Eliana. You escaped them.*

She halted. She had escaped. To her surprise, she'd been able to put them off with her magic. Each time she used it, she could summon the power more easily. And manipulate the magic more precisely, even without amplifiers. Best of all, she could control how much power she used and could stop at any time. While she never thought she'd be practicing her magic while in dire peril, she was grateful for her growing skills. She'd have to be careful not to wear herself out and leave herself helpless against the next threat.

And as lost as she was, she was even more at sea regarding Adakizh. What would she do if she found him? He was much bigger than her, and certainly stronger. Could she restrain him with her magic until the three days had passed?

Even if she succeeded in doing that, Kharan-Khuag wouldn't just admit defeat and slink back to his undersea lair. He'd plotted for too many centuries. He'd persist until he conquered Chorokha and her own realm.

If she'd even be able to call it hers. Her nobles wouldn't want her to rule alone. If they were ignorant of Istvan's role in her parents' deaths, they'd be sure to push for a quick marriage. Without her parents' support, she didn't know how she could break her betrothal. A shudder convulsed her slender frame. Married to that murdering deceiver would be worse than death in a vishapion's jaws. Istvan would use her to keep the people content, thinking she was their sovereign. But he'd be the controlling power and make sure she never forgot it. And what would he do if she failed to provide an heir? Or he wearied of sharing the throne? Even if she bore him a son or two—she cringed at the idea of his hands on her body— once the succession was secure, he'd have no more use for her. She rested a palm against the smooth wall, welcoming its cold support, and tried to control her trembling hands and shaky breath.

Adakizh was her best hope. How could she convince him to work with her? Would he be able to resist the curse long enough? Eliana admired him for fighting the enchantment that compelled him to kill her. That, and the elegant shape of his jaw and large, expressive eyes.

She rubbed her aching head. *I don't know what to do.* If she could break the curse, she could go home. Annul her betrothal. Discover if Istvan had killed her parents. *If only I could ask——.*

Sobs rose in her throat. She'd never be able to ask her parents anything ever again. Eliana's knees wobbled, and she dropped to the ground, wrapping her arms around her head. *I need them. And Istvan killed them.* Anger warred with grief, thoughts of vengeance followed by a new worry. Istvan probably knew she'd run away by now. Had he vented his wrath on Dimitris or Alessia?

Their company would be so welcome. Or Derya's. *I was right to spare Derya this nightmare.* Eliana hoped her friend had managed to get word to the emperor. With each passing moment, she grew less certain she'd be able to completely break the curse. By leaving Adakizh's tower, she might have failed already. Kharan-Khuag and his vile monsters would soon run rampant over Ymittos.

I'm sorry, Derya, you'll never dance at my wedding. I've got two prospects, and both of them want to kill me. A stray tear stung her eyes.

How did she fall into this morass of lies and deceit? She swallowed a lump in her throat. Her parents wanted her to save the kingdom. That was her duty. Preserve the kingdom and the succession. To them, nothing was more important.

And she'd agreed to marry Istvan to please her parents. Which left her betrothed to a violent man who cared only for his ambition and would dispose of her once she gave him an heir.

The tears flowed freely. When she'd agreed to venture into

this dark, damp, and dangerous realm to break the curse, it was more of the same. Sacrifice for the realm. She banged her hands on her knees. *Why didn't anyone tell me it would be like this?*

She huddled in the dark, flinching at every creak of the rock or drip of water. Everyone used her for their own ends. None of them considered what she needed. A tear rolled down her cheek. Did anyone care about her as a person and not just as a princess or political tool? She tugged her cloak tight, her only companion in the shadowy dark the trickle of water running down the rock wall.

But. A sudden thought made her lift her chin. Adakizh was willing to sacrifice himself for her. He didn't even know her, but he refused to kill her for his own gain.

A sliver of the boulder on her soul lifted. Maybe she did have an ally.

But would seeking his help be a mistake? It could easily get her killed. Her only other choice was Istvan, who wasn't worthy of love or trust. His words about her being clever and brave, though, had a foundation in truth. Like the best flattery.

Eliana would use that cleverness and courage. Since she couldn't trust Istvan, that left Adakizh. He hadn't lied to her. In fact, he'd been bluntly honest.

And Adakizh was the only one who would know if she'd failed as a cursebreaker, or still had a chance.

She supposed it didn't matter much. If she'd already failed, Kharan-Khuag would begin his attack within two days. And if not, there was still the thorny problem of how to finish lifting the enchantment without either Adakizh or her ending up dead. But maybe they could conjure up a defense. Or at least warn his people of the impending invasion.

And if Adakizh killed her, well, so be it. No more sacrificing herself for someone else's schemes. She'd die on her own terms.

31

—————

Derya's spine twitched as if an army of lice crawled up its length. She rolled her shoulders and sucked in a breath of crisp, bracing air. Despite the driving snow, they'd left Glyfadu as soon as there was enough light to see the road. The snowfall ceased an hour later, but after a day and a half of travel they'd made little progress to the pass that led to Nafplio.

Not only had the snowy roads kept their pace slower than a plow horse in a muddy field, but the terrain worked against them. A frozen river lined the road on one side and mountains crowded it on the other. This allowed bands of robbers to harry them once the weather cleared. Some shot arrows from unseen perches, others swooped down from the slopes on scruffy horses, killed a few of the Cinarrians' mounts, and rode off. They seemed to particularly enjoy shooting at the horses pulling the wagons.

During their last foray, the bandits had slain four horses and galloped off with triumphant whoops.

Derya led her horse to Chiliarch Bahadir. "Was anyone hurt?"

He shook his head. "Nothing serious. One of the drivers

twisted an ankle jumping off his seat to avoid an arrow. But at this rate, we soon won't have enough horses to pull the wagons."

"Do you think that's their plan? That we'll have to abandon our wagons?"

"It would make them easy to plunder, that's for sure." The chiliarch frowned. "This last gang killed all our birds. I don't know if they intended to, or it just happened."

"So we have no means of sending word to my father?" Derya scratched her ear. "Well, it can't be helped. Besides, we'll be in Nafplio soon enough. How long to the pass?"

He tipped his face to the sky and pointed to the pale sun. "About two hours. Assuming the weather holds." He wrinkled his brow. "But I'm wondering what is waiting for us when we get there."

Derya studied his scowling face. Bahadir was always imagining threats when there weren't any, but he'd been right about the inn in Glyfadu. "Then we'll just have to be prepared, won't we?"

A grim smile stretched his chapped lips, and he nodded. "That we shall. Are you ready to go?"

"On your word, chiliarch." Derya put her knee in his outstretched hand and he boosted her onto her horse. She tugged her fur cloak around her shoulders, watching her breath stream from her mouth in white wisps that spread and dissipated in the frosty air.

Within minutes, they were on their way. Derya mused about the condition of the road. The Ymittosians were clever. Near the villages, they pulled logs behind teams of horses, rolling the wood over the fresh snow to pack it down hard, making it easier to travel on. In between villages, though, her scouts had to ride ahead, tramping the snow, an exhausting task for both horse and rider.

Settling in her saddle, Derya rolled her aching shoulders. *By this time tomorrow, we'll be over the mountains and in Nafplio.* The tiny realm, barely large enough to be considered a dukedom, was sheltered from the harsh north winds by the towering peaks. *Compared to this, it will feel like spring.*

A slow grin spread across Derya's face. A visit to Nafplio would give her a chance to learn about Eliana's betrothed and discover if his brothers were as arrogant and shifty as he was. If they were, Derya decided, she'd assume the persona of the supercilious heir of the empire she'd put on when she initially met Eliana. That could be entertaining. But first, she'd make use of Nafplio's famous hot baths.

On the road, there'd been little chance for them to wash their hands, and, given the bitter cold, even less desire. A gust of wind raced over the frozen river to Derya's right. She ducked her head to shield her stinging eyes, straightening only when the wind relented.

The wind was one enemy. Who were the others who relentlessly attacked? She tried to remember what she knew of Ymittos. Three major clans all vied for power. Eliana's family led the most powerful, the coastal clan that controlled the sea trade. The second lived on the plains and produced much of the food. But here in the hills, what did they have? Goats, perhaps. Maybe they survived by raiding caravans that supplied the king's mines and transported the silver and gold. And her entourage was a tempting prize. She shivered. This line of thinking did nothing to banish the sensation of spiders crawling on her back.

After an hour's travail, Bahadir joined her. She turned to him, smiling, but the smile faded as soon as she spied his furrowed brow. "What is it?"

"Kiral, the rear scouts tell me there is a small party of riders pursuing us. Maybe ten at the most. Following them is another group of twenty."

"Are they travelers like us, do you suppose?"

He shook his head. "The second group is all in black."

Derya's mouth went dry. "Like the midnight attackers."

"Yes."

"And the others?"

"They wear the colors of Cinar, Kiral."

"Cinar? But who of our military would be here?"

"I fear it's a trap," Bahadir said. "That we would turn to help them, only to find ourselves riding to aid enemies primed to attack."

She frowned. "Could they be messengers sent by our ambassador?"

"Unlikely, unless…"

Her breath caught. *Unless something has happened to my father.*

Derya swallowed hard and straightened her shoulders. "What do you advise, chiliarch?"

"We proceed. We're approaching a bend in the road and after that, the ground levels out a bit. If we're about to fight a battle, I'd prefer a little more room. At this pace, they'll overtake us in less than half an hour."

Part of her screamed, "No, we need to find out if they bear a message from Cinar!" The desire to know if her father lived consumed her like a fire in a dry forest.

A sour taste rose in her throat at the thought of her father's death, but Bahadir was correct. They gained nothing by staying still and had much to lose. Better to wait for their pursuers in a more defensible spot.

"And Kiral, if they do overtake us," Bahadir said, "please stay in between your guards. You and your danisman."

She opened her mouth to object, then swallowed her protest. He was right. Her guards were trained to protect her. The last time they'd been ambushed, she'd tried to help and nearly got her horse's head sliced off because she wasn't where the guard expected her to be. "Very well, chiliarch. Let's keep moving."

He saluted her and moved up the line, shouting for his men to advance.

Derya turned to her danisman. "What do you think?"

"That none of us will rest easy until we're back in Cinar."

"True." Derya's head drooped, but she pulled herself upright a heartbeat later. She could not let the soldiers around her see any concern on her part. She patted her waist and boots, assuring herself that her four throwing knives were still in place.

To shake off the worry plaguing her, she concentrated on the tramp of the horses' hoofs on the packed snow and the sound of the wagon wheels, squeaking as if they too were protesting the cold. The vanguard passed out of sight as they followed the road around an outcropping of rock.

Twenty soldiers preceded Derya, who rode in the tenth row, flanked on either side by battle-hardened warriors. Gusts of wind from the mountain slopes pummeled her left cheek and ruffled her furs. She pulled the heavy garment tighter. When they rounded the curve, the wind would blow right in their faces.

Tugging her hood down and sinking into her cloak, she screwed up her face, anticipating the frigid blast of the next gust. Her horse plodded around the rocky outcropping.

Derya jerked upright. What was that she heard? Clanging metal and angry shouts. *Not again.* Another band of robbers, this one clever enough to pounce when her force was effectively split in two. No doubt the riders they'd spotted in the distance were part of this plot, riding to attack the rearguard while the vanguard was busy with this other group.

Her guards pulled their swords, metal scraping the edges of the scabbards.

She reached for her knives. Oh, she'd let the guards defend her. But if anyone broke through, she'd be ready.

A dark shape landed on the rider in front of her. In a heartbeat, her guard toppled from his horse, a black-clad attacker wrestling with him for control of his sword.

Part of her knew she should keep moving forward with the rest of her guards, that stopping would make her an easier target. But she couldn't let her mare trample her own man. She pulled on the reins, halting her mount.

An upward glance revealed shifting shadows on the rocks above. Heat rose to her face. How dare these ruffians assault her party? It was high time they were the recipients of an unpleasant surprise. Derya reached for her magic, summoning her power. While it gathered, she yanked off a glove and shoved her icy fingers into the bag tied at her waist.

Where is it? Between fear and cold, her fingers refused to move swiftly. Another attacker leaped down. The guard to her left held his sword vertically. The attacker fell on it, impaling himself on the blade through his neck. The impact knocked the Cinarrian from his horse. He and his attacker tumbled to the ground with a thud, landing in a bloody heap that spread scarlet across the dirty snow.

Derya's heart galloped like a runaway horse. *Raging winds, that was close.* She resumed searching through the bag of amplifiers. Her fingers closed around the tiny flask of wine. She could use it to induce vomiting. That would be amusing, if she could be sure it would only affect her enemies. No, another amplifier would be safer, and more effective. She located a peppercorn, brought it to her lips, and licked it, savoring the peppery taste.

Directing her magic to a snowbank, she melted it into a puddle. The corners of her mouth twitched. The pepper not only amplified her power but made it work faster. She continued heating the water, keeping an eye on the clifftop above.

A man sprang from the rocks with a shout, a dagger clenched in his fist. She forced herself to wait, counting one, two, three. When he was only a few feet above her, she flung the boiling water in his face.

He shrieked and dropped his weapon, his hands clutching his scalded eyes. He crashed to the ground with a fearsome moan. A moment later, Bahadir sliced off his head.

Derya continued to boil melted snow and fling it in the face of any foe who came near. The clashing swords and shouts of the warriors grew dim and indistinct. Melt, boil, throw. She pulled hard at her magic, frantically drawing on the power, fearful it wouldn't be enough.

In a matter of minutes, six enemies with scalded faces lay dead around her mount. Her cheeks were flushed and sweaty. *If only my toes weren't so cold.* She reached again for her magic, boiled more snow, and downed another foe.

Numbness inched its way up her legs, making it hard to keep her seat on her mare. Her arms were heavy as if they were made of iron, and she strained to lift her hands enough to direct her boiling weapon.

The sounds of the battle faded. *Does that mean we're winning? Or are we losing?*

A man approached, stepping over the corpses on the ground. She squinted. What colors did he wear? She blinked to clear her blurred vision.

"You can stop now, Kiral."

That sounded like Bahadir. But his voice was distorted like he was speaking to her from a long way off.

A horse drew up on her left side. "Kiral, are you unharmed?" The speaker's voice was faint and muffled, as if a pillow pressed against her ears.

Derya turned to her left and squinted. She swayed in her saddle. *I will not faint.* Her eyelids fought to close. The moving horses and people and snowy ground merged into a single gray cloud.

32

———————

Thin fingers gripped Derya's elbow. Slowly, she pulled in a deep breath. *Breathe.*

She peered at the person clutching her. "Danisman?"

Safiye's grip tightened and her lips moved.

Why can't I hear anything? Derya took another uneven breath. "Safiye, are you unhurt?" As the words left her mouth, her eyes widened and her jaw went slack. From the vibration in her throat, she knew she was speaking. But she heard nothing.

The danisman's lips pulled back, exposing her large, yellowed teeth. Her lips pursed, stretched, and flexed, but no sound reached Derya's ears.

What did she say? Derya tried again. "No one got near me. But you?" Still no sound. She sagged over her horse's withers, clinging to her mare's chestnut mane with her ungloved hand. The ice crystals in the rough hair stung her already aching fingers. *What's wrong with me?*

Safiye tugged on her sleeve. Derya shifted her gaze to meet the other woman's dark eyes, noting the lines between her brows were more pronounced than usual. The danisman was talking, her eyes wide and frantic.

Derya struggled to sit straight. With her water magic, she could heal people. She should be helping the wounded.

When Safiye grabbed her ungloved hand, Derya could barely feel the pressure of the other woman's fingers. Now Safiye was waving her other arm frantically. By the looks of it, she was yelling something.

A moment later, four soldiers ran over, preceded by the smell of sweat and horse. *What do they want with me?*

Another moment later, she understood. One of them held out her fur-lined glove. She must have dropped it as she reached for her supply of magic amplifiers.

She thanked the soldier with as wide a smile as she could muster while Safiye slid the black fur over her frozen fingers. The sudden sting of returning sensation in her fingertips made her gasp.

A burly soldier placed a hand on her back. Warmth flooded into her spine, spreading along her ribs and into her head. He must be a healer.

After a few more deep breaths of icy air, Derya's overwhelming urge to sleep had passed. But why was everything as quiet as dawn breaking over a remote meadow? She sensed the vibration of the healer's voice rather than the words of his conversation with Safiye. The shouts of the warriors, whinnying horses, tramping hoofs, all the usual sounds of their entourage, had vanished like the memory of an echo.

Bahadir strode up to her, saluted, and his mouth began moving. She pulled her eyebrows together and frowned. *What was he saying?*

The chiliarch, danisman, and soldiers stared at her. Their mouths were in motion as they pointed at her. But she heard nothing, not even the pulse of blood in her ears.

Safiye rummaged in her saddlebag and extracted a wax tablet and stylus. She wrote on it, then handed it to Derya.

You must have overused your magic. That can cause deafness in water mages.

Deafness? Derya blinked a few times. "Forever?" she asked. Her breath caught in her throat. She was sure she'd uttered the words. But she heard nothing.

The danisman shook her head. She took the tablet, wrote, and handed it back to Derya.

It should pass. Don't use your magic again today.

Derya huffed in relief. Her hearing loss was transient, and at least her advisors could hear what she said. But this couldn't go on. Cinar's heir had to be in control. Relying on others to write things out, not knowing what they were saying behind her back? It was untenable.

Safiye frowned and scribbled more words. *Deafness rarely occurs unless amplifiers are used.*

"I used pepper."

Three startled faces stared at her, then all their mouths went into motion.

What do you know of amplifiers? Safiye scowled as she held up the tablet. *You're not yet eighteen.*

"Does that matter right now?" Derya repressed a grin. It was almost worth being temporarily deaf just to see how shocked they were. "I won't use the magic today, I promise." She turned to Bahadir. "Chiliarch, have we defeated our attackers?"

He nodded.

"How many did we lose?"

He held up both gloved hands, all ten fingers outstretched.

Ten. That was ten too many. "Wounded?"

Holding his hands out with his palms up, he shrugged.

"That means you don't know, right?"

Another nod.

Derya huffed. How infuriating to not be able to simply ask and hear a reply. "What about the people we saw in the distance?"

Bahadir pressed his lips together, then took the tablet from Safiye. *Almost here. I sent some of the rearguard to engage them.*

"I want to see what's happening."

"Kiral—"

She could read his lips well enough to make out that word. She stopped him with a glare. "I will observe, not act. You can handle the fighting."

Without waiting for a reply, she pulled on her reins and turned her horse. When six guards surrounded her, their mounts moving in step with hers, she smiled. Bahadir wasn't going to fight her on this. But he wasn't giving in completely.

Gripping the reins in one hand, she slid the fingers of the other hand out of her glove, curling her hand into a fist. Tiny tendrils of warmth arched through her frozen flesh.

Derya twisted her mouth into a wry smile. *So, I wounded seven men, lost my hearing, and almost froze half my fingers off. Not exactly what I was planning today. Guess I won't be having a hot bath any time soon. Unless I boil my own water. Warm water would be a small price to pay for going deaf again.*

Her horse's head bobbed. Was that a nicker she heard? Or her imagination?

Squeezing her knees against her mare's sides, Derya urged her to walk faster. She needed to see what was happening.

Kentarch Farooq maneuvered his horse next to hers. He touched her arm and pointed.

One brigade of her men cantered toward the approaching riders, the group they'd spotted earlier wearing the turquoise and black of Cinar. The black-clad pursuers were gaining on the fleeing Cinarrians—if that was who they were—and loosed a hail of arrows.

Five riders tumbled from their horses. Derya sucked in a breath. She wondered if she'd witnessed the deaths of friends or foes. Whoever the pursuers were, they were impressive archers.

Just then, her soldiers overtook the riders, some with swords drawn, others with arrows nocked in their longbows.

Half of the pursuers wheeled to meet them. They sent a volley of arrows soaring through the air toward Derya's warriors. A gust of wind, the work of a Cinarrian air mage, brushed them to the side.

Next to her, Bahadir was shouting orders. At least, that's what she assumed he was doing from the spray of spittle that flew from his mouth. The meaning of his words became clear when another twenty men galloped toward the battle.

Bahadir continued to issue commands. The only word she could read on his lips was "Kiral."

I'm a liability, when he needs every sword and bow in this battle—or to watch for more ambushes.

Four of her soldiers went down. How many attackers were left? She tried to count, but their ceaseless motion made it hard to be sure. Only the growing number of corpses on the snowy ground gave her any indication of the tide of the battle.

What had Bahadir told her? Ten men in her colors, twenty in pursuit. Fifteen black-clad men lay motionless on the ground. Eight of those they'd pursued were also dead, their crimson blood staining the turquoise of their cloaks.

Pressing a hand to her mouth, she stifled her scream of frustration and anguish. She couldn't help. She could only watch more of her loyal subjects meet their deaths.

Three of the living pursuers turned their mounts and galloped to the south. Derya's archers sent arrow after arrow in pursuit.

One man tumbled from his saddle, an arrow through his neck. Two more fell to the ground, their wounded mounts thrashing on the blood-stained snow.

In a few moments, the rest of the pursuers lay dead. Only two of their quarry lived. Derya's breath caught. One of them embraced the kentarch. They were Cinarrians. Which meant they must bear urgent news. *Does my father live?*

She urged her horse forward. Bahadir was waving his arms, apparently shouting orders. This time, she could guess a few more words. *Wounded. Enemy.*

Leaving him to his task of dealing with the injured and dead, Derya rode to meet the newcomers.

As she drew near, her heart raced. Surely, she was seeing things. The gray-haired man talking with the kentarch, was he the deputy ambassador to Ymittos? What would drive him from the capital?

Derya urged her mare to a canter, her heart throbbing in her ears. She stiffened her spine. *Whatever the news, I will accept it with stout heart and steely resolve. Cinar's heir will not be shaken.*

The kentarch and the gray-haired man turned toward her and her heart skipped a beat. There was no mistaking the hooked nose perched over full lips. Sweat dripped from his flushed olive face and a smear of blood crossed his wrinkled cheek.

This man had argued hard for her cousin Nazif to be named heir, rather than her. He'd insisted that a girl had no business ruling the empire. That empresses had ruled successfully in the past made no difference to him. He clung to his belief that since women were usually physically weaker than men, they were mentally weaker as well. It was clear he still resented the pranks she'd played on him when she was small.

Putting vinegar in his wine and hiding his shoes were the opening sorties in the battle between them. Her last prank incensed him so much he complained to her father. That was when the emperor appeased his outraged pride by promoting him to deputy ambassador to Ymittos. He'd been sent out of Derya's life.

From the sneer on the man's face, it didn't appear he'd forgiven her. Having lost her hearing wasn't going to help convince him that her father had made the right choice in naming her his heir.

When Derya slid from her chestnut mare, her knees buckled. Her head was spinning. Maybe better not to walk over. With one hand on her horse's side for support, she fixed her gaze on the man. "Well met, Oikeios Kelebek." She suppressed her grin, the smirk that always threatened to spread across her face when she used his formal title. While it meant "Honored Official" and was only awarded to high-ranking diplomats, she always thought of something oily when she paired it with Kelebek's given name.

Kelebek bowed. She caught a whiff of ginger and musk over stale sweat. The man's mouth moved.

"I'm sorry, Oikeios, I can't hear you."

She jumped when Safiye touched her arm. She'd been so focused on the deputy ambassador, she hadn't noticed her danisman approach.

Safiye began speaking. Derya still couldn't make out the words. She watched Kelebek's reaction. His eyes widened, and he looked from Derya to Safiye, to the dead men on the ground. He narrowed his eyes, giving Derya a fleeting scowl before the neutral mask of a trained diplomat slid over his face.

When Safiye stopped talking, Derya said, "Danisman, please. Oikeios Kelebek needs your tablet."

After Safiye handed the writing implements to Kelebek, Derya gestured to them. "Oikeios Kelebek, while I'm always delighted to see you, why are you here?"

Pressing his lips together, he wrote and then held up the tablet. Derya gasped when she read the words:

I regret to inform you, Kiral, that the king and queen of Ymittos are dead.

"How?" Derya asked.

The Nafplian ambassador held a banquet to celebrate the upcoming nuptials of Dochan Istvan and Princess Eliana. The next morning, the king, queen, and several of their nobles were dead.

"What?" It was impossible, except in times of plague, that so many would die so suddenly. Or… "Poison?"

The official story was plague. Which wasn't credible, since the supposed illness killed the sovereigns of Ymittos and a handful of Ymittosian and Nafplian nobles, but didn't spread any further.

"Who is ruling Ymittos?"

One of the Nafplian lords declared himself regent, holding the throne for Dochan Istvan and Queen Eliana until they return.

Derya frowned. "But they aren't married yet. So it should be one of the Ymittosians serving as regent."

The Nafplians produced a copy of the betrothal contract. It stated that since the dochan was accompanying the princess on a dangerous quest, the betrothal would be considered as legally binding as a marriage.

"I don't believe it." She crossed her arms, her frown deepening into a scowl.

Kelebek turned the tablet over and continued writing. *Neither did many of the Ymittosians. But a few of the scribes all swore it was genuine. You can imagine how the lawyers and philosophers started debating the issue. They stopped when two of the Ymittosian generals supported the Nafplians' claim.*

Derya and Safiye exchanged perplexed and dismayed glances. Something was wrong. Derya was as sure of it as she was that snakes could bite. "What did our ambassador think?"

A muscle twitched in Kelebek's jaw. *She suspected treachery, as she'd discussed the terms of the betrothal in a general fashion with the king, and nothing he'd said implied he gave the dochan any legal claims before the marriage took place. She guessed the Nafplians prepared a forged betrothal contract and bribed the scribes and generals to swear it was genuine. The ambassador's first act was to write to your father. But her page was caught as he was readying the bird. The regent imprisoned our ambassador and nearly all the embassy staff as spies.*

"How did you escape?"

We were in Merousi, meeting with a group of our merchants. One of the ambassador's guards managed to escape the capital and intercepted us before we returned to Ptolemaida. We decided to find you and give you the news.

Derya closed her eyes. Relief warmed her. Her father wasn't dead or dying. But the kind king and queen of Ymittos were gone. Her eyes flew open. "Does Eliana know?"

I don't think so. How would word have gotten to her? If, as we suspect, this was a Nafplian plot, they won't tell her until she breaks the curse.

"But would Istvan poison his own people in an attempt to seize the throne of Ymittos?" As soon as she uttered the words, she knew. He was ruthless enough, she was certain of it. She hugged the tablet to her chest. *Oh, Eliana. May the Rider protect you. No one else can.*

Kelebek reached for the tablet. *The other concern is that the guards at the rift, the ones waiting for the princess's return, were supposed to rotate. None of the Ymittosians returned to the capital. Only a handful of Nafplians.*

"Please find the chiliarch," Derya said to the kentarch, "and tell him I need to speak with him."

Farooq saluted, leaped onto his horse, and rode away.

Not wanting Kelebek to read any weakness or distress on her face, she forced herself to stand straight as she patted her horse's neck, trying to appear calm. The coppery taste of blood filled her mouth, and she clamped her jaw to stop gnawing on the inside of her cheek. *Raging waters, what is going on in Ymittos?*

When she felt she had her emotions in check, she turned to face her advisors. Safiye was talking with Kelebek. Perhaps she was filling him in on the events of the past few days. Good. She thought it would make him more able to advise her, but as he answered, he waved his arms in the air and pointed at her. It appeared he was going to be difficult.

She stifled a moan. What she wanted was to lie down and

sleep. Or recover her hearing. Or have a hot bath. It didn't seem she'd get any of them soon.

Instead, she had an uncooperative diplomat to appease and a decision to make. She sorted through her options. What would her father do?

He would seize control of the situation. She hadn't thought beyond that by the time a man with bloodstains on his tunic and cloak strode up to her and saluted.

"Chiliarch, thank you for coming so promptly." The princess fixed her eyes on his. "Did your kentarch advise you of recent events in Ymittos?"

His face grim, Bahadir nodded.

Derya turned to the others. "Then we have three choices. We can return to the rift and offer what aid we can to Princess Eliana." She gulped. She hoped her friend still lived. "Second, we can continue to Nafplio, which we had previously thought was our safest option. Third, we abandon that plan and head north for Cinar with all possible speed."

Kelebek scratched on the tablet. *For what purpose would we go to Nafplio? We already know the treachery of their dochan. We'd most likely end up imprisoned like our ambassador.*

Bahadir nodded and took the stylus. *I agree. And we've lost too many men to fight the diodochi's entire army.*

"Is it possible that the men who've been attacking us are Nafplian?" Derya asked.

The chiliarch frowned, then wrote. *What would they gain from attacking the heir of Cinar?*

What indeed, Derya thought. She bit her lip. "Danisman?"

Safiye took the tablet from Bahadir. She tipped her head to the side, then wrote. *I concur. We should discard any thought of traveling through Nafplio.*

"Princess Eliana is in danger. Should we go to her aid?" Derya kept her tone neutral. She'd like nothing more than to leap on her mare and gallop to the rift. But she had nearly two hundred people to consider.

Her danisman placed a hand on her arm. "Kiral."

Derya didn't hear the word, but from the motion of Safiye's lips, she knew what her danisman was about to write. A lump formed in her throat.

We don't know if the princess still lives.

A sudden memory of Eliana's laughter—when she'd used her magic to speed Derya's bird on its way to Cinar—brought stinging tears to her eyes. She swallowed hard. "Oikeios, did the ambassador send birds to my father, informing him of the curse Princess Eliana was to break?"

He shook his head and sighed as he wrote. *King Archelaos forbade any birds to be sent unless he approved the message. He didn't want anyone to know his heir was in danger, lest someone try to exploit the situation.*

"Then," Derya said, "unless the birds I sent got through, my father has no idea what's happening."

Kelebek nodded.

Her duty was clear. Derya took a few steps away from her advisers, staring across the snowy plain toward the rift, clenching her jaw and narrowing her eyes to fight the tears. *Oh, Eliana. If Istvan has ended you, if the Malkhians have hurt you, I will avenge you.*

She whirled in place. "As I see it, we have no choice. We must head north for Cinar as fast as we can."

Three nodding heads told her they agreed. "Should we leave the wagons?" Derya asked. She refused to give any attention to the pang she felt over abandoning her clothes and other comforts, and forced her thoughts to practicalities. Would their wounded be able to make the journey on horseback? Would any of them survive the bitter nights without their tents and braziers?

Bahadir reached for the tablet. *I would say not yet. We might want to use them as firewood in the high passes if we encounter bad weather.*

"When can we leave?" Derya asked.

As soon as we've taken care of our dead.

The chiliarch had written the words in tiny script crammed at the very bottom of the tablet. There was no more room to write, nothing left to say.

Derya straightened her shoulders. "Then, Chiliarch Bahadir, lead us north."

His mouth moved as he saluted, accepting her order. Derya watched him stride off. She strained to hear anything, a whinny or a shout. Even a complaint from one of her maids would be welcome.

Nothing. Even surrounded by people, she was solitary in a silent world, carrying the burden of ruling alone. The silence, she assumed, would end shortly. The burden, she knew, was hers to bear until she died. Which she hoped wouldn't be at the hands of an assassin in an icy pass.

33

The rhythm of her footfalls accompanied by the steady dripping of water, Eliana sprinted through the bleak blue light until she was out of breath. *Rider willing, I've lost my would-be captors.* She rested a hand on the rock wall and stood panting, sweat seeping into her eyes. She blinked to chase away the sting. After racing through the serpentine tunnels, she did not know if she was getting farther from Istvan, closer to Adakizh, or, she thought with a gulp, approaching the lair of another beast.

She wandered down a passage, not knowing where she was going. Emptiness in her stomach reminded her she hadn't eaten since the day before. Perhaps she could find some edible mushrooms. *At least I didn't lose my last meal in the necessary ditch.* She smirked. Maybe the flux still occupied Istvan and his men. Unless a water mage had healed them. She screwed up her face. That wasn't a helpful thought.

The tunnel widened, and she found herself on the bank of the Qvirila River where it spread to form a pool. Eliana gazed longingly at the water but didn't dare drink.

Eliana dropped onto a large boulder near the rippling water and put her head in her hands. Exhaustion weakened her muscles, hunger gnawed her stomach, thirst soured her dry mouth. And she was lost and alone in the dark. Every time she thought she'd reached the bottom of the pit, she slid deeper into the abyss.

A splash sent a spray of water her way, dampening her arms. She jumped to her feet. Adakizh was treading water in the middle of the river. He dove under the water like a dolphin, surfaced, and swam toward her with a smooth, lazy stroke.

"Where did you come from?" she asked.

He rested his muscular forearms on the riverbank. "From where you left me. Since I wasn't sure if your friends would chase me, I decided the river was my best escape."

"But I didn't see you a moment ago."

"Of course not. I was underwater."

"I thought the stories about your people being half goat and half fish weren't true."

He laughed. "Didn't they tell you? We climb like goats and swim like fish. It's a gift from our water fae ancestors, the ability to breathe underwater." He tapped the three slits on the side of his neck.

She blinked, trying to make sense of it. "I don't mean to be rude, but doesn't all the water flow into the river? Even the water that flows near the orange mushrooms? Surely you're about to be ill."

With another laugh, he shook his head, letting his long, curly, dark hair spray droplets into the air. "No, I'm not. We channel all the water through filters made of sand, gravel, and charcoal before it joins the river." He pointed at a small rivulet that drained into the larger flow. "That's the purest water."

"Oh. Thank you." She plunged a hand into the stream and lifted it to her lips. The cool wetness in her dry mouth was like spring rain in the desert.

Adakizh waited until she finished drinking. "And now, Eliana, please go." He said the words as blandly as if he was suggesting she pour a cup of tea. "I'm feeling the urge to kill you and I don't want to do that." With a single, fluid motion, he hoisted himself from the water and stared into her eyes. "Go."

She met his gaze, suddenly unable to remember what she wanted to ask him. Or why her question was of greater consequence than staring into the depths of his mournful blue eyes.

A heartbeat later, his long fingers wrapped around her throat.

She clutched his hand and strained to pull it away, struggling to breathe.

A shout echoed through the cavern. "Eliana!"

Adakizh loosened his grip and Eliana staggered back, rubbing her bruised neck. In spite of his murderous attack, the voice was more terrifying than Adakizh, or any vishapion. It was Istvan.

"That one shows up like a puppet pulled by a string." Adakizh let out an exaggerated huff. "But I suppose I should be grateful. Please leave my realm before I find you again. Your Istvan might not be around to save you."

He dove under the water and disappeared, barely leaving a ripple behind.

Eliana longed to dive after him. If Adakizh thought Istvan was her refuge, he was mistaken. She squinted into the dusky light, spotting Istvan on the river's opposite bank, accompanied by a handful of men.

"Wait for me there," he yelled. "I'll come for you."

Oh, no you won't. Gathering her air magic, she sent up a mist and ran upstream, hoping that was the direction Adakizh had taken. She needed to talk to him without him assaulting her. If only she could figure out how.

Istvan's shouts faded in the distance. Rider willing, the Saumarotas would find him. Or a vishapion.

A stitch stabbed her side. Eliana halted and rubbed a hand over the pain. Shoulders slumping, she watched the ripples in the river. The one she wanted to talk with fled from her, and the one she wanted to evade wouldn't leave her alone. She listened for any hint of Istvan's presence. Faint sounds from downstream sent quivers along her spine. Better not try that way. And if Istvan's flux had passed, he'd have time to search for her. She turned and trotted upstream, hoping Adakizh would continue to swim in that direction.

When she came to a side tunnel, the faint burbling and hiss of a waterfall made her parched throat itch. Eliana followed the sound of the water, relying on the glowing mushrooms for light.

The gush of the waterfall grew into a roar. She hurried to it, aching to be free of the dusty feeling in her mouth.

Dropping to her knees, she held a hand under the spray, letting the cold water cool her sweaty face and clean the dirt and grime from her hands. Once they were clean, she cupped her fingers together and drank the frigid water that glowed pale blue in the light from the mushrooms that clung to the damp rock walls.

Eliana closed her eyes, savoring the chill in her mouth that washed away the sticky, sour taste. She drank and drank until her thirst was appeased.

"If you're hungry, I have food."

She started at the soft baritone voice behind her. Adakizh stepped out of the shadows.

"How did you find me?" Eliana asked.

He shrugged. "I don't know. The same reason you can find me, I suppose. The curse draws us to each other."

"You almost killed me back there."

"Almost. I can resist the compulsion if I concentrate. You…" He paused. "You distracted me." He rummaged in a bag and pulled out a handful of figs. Holding them out to Eliana, he gave her an impish smile. "I hope your Istvan isn't too angry that I stole this from him."

Returning his grin as she accepted the figs, Eliana bit into one. "Adakizh, we have to break the enchantment without either of us ending up dead."

"I'd like that." He bit into a fig and chewed thoughtfully. "I have a vague memory of a counterspell, but I can't remember the specifics."

"Try."

"What do you think I've been doing when I haven't been trying to kill you? Speaking of which, you need to go. Now."

He lunged for her. His long fingers reached for her throat.

She ducked and surged toward him, one shoulder dropped. He grunted when she crashed into his abdomen. Off balance, he toppled to the ground.

Eliana stood over him, blinking in surprise that she'd downed him. She bitterly regretted every complaint she'd ever made about the wrestling lessons her father had forced on her. He'd been right to insist. If only she could tell him.

Adakizh rolled onto his back, grinning, his teeth gleaming blue under the mushroom's illumination. "Who taught you that move?"

"I had tutors," she said stiffly.

"You studied well." He surveyed her face for a moment before allowing his gaze to drift lower.

Under his stare, heat spread up from her chest. "I took advantage of every opportunity my parents gave me." Her voice broke on the last words.

"Well, you didn't disappoint them."

While she appreciated his compliment, hadn't that been her problem? She'd done almost everything her parents wanted her to do, desperate to fulfill her duty, even if it went against what she wished.

With a grunt, Adakizh sat up and rubbed his arms. "I'm a little stiff, you know, from all that sleeping." He gave her half a smile. "But even at my best, you might have taken me by surprise enough to throw me. Well done, princess."

Eliana couldn't help but smile. What was she thinking? It

was absurd how pleased she was by his praise. She forced a severe frown onto her face as Adakizh clambered to his feet.

When he straightened to his full height, Eliana had to look up to meet his eyes. She hadn't realized he was so tall.

They stood staring at one another. For the first time, Eliana noticed his kind eyes, rimmed by long, dark eyelashes. Were his eyes black, or midnight blue? It was hard to tell in the mushrooms' light. High cheekbones under olive skin, an aquiline nose, and a square jaw formed his handsome face. Despite his long sleep, he hadn't lost his muscles. They bulged under his damp tunic.

An intensity burned in his eyes, obvious even in the shadowy light. "Eliana." He breathed her name, almost like a prayer. With a trembling hand, he stroked her hair and laid one finger on her cheek. "Eliana."

Heat coursed through her and her breath came in pants as if she'd been running. She swayed toward him, her gaze locked onto his as if she were staring into a fire.

Adakizh jumped back as if her skin had scorched his finger. "Go! You need to go now!"

His last word was a shout, not of rage but of anguish.

But to leave him now, to break away from those kind dark eyes, when tingles spread to her feet and blood pulsed in her core? She couldn't do it. One kiss, that's all she wanted.

"Do you have a death wish, princess?" Adakizh snarled. He put a hand on her throat.

Eliana shrieked. She kneed him between the legs, and fled, the echoes of his groan chasing her as she ran.

34

———

Eliana bolted to the nearest tunnel and plunged into it. She dashed around a corner and crashed into a rock wall. With a gasp, she slumped against the slimy stone, its red surface taking on a lavender hue in the blue mushrooms' light. There had to be a way out of this dead end. She ran her hands over the walls. After a frantic search, she found a narrow crack. If she crouched, she just might be able to squeeze through it.

She heard steps in the tunnel behind her. Were they slow and deliberate footsteps, as if Adakizh was giving her time to flee? Or were they the uneven, staggering footsteps of a man in pain? With all the echoes, it was hard to tell. She winced, hoping she hadn't hurt him too badly.

Her fingers clawed at the sides of the crack. Turning her shoulders, she slid her head and right arm into the crevice.

The rock walls pressed against her like a vise, clamping her in place. She pushed and tugged, her feet scrabbling on the pebbly ground. Inch by inch, she squeezed through.

The footsteps grew closer. Eliana paused her squirming and held her breath to listen. The echoes made it sound as if more than one person was stalking her. Whoever they were, she didn't want them to find her stuck between two rocks. With an extra effort, she flattened her right hand on the edge and pulled. Her ribs scraped through the crack, her sword's scabbard digging into her hip. She yanked her legs and the trailing end of her cloak inside and leaned against the rock wall, panting.

The air was damper than in the tunnel. Its musty smell tickled Eliana's nose, making her want to sneeze.

"No one's here," a man said.

Another man cursed. "I could swear I saw her go this way."

Istvan. Eliana's nose twitched. The princess pressed a hand over her mouth to suppress a sneeze. Her heartbeat thumped in her ears. She took only shallow breaths, trying to avoid disturbing even the smallest mote of dust.

Something metallic tapped the rock wall over the crack. "Look at this," Istvan's companion said.

The tickling in her nose intensified. She squeezed her nostrils shut, holding her breath. Tears streamed from her eyes. *I can't let them catch me.*

Istvan snorted. "She's too big to fit through there. Let's try near the river again. See if we can catch that slippery prince." He hawked and spat. "I'm sure that troglodyte is lurking around here somewhere."

Eliana closed her eyes and stood motionless until their footsteps were drowned out by the dripping of water.

When she was certain Istvan had gone, she moved from the wall and turned in a circle, inspecting her surroundings as best she could under the mushroom's feeble light. She hadn't forced her way into another tunnel, but into a chamber with high walls covered with jagged, pale-yellow crystals as far as she could see. Ledges like small shelves protruded at irregular intervals. Mushrooms glowing the color of faded cornflowers perched on the crags. Water trickled down from the darkness above, adding to the chilly dampness.

Caught like a fish in a trap, Eliana wondered if she'd ever escape. The clammy walls seemed to close in on her, striving to hold her in a stony embrace and sucking the air out of the tiny enclosure. She gasped, each breath shallower and quicker than the last. This rock chamber would be her tomb.

She clenched her jaw, willing herself to breathe slowly and calm her racing heart. No, she wasn't trapped. If she'd gotten in, she could get out. She ran a hand through her hair. Fatigue weakened her desire to battle her way back into the tunnel. She needed sleep. And this hidden room was the perfect place for getting some undisturbed rest.

After surveying the cold stone floor, she chose what looked like the smoothest and driest area. She wrapped her cloak around herself and lay down, tucking one arm under her head. Gradually, her pounding heart slowed.

While she was safe for the moment, the question of what to do nagged her. She couldn't run away from Adakizh every time they found each other. Sooner or later, either he would kill her or Istvan would find them. Then Adakizh would be dead and she'd be Istvan's tool. And she'd still have the problem of Cetus, his threatened invasion and his deviant plans for her.

She needed to talk with Adakizh long enough to convince him they needed to work together. But how? His cursed fingers longed to wrap themselves around her throat. When they weren't gently caressing her cheek…

Eliana hunched her shoulders and winced. What kind of girl finds pleasure in the attentions of princes who want to kill her? *At least when I enjoyed flirting with Istvan, I didn't know what he was.*

A drop of water fell on her face. She whisked it away. *I can't physically overpower Adakizh. But maybe my magic can.* She pursed her lips. He hadn't used any magic in front of her. Could it be possible that she was the more powerful mage? A single drop of hope fell on her shriveled courage, coaxing it to rally. If she was more powerful, she might be able to restrain him. But there was no way to know unless she tried.

Eliana sighed. While it was theoretically possible to bind someone using bands of air, she'd never attempted it. How draining would it be? She only needed to keep Adakizh in check until they formed an alliance and devised a plan. Then, they could resume chasing each other in the dark and their game of cat and mouse would no longer be aimless. She shifted position, seeking a less bumpy section of the floor, and slid into an uneasy sleep.

Tapping on stone roused her. Her eyes flared open. The tapping continued. Restless feet shuffled on the loose pebbles in the tunnel. Maybe if she stayed perfectly still, whoever it was would go away.

"I know you're in there, Eliana," Adakizh said.

35

No. Eliana's breath caught and she sagged against the rocky floor. He'd found her. *Again.* She lay blinking in the darkness.

"I'm coming in," Adakizh said.

The princess scrambled to her feet. "Good luck. I could barely fit."

A low chuckle reached her. "Did you not know? I am a stone mage."

Eliana's tutor had told her only the most powerful mages had more than one magic. She didn't know if this was welcome or bad news, that Adakizh wielded two magics, water and stone. He'd be harder to contain but would make a stronger ally against both Istvan and Cetus.

The stone at the crack's edge steamed and hissed. A chunk broke off and smashed on the ground.

"What did you do?" Eliana jumped back, pressing against the rock wall.

"I heated the rock until it turned brittle." A piece of stone cracked and fell.

She let out a huff. "I don't suppose you'll leave so I can get out?"

"Oh, are you trapped?" He sounded like he was sorry. "I hoped that you'd escape before I broke my way in." Another chunk of rock shattered on the ground. "I walked as slowly as I could. And yes, walking was difficult at first, thank you very much."

"I'm sorry," she said. "It was either that or let you choke me. Can you forgive me?"

"Let's call it even, shall we?" A slab of rock crashed to the floor. "I knew you came this way, so I took the opposite tunnel. Every time I felt compelled to turn, I went the other direction. But somehow, I was drawn to you. As time runs out, the compulsion to kill you grows stronger."

Weariness pulled on her. "How long have you been awake?"

"I'd say a little over a full day."

His cheerful tone seemed out of place to Eliana. Every moment that passed was one less minute they had to lift Kharan-Khuag's curse. Her short sleep had only dulled the fatigue. Part of her wanted to lie down and let Adakizh give in to the spell's compulsion. Perhaps she could trust him to kill her quickly.

What was she thinking? She couldn't allow a little tiredness deter her from rescuing her people.

There had to be a way out. Tipping her head up, she spied a ledge about twenty feet overhead. Maybe she could climb out of Adakizh's reach. She grasped a jutting crystal and pulled herself up.

"Eliana. You have a beautiful name." Another stone shattered.

His voice had a reassuring quality to it, an artlessness that made her believe he was sincere. "Thank you. Yours is…"

"Unusual?" He snorted. "That's a polite way of putting it. It belonged to a distant ancestor. He didn't do anything memorable; my mother just fancied the name, so I got stuck with it."

"I rather like it." Which was true. "It's strong. Masculine." She snapped her jaw shut. She hadn't meant to say that last part out loud.

"Are you trying to distract me with compliments?" He sounded amused.

"No. Are you?"

While she waited for his reply, Eliana studied the ledge over her head. One burst of air should be sufficient. She sucked in a breath, pulled on her magic, and launched into the air, arms outstretched. Her right hand missed. The left one grabbed a piece of jutting rock. She clung to it, her feet scrabbling for footholds. Then her right foot found a tiny support, and she pushed herself high enough to slide her forearm onto the top of the ledge.

Sharp rocks bit into her arm as she pulled herself up, grunting with the effort.

"Eliana, what are you doing?"

She lay on the ledge, panting. When she caught her breath, she replied. "Getting away, like you said." She rolled onto her back, ignoring the pebbles that dug into her ribs.

After a few more crashes from below, Eliana peeked over the edge. Adakizh had widened the crack, allowing more air to flow into the tiny room. The light dimmed as he pressed himself through the narrow opening.

The tagavlon rested a hand on the rock wall and looked up. His face broke into a wide smile. "There you are." He shook his head. "You know it won't take me long to break that wall down. Or to cut steps so I can climb up to you."

"Whatever you do, do it slowly," she replied.

"Does it matter if I kill you in an hour or three?"

"Why, yes." She scooted back from the edge of her perch. As she reached behind herself, her hand moved through nothingness and she tipped backward. Between the ledge and the wall was a crevasse that dropped into another chasm. With a lurch and a jerk, she saved herself from toppling into the abyss.

Heart pounding, she clenched her jaw. She would not scream. The ledge she sat on was more like a bridge than a shelf. There was no escape for her, teetering on the narrow beam.

"Adakizh. You know Istvan will kill you when he finds you."

"That's not a problem." He waved a hand and the chunks of stone lying on the ground glowed, first red, then white. "Now, if you'd use your air to cover the crack."

For a moment, she didn't understand. Then she blew air magic at the rocks. They flew into place and cooled, sealing her and Adakizh into the tiny chamber.

He nodded. "Impressive. I had no idea you were so powerful."

"I didn't either. The power seems to grow every time I use it."

"Consider it a gift from the Rider of the Ancient Skies." He paced around the chamber, ten steps for each circuit.

"I suppose." She didn't want to get mired in a theological conversation. They had more important things to discuss. "Adakizh, we need to decide what to do. Other than killing each other. Or chasing each other through these tunnels until we drop from exhaustion."

"Well, that last would be disappointing. I don't want to end up as food for a vishapion."

"Right. So we have to figure something out."

"But what?

"I don't know."

"It's rather hopeless. I am, after all, cursed to kill you."

She shivered. "I don't want you to kill me. I don't want to kill you. And I don't want Istvan to kill either of us."

"Add to your list that I don't want Kharan-Khuag to claim my kingdom. Or yours."

"I agree. So, will you?"

"Will I what?"

"Help me find another way."

"There isn't one."

"I thought you said—"

He held up a hand. "It was a vain hope."

Her heart fell. All this time, she'd hoped Adakizh knew of some counterspell they could use or some arcane magic they could wield. How foolish she'd been. If there was another solution, he would have mentioned it earlier.

Was her only hope to kill him?

Steam rose from below, bringing the scent of hot stone. She stuck her head over the edge. "Now what are you doing?"

"Making myself a staircase."

Adakizh had already cut three steps. Once he ascended to her ledge, then what? Eliana would have to kill him. Maybe pushing him over the edge would do it. Or would she be able to bind him with her air magic?

Warmth spread through her as she watched his lips twitch while he pushed his magic to carve another step, the muscles of his forearm flexing as he waved his arm. She most definitely didn't want to kill him.

What if she tried to stop him? She sent a flash of light magic at him. He yelled and covered his eyes. With a burst of air, she knocked him to the ground and held him there.

Now she'd have a chance to put some distance between them. She assessed the wall behind her. Could she climb up while holding him on the floor?

A shower of stones told her probably not. Even held down by her air, he could throw rocks at her. She created an air shield. The rocks bounced off.

Laughing, Adakizh hurled a second volley of rocks. "Truce?" he asked.

"Truce." Another third group of rocks soaring towards her suddenly veered downward, hitting the crystal wall below her ledge. She dropped the air shield and sagged over her knees.

"Good." Adakizh's chuckle echoed through the chamber. "I didn't think I could keep that up much longer."

Eliana snickered at his confession, not certain she believed him. "I was getting tired myself." She peered down at him.

He was gazing at her, his head tipped back and to the side. "We're evenly matched, you and I," he said.

She knelt on the edge of her perch. "We are." She let out a heavy sigh. Fighting him with magic would only wear both of them out. They'd have nothing left to fight Istvan or Kharan-Khuag.

Adakizh waved a casual hand in the air. After a protesting groan, a chunk of rock fell from the wall. He mounted his staircase and began to climb. Eliana watched, horrified, as the top of his head came level with the ledge. One, two more steps and she'd be within his grasp.

Her vision blurred and her throat ached. The thought of killing Adakizh was repugnant, but she was out of choices.

Eyeing the chasm on the other side of her ledge, she wondered if she could tip him into it. She flung a ball of light into the chasm. It descended thirty or forty feet before reaching the rock floor below. Would Adakizh survive that fall?

It wouldn't be long before Adakizh stood in front of her. Another waft of steam, a little scuffling, and he climbed onto the ledge. She stood up and regarded him. *Merciful winds, he was handsome.* A flawless olive complexion and regal nose added to his beauty.

His shoulders were broad, his arms well-muscled. She'd need to use a lot of her magic to knock him over. Eliana shifted her gaze and found him staring at her as if gazing into a star-studded night sky.

"What?" she said.

"I'm sorry. You're beautiful and clever. And very good-natured about me having to kill you and all. I wish I didn't have to do this. But I can't help it."

"You can't?"

"Something pulls on my hands like a fisherman reels in a fish, directing my fingers to break your neck. I get an excruciating headache when I fight the compulsion. Resisting is like being unable to scratch an itch. It gets worse and worse until I can hardly stand the pounding in my skull. Like now." He took a step closer, his hands reaching for her throat.

"I can help you." She hit him with her air magic, a blast that knocked him off balance and sent him tumbling into the abyss.

His startled cry cut through her like an icy blast of wind, ripping the breath from her lungs. What had she done? Even if he was trying to kill her, she didn't want him to die.

She hurled another blast of air, this time to the bottom of the chasm, bouncing it off the hard surface. If she used enough power, the air would cushion his fall.

Still, the thump when he landed sent a shudder through her. Then there was silence.

Eliana waited a few long minutes. Water dripped on rock. A pebble dropped from the ceiling and rattled its way into the chasm. The echoes of its fall died away and still no sound from the prince.

"Adakizh?"

36

———————

"**A**dakizh?" Eliana's pulse throbbed in her throat as she repeated her call.

Please. He had to answer. She didn't want him dead. Or damaged. Just not able to strangle the life out of her.

Darkness obscured his form like a shroud. After several agonizing moments, he sat up. He took a few long breaths before he spoke. "You tried to kill me," he said, as if he was informing her that the sun had come out after a rain.

"Not true. I can explain."

He scoffed. "I'd like to hear it."

"I couldn't let you throttle me. Knocking you into the pit was all I could think of. But I didn't want you to die. So, I saved you."

Scrambling to his feet, he said, "Saved me for what, precisely? If you'd have let me die, we'd both be free."

"But we wouldn't have broken the curse."

"No, I suppose not. But what else will we do? Stay here until we starve to death? Or one of us slays the other?"

"Of course not. We owe it to our people to thwart Kharan-Khuag's plans."

"We owe it to ourselves." He rubbed his chin. "Well, we're

caught between two enemies. Your Istvan and Kharan-Khuag."

"Istvan is not mine." She snapped out the words. "But he is the more immediate threat."

"I agree, but why do you think that?"

"He's here."

"Intent on killing me. Why is he a threat to you?"

He killed my parents. Her breath hitched and tears stung her eyes. If she said the words out loud, she'd break into sobs. *He's going to force me to marry him and then seize my kingdom.* That information alone would do nothing to convince Adakizh to help her. "He intends to gain control of Ymittos and Chorokha, along with Nafplio."

"So, what do we do?" Adakizh scratched his head. "We are two mages, powerful ones, but only two. We have about a day and a half to break the curse—"

"But my birthday was only eleven days ago. I think." She frowned. "So we have four days."

"You forget, it's been more than a day since you woke me. We only had three days from that time. Assuming that us leaving my tower didn't erase any chance we had of meeting the terms of the enchantment." When she nodded, he continued. "A day and a half or Kharan-Khuag will enslave our people. That doesn't give us time to raise an army, even if we thought we could successfully repel an invasion. Our best hope is to make a valiant but doomed stand and die honorable deaths."

She crossed her arms. "That kind of thinking will get us nowhere."

"I'm being realistic. What other kind of thinking is there?"

"My tutor always told me to think the unthinkable."

He snorted. "What does that mean?"

"It means to consider every option, even those you think are impossible. Or unacceptable." She tipped her head to the side. "We've both been doing some of that already."

"You mean my willingness to die rather than kill you?"

"Yes. And my decision to work with you instead of Istvan. I thought it better to ally with the man who's been honest about killing me, not the one who adds a new lie every time he opens his mouth." A sour taste burned her tongue. She gulped it back and faced the truth. "I believe we have no choice," she said slowly, reluctant to say her thought out loud. "We have to kill Istvan."

She let the words fall from her mouth and drop to the bottom of the shaft to Adakizh.

"Yes." He tipped his head back, his expression unreadable in the shadows. "If it makes you feel better, I'll do it."

He waved a hand at the rock wall. Steam rose, the mineral-laden scent of heated rocks to tickling Eliana's nose.

"Thank you. But what are you doing?"

"You're welcome. I'm cutting some steps. Whatever plan you want to concoct, we don't have much time. The pain of not killing you is about to split my skull."

"What if we pretend I've captured you?" she said. "We find Istvan and I'll tell him the truth, that I didn't want to kill you. I'll free you so you can..." The words died in her throat.

"That might work," he said. "But promise me you'll flee for your life once Istvan is dead. No matter what. Even if I'm surrounded by twenty of his men. Get away. Don't let me kill you."

"That only delays the inevitable," she said. "Kharan-Khuag will invade and you'll be cursed forever." *And I—* She didn't want to think about her own fate.

"Not forever. Kharan-Khuag will make sure I die a slow and agonizing death once he takes over. Anyway, if I somehow survived, I'd rather live with this agony than kill you." He shook his head and looked at the ground. "Just before Kharan-Khuag put me in that cursed sleep, he informed me that if I died before the three days were up, the curse would not be broken. Then he taunted me with the second curse."

He slammed his fist into his hand. "There I was, doomed to sleep for a century, after which I'd have to murder the one who woke me. Letting her kill me in self-defense wouldn't work. Right then, I vowed not to kill her, whoever she was. Not for anything." He chuckled. "I didn't imagine keeping that vow would be so painful. But now..." His voice trailed off, and he rubbed his face. "But now, having met you, I don't think I want to live if you are dead."

Eliana longed to throw her arms around him, to rest her head on his shoulder, to lose herself in his embrace. "Thank you." Her words felt inadequate, but she didn't know what else to say. "I'm more grateful than I can express, but we need to get back to the plan. Once Istvan is dead, what will we do about Kharan-Khuag?"

Adakizh ran a hand through his midnight black hair. "Do you know how Chorokha was created?"

She frowned, not sure how that related to their current problem. "Kharan-Khuag made his last attempt to conquer Chorokha. When he realized he was about to lose, he unleashed his power. And sank the Qvirila River."

"Is that what they told you?" He chuckled. "That's not exactly how it happened."

"All our histories say it is."

"Your historians labeled us barbarians, remember? Think, Eliana. If Kharan-Khuag caused the cataclysm, how did any of my ancestors survive?"

Her jaw went slack. She'd never considered that.

"Kharan-Khuag didn't cause the cataclysm," he continued. "My ancestors did, using a complex magical spell. When they saw the fight against Kharan-Khuag was hopeless, the tagavoi and tagavli—who you would call king and queen—unleashed the spell, causing a massive earthquake."

Adakizh pointed up. "The riverbed collapsed and fell through the ground to land hundreds of feet below. A massive cave formed around the river. The tunnels took shape, following underground streams and channels." He took a breath. "The water fae, of course, dove into the water and rode out the earthquake. Some perished, crushed to death by rock and soil, but most survived by seeking the deepest waters."

"What about the humans?"

"Those with any powers used them. To move the stone, to cushion their falls, to send the waters away or draw them near."

"But many died?" She couldn't comprehend how much death and destruction had been unleashed that day.

He shook his head. "Many more would have perished without the magical protections of the spell."

Eliana rolled her head on her shoulders. Her neck ached from looking down at him. "And how does this help us now?" she asked.

"By causing the cataclysm, the spell broke any hold dark magic had on the realm."

She let out a slow breath. "That means if we used it, we'd break all the curses. Can we?"

"The incantation requires the use of four powers at once: light, air, water, and stone."

"We have those four." Her heart skipped a beat. His words gave her a glimmer of hope, like a single firefly in a forest.

"We do."

"Do you know the spell?"

"Yes."

"Merciful winds, why didn't you tell me this before?"

"I didn't think you were powerful enough to even consider it." He cut off her protest with a wave of his hand. "I'm not certain I'm powerful enough. Our traditions say that if you try the spell and don't have enough power to wield it properly, it will kill you. But you've convinced me we should try. Think the unthinkable, as you say."

A weight lifted from Eliana's shoulders and her breathing

grew less labored. Finally, she had an ally and was no longer blundering alone in the dark. "If we do break all the curses and survive, won't Kharan-Khuag come after us anyway?"

"Probably. But in breaking the spells, he loses the power behind them."

"Even weakened, we still might not be able to fight him off."

"We might not have to do that right away." When she stared at him with a puzzled frown, he continued. "Kharan-Khuag knows we haven't broken the original curse."

"Yes."

"In about a day, he'll come here to claim my kingdom and conquer yours."

"And?"

"But he won't if he thinks both kingdoms are destroyed."

"What are you talking about?"

"Don't you see? The original cataclysm was a trick devised by my ancestors. They made it appear that everyone had died. It took Kharan-Khuag nine hundred years to learn the truth."

"Your realm is already underground."

"We collapse yours. The whole surface will turn into desert."

"Oh, no. I can't do that to Ymittos."

"How else will we stop Kharan-Khuag? Or at least slow him down?"

Adakizh was right. Sinking Ymittos under the earth, destroying the olive groves and sunny villages, the vineyards and meadows, the schools and stadiums, was unthinkable, but it was the only way to save her people from conquest and slavery. "Even if we survive the cataclysm, how will we go on?"

"The same way my people did for centuries. We only use our magic to hide traces of our survival. We adapt."

"Will your people help mine?"

"Will yours help mine?"

Would the Ymittosians aid those they disdained as barbarians? "I suppose they would, if they suddenly plunged into this dark realm and realized they needed to cooperate to survive. They're not going to like it."

"I can imagine. But they'd like being overrun by Kharan-Khuag less."

"Won't the people turn on us once they know what we've done?"

He shrugged. "They might. I wouldn't blame them."

"Maybe they'll be too busy trying to rebuild. That will give us time to explain. And help them."

His laugh echoed around the chasm. "Oh Eliana, ever the optimist. But the people aren't my biggest concern."

"You mean Kharan-Khuag?" She nibbled her lower lip. "Will he fall for the same trick twice?"

"That's what worries me. It depends on whether he thinks we—you and I—are powerful enough to work the spell. And my family worked hard to hide any records of it. I'm hoping Kharan-Khuag believes we lost the knowledge centuries ago."

"Before he figures out what we're up to, we might have enough time to build our defenses and send word to the other kingdoms."

"We might."

Something in his tone bothered her. "What else is worrying you?" she asked.

"The old stories never said whether my ancestors who created the cataclysm survived. Using that much magic may have killed them."

The blood pounded in her ears as she considered his words. "Meaning, if we try the spell, we might never know if it worked because we ended up dead."

He smiled, his white teeth gleaming in the darkness. "I have to say, it's a joy working with you. You understand so quickly. I don't have to explain everything."

Heat bloomed in her cheeks, making her grateful for the

dim light that obscured the signs of her delight in his praise. "You speak clearly, so lengthy explanations aren't necessary."

"Such a shame." He said this quietly, as if to himself.

"What is?"

"That as soon as I find you, I have to kill you or lead you to your death."

Did that mean he felt an attraction to her? Or was it just the curse, making him desire her company long enough for him to kill her?

Eliana's throat tightened. She didn't want to know the answer to that question. "Why are you so sure we'll die?"

"Because only the most powerful mages can wield the spell. We'll probably burn ourselves out in the attempt. If only…"

His pessimism spread through her, dragging her spirits to her feet. "What?"

"If only we had amplifiers. That might make all the difference."

She jerked her head up. "Why didn't you say so? I have some."

"You do?"

"Yes, I brought them with me."

"Does Istvan know?"

"No one knows. Except Alessia."

"Who?"

"My maid." Her stomach knotted to think of Alessia all alone. "She helped me escape Istvan. I don't know what he's done to her."

"Once Istvan's dead, I'll help you find her and free her, if need be."

"Thank you." Heart racing, she pulled out her bag. "I have salt."

"Excellent. That will make your air flow faster. We'll need that."

"Right. Here's pepper."

"Not sure what we can do with it. We don't want to boil or scorch people to death."

"Certainly not." Eliana shoved the spice back into her bag and held up a tiny vial. "What about citrus? I have lemon juice. You can use it to pull the water."

"Right you are. What else do you have?"

"Berries. They would help you push the stone away."

"Yes. Do you have wine?"

"Why? Do you feel the need to purge your stomach?" *I do.*

He laughed. "No. But it intensifies your air into gusts. That could be useful. Added to the salt for speed, that's exactly what we need."

She nodded. "What about dates?"

"Hmm. I don't see a use for them. Do you have beer?"

"Yes, but how would it help us now?"

"It wouldn't, but we could at least have a toast before we go to our deaths."

They laughed and tears pricked Eliana's eyes. Adakizh was such good company. Such a shame they would never be able to explore their growing attraction to find out if it was real.

"The only amplifier left is bitter herbs," Adakizh said, his tone now pensive.

"I have quite a few. They'll help you fix the stones once they fall."

"They will. And aid the healers, after."

"Then you take them."

"Not all of them. You can infuse some into your air magic to drug people if they are in pain."

"Or if they want to attack us."

"Oh, good point. Which herbs do you have?"

She sniffed the tiny packets. "Artemisia, elecampane, marrubium, angelica, chamomile, and rue."

"Don't give me the chamomile. It gives me a rash."

Eliana chuckled while he counted on his fingers. When he

looked up, he wore a puzzled frown. "What do the herbs do for light magic?"

"I don't know. Everything I've read says no one has ever used herbs to amplify it."

He absently pulled at his hair. "Where have I heard that before?"

Shouts in the distance made her glance from him to the crack leading to the tunnel. She leaned over the edge. "That's Istvan's voice."

"Are you ready?"

Her stomach turned over. "I don't know."

"Don't worry. I think I can channel the desire to kill you into ending him."

Eliana rubbed her forehead. It felt so wrong to calmly discuss Istvan's demise. But she didn't see any other way forward.

Think the unthinkable and kill your betrothed.

She squared her shoulders. "Then let's get on with it. Before you change your mind and try to kill me first."

37

Adakizh's laugh echoed through the dark shaft. "You forget, I'm trapped in this hole."

Peeking over the edge, Eliana smirked. "You underestimate me." She readied her air magic. "When I tell you, jump." With a wave of her hand, she sent a blast of air down the shaft. "Jump!"

When he leaped upwards, she gusted more air beneath him, lifting him to the ledge. He scrambled onto the rock. "That's a useful trick," he said. "Did your tutor teach you that?"

"No." Her breath caught at the memory. "A friend." She gestured to the steps he had cut earlier. "Go."

"One compliment, and she gets bossy. I'll have to watch what I say." She snatched a glimpse of his grin as he lowered himself over the edge. A moment later, she heard the thump of his boots when he landed on the ground below.

"Stand back," Eliana told him. "Please." Using a puff of air magic, she dropped lightly to land beside him. "Now, if you would be so kind as to hold out your hands," she continued, a hint of teasing in her tone.

"What? Oh, right." He held them out, wrists together.

Eliana scrunched up her face, concentrating. *All I have to do is compress the air.* She extended her hand and waved it in a small circle, willing the air to create cords.

Adakizh grimaced. "A little looser, if you don't mind. I just need my hands bound, not severed from my wrists."

"Oh. Sorry." Eliana winced and released the magic slightly. Then she added a tendril of light. Adakizh raised his hands to study his shackled hands. She grinned. "The light is so Istvan will see the bonds clearly," she said. "And assume I want you dead."

He raised his eyebrows. "Do you?"

"No. I told you that."

"Just checking to make sure you haven't changed your mind."

"Silly." The echoing shouts of Istvan's men in the caverns had faded. "Let's go before we lose them," she said.

"I'm in your hands, princess." He winked.

She nudged him in the back. "After you."

Using his magic, he heated the stone wall. Cracks spread over its surface. With a crash, the wall fractured and collapsed, and a cloud of fine dust rose from the shattered fragments of rock.

"Sorry about that," Adakizh said.

She coughed and waved a hand to clear the air. "It's fine." She picked her way over the rubble into the main tunnel.

Adakizh joined her. "Are you sure you're ready?" After she nodded, he turned right and walked in the direction of the shouting men, Eliana on his heels. "Just don't let your betrothed murder me." Adakizh's tone grew wistful. "Although, if he does, I suppose that's better than me killing you."

Or not. Then Eliana would be stuck with Istvan because she didn't believe she'd be able to kill him. As deceptive and murderous as he was, slaying him in cold blood was more than she could stomach. She stretched her backbone until it was ramrod straight. For poisoning her parents, Istvan deserved to die, but that thought didn't remove the taste of curdled milk from her mouth. She wasn't prepared for this aspect of ruling —making judgments and sentencing people to death. No escaping it, though. It was her duty. Her personal feelings were of no account.

Eliana and Adakizh followed the tunnel beside the narrow river. A blue-scaled fish leaped from the water and fell back with a splash. "This branch flows into the Qvirila River rather close to the sea," Adakizh said. "And that, I'm afraid, is where our enemy will invade."

Not wanting to think about Kharan-Khuag and his army of monsters, Eliana turned her thoughts to Istvan. If the dochan attacked the tagavlon, that would give her another reason to kill him. Still, she hoped Adakizh would be the one to strike the killing blow.

The tunnel broadened, and she took a few quick steps to walk next to Adakizh, near enough to rub shoulders with him.

"You might not want to walk so close," he said.

"Why not?"

"What if I shoved you into a pit?"

"You wouldn't."

"I might not be able to stop myself."

She nudged him with her elbow. "Then you'd be free to make a play for Istvan."

"Ha. He'd never look at me. He has you."

"No, he doesn't have me. And never will."

"Not if I can help it."

Eliana smiled to herself in the darkness, warmed by his words, hoping he meant more than just freeing her from a bloodthirsty suitor. She was surprisingly comfortable in his company and grateful for the banter that distracted her from the confrontation ahead. Then there was the tingling that spread through her body at his touch. How did she feel about that?

They rounded a bend. Istvan and five of his soldiers stood near a waterfall illuminated by pale green mushrooms. Istvan's arm was extended under the flow, filling a waterskin. Alerted by his men, he jerked around to face Eliana and Adakizh. He dropped the waterskin and strode toward the princess. His warriors drew their swords, the echoes of scraping metal sounding like a brigade of ghostly warriors preparing for battle.

"Istvan!" Eliana attempted to put longing and happiness into her tone. She wasn't sure she succeeded.

He stalked nearer, his steps like a mountain lion approaching a baby goat. "Eliana! Where have you been?"

Not a trace of concern or relief mingled with the anger and irritation in his tone. Eliana tipped her chin up and looked him in the eye. "I was busy. Capturing the prince." She jerked her head at Adakizh, who was staring at the ceiling.

Why would he be doing that? She glanced up and spotted a massive stalactite a few paces in front of them, just over the empty spot between her and Istvan. She shuffled forward.

"What do you think you're doing with him?" Istvan stepped closer.

"I'm taking him back to his tower, of course. To finish breaking the curse." She took another step. *Come on, Istvan. One more step.*

Drawing his sword, Istvan pointed it at Adakizh. "I think it's too late for that. All I can do is kill him."

"Is that really necessary? Why does he have to die?"

Eliana knew she was talking nonsense, but she had to keep Istvan's attention. She wondered how much control Adakizh would have over his magic with his hands tied, or if she'd have to free him first.

"He dies so we can rule his kingdom."

"Why would we want to do that?" Eliana snorted. "I don't know about you, but I can't wait to get out of this damp, nasty place."

"Is that your opinion of it?" Adakizh asked. "I think my realm has been insulted."

"Quiet, you." One of Istvan's men held his sword to Adakizh's throat.

"You don't need to do that," Eliana said. "My magic has him bound."

Istvan waved for his guard to back away. "To answer your question," he said, "of course, we want to rule Malkh, or Chorokha, whatever they call it."

"But we have no right to it."

"Of course we do. We have the best right of all. The right of conquest. How do you think your family came to rule Ymittos? They defeated my ancestors through treachery and pushed them over the mountains, allowing them to govern territory barely large enough to call a dochandom."

"That was a long time ago—"

"The spoils go to the cleverest in conquest. To the person best suited to rule a united kingdom, to unify the riches and culture of Ymittos, the military brilliance and resources of Nafplio, and the wealth of Chorokha." He looked down at her. "And that would be me."

"Wealth of Chorokha?" Eliana shook her head. "How can people who survive by stealing cattle and beer be wealthy? All they have are mushrooms."

Istvan laughed. "There's silver in these tunnels. Haven't you seen it? And precious gems. Not just the lesser ones, like turquoise, agate, or onyx. Every tunnel is crammed with emeralds, lapis lazuli, and amethyst. We might even find rubies. Don't you see? We could mine the gems easily, at much less expense than anywhere else. We'd be the richest kingdom on the continent. Perhaps even rival Cinar. Or Tinaxia."

So that was why the Chorokhese wore clothing embellished with gems. The stones were so plentiful they were of little value. Eliana glanced at Adakizh. He was still staring at the stalactite with a bored expression. She turned back to

Istvan, meeting his haughty gaze with one of her own. "We've moved on from the days of constant warfare. There are treaties in place. Cinar guarantees the peace in this part of the continent."

"Cinar? Bah. That empire is a sick old wretch, scarcely able to walk, ruled by a man more suited to be a playwright than a diplomat. The heir is a frivolous girl whose biggest accomplishment is playing pranks."

Eliana lowered her eyes. Derya had fooled him with her facade, but Eliana hoped that reputation hadn't spread throughout the empire. People other than Istvan might have drawn the same conclusion and be reluctant to support Derya when she inherited the throne.

"Don't place your hope in Cinar, Eliana," Istvan said. "This is the time for the wise to make their moves."

She swayed toward him, widening her eyes, adopting a guileless expression. "What moves do you mean?"

"Allying with the right power, of course. Cinar is weak. The kings in the west are fractured and can't agree on anything. Pasargadae is in decline, harassed by roving tribes from the south and east. And Tinaxia is so far away it is of no account."

His analysis, she had to admit, was mostly correct. "Yes, that's true enough. But what other power is there?"

As she spoke the words, her heart skipped a beat. He couldn't possibly mean what she feared he did.

Adakizh ceased his examination of the stalactites and leveled his attention on Istvan. "Good question. Who is this 'right power' you mention?"

"Quiet, fool. You are not a part of this conversation." Istvan spoke as if rebuking an impudent servant. He locked his eyes on Eliana's. "Listen to me with both your ears. There is one other power, far under the sea."

Eliana stared at him with wide, horrified eyes. "You don't mean…"

"Of course, I mean Cetus."

Rage boiled in her belly and her neck stiffened. Her lip curled into a sneer. "You would ally with him?"

"Why not? Who else is there?"

"The Rider of the Ancient Skies," said Adakizh.

Istvan threw his head back and laughed. "That myth?" His men joined in his guffaws, the taunting echoes of their mirth amplifying their derision.

"That myth," said Adakizh, "banished Cetus, as you call him, to an underwater realm in the far western sea."

"Bah. We all know history is written by those in power."

"If Cetus wasn't banished," Eliana asked, "why did he abandon this continent?"

"He doesn't confide in me," Istvan said. "But since he left Ardebil, he's taken over the western continent. I think he enjoys reigning there—a continent of great wealth that's free of petty monarchs constantly fighting among themselves."

"Then why come back here?" Eliana pressed. "If he's so wealthy, why bother us?"

"Cetus sees the unrest and injustice and wants to put an end to it. That he has persevered against all odds for a millennium is admirable."

While Eliana couldn't argue that the continent of Ardebil was often in turmoil, the idea of Cetus choosing the overlords made her stomach churn. Istvan's admiration of the sorcerer added to her unease. If Istvan thought Cetus would be a better ruler, the Saumarotas might feel the same way. Maybe that was why they didn't want the curse broken.

Istvan seemed oblivious to her silence. "Once Cetus establishes peace," he said, "he'll install wise rulers who will keep order. Sovereigns who will use the riches of the lands properly."

Eliana suspected Istvan's idea of using resources properly would mean nothing good for the peasants, fishers, and merchants. "Just to be clear," she said through gritted teeth,

"You've allied with Cetus so you can rule not only Chorokha, but Ymittos and Nafplio?"

"How else would I come to power?"

His matter-of-fact expression further enraged her. "Did you order your family killed?"

"What makes you think they're dead?"

"You as good as told me when you boasted you'd be ruling three kingdoms. But I heard through other means." Was it wise to tell him this? But she needed to distract him from whatever Adakizh was doing to the stalactites.

Istvan's eyebrows pulled together. "Such as?"

"The same way I learned you assassinated my parents. Your men talk, you know."

Even in the dim light, she could see the angry flush rise to his face.

"That spying maid of yours." He gestured to one of his men. "Fetch the wench."

Eliana pointed a finger at Istvan. "If you hurt her—"

"Oh, don't worry. She's mostly unharmed."

Unsure of his meaning, she pulled in a deep breath. "If you think I'll marry you and hand over my kingdom, you've miscalculated."

Faint scuffling noises in the tunnel grew louder and Istvan smirked. A guard appeared, leading a gagged Alessia, her hands tied in front of her.

With a hand pressed to her mouth, Eliana stared at Alessia. Red streaked the maid's cheek, a purple bruise ringed one eye. Dark stains on her tunic looked like dried blood. Her shoulders were hunched over her bound hands, and she pressed one arm to her side as she limped. Without her cloak, she shivered in the dank cold.

Istvan waved a hand at Alessia. "She wouldn't tell us where you'd gone. Pity." He grabbed the maid's hands and held them up. One was wrapped in a filthy bandage. "Not even when we cut off a finger."

Fury pulsed in Eliana's veins. She took a step toward Istvan and glared. "Release her. Now."

He stepped back. "Oh, no. Not so fast. I'll give her to you for a wedding present. After we have consummated our marriage. And only if I'm pleased."

Ice chased heat through Eliana's body. Had Cetus promised her to Istvan? And would the sorcerer hand her over before or after he fulfilled his own personal plans for her? A shudder convulsed her. *No.* The princess infused her backbone with steel. She would not give herself to Istvan or allow Cetus to have her. Either way, her people would serve under a merciless tyrant. Let alone the agony her own life would become. This was one sacrifice she refused to make.

Alessia shook her head.

"No." Eliana stiffened her shaking knees and thrust her nose in the air. "I will not marry you."

"Then she dies." Istvan jerked his chin at his men. "You can have her. Kill her when you're done."

38

Rage surged through Eliana's veins, scorching her face and neck. She pulled on her magic, preparing to unleash it on Istvan, to choke the smirk from his lips and end him forever.

A stocky man with a pinched nose stepped forward and grabbed Alessia's arm. "I won first dibs." A heartbeat later, his eyes flared open, and he fell to his knees.

A sword protruded from his abdomen. Dimitris stood over him, his eyes fierce and his mouth in a snarl. He jerked the blade out and spun to the next man while blood gushed from the stocky man's gaping wound. He twitched and lay still.

Dimitris parried a blow, then swung. The tip of his sword scraped his opponent's tunic. With the return stroke, he sliced the man's calf. The man collapsed, shrieking.

"Dimitris! Behind you!" Eliana yelled. She pulled at her power and blasted the Nafplian readying to strike, a thin man with a receding chin that made him resemble a rat. He fell backward and lay still. A barrage of stones pummeled a fourth man. He retreated, hands covering his head. Dimitris slit the fallen man's throat.

Istvan's fifth man, a wiry, long-legged youth, flung a knife at Eliana. The blade scraped her cheek as the weapon flew by. She pulled at her magic, readying another puff of air. She dodged another knife and stumbled. Her hand scraped the rocky floor before she regained her footing. A knife clattered on the stone next to her foot. She clamped her jaw and released her power. The youth toppled to the ground, a knife gripped in his fingers. He rolled and staggered to his feet.

The rat-faced man charged toward her, followed by the youth. Eliana pushed another gust of wind. Adakizh added a storm of rocks. The Nafplians staggered and cowered, holding their arms over their heads.

Istvan let out a triumphant yell. She whirled as he thrust his rapier into Dimitris' side. Her guard crumpled to the ground and lay still.

Eliana screamed. Anguish stabbed at her chest. Her throat tightened and fiery wrath scalded her face.

Istvan kicked Dimitris in the jaw. "I wondered where this one had slunk off to. He should have died when I gave him the chance." He shook his head in mock disgust. "Oh, simple Eliana. Did you never wonder why he fell when we were climbing down here?"

Bile crept up the back of Eliana's throat. "You planned that?"

He raised his eyebrows, grinned, and nodded. Then he raked Eliana's body with his eyes. "Now, princess, let's finish the curse-breaking and have a wedding." He took a step toward Adakizh, his sword arm lifted, the metal blade shining green in the mushroom's light.

"You'll have to kill me first," Eliana said, stepping in front of Adakizh. With a thought, she released the air magic binding his hands, leaving the band of light in place. *Just so Istvan will think Adakizh was still bound.*

"Killing you only makes things easier for me," Istvan said with a sneer. "Your people will beg me to take over once they learn you sided with one of these savages."

"Princess Derya knows what you are. She'll avenge my death."

"You really are innocent, aren't you?" Istvan held his sword up vertically, letting the green light shimmer on its blade. "Sadly for the Princess of Cinar, she's on her way to Nafplio. Rumors have been flying about her. Some say her father would pay a huge ransom if she was kidnapped. Others murmur that she intends to annex Nafplio. Still others whisper that she killed the royal family of Ymittos. Or that the girl calling herself the Heir of Cinar is an agent of Cetus, or else an escaped slave. Whichever rumor my people believe, they won't let her live. No, you won't get any help from her."

Eliana's stomach clenched. He was lying. He had to be. *Rider help Derya if he's not.*

Hot blood throbbed in her ears. It was time to end Istvan. Then she'd deal with his remaining soldiers. She put a hand on Adakizh's arm and tugged him forward. His muscles tensed and a vein in his forehead pulsed a frantic rhythm. Which was only natural, Eliana thought, given that a fierce man with a sword was preparing to lop off his head.

Istvan was a step away from the spot directly below the stalactite. The tagavlon raised a hand. A loud crack like the splitting of marble cut through the cavern.

Adakizh grabbed the neck of Eliana's tunic and yanked her backward. An instant later, the stalactite fell and pinned Istvan to the floor.

When Istvan's three remaining soldiers yelled and ran toward Adakizh, Eliana didn't hesitate. She hurled a gust of air at them, knocking them to the ground. They lay gasping for breath, one moaning about his injured head.

Sprinting to the squirming Istvan, Adakizh seized the dochan's sword and handed it to Eliana.

"Go ahead, barbarian," Istvan gasped. "Kill me, for whatever good it will do you."

"Oh, I can think of a lot of good it will do."

Istvan sneered. "You think Cetus will accept defeat? Never."

"How would you know that?" Eliana asked.

"Wouldn't you like to know? A meddling little girl who involves herself in men's business. When you were born, your father should have left you on a mountain to die." He spat. "You'll never rule Ymittos. The best you can hope for is to live to serve me. Unless I tire of you. Then you'll be a slave in Cetus's household. Who knows, he might take a liking to you."

Eliana shuddered and gasped when, with a mighty heave, Istvan shoved the stalactite aside. He brushed the dust from his torn and bloody clothing and stood up.

Unable to comprehend what she was seeing, Eliana gaped. Why hadn't the falling rock fatally wounded him?

"What, surprised I'm not dead?" Istvan sneered at Adakizh. "You'll have to drop your rocks more accurately next time. A blind old hag could have done better." He extended a hand. "Now, give me my sword. I promise to kill you quickly."

"I don't think I want to do that." Adakizh lunged and snatched a sword from a dead Nafplian's hand.

"You sure you know how to use that?" Istvan scoffed. He glanced over his shoulder at his soldiers. "Are you three going to stand there all day? Give me a sword." Turning back to Adakizh, he smirked. "We can stand here until you succumb to the compulsion to kill Eliana. Then I'll finish you off. Or you can allow me to kill you. And I'll let her live."

Adakizh looked into Eliana's eyes. "I don't want you to die."

She readied her magic. "I'm not going to." She flashed light in Istvan's direction. The dochan and his men howled and covered their eyes. She followed up with a burst of air.

Two of Istvan's men toppled over. One flew into the stone wall near the celery green mushrooms and dropped to the ground with a thump, shrieking in pain.

The man held up the stump of his arm, the skin and bone

dissolving. Adakizh darted toward him and, with a swipe of his sword, severed the man's arm from the shoulder. He turned to Eliana. "Tie that up for him. And watch out for poison centipedes."

Eliana blinked. Poison centipedes lived near the pale green mushrooms. *As did—*

"Stinging worms!" Adakizh grabbed the man's tunic and pulled him away from the wall. The man writhed, his mouth frothing. "I'm sorry," the tagavlon said. "There's nothing else to do." He slit the man's throat, silencing his screams.

"Behind you!" Eliana shouted.

His weapon raised, Adakizh whirled to face the threat. Istvan lunged for him, swinging a sword he'd snatched from one of his soldiers.

Istvan's first slash cut Adakizh's sword arm. The tagavlon yelped and jumped sideways, parrying Istvan's next blow. Eliana held her breath, wondering if Adakizh could best Istvan. The two remaining Nafplians had risen to their feet again, clutching their weapons. Eliana bound their hands with air magic the same way she'd restrained Adakizh. To her surprise, neither of the soldiers seemed too interested in freeing themselves to help Istvan.

A cold hand touched hers. Alessia. With a quick motion, Eliana snatched the gag from her maid's mouth. "Thank you," Alessia said.

"I never should have left you." Eliana tugged at the bonds on Alessia's hands while keeping Adakizh and Istvan in her sights.

The two exchanged blows, sweat dripping from their faces. Istvan swung at Adakizh. The tagavlon dodged, but not enough. Blood seeped through the sleeve of his tunic where Istvan had sliced the muscle of his upper arm.

The fight couldn't go on. Eliana knew she had to stop it. Her hands tingled and the pressure of the power grew within her as she waited for the perfect moment. The dochan and the tagavlon circled each other, trading blows. Adakizh dropped another stalactite, crashing it next to where Istvan had been a heartbeat earlier.

"Think you're clever?" Istvan snarled. "How about this?" He darted back a few paces. With a wave of his hand, he caused Adakizh's sword to bend and twist.

The tagavlon stared at his ruined blade. Eliana reeled back a step. She'd never known Istvan had metal magic.

The princess sucked in a breath. She still held Istvan's first sword, but he could easily ruin it like the Adakizh's. There was only one thing she could do to keep the tagavlon from being slaughtered.

Istvan threw his head back and laughed. Then he charged.

Adakizh hurled the crooked sword at Istvan. With a sweep of his weapon, Istvan batted it away and sneered. "Giving up, are you?"

Seizing the moment, Eliana flashed her light into Istvan's eyes. He yelled and stumbled, eyes screwed shut.

With a grunt and a wave of his hand, Adakizh raised the fallen stalactite. He plunged it into Istvan's chest. The dochan collapsed to his knees and dropped his sword. Adakizh grabbed the blade and swung for Istvan's neck.

The dochan lurched to the side, causing the blow to miss its mark. Instead, it severed Istvan's right arm above his elbow. A geyser of blood surged from the wound.

Istvan roared a curse and grabbed the bloody stump. "Fools. Such sss…" His words trailed off, and he toppled over.

With a fierce final blow, Adakizh lopped off the dead man's head. "Just to be sure."

Eliana snatched the sword from Adakizh's hand. "Just to be sure."

He grinned.

The princess stared at the lifeless Istvan. She'd been infatuated with him, flattered by his attention. To her shame, she'd even believed she loved him, or was well on the way to it.

What had turned him into such a cruel and selfish man? And how could she have been so blind?

"I'm sorry, Eliana." Adakizh's tone was insistent. "But we have things to do."

Adakizh was right. Sorting out her feelings about Istvan and his death could wait. She sped to Dimitris, who lay crumpled in a puddle of blood mixed with water on the stone floor. She knelt by him and slid her hand into his clammy fingers. "Oh, Dimitris."

His eyes fluttered open. "Highness."

"You're alive." She choked on the words.

"Not for long." He took a shuddering breath. "I couldn't find you."

"I know. It's alright. You saved Alessia." She glanced over her shoulder. Adakizh was studying the bloody stump of Alessia's left forefinger.

"Couldn't save you…" Dimitris squeezed Eliana's hand.

"You served me well." She ran a hand over his tunic. So much blood. Would Adakizh be able to use his water magic to heal even these wounds?

Dimitris coughed. Blood gushed from his mouth and he went still. His lifeless eyes stared up at the cavern's murky ceiling.

Eliana sobbed and dropped her chin to her chest. *Dimitris. I should have looked after you better.*

A small hand gripped her shoulder. "We searched for you," Alessia said. "But you were nowhere to be found. We thought the Saumarotas had captured you."

"They tried," Eliana said. Creaking leathers made her stand and turn. Istvan's two remaining soldiers were slowly approaching.

Adakizh stood with arms crossed, staring at them. "Don't try anything," he said. "There are plenty more stalactites just waiting to become spears."

The men exchanged furtive glances. The rat-faced one

with gray strands in his hair held up his bound hands. "Whatever you say, Your Highness."

Eliana rose to her feet. "I didn't want to kill Istvan. He—"

"Why not?" The wiry youth's voice held a note of surprise.

"What?" Adakizh glanced from the soldiers to Eliana.

They shrank back. "You're not working for Cetus, too, are you?" the older one asked.

"No." Adakizh nudged Eliana and raised an eyebrow. She crossed her arms and studied the Nafplians' faces. They were bruised and grimy, with several days' growth of beard and wide, staring eyes.

"We're not allied with Cetus. We want to destroy him," she said.

The rat-faced man rubbed a trickle of sweat from his face with his forearm. "Well, that's a relief." He curled his lip at Istvan's corpse. "In exchange for killing both of you, Cetus was going to give the dochan your kingdoms."

With the intensity of the skirmish behind her, fatigue crept through Eliana's body. And worse. She swayed on her feet. How could she have not seen through Istvan's deceit sooner? Derya and Alessia had known from the start something was wrong with him. They'd warned her, and she hadn't listened, the only idiot among them. Her breath came faster as her anger grew. "Then Istvan was a fool. Cetus would have installed him as a puppet ruler at best."

"Who else is working with Kharan-Khuag?" Adakizh asked. When the man gave him a puzzled look, the tagavlon added, "Cetus, you call him."

The rat-faced Nafplian nodded. "From what I overheard, the Saumarotas. They didn't want the curse broken because Cetus promised they would govern this kingdom once he conquered it."

"Cetus made a lot of promises, it seems." Eliana gave the soldiers a pointed stare. "And where do you stand?"

Two frowning faces looked into hers. They glanced at each other. The older man shrugged. "I honestly don't know," he said. "You killed my dochan, and for that, I should kill you. But he turned traitor, and you stand against the biggest evil our world knows. I suppose that puts us with you."

"That's good enough for me," Adakizh said. "We plan to break the curse before Kharan-Khuag makes his move."

As if on cue, the earth trembled. The water in the river churned and flowed backward.

"I think you're too late for that," the Nafplian said. "He has already attacked."

39

———

The waves on the river thrashed as if they had been scourged with a whip. Eliana stared at the rising water, her feet frozen in place. *No. It can't be. We can't be too late.*

Adakizh tugged her hand. "We must get to higher ground."

Eliana shook off her growing panic. "Warn everyone you see," Eliana said to the Nafplians. "Tell them to climb high and to find places to hide—alcoves, niches, wherever. Alessia, go with them. Find Shirdona and stay close to her. Warn everyone to have their magic ready to use when they need it."

"But not until they have to," Adakizh added.

"What are you waiting for? Go!" Eliana barked at the Nafplians.

"Yes, highness." After shooting a startled and confused glance at the princess, Alessia dashed after the two men, who were sprinting upstream.

Blinking the tears from her eyes, Eliana stumbled to Dimitris's lifeless form. "I don't want to leave him," she said.

"You don't have to." Adakizh scooped up Dimitris's corpse

and hoisted it over his shoulder. "Come on." Without waiting to see if she followed, he hastened upstream.

"Where are we going?" Eliana asked.

"Somewhere further from the sea." His breath came in gasps. "Away from Kharan-Khuag. To give us time."

They ascended until they arrived at an outcropping. Adakizh pointed at the rock, feeding it with his power. The stone steamed where the outthrust part met the wall. A crack formed, and the rock shattered.

He gave Eliana an apologetic look. "I'm sorry, it's the best I can do." He laid Dimitris' body on the ground. With a wave of his hands, he covered the corpse with a pile of broken rocks. "At least nothing will bother him."

"Thank you." Eliana stooped and picked up a few pebbles. After shaking them in her hand, she scattered them over the cairn. "May the Rider take you home to the ancient skies." She stood motionless for a few moments, staring at the mound of stones. A pair of tears trickled down her face. After letting out a long sigh, she stirred. "Now what?"

"We find a place to work our magic." Adakizh pointed at an ornate staircase carved into the rock. "Let's try up that way."

Eliana followed him up the steps. As she ran, she noted a repeated pattern of fish jumping over goats climbing up the banister along the side wall. Some of the animals' eyes were gemstones and glinted in the dusky light. Eliana ran her fingers over the carving as she climbed. "Who made this?"

"My grandfather's grandfather, or something like that. Does it matter? Run!"

She scurried up the steps after him, grateful she didn't have to scale a wall. Adakizh slowed as they neared the top. Just as Eliana opened her mouth to ask why, she heard shouts and clangs. "No! They can't already be here," she cried.

"If they are, it might not be all bad." Adakizh's lips twisted in a wry smile. "I'm feeling the compulsion to kill you again.

Maybe a little swordplay with someone else will burn it out of me for a while." He drew his sword. "Princess, are you ready?"

Eliana nodded. They burst into a large, shadowy chamber filled with fighting figures.

Some of them were Chorokhese, tall men swinging swords. Eliana recognized some of them as Shirdona's relatives, along with the two Nafplians.

But the others? Something with a slug's gray body and tiger's legs scurried back and forth between the combatants. Its head looked like a domed helmet and long spikes protruded from its face between its eyes and nose.

"A tsovul." Adakizh drew his sword. "The spikes carry stinging poison."

One of Istvan's men, the wiry youth, swung a sword down on the creature's head. The blade bounced off the bony skull.

"No!" Adakizh yelled. "That's a good way to make it mad and break your sword. Go for the throat."

His warning came too late. The tsovul seized the man's sword in its curved claw and snapped the metal. With a sweep of its arm, it knocked the unarmed Nafplian to the ground.

An octopus slithered over, blue rings glowing on its slimy black skin. It brushed a tentacle over the downed man's face. The man shrieked, his wails echoing throughout the cavern. He writhed on the ground, his agonized cries intensifying until they broke off in a choking gurgle. Then he went still.

Adakizh gripped Eliana's arm. "See the blue rings on the octopus? Just a drop of its poison means a painful death." His voice was strained. "Whatever you do, don't let it touch you."

Shouts from the center of the chamber tore Eliana's horrified stare away from the dying man. Was that Shirdona brandishing a long whip? But what was she fighting?

Along with five of the tsovuls, the woman and seven of her warriors were battling a pair of men with shark's heads. *Karcharia.* Shirdona had described them to Eliana once.

Circling the clump of fighters were six or seven beings with the elongated limbs of the fae. But these were no ordinary water fae. They looked like mutants from a feverish nightmare. Beady lidless eyes bulged in angry glares from fishlike heads. Two long tentacles sprang from their shoulders, waving hooked ends at Shirdona and her allies.

One of Shirdona's warriors stabbed the nearest karcharia. It whirled and seized him around the middle, its jaws wide in a soundless howl. As the man struggled to free himself from the monster's grasp, it dragged him toward the river. Several of Shirdona's men hacked at the monster's sides. Gray blood oozed out of the wounds, emitting a putrid stench. The karcharia grabbed a second man and dove into the river, taking its two captives with it into the depths. Eliana's heart thudded in her chest. Horror made her stomach churn, sending the bile surging up her throat as if it, too, wanted to flee.

A howl from Shirdona yanked Eliana's attention from the terrifying scene to the tavkatseen. Shirdona was holding her own. She'd beheaded the other karcharia and three of the mutant fae. Adakizh had already sprung into the melee, battling with the tsovuls. With smooth swings of his sword, he severed tentacles and legs from the bodies of their owners. When he'd wounded the nearest five to the point they couldn't move, he drove the sword into their eye sockets, one at a time.

Eliana reached for her own sword. Her fingers found the scabbard, but the weapon was gone. Her breath hitched. Somewhere in all the running through the tunnels, she'd lost her weapon. And what had she done with the one Adakizh had handed her? It didn't matter. In a close battle like this, she'd be just as likely to harm one of her allies as the monsters.

She stooped and yanked the dagger Derya had given her from her boot. She jumped upright when she heard Alessia scream. A mutant fae wrapped a tentacle around Alessia's waist.

Raising her dagger, Eliana steeled herself. She'd lost Dimitris. She couldn't—wouldn't—lose her maid.

Alessia shrieked and hacked at the tentacle with her knife. The blade bounced off the scaly flesh. The water fae hissed, grabbed her arm, and twisted. Alessia dropped the weapon and it clattered on the stone floor.

Adakizh bounded to her. He sliced through a tentacle. "Go for the place it joins the body," he shouted. The tagavlon leaped backwards as the mutant fae lurched forward, its mouth wide open.

The fae snapped its jaws shut on Adakizh's shoulder of his sword arm. The tagavlon yelped and dropped his sword. He punched the fae in the throat. It shook its head but didn't let go.

Eliana darted around them, gritting her teeth. Adakizh was writhing and twisting, his fingers clawing at the fae's eyes. The princess waiting until the fae's back was to her. Then she bolted forward and stabbed the monster at the root of the tentacle holding Alessia. Gray blood spurted into her face.

Released from its grasp, Alessia fell to the ground. Nearly blind from the blood dripping down her face, Eliana thrust her dagger forward, deep into the fae's throat. It jerked its head back and collapsed.

Adakizh toppled to the ground, pulled down by the fae's teeth imbedded in his shoulder. Panting, Eliana dropped to her knees and yanked the fae's jaws open.

Adakizh moaned. "Thank you. Is Alessia—"

Eliana scrambled to Alessia's side. She wrapped her arms around the shuddering girl. "I'm so sorry."

Alessia sobbed. "It's not your fault. This is all Istvan's fault."

Adakizh clambered to his feet. A red spreading stain soaked the shoulder of his tunic.

"You're hurt!" Eliana cried.

Without answering, Adakizh retrieved his sword and scooped up one that had belonged to the Nafplian. The tagavlon handed it to Eliana. "This'll be more useful than that dagger."

"What—" The words stuck in Eliana's throat. The blue-ringed octopus slithered toward them. Two tentacles reached forward, then contracted, dragging the bulbous head forward, the other six tentacles trailing behind.

"Don't let it touch you. Use the sword to keep it at bay." Adakizh advanced on the creature, his blade extended.

Eliana's eyes flared wide. The thing was creeping nearer, her doom approaching inexorably on eight legs. She sheathed her dagger, knowing the sword was her best hope. *How can Adakizh fight with that wounded shoulder?*

Adakizh darted around the octopus. When he stabbed a tentacle, it snapped toward his face. The tagavlon leaped backward and tripped over a tsovul. He stumbled and fell. The tsovul lunged for Adakizh's face, its spiked claws aiming for his eyes.

40

———

"No!" Eliana screamed. She darted to Adakizh, running in an arc to give the octopus a wide berth. The creature's tentacles lashed in her direction but fell short.

It swiveled its head and turned, pulsing its way toward Adakizh.

Pinned under the tsovul, the tagavlon grasped its throat, holding it as far from his face as he could. The beast's facial spikes scourged Adakizh's forearms. Blood ran down his arms and splattered into his eyes.

Eliana dropped the sword and retrieved her dagger. She darted close and stabbed the tsovul in the eye. With a screech, it retracted its lashing tentacles.

Adakizh seized the tsovul's head and hurled the beast at the octopus. It landed with a thud. The octopus wrapped two tentacles around the tsovul and the creature stopped moving.

Adakizh staggered to his feet. "Where's my sword?"

"I don't know." Eliana picked up the one she'd dropped and handed it to him before glancing at Shirdona. The woman and her followers had downed all the monsters except one of the fae and two eight-legged terrors. With a crack of her whip, Shirdona beheaded one octopus.

"So, that's how you do it," Adakizh said. He shoved Eliana behind him just as the second octopus swung a tentacle at her. Adakizh lopped it off.

Blue blood squirted like a geyser, creating a deadly rainfall. "Stay back!" the tagavlon said as he advanced on the octopus. It opened its maw, revealing a double row of pointed teeth. It hissed and snapped its mouth open and shut. Then it launched itself into the air at Adakizh.

"No!" Eliana's shriek echoed through the chamber. Adakizh stood motionless, as if he wasn't going to defend himself against the octopus' thrashing tentacles and razor-sharp teeth.

Dread constricted Eliana's throat. She tried to scream again but couldn't find the breath.

Just as the octopus was about to descend, Adakizh hurled his sword like a javelin into the creature's open mouth. He dove to the side, rolling on through puddles of gray and blue blood when he fell. The writhing octopus smashed into the ground where Adakizh stood a heartbeat before. Its tentacles waved in the air, then fell, limp as parchment drenched in rain.

Eliana ran to the tagavlon. "Adakizh?"

He groaned. "That hurt." With a wince, he sat up, clutching his wounded shoulder.

She turned her head when Shirdona and her warriors gave a triumphant shout. A woman nearly as tall as Shirdona extracted her sword from the eye of the last tsovul. The rest of Shirdona's band surrounded the surviving octopus. "Um, it's not over yet." She held out a hand.

Adakizh took it and she helped him stand. He grunted and flexed his wounded arm. "Would you mind?" He gestured to his sword protruding from the gullet of the dead octopus.

Holding her breath against the foul stench, she retrieved

the blade and handed it to him. He pointed to the swords on the ground, the blades of the dead. "You and Alessia need weapons."

Darting to a pair of swords lying on the rock floor, Eliana snatched them up and pressed the hilt of one into Alessia's shaking hand.

A muffled thump behind her made Eliana turn. Adakizh had sunk to his knees. His eyes were shut. Even in the blue light, she could see his normally olive complexion had turned pale.

"What's wrong?" she asked.

"That cursed tsovul stung me." He held up his arms. Through the tattered sleeves and spatters of gray and blue blood, purplish-black welts crisscrossed his skin. "Find some blue mushrooms."

Eliana sprinted to the nearest wall and scraped four mushrooms off the rock. At the prince's direction, she cut the fungi into halves and laid the pieces on the welts.

Adakizh let out a long sigh. "That takes away the sting. But the poison is still there. My hands are going numb."

"Can't you use your water magic?" she asked.

He clenched his jaw. "Water mages can only heal others, not themselves." Sweat beaded on his forehead. He took a shuddering breath and screwed his eyes shut, his head drooping over his knees.

The princess sped to Shirdona, who, along with her surviving men, was gathering the bodies of her dead.

The woman glared at Eliana as she approached. "It's about time you showed up." Shirdona's voice was hoarse, as if she'd been shouting for hours.

Eliana glanced over her shoulder at Adakizh. "I've been busy." She jerked her chin at the wounded tagavlon. "He could use a healer, if it's not too much trouble. One of those tsovuls stung him. And a fae bit his shoulder."

Shirdona let out a huff. "I'll do it myself." She went to

Adakizh and squatted next to him. "Got a bit too close, did you?" She shook her head. "If you're going to tangle with monsters, you need to be smarter about it." After breathing deeply a few times, she held a hand over Adakizh's wounded arms. The black faded from the purple marks, with red appearing against the darkness like a sunrise. The slash Istvan cut into his arm knit together, leaving a thin pink line.

"Where's the bite?" Shirdona asked.

Adakizh shifted his tunic to expose the eight punctures, the skin around them a sickly gray. Shirdona tsked and waved a hand. The gray faded to olive.

Adakizh straightened his back, rolled his shoulders, and offered Shirdona a feeble smile. "Thank you."

"Well." Shirdona leveled her eyes on Eliana. "I don't know what you've been up to, my sunshine, but it wasn't curse breaking." Her tone dripped with exasperation. "The Saumarotas have taken advantage of that. While you were taking a stroll along the river, they allied with Kharan-Khuag."

"We know." Adakizh stretched his arms above his head, grimacing. "Where else did Kharan-Khuag attack?"

"Who are you, anyway?" Shirdona asked.

"Really?" Eliana said. "You don't recognize your own tagavlon?"

Shirdona gave him a cool glance. "He wasn't so grimy the last time I saw him. Not so much blood on his face."

"Tagavlon Adakizh to you," he said. "And you are?"

"Shirdona, Tavkatseen of the Kambadas." She raised an eyebrow. "The one who's mounted the best defense against Kharan-Khuag, I'll thank you to remember."

"I'm grateful for your efforts." The tagavlon placed a hand on his heart and inclined his head. "What do you think our chances are?"

"Against Kharan-Khuag?" Shirdona scoffed. "None. He's got armies of those things. This was only the beginning, his way of taunting us, of toying with us like a shark circles its prey. If he sends a larger force, we'll be begging him to rule over us just to be free of them."

Eliana and Adakizh stared at each other. Her core turned to ice at the thought of Kharan-Khuag looting her land, torturing and raping her people. Or anyone's land and people. He had to be stopped.

But the alternative? Adakizh wasn't sure how the spell worked. And even if they successfully cast it, the attempt would likely mean death for her and Adakizh.

If they failed, then what? Kharan-Khuag would conquer and enslave Ymittos and Chorokha. Cinar would be next. The emperor commanded large armies, but Eliana doubted they'd be enough to fight off Kharan-Khuag's monsters.

Eliana's optimism drained from her as she breathed out. A day ago, she would have been able to count on her parents. Now, she didn't know what else had gone wrong in the world above. Maybe Derya had already fallen prey to some scheme of Istvan, Kharan-Khuag, or an unknown enemy. There might be no one left to help them.

Each breath became an effort as Eliana's chest tightened. She pulled Adakizh to the side. "What do you think?"

"We seem to be out of choices."

"Except for—" She wasn't able to push the words past the lump in her throat.

He gazed into her eyes. "Lovely Eliana. I have not forgotten. But are you sure you want to sacrifice yourself?"

She wasn't. *But.* She wrapped her arms around herself. "I have to save my people." To stifle the tremor in her voice, she bit down hard on her lower lip. She'd made her choice and refused to waver or give in to fear.

"Even if we die?"

"We die together." She tipped her chin up. "It will be an honor."

"What a pair we are," Adakizh said. "You had to lure your

betrothed to his death. I'm attracted to a girl I am compelled to kill. And now, I'm doomed to join her in death."

"Cheery thoughts," Shirdona said. "Why so gloomy? Just because the most evil sorcerer the world has ever known is preparing to invade and we have no means of repelling him?"

Eliana glared at her. "You were eavesdropping."

"I need to know what's happening, my sunshine. What's your plan?"

"We," Eliana said, "are going to conjure up some help." *At least we hope that's what we're doing.* "You need to prepare the people. As many as you can."

"Prepare for what? An invasion?"

"No," Adakizh said. "A cataclysm. Floods. Cave-ins. Earthquakes. Rain. Snow."

"Rain dripping from above, I understand. But how will it snow down here?" Shirdona asked.

"I don't know. I just threw that in to make my point." Adakizh winked at Eliana. "Anything can happen. Have everyone prepare their magic. But don't use it until we give the signal."

Shirdona narrowed her eyes. "Sounds like you two have something magical in mind. I hope you know what you're doing. Magical weapons have a way of getting out of control." She regarded Eliana and Adakizh for a few moments. "What's this signal I'm waiting for?"

Eliana wanted to know that, too.

"You'll know when you hear it," Adakizh said. He paused. A muscle twitched in his jaw. "Tavkatseen, the princess and I may not survive what we're about to do. If we don't, will you send word to Ymittos and Cinar and anyone else you can think of? Warn them of the coming invasion."

In all her time in Chorokha, Eliana had never seen Shirdona without a smirk or a smile, a glare or a glower. But now, the woman's face went blank. The tavkatseen bowed her head. "If I'm still breathing, I will."

"Thank you." Adakizh tipped his head to the side. "And now, Princess Eliana, are you ready to save the realm?"

Straightening her shoulders, Eliana met his gaze. *If we die, we die.* She swallowed hard, willing her answer to come out in a steady voice. "Yes."

41

———

Eliana stumbled as the earth shook, her feet sliding over the damp rock of the tunnel's uneven floor. The sound of gushing water filled the cavern, the echoes making it sound like hundreds of waterfalls dumping their torrents over lofty cliffs.

Shirdona spat out a curse. "That's how he started his invasion the last time. Earthquakes and flooding the land."

Eliana grabbed Adakizh's hand. "Then we need to go. Now."

They charged up a slope. Tiny rocks fell around them, and the roof of the passage creaked and groaned. A stalactite dropped from the ceiling and shattered a crystal formation shaped like a banqueting table for giants. The rock split in the middle, collapsing under its own weight.

It's going to cave in. We'll die in the rubble. Eliana's heart thumped hard in her throat. She choked on the dusty air.

As if he could sense her panic, Adakizh squeezed her hand. "We can do this," he said. "We must."

When the slope leveled, Eliana stopped him. "Adakizh, where should we perform the spell?"

There was a long pause before he answered. Rocks rasped

against each other, while stones rattled along the crystal walls as they tumbled from above. The roaring of the earthquake subsided, replaced by the whooshing of blood in Eliana's ears.

"I was thinking about that," Adakizh said. "Maybe the top of my tower?"

"Or at a sinkhole, like where Shirdona brings in the stolen cattle?"

"We need to find the right spot to make sure all of Ymittos sinks."

She rubbed her chin. "How did they do it before?"

He shook his head. "We only have old legends. They're long on flowery tales of drama and heroics, but a bit lacking in precise details."

"Then…" A horrifying thought overcame her. "Are you certain you have the correct spell?"

"I am. My family handed it down, from father to son, mother to daughter. We all had to recite it four times a day. Every day. I'm sure I have it right."

Looking into his eyes, she searched for any trace of doubt.

He met her gaze without flinching. "Eliana, that incantation is all we have. If it doesn't work, will it matter to us?"

She dropped her gaze. If the spell failed, they'd be dead. "Not for long."

"No." Adakizh stood lost in thought, the only sounds dripping water and creaking rock. He let out a long breath. "The cursebreakers chose to stand under the widest part of the Qvirila River."

"I know the perfect place," Eliana said. "Underneath the Bisaltes River, where it widens in the central plain."

His teeth gleamed like pale-blue pearls when he smiled. "You're brilliant. That river drains most of your land. If we pull on the Bisaltes, we can channel its water to the Qvirila."

"Do you know the way?"

"Up there." He pointed to a sloping side tunnel illuminated with blue mushrooms. "It will take us only an hour or so."

"We're that close? That's three day's journey from where we climbed down."

He chuckled. "On the surface, yes. But all this chasing each other in the tunnels has brought us far from the rift. Let's go, shall we?" He strode into the darkness, but Eliana didn't follow.

Adakizh turned and retraced his steps. "What's wrong?"

She didn't want to utter the words. That she still had hidden doubts. That she feared she was making an impulsive decision she'd regret. She'd trusted Istvan, and he betrayed her. Was she about to repeat her mistake?

"Are you worried that I'll get you alone and kill you? Or force you to use your magic so much that you become paralyzed, so I can have my way with you and then murder you?" The corners of his mouth drooped. "I thought we were beyond all that. If we're going to break the enchantment, you'll need to trust me. Will you?"

Eliana had no reason to trust him other than the way he'd resisted the curse that compelled him to slay her. And he seemed sincere in wanting to save both their peoples. She nodded.

"Thank you. I'm relieved to hear that." He rubbed his eyes. "Besides, after getting stung by that tsovul, I'm too tired to kill anyone else."

They walked without speaking, the only sounds the trickling water, the occasional crash of a tumbling rock, and their echoing footsteps. From time to time, Adakizh muttered to himself. The only words she understood were, "Don't do it." Hopefully, he was convincing himself to refrain from killing her. They didn't need to waste time chasing each other in the darkness. Or tumbling over a precipice, getting eaten by a vishapion, or falling prey to a stinging worm. The more she thought of the obstacles in their path, the more hopeless she judged their situation.

To distract herself, she considered the young man striding in front of her. His steps were easy and athletic. Loose curls bounced on his broad shoulders. And those kind eyes. So very kind, with an underlying sadness. Eyes that understood pain and weakness. He treated her like an equal, a partner. No man since Evander had treated her that way. This barbarian tagavlon was far more noble than the cultured Istvan.

What an idiot she'd been with Istvan. No point whining over that now. She and Adakizh would die saving their kingdoms. *We will have thwarted Kharan-Khuag's evil schemes.* The problem of opposing him long term would fall to others.

She trotted after Adakizh, her breath growing ragged. Her legs ached and sweat stung her eyes. Just when she thought she couldn't take one more step, he stopped and stared at the rocky ceiling.

"Your Bisaltes River is up there."

Eliana struggled to speak through her panting breaths. "How do you know?"

"I've been running through these tunnels all my life."

All his life. "Adakizh. How long was your life?"

"It's not over yet, I hope."

"That's not what I mean."

"Are you wondering how old I am? Why is that important?"

"Well, it's not, I suppose." She rested a hand on the wall of the tunnel, her head spinning, her breathing labored and shallow.

"Why don't we sit?" Adakizh said. He lowered himself to a rock and pointed at another several feet away.

"Don't we have a spell to perform?"

"We do. But I'm feeling a bit winded. Maybe we should have a rest before we attempt it." He dug in a pouch tied to his belt. "Here." He held out a strip of dried meat.

Eliana tottered to the rock and sat, slumping against the wall. "But Kharan-Khuag—"

"Won't invade in the next ten minutes." He tossed the meat into her lap. "I'm not sure how to answer your question."

"You just did." She took a bite of the salty dried goat.

"No, about my age. How long was I asleep?"

"They tell me the hundred years were almost done."

"And you turned eighteen, what, ten days ago?"

"Eleven."

He chewed and swallowed. "That betrothed of yours looked a bit older."

She furrowed her brow. "My parents led me to believe he was only a few years older than me. But he was twenty-five."

"What did you think about a seven-year difference?"

"I would have preferred someone closer to my age." She crossed her arms. "Someone who wouldn't consider me a little girl." The insult still stung.

He studied her face. "Do you want to know how old I am, or how old I was when Kharan-Khuag put me in that cursed sleep?"

"The second."

"Three months shy of my twentieth birthday. Which makes me almost one hundred and twenty."

"Or maybe not. It's not like you lived all those years."

"I can't claim that many years of experience, true." He picked up a pebble and hurled it against the wall. "So here I am, an old man. But I've never had a wife, a child, or anything that should come with more than a century of living."

A new question bubbled in Eliana's mind. "You look twenty. Is that your actual age now, or will you grow older faster to catch up to the age you should be?"

"I don't know. Kharan-Khuag didn't tell me what my life would be like if I broke the curse. Perhaps he thought I wouldn't." He tossed a rock. It broke in two when it hit the wall. "The problem is, curses don't have many rules. They can be as complicated or simple as their maker wants them to be. The only law I know is that the curse maker has to reveal to the cursed one how to escape the enchantment. They're not obliged to explain all the consequences."

"The only way to find out is to break the curse." She wrinkled her brow. "Do you think we have a full day left? Or since we didn't stay in your tower, does Kharan-Khuag believe his curse is intact?"

"I don't know." He shrugged. "We gain nothing by waiting. So I say whenever you're ready."

She gripped her hands together, not sure if they were shaking from cold or fright. "Something puzzles me about all this."

"Only one thing?"

"Fine." She huffed and glared at him. "Several. For one, I've been thinking about Kharan-Khuag."

"Don't tell me he was another potential suitor."

Eliana kicked a rock in his direction. "Don't even joke about that. You say Kharan-Khuag told you the terms of the curse. Did you see him? What did he look like?"

Adakizh tapped his lips. "He came to the mouth of the Qvirila where it pours into the sea. Scores of karcharia and mutant fae lined up around him in a silent demonstration of what he could unleash upon us. He rode a massive shark with teeth as long as my arm. But Kharan-Khuag himself? He looked like an ordinary water fae except for his dead, ashen eyes."

"I thought he was some kind of creature with the body of a snake, six arms with sharp claws, and five heads."

"Five?"

"Yes. Boar, shark, vulture, goat and man. At least, that's what our legends say."

He shrugged. "There might be a drop of truth in those

legends. Who knows what dark magic he's perfected? It's possible he learned how to shape shift. Or can glamour himself to appear as he wishes. But we always understood him to be one of the fae, deformed by his own evil incantations."

Her stomach twisted as she cringed, imagining herself in Kharan-Khuag's clutches. To rid her mouth of the bitter bile, she took a bite of dried meat. "Another question. If I understand it, he tried to conquer our continent a thousand years ago, right?"

Adakizh nodded. "The Rider destroyed his military and he lost most of his power."

"So, he's spent a millennium regaining power and conquering the western continent."

"That's what we thought, at least at the time he cursed me. I don't know about Ymittos, but we had hoped he'd be content to stay far away."

"So why curse you?"

"He was enraged to discover we'd survived. Isn't that enough?"

"He has a bigger plan." Eliana drank from her waterskin, her dry mouth making it hard to speak. "Chorokha and Ymittos are just the beginning. When Kharan-Khuag informed Ymittos of the curse, the last line read, 'nothing will stop me from taking the rest.' He plans to use us as his foothold to invade the continent."

"So Kharan-Khuag is ready to try again to dominate Ardebil." Adakizh sucked in a breath.

"All the more reason we must succeed." She paused, gulping down her fear. "Are you ready?"

"Yes." He swallowed his last bite of dried goat and stared at his empty hands. "There's one other thing you should know. Before I was cursed, I did my share of cattle raiding. And enjoyed every moment stealing from the ox-footed over-worlders of Ymittos."

She jerked upright. "Is that what you thought of us?"

A wry smile spread across his face. "Is that worse than half-goat, half-fish savages?" His grin faded. "Please understand. We had very little meat other than our stringy goats. Raiding cattle became our national sport, one of the few joys in a dark existence where we feared discovery and annihilation at any moment. It was our single act of defiance." He blew out a long sigh. "I know you see it differently. Those who lost their herds suffered greatly, I'm sure."

Eliana gazed into his eyes. He was an unusual person. Not many had such empathy. *He is someone I could love.* Regret and longing gripped her heart. But there was no time for that now, no time to waste mourning what could never be. "So, how do we perform this spell?"

42

———————

Adakizh didn't answer Eliana right away.

Her stomach knotted. "You do remember the spell, don't you?"

The tagavlon stared at his hands, stretching his fingers. Then he balled them into fists. "I'll recite the incantation. Then we use our magic." His head sagged. "I'm worried we're not strong enough to make it work, let alone protect our people from drowning or getting crushed."

"There has to be something we haven't thought of. Some arcane power no one's ever wielded before."

"Eliana, say that again."

"Why?"

"You might have given me the answer."

"What did I say? To try something no one ever used?"

Adakizh bit his lip. "Where have I heard that before?"

"I just said it."

He shot her a frustrated glare. "I mean, from before I was cursed." He sighed. "My grandfather told me something." He sprang from his boulder and paced back and forth, muttering to himself.

Eliana strained to hear what he was saying. The only

words she caught made no sense to her. All she understood was 'cataclysm' and 'secret.'

With a shout, Adakizh whirled to face her. Eliana jerked backward and nearly tumbled off her rock. Warily, she rose to her feet.

"I remember!" He laughed. "I know what it is."

"Are you going to tell me?"

"The spell to cause the cataclysm involves water, stone, air, and light magic, right? How the first three are involved is obvious."

"Of course. Pull the water down and use the air and stone to create new tunnels and caverns."

"But what about the light magic? The ancient scrolls only said to use the secret power to break the dark."

Break the dark? Eliana didn't know what he was talking about. But he'd complimented her on how quick she was to understand, so she wanted to work it out for herself. What was this secret power nobody knew how to employ? Her lips parted as the realization swept through her mind. The amplifier that no one knew how to use with light magic. "Amplify my light with bitter herbs?"

"That must be it. Can you think of anything else?"

"No. But I don't know how to use the herbs with light magic. I don't even know if I can."

"How do you use the other amplifiers?"

"I summon the magic. I put the amplifier in my mouth. Then I release the power."

"Good. Do that."

"Before or after you say the incantation?"

"Both. Gather and amplify your magic. All of it. Air and light. I'll do the same with my water and stone. Then I'll recite the spell. When I'm done, we release the magic."

"Then what?"

"We find out if we live or die." Adakizh took her face in his hands and stroked her cheek. Then his hands slid down to her neck and his fingers wrapped around it. With a curse, he snatched his hands back. "Sorry. I still get the urge to kill you."

His fingers had been so gentle and tender on her face. Eliana longed for more of his touch, a touch that spread hot yearning through her veins. "I understand." She kept her tone soft, trying to keep the desire out of it. "This should work, right?"

"Only the Rider knows." Adakizh rubbed his forehead. "The best outcome I see is we break the curse, but we die. The worst? We kill most of our people and the survivors are Kharan-Khuag's slaves."

"And if we fail and don't die..." He'd be tortured and killed. She'd be tormented and enslaved. *No.* "I'd rather go down fighting. If that means offering my life for my people, so be it."

"That's how I feel." He smiled. "It's amazing, Eliana, how often you say precisely what I'm thinking."

Her gaze fell from his face to his chest as she felt a blush spread over her face. *I've thought the same about you.*

"Too bad we have no hope of survival." His tone was pensive and sad.

"We have to survive," Eliana said.

"But in case we don't," he held his hands out to her, "bind me."

Eliana frowned. She didn't understand, but did as he asked, using her air to tie his wrists together.

Adakizh stepped toward her, tilted his head, and kissed her. At first, his lips met hers like the brush of a silk scarf. Then he deepened the kiss. Through his touch, she sensed his hunger and desire for her, feelings that mirrored her own. Tingles spread through Eliana's body, tingles that grew into flashes like lightning. She'd die if he pulled his mouth away from hers.

When he stepped back, she was gasping for breath.

"Thank you. I die content." He held his bound hands out. "You can release me now."

With a chuckle, she freed him. "Thank you for taking precautions. But if you wanted to kill me, a kiss like that would be a good distraction."

He smirked. "I hope you live long enough to require distraction again."

Eliana swallowed the lump in her throat. "Adakizh, when I came to Chorokha, I thought your people were savages. Since then, I've come to know them as joyful and hospitable. More compassionate and noble than my own." She took a deep breath. "As for you, I only wanted to break your curse and leave you to rule your barbarians, hoping never to see you again. Now, I'm grateful that the last person I'll see, I'll talk with, is you. That I will spend my final moments in this world with you."

His eyes glittered. "I'm sorry you have to give your life for my kingdom. But I'm not sorry I met you. And that my last moments alive have been with you."

Their eyes locked on each other. After a long moment, Eliana broke away. She fumbled for her bag, her hands trembling. *I'm just nervous about dying. It has nothing to do with him.*

"Let's see. Here's the citrus." She handed him a vial of lemon juice. "And the berries." She passed him another vial.

After more digging, she found the salt and a vial of wine, along with a bag filled with tiny packets of bitter herbs. "Which herbs do you want?"

"I think they all work the same way, don't you?" Adakizh said. "I'll take anything but the chamomile."

She smiled. "I didn't forget. Here, you can have the artemisia, marrubium, and angelica. I'll use the others."

"Are you sure? I don't need them."

"I know we expect to die. But just in case we don't, you can use the herbs for healing."

"Ever the optimist, Eliana." He juggled the tiny packets in his hands. "How did you get artemisia?"

Istvan gave it to me, pretending to be kind. "It was a gift."

"This much artemisia is worth a herd of cows. That was some gift." He handed the packet to her. "You should use it. It's the strongest of the herbal amplifiers."

Reluctantly, she accepted. Istvan had used this herb to win her favor, to manipulate her into thinking he was thoughtful and generous. She didn't even want to touch it. "Which would you like in its place?" She attempted to speak lightly. "The elecampane?"

"No, give me something I can pronounce. I'll take the rue."

Eliana handed it over. Frowning, she considered the packets of herbs and salt in her hand. "I've never tried to manage three tastes at once. Not even two."

"One on the left, one on the right, one under the tongue?"

She shrugged. "I suppose first, we summon the magic, add the amplifiers, and then you say the spell?"

"Right."

He answered patiently, humoring her, as if he knew she was asking him to repeat what he'd already told her simply to delay the inevitable.

"You haven't forgotten it?" Eliana took deep even breaths. Corban had told her only the most experienced mages tried combining amplifiers into spells. Many who'd experimented met painful ends. She and the tagavlon had no hope of surviving. This was the end of her life. The end of her partnership with Adakizh. The end of whatever had blossomed between them.

Adakizh shook his head. "No."

"Our generals have a saying," Eliana said. "To win a battle, you need might and luck. We don't have much might. Let's hope we have luck."

"Or perhaps the favor of the Rider. Far better than luck."

She nodded. The Rider's favor could be their only hope. She stood facing Adakizh, keeping her eyes on his. Her breath flowed from her lungs in a long stream. With a determined nod, she sucked in a deep breath. She summoned her air and light magic, feeling the familiar warmth spread through her, the power surging in her veins. When the magic ached to be released, she put a pinch of salt in her mouth.

His forehead creased in concentration, Adakizh dropped a berry into his mouth. Then he placed some salt under his tongue. Slowly, Eliana did the same with her herbs, grimacing at the bitter taste. She raised the tiny vial of wine while he held up the vial of lemon. "To the Rider of the Ancient Skies," she said.

"To the Rider."

In unison, they poured the contents of their vials into their mouths.

By now, power hummed through her veins, beating against her skin and skull like a thundercloud about to burst.

Adakizh recited words in a language she'd never heard, his cadence insistent and fierce.

The power surrounding her intensified. Eliana sensed the motion of water and stone. The freshness of air rushed through her as the warmth of light welled inside her. She was light, she was air. In another moment, she'd float off the ground. Her flesh was snow melting under a summer sun. She couldn't contain the magic much longer.

As he chanted the spell, Adakizh's voice grew louder. He shouted the final words. He placed his hands on Eliana's shoulders. "Now."

She raised a hand and released her magic. Gusty winds whipped her hair around her face. Stone cracked and crashed, and thundering booms echoed through the caverns. Water gushed beside Eliana in a torrent.

Over the deafening noise and chaotic motion shined one power. A blinding burst of light arced through the gloom and made the stones around Eliana transparent. She saw the bones in her upraised hand, every detail of the veins and tendons, every drop of blood pulsing its way back to her heart.

Eliana fell to her knees and tumbled to the ground, her limbs tangled with Adakizh's.

"Push!" he yelled.

Gritting her teeth, she pushed. With all she had, she drew on her reserves of power, sending out her air and light magic, amplified by the salt, wine, and bitter herbs.

Air bit in hard gusts, stones cracked and fell, water surged. Light flashed, showing her glimpses of Adakizh's sweating, strained face. At other times, boulders bounced around them, carried away in torrents of water.

As she continued to push on her power, a stone dug into Eliana's thigh. She tried to shift her leg, gasping when she realized she couldn't move the limb. And not because Adakizh's heavy leg pinned hers. She'd lost the feeling in her lower legs.

"Push." The tagavlon's voice was weak and shaky, as if he had aged one hundred years in the past few moments.

Eliana clamped her eyes shut and pushed. She knew she'd fallen on pebbles, but could no longer feel them. Air rushed with the speed of an approaching hurricane, its roar surrounding her like a pack of hungry vishapions.

Water gushed and stone creaked. The winds intensified, pulling Eliana's breath from her lungs. "Push." Adakizh's voice sounded far away, as if raging currents had carried him deep under the stone.

The light magnified. She shoved at it with her last reserve of strength and the radiance grew to rival the intensity of a summer sun at midday. Rocks and crystals shone as if lit from within.

Colors spun before her, illuminating the cavern in shades for which she had no name. Scarlet, cobalt, emerald—none were the least bit adequate. Vermillion warred with indigo and exploded into violet. Turquoise melted into teal. The dark was writhing. She had no other word for it. It writhed like a beast in pain. Then the dark shattered in a multi-hued burst of light. Tears streamed down Eliana's face, and she closed her eyes, unable to gaze at the brilliance that danced around her.

Icy water drenched her head, turning the dust on her face to sticky mud. She swiped her left hand over her face to clear her eyes, but her fingers were like sausages attached to her hand and she couldn't bend them. Her right hand, the one she used to channel her power, was numb and lifeless.

As she lay immobile on the wet stone, the howling wind calmed. A few boulders thumped to the ground, followed by the rattling of pebbles. The torrent of water slowed to a trickle. She tried to grope for Adakizh, but her arm refused to move. "Adakizh." Her word came out in a pant no louder than a whisper.

The light faded, leaving only thick darkness. No air remained in her lungs.

Her eyelids fluttered and she let them close, too weary to fight. Fatigue crushed her bones. Even drawing a breath was a struggle. Each one grew more labored, each one felt like her last. Her worst fear had been realized. She'd die in the dark, trapped under a mountain of rock, alone and forgotten. A tear leaked from her eye. It was over. Success or failure, she didn't know. She was finished.

43

A blast of icy wind battered Derya's head, chafing her wind-scorched skin. She pulled the hood of her heavy cloak over her face and winced as the snowflakes on the fur melted on her cheeks, adding a sharp burn to the stinging cold. Snow built up on the mane of her horse, white crystals decorating the chestnut hairs like tiny diamonds. Her mare's breath formed plumes in the air, clouds that turned to frozen mist.

They'd been traveling for three hours since she learned the news from Ymittos, of Istvan's treachery and her own peril. Three hours of plodding into the north wind that swirled around them, sometimes pummeling them from the right after sweeping down the mountain slopes, sometimes barreling full into their faces. They'd crossed a bridge that soared over a deep chasm between two outthrust spurs of the mountain, where the winds unimpeded by rocky crags battered them without mercy. At least that was behind them.

As cold and miserable as she was, Derya would not complain. Instead, she set her jaw and occupied her mind with speculation. How long had Istvan been scheming against Ymittos? He must have laid his plans long before he agreed to marry Eliana. No wonder he was so willing to accompany her to find the cursed prince. His agents poisoned Eliana's parents while he was far away. And if an unfortunate accident had occurred in the lower realm, then Istvan could assume the throne, based on the terms of the supposed betrothal contract. That he was a distant relative of Ymittos' royal family might make it easier for many to accept him as sovereign. A sour taste like an unripe persimmon filled Derya's mouth, and she pursed her lips. Were Cinar's southern vassal states also plotting coups or rebellions?

Overriding these questions was the twist of her stomach every time she thought of Eliana. Between the wild Malkhians and the devious Istvan, Eliana was in grave danger. Assuming she was still alive. *Rider preserve her.*

Derya scowled. She'd always suspected something was wrong with Istvan. The way his eyes didn't match his smile. The latest news convinced her that Istvan, if he even permitted Eliana to live, would never allow her to rule beside him. Ymittos would belong to him and him alone. Unless Eliana could prove Istvan's murderous plot, there would be nothing she could do to get rid of him.

Derya knocked the snow from the leather overskirt covering her thighs and brushed her gloomy thoughts aside. She was powerless to change any of that now. At least there was one bright spot: the roaring in her ears. The sound had started gently, like the whisper of a falling leaf. After a mile, it hissed like a retreating wave. Another mile or two, and the noise intensified to that of surf pounding against the shore. The roar blocked out any other sound, but at least it wasn't that ghastly dead silence, an absence of sound that made her feel alone. Her hearing was coming back.

Perhaps in another mile or two, she'd be able to hear conversations. Grinning, she decided to keep the fact of her returning hearing to herself. She could overhear what her advisors were saying about her. And give them a good shock when she responded.

Soon, she thought, they'd reach the pass. Once over it, they'd be sheltered from the wind. And at lower elevations, the air would be warmer. Not the gentle climate of Nafplio, but at least not this soul-sapping cold. She hoped.

A rumbling sound grew beneath her, one she felt rather than heard. Her mare tossed its head and shied. The ground shook. An earthquake? To her right, Danisman Safiye's mouth was open, her eyes wide as she struggled to control her own frightened horse. Derya's mount stood still, head lowered, its limbs quivering. The princess patted the mare's neck and murmured to it. Along with the roaring in her ears, she heard shouts. Her heart pounded in her chest—part fear of the earthquake, part joy for her returning hearing.

The shaking intensified, accompanied by a deep rumbling. A loud crack pierced the air as if the land was breaking in two.

Derya gasped. Her first thought was that she could hear. Her second was that the splitting of the earth might be the last sound she'd ever hear.

A horse reared and threw his rider. The soldier tumbled to the ground. With a frightened neigh, the gelding bolted down the slope into a snowy meadow.

The horse frantically pawed its way through the snow. As Derya watched, lines formed on the expanse of snow, spreading and thickening, irregular lines that covered the land. The snow sagged into the grooves and then collapsed as if slits had opened underneath.

The fleeing horse stepped on one of the lines. It threw back its head, eyes wide and mouth frothing. With a scream, it sank beneath the ground.

The grooves traversed the snowy fields, some carving their way toward the road where Derya sat astride her mare, staring in fascinated horror. Trapped between the cliffs behind and the collapsing land before, there was no place to run, to escape. Her heartbeat pulsed in her ears and sweat dampened her neck. Was this the end?

The dark tracks surged closer. Bahadir guided his mount to Derya's side and gripped her arm. The lines were less than ten feet away. Derya tensed, readying herself for the plunge under the earth to what was sure to be an agonizing death. She sucked in a breath and screwed up her face.

The lines sped toward the road. One heartbeat more and they would slice through the ground underfoot. She clutched Bahadir's hand, willing herself not to scream. She would not flinch, not even in the face of an inescapable doom.

The grooves crashed into the road's edge and halted, ceasing their advance as if restrained by a leash. Derya stared, holding her breath and counting the moments. When she reached ten, she exhaled and let her shoulders droop. *Perhaps I won't die today.* But what was that disaster she just witnessed?

Bahadir urged his mount to the edge of the meadow, dismounted, and scooped up some of the white substance that covered the ground. He returned to Derya.

She extended her hand, palm up. The chiliarch trickled the white grains through his fingers onto her glove. Sand. The snow had vanished. Only sand remained, as though all the water had sucked away.

Derya sat limply on her mare, her jaw slack. The nearest village in the valley below lay in ruins. A fine dust filled the air as the broken pieces of houses and barns slid under the sand. She coughed, fighting a spasm of nausea. How many people had died? And why?

Safiye touched her arm and pointed up the slope. Chiliarch Bahadir and Oikeios Kelebek were already picking their way along a goat trail. Derya nodded, assuming they wanted to look from a higher place.

So did she. Derya leaped from her mare and handed the

reins to one of her guards. She glanced at her danisman and jerked her chin towards the climbing men. "Are you coming?"

With a nod, Safiye slid from her horse. They jogged up the slope after Bahadir and Kelebek. A foul odor of decay pricked Derya's nose but dissipated as quickly as it had come.

Before she could wonder what the smell had been, Bahadir and Kelebek waved their arms. They seemed to be shouting. Through the roaring in her ears, Derya heard only muffled words.

She was panting and spent by the time she reached Bahadir's side. He pointed at the valley with a shaking hand. Derya turned to discover what had him and Kelebek so agitated. Miles of fields covered in lines spread out below like a map unfurled on a giant's table.

As she watched, a series of fissures formed where the lines had been, some wide and straight, others narrow and winding. Everything was pouring into the rifts like water flowing down a drain. The faint silhouette of a village collapsed. A cloud of dust rose over it.

The land they'd visited was no more. Olive trees and vineyards had vanished. No buildings stood, neither near nor on the horizon. Even the roads were gone, as was the shining snow that had blanketed the barren fields. All that remained were the rifts that crisscrossed the white sandy fields like the slashes of a sword, crusted black like dried blood.

Derya shuddered and pressed her hand to her throat. "Raging waters, what just happened?"

For a long moment, no one replied. Then Kelebek said, "It looks like Ymittos has collapsed into Malkh. At least this part of it."

The fact that Derya could indistinctly hear his words was overshadowed by the horror of the destruction before her. She blinked a few times and shook her head.

Safiye pulled out a tablet and wrote: *It appears Princess Eliana not only failed to break the curse, her land was cursed as well.*

"We don't know that," Derya said. She pressed a hand on her plummeting stomach. Eliana couldn't be dead.

Kelebek took the tablet. *We need to report to the emperor.*

Bahadir opened his mouth to reply, but more rumbling under the earth drowned his words. The ground trembled and shook, groaning and roaring.

The chiliarch grabbed Derya's arm and tugged. "Get down, Kiral."

Even with her impaired hearing, Derya could not mistake the terror in his voice. She dropped to the rocky ground, clutching Safiye. The two men staggered and lurched to sit beside them.

Sweat beaded on Derya's forehead. Her stomach turned over. Safiye's olive skin was a sickly green and Kelebek's didn't look much healthier. Bahadir's wide eyes darted all around. Sweat dripped from his forehead, his nostrils flared, and his lips trembled. She'd never seen Bahadir frightened before. Now he was terrified.

A crash on her right made her pivot toward the noise. Boulders rolled down the slope toward their entourage. One massive rock bounced onto a guard and knocked him from his horse. The animal bolted off the road into the white sand meadow. After a few strides, it was floundering and flailing. This time, its screams pierced Derya's ears. And then it was gone. She stared at the depression in the sand where the horse had been a mere heartbeat before. The sands shifted, leaving no trace that anything had passed through them to the unknown depths below.

More rocks sped past them. Some tumbled end over end. Others flew by, bouncing their way down the slope. Bahadir yanked Derya to her feet and pulled her to the shelter of a large outcropping. Kelebek and Safiye crowded next to them. They huddled together, all shaken into silence except for their gasping breaths.

Derya stretched out a hand and let it fall. There was

nothing she could do. Even if she could wield stone magic, she had no power left. She was empty inside, her magic just a tiny trickle being replenished drip by drip. It would be hours, no days, before she'd be able to use her power again.

The tremor ceased. A few rocks rolled down the slope, rattling as they bounced over stones and scrub bushes. Derya started to stand, but Bahadir put a hand on her arm. "Wait, Kiral, please. There may be aftershocks."

His voice shook, and she didn't want to upset him further. "As you wish, chiliarch."

"You can hear?"

"Faintly. Enough to make out the meaning of what you say. What do you advise we do when it's safe to move?"

Bahadir squinted and held a hand over his eyes. "Kiral, I think we need to cross the mountains. Get away from the destruction while we can."

44

erya opened her mouth to agree, then thought better of it. "No. First, we need to investigate. We saw two horses sink under that sand. Is the ground still falling? Or is it stable?"

She expected an argument, but her danisman nodded. "You're right. Perhaps we should dispatch some men to scout out the destruction and search for survivors."

"I'm glad you agree. But I need to see for myself." The princess was silent as she gingerly made her way down the path, fatigue weighting her limbs. Indistinct sounds reached her ears, what seemed like soldiers' shouts and horses' whinnies, but she couldn't be sure. At least she heard something. Vainly, she sought a reason for the cataclysm. Anything but the obvious conclusion that Eliana had failed and met her death.

When they rejoined their entourage, Bahadir ordered a scout to test the sand. "Carefully, Irmak. We don't want any more disappearances."

With a confident nod, Irmak stepped to the edge of the road. He scuffed the surface with the toe of one boot. "It's hard here." He stamped his foot. "All good. It doesn't crack under me."

"That's a mercy from the Rider," Bahadir said. "The last thing we need is the road collapsing under us."

Derya stared at the ground. That possibility hadn't occurred to her.

"Go slow," Bahadir said.

Irmak held up a hand in agreement. He extended that hand to a second scout, who grasped it.

Gripping her hands together, Derya watched the man take a tentative step onto the sand, leaving one foot on the road.

He leaned forward. "It feels solid."

Derya fought the impulse to look away as Irmak lifted his left foot from the road and brought it next to his right. Her heart sped up and she held her breath.

"It's fine," Irmak said as he took another step. He shot an arm in the air and shouted. The sand covered his legs to his knees. The second scout yanked Irmak's hand. In a heartbeat, he, too, had toppled onto the sand. Two others lunged for his feet and missed. Irmak and the second man slipped underground as if sucked down by the ocean's undertow.

Frozen with shock and horror, Derya stared at the spot where the soldiers had disappeared. She winced, thinking of their painful deaths, choked by the white sand, smashed under the earth.

"What happened?" The mutters and curses of the nearby soldiers echoed Derya's question.

Bahadir squatted by the place his warriors had vanished. "Oh, Irmak. Oh, Makbule." He stood up and walked back to Derya, head drooping. "Kiral—"

"You are not to blame, chiliarch." Derya swallowed hard. "This means Eliana and Istvan are dead. Along with everyone in both Ymittos and Malkh."

"Leaving these lands desolate and empty, with nothing

standing in the way of Cetus's invasion." Bahadir's tone was flat.

Derya squared her shoulders. "Which makes Cinar next." She jerked her chin in the direction they had been traveling. "Is the road ahead safe?"

"I'll send some scouts." Bahadir frowned and wiped the sweat from his face.

Derya noticed his hand was still shaking. She pursed her lips, wondering what had happened to her usually stoic chiliarch.

He turned to his kentarchs. "One of you, send a pair of scouts north. Find out if the road is clear. And stable."

"I'll go," Kentarch Farooq said. "Better one of us takes the risk this time."

Bahadir's eyes flicked to the sands before settling on his kentarch's face. "Thank you, but take someone with you. Be careful, and return quickly. We can't wait here long. And send a few scouts south. Find out how far the devastation extends."

Farooq saluted and walked away. Bahadir watched him for a moment, his frown deepening.

"Chiliarch," Safiye said, "I think you should have the kiral's tent put up. Tending the wounded could take a while, and she needs refreshment."

"Kiral, I'm not sure that's a good idea," Bahadir said, his eyes darting from the danisman to Derya. "But if you desire it—"

Derya shook her head. "Thank you, but no. I'll assist the healers. Danisman, could you arrange for hot tea for everyone? And maybe something to eat?"

Safiye huffed. "I'll talk to the provisioners," she said. "You make sure you don't use your magic or overdo things again. You need to rest."

Rest sounded wonderful to Derya. To retreat under a thick fur blanket, out of the wind and snow, away from observing eyes, she could let her tears flow for Eliana. She squared her shoulders and shoved her grief away. While her entourage labored, she would not indulge herself. She had to remain strong, especially under Kelebek's critical eye.

"Then we concur," Derya said. "We eat, aid the wounded, and move on as soon as possible."

"Kiral." The three scars on Bahadir's cheek twitched. "We have to be prepared. We don't know what damage the earthquake caused up north."

The princess straightened her sagging shoulders. "We'll have to deal with that when we meet it, chiliarch."

Kelebek pointed a bony finger at her. "Kiral, you must get word to the emperor. Now."

"Yes, Oikeios," Derya said in a placating tone. "I must. Did you bring any messenger birds with you?"

Kelebek scowled. "Since we were fleeing for our lives, no."

"It's a pity," Derya said gently. "That would have been a great help. Ours were killed in a bandit attack. All we can do is cross the mountains and find someone with the right birds. Believe me, I want to inform my father as much as you do."

The oikeios shook his head. "You don't understand, Kiral."

The princess tamped down her anger. Kelebek was proper to a fault, and at times annoying, but his condescension was more than she could bear on this horrible day. "What don't I understand?" Irritation crept into her tone.

"The emperor doesn't know you've left Ptolemaida, let alone Ymittos, correct?" Kelebek twisted his hands together. "If he thinks you remained in Ymittos and hears of all this…" He gestured at the empty sands.

Derya pressed a hand to her mouth. She could finish Kelebek's thought easily enough. Her father would assume she was dead, even if the birds she'd sent from Ptolemaida had reached him.

Bahadir's eyes widened. "If word gets around that Cinar's heir is dead…"

That didn't bear thinking about. Derya closed her eyes. Her male cousins, all resentful that she'd been named heir, would swarm around her father, jockeying for her place. The nations she'd just visited, solidifying treaties and trade agreements, would have a pretext to renege on their word. And the unstable southern vassal nations might seize on the disruption as an excuse to secede from the empire.

Hoofbeats broke into her thoughts. Kentarch Farooq and the scout had returned.

She waited impatiently for them to threading their way through the groups of soldiers strung along the road. Was it good or bad that they'd returned so quickly?

Farooq saluted and leaned forward in his saddle. "Kiral, chiliarch, we rode only a mile or so. The last bridge we crossed earlier crumbled and fell. We can't reach the northern pass that way."

"Are you sure?" Bahadir asked.

"Half the mountain has collapsed, chiliarch," Farooq said. "The stones are piled up three times a man's height."

"A tall man," put in the scout.

Bahadir's head jerked to one side, and he cursed.

Derya raised her eyebrows. "Chiliarch, what's wrong?"

The man's olive face flushed. "A thousand pardons, Kiral. The scouts who went south are back. This can't be good."

Derya watched two men ride along the line of their entourage. "Maybe they bring good news," Derya said, "that the cataclysm only affected this region."

"And pigs will fly," said Kelebek.

"Shall we place bets?"

"Kiral, that would not be advisable," Safiye said.

Derya suppressed a grin. Safiye, as worthy as she was, lacked a sense of humor. Which, the princess noted to herself, was a valuable commodity in disasters. One could either allow despair to destroy hope or laugh at the obstacles ahead. Sometimes, a feeble joke was the only thing that kept her going.

She shifted her weight from side to side, wishing the scouts would hurry.

After a salute to her and the chiliarch, the older one reported. "A mile south, an avalanche tore out the road. You'd need a bridge to cross the chasm it left. We'll have to head north."

Bahadir shook his head. "The road north is blocked. Is there no other way?"

The scout nodded. "I spotted a trail, wide enough in spots for a wagon. It winds up the mountain but was unblocked as far as we could see."

"Does the trail twist more north or south?" Derya asked.

"It goes around the south face of this mountain."

"Kiral," Bahadir said, "that would lead to Nafplio."

Derya froze. Nafplio could be more treacherous than the white sands of Ymittos. If Istvan had no scruples about poisoning a handful of his own nobles to serve his ambition, she couldn't expect she'd be treated any better by his surviving relatives. "If that's the way our road home leads, chiliarch, then that's the way we'll go."

Kelebek shook his head. "Kiral, I strongly advise against going into Nafplio. My instincts tell me war will soon convulse the continent, and that Nafplio is one of the flashpoints. The only way to save the empire—and all of Ardebil—from Cetus is for Cinar to act quickly to contain the unrest."

"I quite agree with you, Oikeios," she answered. "But it appears we have no other choice. And I don't know about you, but I would prefer to move away from these sands before the road crumbles beneath us."

Kelebek's startled expression nearly made Derya laugh. "Oh, I have no reason to believe that it will," she said softly. "But I'd rather not wait to find out."

Bahadir's wry smile was a welcome sight. "I have to say I agree with you, Kiral," he said. "Oikeios Kelebek, if you would kindly assist the kiral and our healers attend to the wounded, that will speed up our departure." He saluted Derya and strode off.

Sliding her arm through Kelebek's, Derya smirked to herself as the man stiffened. She'd shocked him. Young women would only be so familiar when they were making a naughty advance. But when a member of the royal family made such a gesture, it indicated the recipient had earned high favor. She'd let Kelebek work out for himself which she meant.

Too bad for him, it was neither. Still depleted by her use of magic, the walk up the goat trail earlier and the effort to project a confidence she didn't feel left her so exhausted she feared she would stumble without some support. "Come, Oikeios, let's help however we can. Unless you'd like to try some winter camping here?"

"No, Kiral, I would not."

She patted his arm. "We'll be on the move shortly. Home in a little over a week. Then we can set to work saving the continent."

45

———————

A rock dug into Eliana's spine. She shifted her position, every muscle protesting. That small motion left her weak and spent, gasping for air. Her head pounded and dust filled her mouth. She wanted to open her eyes, but that seemed like too much work. The fingers of her left hand grazed a puddle of slimy water.

What was she doing lying on a stony floor? The last thing she remembered was riding with the annoying Princess Derya. More memories trickled through her mind. She and Derya had overused their magic while rescuing canal workers. They'd ended up sleeping for days. Her chest tightened. She should be in her room in the palace, surrounded by her parents and servants, not in a chilly, dark, damp cave. The cold, more than anything else, convinced her she wasn't dreaming.

Then the trickle of memories became a flood, choking her with anger, sadness, and fear. The descent into Malkh, which turned out to be Chorokha. The cursed tagavlon. Istvan's treachery. Her parents' death. And working with Adakizh to cause a cataclysm.

The spell had worked, at least to some extent. The

crashing stone, the rushing wind and water, and most of all, that blinding, overwhelming light were proof. And, wonder of wonders, she was still alive.

But why was it so dark? She blinked several times. Everything was black. Not even a lone mushroom gave off its pale glow.

Her heart beat a jerky rhythm, skipping and fluttering. Eliana pressed her shaking hands against her chest and blinked her eyes a few times more, trying to discern something, anything, in the inky blackness. No glowing mushrooms. Or water glinting on smooth, crystalline rocks. Or a ray of sunlight shooting through a shaft from the world above. Nothing but the thick, damp, suffocating dark.

Where was Adakizh? She groped in the darkness, her hands finding only cold emptiness and slimy stone.

Eliana let her arms fall slack. Her body ached and was bruised and sore, as if gigantic fists had punched and pummeled her. With a moan, she wiggled her toes. At least she could move them, as frigid and numb as they were. She shivered. Maybe she should stand up and explore. There had to be a way out. But where would she go in the dark? It would be too easy to fall into a crevasse or stumble into a vishapion's lair.

She sighed. It was pointless, anyway. Just the idea of standing fatigued her. She had no strength to sit up, let alone walk.

The rock overhead creaked and groaned. A sob rose in her throat as she imagined tons of earth falling to crush her. She was buried alive in this dark cavern, isolated, trapped in complete darkness and doomed to die where no one would hear her scream except the silent, lifeless rocks.

But since she had survived, perhaps Adakizh had as well. He must be somewhere nearby. Eliana strained to listen for any sound that would indicate his presence. All she heard were pebbles falling from the ceiling, trickling water, and her own ragged breathing.

Where was he? She stretched her hand, searching for Adakizh. She screwed up her face, hoping she wouldn't grasp a stinging worm or other creature of the night.

To her right, she found stones, some cracked and broken like smashed nutshells. Same on the left. Her breath came in labored pants. Despite the cold, sweat dripped from her forehead. He couldn't be dead.

"Adakizh?" she said to the darkness. She tried again. "Adakizh!" She shouted his name over and over until the echoes multiplied, mocking her desperate calls.

Scraping on her left made her clamp her lips shut. Something was crawling over the floor, rattling the broken stone. She listened, trying to guess how close it was. Her fingers closed around a rock.

The slithering noise stopped, replaced by retching. Someone—or something—was vomiting. Eliana frowned. Was that human or beast?

The gagging ceased. Eliana strained to listen over the thumping of her pulse. A low moan filled the chamber. Whatever it was, it was in pain. A wisp of air told her the thing was moving toward her. Something nudged her foot. She screamed and slammed the rock onto whatever it was. The grip on her foot released and a howl filled the cavern.

Eliana froze. That was no beast. That was a man.

"Don't hit me again," said a weak, trembling voice.

"Adakizh?" That baritone sounded like his. "Is that you?"

"Don't hit me."

The tagavlon. Tears pricked Eliana's eyes. He was alive, not crushed under a boulder or drowned in the floodwaters. She wasn't alone in the dark, doomed to perish in a lonely crypt. She flung herself toward his voice.

After a few heartbeats of frantic groping, she found his thigh. A sticky wetness covered his skin.

"By the Rider, that hurts," he said. "Who are you? Move to where I can see you."

How could he see in such darkness? "Adakizh, it's me. Eliana." She groped her way up his leg.

He jerked away. "Who are you?"

Her hands flailed in the darkness. "Don't leave me. Please." The last word was a wail, but she didn't care. She'd beg him to stay with her. Why didn't he recognize her voice?

Eliana inched toward the sound of his heavy breathing. A rock bit into her knee and she gasped. She ignored the pain and kept moving.

"Don't come any closer." From the sounds Adakizh was making, she guessed he was lying on the ground, sliding away from her.

"I don't care if you kill me. Just don't leave me alone." Eliana brushed her hand over the floor, knocking pebbles out of her way. She crept forward, favoring her wounded knee. Her hand bumped Adakizh's leg. She grasped the fabric of his trousers and edged closer. "Adakizh, please…"

A hand gripped her chin and forced her face upwards. "Eliana! It's you! You're alive!" His fingers stroked her cheek.

Seeking his face, Eliana felt along his arm. She wondered why he was lying down. "Are you wounded?" She pulled herself to him and laid her head on his chest with a sigh. "I can't believe we survived. Do you think we broke the curse?"

His hand stroked her hair. "Are you alright? Let me look at you."

Eliana stiffened. Had he gone mad? There was no light to see by.

He lifted her head from his chest with his hands on either side of her face. "Did you answer me?"

"Adakizh…"

"I see your lips move. But I hear nothing." He pushed the damp hair back from her forehead. "We clearly overused our magic."

Of course. Expending too much magic was dangerous, especially when using amplifiers. Water mages could lose their hearing and light mages, their sight. She dropped her head back onto Adakizh's chest and sobbed with relief. She wasn't in a black hole with no light. Her sight should return.

Adakizh patted her back until her sobs subsided. "I'm guessing you can hear me. Squeeze my hand if you can."

She found one of his hands and squeezed it in her chilly fingers.

"Good. Now, squeeze once for yes, twice for no. Can you see anything?"

She squeezed twice.

His warm breath tickled her ear as he sighed. "Right. And what about smell?"

Now that he mentioned it, she hadn't detected the damp odor of the caverns since she regained consciousness. The price of overusing air magic.

"Did you lose your sense of smell?"

She squeezed his hand once.

"I hope you're feeling strong," he said, "just in case a vishapion survived the cataclysm. I can't get up."

Overuse of stone magic, what did that cause? Or was he injured, more than the gash on his leg? Her heart raced and her breath came in jagged pants. She bit hard on her lip to calm herself. *I will not panic. He needs me.*

"Don't worry, it's not fatal. Just no sense of balance. I'm fine as long as I don't move my head." He shifted and coughed. "Which is why I've been ill. Whenever the dizziness ebbs, the stench gives me the urge to vomit all over again."

"Overusing air magic does have some benefits."

When he didn't respond, she remembered. He couldn't hear her. She stroked his face, the rough stubble on his chin scraping her fingertips. "Then we'll just have to wait. Unless…"

Jerking away from him, she scrambled over the pebbly floor, out of his reach. As soon as he could stand, he'd come after her with those elegant fingers, intending not to caress, but to kill.

"Eliana, what's wrong?"

Her mouth went dry. Her sole companion in this lightless pit was driven to murder her.

She heard him suck in a breath. "Eliana, where are you? What happened? You can't see, so what startled you? Did you hear something?" His questions came fast and frantic. "Oh. Wait. Is it me? Don't be afraid. The compulsion to kill you has vanished."

Was he sure? She didn't want to risk being too close, especially not while she was blind.

"Don't you see?" he asked.

"No, I see nothing, in case you forgot." She spat out the words. Then chided herself. He could hear nothing.

"Eliana, we must have succeeded! By causing the cataclysm, we broke the dark curses on Chorokha. Our magic overpowered Kharan-Khuag's. At least, I think so. My desire to kill you is gone."

The princess sucked in a breath. Could he be right? She edged back to him and found his hand.

Adakizh pulled her closer. Feeling like she'd returned to a sheltering haven, she stretched out beside him, her head on his chest.

His heart thumped under her ear, a strong, steady beat. She let her breathing match his.

He placed a hand on her head and stroked her hair. "You broke the dark."

Her breath caught. She had. And survived.

"A strange expression, breaking the dark," he said while playing with her hair. "My ancestors, the ones who caused the first cataclysm, called it that—using light to break the dark magic that threatened our land. No one would dare attempt such a destructive spell unless it was the only way to defeat a powerful magical evil. And you did it."

"We did it together." She said the words aloud, not caring that he couldn't hear her now. She'd tell him later. And she had more important questions, questions she'd pose later.

"I suppose you're wondering what we should do next."

Well, yes. She squeezed his hand once.

"As I see it, we have two choices. We can imitate my ancestors and hide any trace of survivors. Or we can openly prepare defenses against Kharan-Khuag." He massaged the back of her neck. "Which would you like to do? The first?"

She didn't have to think about it. Her face heated just thinking about Kharan-Khuag and his heinous crimes. She gave Adakizh's hand two vigorous squeezes.

He chuckled. "You don't have to break my bones. I take it you want to fight."

This time, she pressed his fingers gently.

He wrapped his arms around her. "I was hoping you'd say that."

46

___

Adakizh kept talking, but Eliana barely heard his words. They were lost in the soothing rumble of his voice, the reassuring warmth of his arms circling her ribs, the muscle of his thigh pressed against hers, and the tingling in her toes. For a heartbeat, she entertained the fleeting wish that they could lie there forever.

But no. They had a duty to their people.

"What do you say?" Adakizh squeezed her hand.

What had he asked? She buried her face in his chest, hoping he couldn't see the simmering desire for him in her eyes. What were these unsettling feelings she had for this supposedly barbarian prince who was anything but savage?

"We need to find the survivors," Adakizh said.

Eliana squeezed his hand once.

"Then unify them."

That won't be easy. Eliana squeezed his hand again.

"And develop defenses."

Eliana stiffened. They'd broken Kharan-Khuag's dark spells. That removed the immediate danger. But she had to believe that once Kharan-Khuag learned who had destroyed his plan, he'd direct his wrath in their direction. The sorcerer would be more determined to give Adakizh the agonizing death he'd promised; his intimate plans for Eliana would become more vile and degrading. They had no time to waste.

She raised her head and spoke with an exaggerated motion of her lips. "Saumarotas." She had to repeat it twice before he understood.

"The Saumarotas," he said. "You're right. We also need to discover who else is working against us." He let out a mirthless chuckle. "After what we did, I wouldn't blame anyone if they chained us to a raft and sent us straight to Kharan-Khuag."

Eliana squeezed his hand twice.

"You mean, no, they won't do that?"

Another two squeezes.

"No, we won't let them? We'll have to convince them not to?"

She smiled and gave him one squeeze.

"What a joy we think alike." He rested his hands on either side of her face. "I know it was a sacrifice when you kissed me to break the curse. And agreeing to destroy your kingdom was another."

He was right. She'd sacrificed much. But she'd done it not to appease her sense of duty or guilt, or compromise her values while she was at it. But because it was the right thing to do for her and the people of Ymittos and Chorokha, the only way to thwart Kharan-Khuag.

He brushed a tear from her cheek. "Maybe you'll be willing to offer yourself in another way."

What was he talking about? How she wished she could gaze into his face. It was hardly fair that he could see hers. Her cheeks heated as she wondered what he could read in her expression.

"We can talk about that later." He stroked her face, his touch rose-petal soft. "But first," he yawned, "some sleep."

Eliana settled into his arms, listening to his breathing

subside into a slow cadence. He was right. Sleep was the fastest way to regain their senses and recover their strength.

Fatigue pulled at her, luring her into unconsciousness. The thought of rescuing the survivors among their people and fighting off Kharan-Khuag made her weary. Sleep would be so delicious.

Perhaps someone should stay awake to watch for vishapions or other dangers. Rider help us if something comes. Neither of them could fight off anything more threatening than a butterfly. Her eyelids drooped, too heavy to keep open any longer.

She ran her hand over Adakizh's broad chest. Someday, she hoped they'd find time for a much different cat-and-mouse game, one that they both could win. Or one that to lose would involve no sacrifice at all. That thought curved her lips into a smile and she slid into sleep.

SOMETHING WAS JOSTLING HER LEG. A stabbing pain shot through Eliana's stiff neck and every muscle ached. Bands of tension tightened across her forehead.

The poking continued. "Wake up, my sunshine."

That mocking voice could only belong to Shirdona. Eliana opened her eyes, hoping to see the woman's face. She sagged against Adakizh. Her sight hadn't returned. Everything was as solidly black as when she fell asleep except for a weak streak of gray in the center.

Her olfactory sense was a different matter. She choked on a whiff of stale sweat and an acrid, rotting smell that could only be Adakizh's vomit. Even though the stench made her stomach churn, she felt a tiny bit of relief. Maybe one of Adakizh's senses had also returned.

"My sunshine, are you going to lie there forever?"

"I'm so happy to hear your voice, Shirdona! You have no idea." She shook Adakizh. "Wake up."

He jerked, his arm tightening around Eliana. "What's wrong?"

"Shirdona's here." She uttered the words aloud, hoping Adakizh could hear her. That would be one less complication.

His fingers groped for hers. "Eliana, give me your hand."

"This is all very sweet," Shirdona said, "but you two caused quite a ruckus. People are not happy."

With a groan, Adakizh sat up. "It's lovely to see you, tavkatseen." He clasped Eliana's fingers more firmly. "How did you fare during the cataclysm?"

From the sputtering noises, Eliana guessed the question irked Shirdona. "Not well," the tavkatseen said. "What are you going to do about it?"

Adakizh yawned. "How long were we asleep?" he asked.

"Three days." Shirdona spat the words out.

Eliana squeezed Adakizh's hand three times.

"Three days? Did I get that right?" he asked.

She gave his hand a single squeeze.

"No wonder I'm so stiff. And in such need of a ditch." He staggered to his feet, pulling Eliana up with him. "I'm assuming you have the same need, hmm?" He tucked her hand under his arm. "Give us a moment, tavkatseen."

Shirdona muttered a few colorful curses. Eliana tried not to grin. She allowed Adakizh to shuffle her from the sound of Shirdona's voice, supporting her when she slipped on a slick spot.

"Here, Eliana. I don't see any spiders or worms, so you should be fine." He released her hand and stepped away.

Hopefully, he'd led her behind a rock, or at least into a shadowy place. With a few hurried motions, she squatted, relieved herself, readjusted her clothing, and stood up. Holding her hand out, she reached where she thought he'd be.

He grasped her fingers and led her a few steps. "I'll only be a moment."

She focused on the sound of water hitting rock. Her

mouth was gummy and sour. Thirst and hunger were making her nauseous, weak, and dizzy. If he didn't hurry, she'd topple over, face first into the slime-covered rocks. She clenched her teeth, willing herself not to faint.

Eliana relaxed her jaw when the tagavlon slid his hand under her elbow. She leaned on him, clinging to his muscular arm. He led her back to the waiting Shirdona.

"Now, tavkatseen, do you have any water?" he asked.

Shirdona huffed. The woman must have held out a waterskin, because Adakizh pressed one into Eliana's hand a moment later. She gulped the water, the cool wetness reviving her like rain after a drought. After swallowing half the contents, she offered it to Adakizh.

The princess listened as he rinsed his mouth and spat. When he'd finished drinking, he spoke. "Thank you, tavkatseen. Please tell us what's been happening."

"After you worked your magic, whatever it was you two cooked up, the disaster struck. First, rivers and lakes poured down from above. The floodwaters washed away a few people. They all had the sense to dive deep and wait it out. Then the rocks shifted. Tunnels collapsed. Others formed. Falling stalactites speared a few." She paused. "At least our people had warning. The Ymittosians, well, suddenly they were here. The fall injured many, but not as badly as I expected. Just what was that magic you performed?"

Eliana gripped Adakizh's arm. She wasn't sure how to explain to Shirdona. "Where are the Ymittosians?" she asked.

"They've huddled together in groups, at least the ones I've found. They won't let anyone get near them. The Saumarotas killed a few."

"We've got to help them."

"Maybe," Shirdona answered. "But first, my sunshine, you and the tagavlon have some explaining to do. I want to hear from him first."

"You can't. I mean, he can't."

"Why not? Did you ensorcel him and force him to destroy his own realm?"

Eliana took a deep breath. Hunger twisted her stomach, fatigue weakened her knees. She could barely stand up, let alone get involved in a verbal duel with Shirdona. If only Adakizh could help. But he stood by her side, silent as a statue. He probably didn't want to reveal his deafness or her blindness yet.

"What's wrong with him?" Shirdona demanded. "He's moving like my old granddad."

"We broke the curse," Eliana said. She gripped Adakizh's hand, wishing he could guess what they were talking about.

"Tavkatseen, do you have something to eat?" he asked. Eliana mentally cursed his timing.

"By the Rider, you're in a demanding mood," Shirdona snarled.

"Please," Eliana said. "We've been asleep for three days and we overused our magic. We'll be better able to discuss matters once we've eaten."

"Hmph. But I'll want the tagavlon to tell me everything."

Eliana nudged him with her elbow, hoping he'd get the idea that he needed to say something. This time, he didn't disappoint. "We broke the curse," he said. "We used our combined magic, water, stone, air and light, to mimic the spell that created Chorokha a millennium ago."

"That's impossible," Shirdona said.

"I would have thought so, too," Eliana said, "except it worked. The curse is gone. Kharan-Khuag's spell to enslave Ymittos and Chorokha has been broken." She took a deep breath. "We're afraid he won't give up. We must prepare for an invasion." She clung to Adakizh's hand, willing him to join the conversation.

As if he'd read her thought, he spoke. "Tavkatseen, we need your help to unify our people with the Ymittosians. To teach them how to live underground. And to persuade them to ally with us against Kharan-Khuag. Will you do that?"

Shirdona took a few steps toward Eliana, or so it sounded to the girl. "You destroyed my family hearth and extinguished my fire. Everything is in ruins, and you expect people to work with you?"

Heat raced up Eliana's neck. "We risked our lives to break the curse, and to save both kingdoms from immediate conquest and enslavement. Now we have a chance to fight back. Maybe it's a small chance and perhaps it's hopeless. But for at least today, we are free from Kharan-Khuag's tyranny. Tell me you would have chosen differently."

A long silence followed, broken solely by a faint trickle of water. Eliana balled her free hand into a fist. How could she negotiate with Shirdona if she couldn't read the other woman's face?

"You're right, my sunshine. I would choose one hour of freedom in place of a century of life under Kharan-Khuag."

"Will you work with us?" Adakizh said, which startled Eliana.

She frowned. How did he know what Shirdona had said? Unless he could see her face well enough to guess at her words.

"Yes, Tagavlon," Shirdona replied.

Eliana squeezed his hand once. He squeezed hers in response. "Then we are agreed," he said. "Can we count on your family to spread the word to the others? And to the Ymittosians?"

"Oh, now there's the problem," Shirdona answered. "You'll need someone whose words can shatter a cliff to get them to settle down."

"Why? What happened?" Eliana asked.

"Naturally, falling into Chorokha was unnerving for them." Shirdona chuckled. "And like you, my sunshine, they were expecting half-goat, half-fish monsters. When we approached them, they attacked us. Some panicked and fled right into the path of a vishapion. After we rescued them, they calmed down. At least enough to stop flinging rocks at us. But turning them into allies? That's like sewing mountain peaks together with a needle."

"We'll need a big needle, then," Eliana said. "What do you think will convince them?"

"Most of our people will rally around the tagavlon here, especially now that he's proven how powerful a mage he is. Are yours loyal to you?"

"I think so." *Were they?* Who knew what lies Istvan's people had told her court? Maybe they believed she'd been in on the plot to kill her parents. "I can try to persuade the Ymittosian leaders that allying with you is their best chance."

"You planning on going alone?"

"I—"

Shirdona's laugh echoed through the cavern. "From the looks of it, you two got pretty friendly after the cataclysm. You haven't let go of his hand for a heartbeat."

"What do you mean?" Eliana thought she understood Shirdona's veiled hints, but she didn't want to be the one to give voice to them.

"I can tell you this. Your people want one of their own to lead them. As do mine. There's only one way around that. When you two meet with people, ask them what it will take for them to work with you. Let them demand that you wed, to unify the kingdoms."

Eliana huffed. She wanted to look at Adakizh, to read his expression, but she still couldn't see. He most likely hadn't heard Shirdona's proposal. From his lack of a reaction, she guessed he hadn't been able to discern the tavkatseen's meaning just by watching her face.

"Of course, princess, if marrying him is too big of a sacrifice…"

Would it be? No. She'd be giving up her dreams of ruling

Ymittos, but they had died in the cataclysm. Marrying Adakizh was a tantalizing prospect. She shifted to stand a little closer to him so that the length of her arm touched his.

"Not at all," she said. "I would only give up things I can't have, anyway." But would Adakizh feel the same? He'd said some pretty things to her just before they broke the curse. But he'd thought they were about to die. With a full life ahead of him, he might have different desires.

It wasn't that she was against marrying Adakizh, and she hoped he wasn't opposed to the idea. It was, she conceded, a convenient political solution. But what about her personal feelings? And his? They both needed time to sort them out. Eliana bit her lower lip. She didn't want to make a public commitment without his consent. "Shouldn't we think about this some more?" she said.

"Don't drown yourself in a teaspoon, my sunshine," Shirdona said. "What else are you going to do?" When Eliana didn't respond, the woman continued. "Then it's settled. Follow me, and we'll give the joyful news to my family. And try to scrounge up some food for you."

Adakizh squeezed Eliana's hand. "Thank you, tavkatseen."

Eliana hoped Adakizh would be pleased, not angered, by the betrothal she'd committed him to. He tugged her hand, leading her in Shirdona's wake. The princess slid her arm under his and her lips curled up when he laced his fingers with hers.

The smile melted from her face when the enormity of the task ahead settled on her slim shoulders. *How will we save Chorokha?* Yes, they'd broken the dark. But the war had just begun.

WANT to know if Eliana and Adakizh succeed in protecting their realm? And what perils Derya faces in fighting off Kharan-Khuag? Read on for a sample of The Girl Who Wrote on Water.

Chapter 1

Surviving a cataclysm only to die in an earthquake was not how Princess Derya wanted her life to end. The road rumbled under her feet, competing with the roar in her ears. The stony roadbed was an untrustworthy mire, as deceitful as ice on a lake after spring's first caress. She staggered on wobbling knees to keep from tumbling to the ground. Dusky rocks the color of ash tumbled down the mountain slope, attacking the road like an invading army.

A boulder grazed her shin as it rolled by, its rough surface stabbing her flesh. Derya reached down to clutch the wound, but the ground under her feet shimmied as if the rocky soil had turned to churning mud. She stumbled and flailed her arms, as unsteady as if she was walking on the deck of a ship in a stormy sea. She grabbed the mane of the mare standing alongside her, trying both to regain her footing and to calm her panicked horse.

A few moments of murmuring to the mare quieted it. Derya rested her head on the horse's withers, panting. When she caught her breath, she glanced at her throbbing leg. Her leggings were torn, but only a thin smear of blood trickled down her olive skin.

All around her, horses were plunging, straining at the reins, eyes wide and frightened. Soldiers clung to the reins, trying to calm the rearing, plunging animals. She watched, wishing she could hear anything other than the steady roar in her ears.

Several soldiers pointed at the foot of the mountain,

mouths moving in silent, frantic cries. Several pulled their swords and assumed fighting stances.

Heart thumping, she looked to where they were pointing. The earthquake had opened a small cave in the hillside, tall enough for a horse to walk into. But what was it that frightened her men? Chiliarch Bahadir, the captain of her soldiers, ran over, waving his sword, gesturing, and by the looks of it, shouting orders.

Then she heard it. A higher-pitched roaring than the constant thundering in her ears, more like a frantic bellow. Chilled fingers of fear gripped her heart and sweat dampened her palms.

Bahadir slowed as he approached the cave. Suddenly, he sprang to the side, tripped, and fell on his back. A soldier rushed to help him up, glancing nervously at the cavern.

An enormous beast leaped from the cave, its boar-like head covered with dust and blood. One of its massive tusks was broken off about a foot from its jaw. Its mouth was wide open, revealing two rows of spiked teeth.

AFTERWORD

I hope you enjoyed **The Girl Who Broke the Dark!**

If you'd like to receive updates about upcoming releases, books recommendations, bonus content and sneak peeks of my work, please subscribe to my newsletter at:

newsletter.evelynpuerto.com

As a thank you, I'll send you a free short story about a time Eliana used her air magic with disastrous results.

And if you did enjoy **The Girl Who Broke the Dark**, I would be deeply grateful if you would leave an honest review on BookBub, Goodreads or your favorite online retailer. Book reviews mean a ton to a self-published author like myself. More reviews help my books get better visibility and perform better in search algorithms. Your review will help others find my work and will make my day!

Even one sentence will help a lot.
Thank you!

ACKNOWLEDGMENTS

First, a big thank you to you, my readers, for following the adventures of Eliana and Derya in the world I created for you. I'm especially grateful to those of you who read my earlier works (The Outlawed Myth series) and decided to give this new series a try.

Special thanks to Joe Bunting and the gang over at the Write Practice. Lyn Blair, John King, Antonio Roberts, Robert Harrell, Lori Palmer, Monica MacKinnon, Wendy Pearson, and many others faithfully read and critiqued early versions of this book. Your feedback was priceless, as was your encouragement and enthusiasm about this story. The science fiction and fantasy chapter of the South Carolina Writers' Association also provided excellent suggestions for making the story more exciting.

My editor Elizabeth Doyle offered valuable suggestions and pointed out inconsistencies that no one else, including me, noticed.

Sebastian Breit of Foreign Worlds Cartography did an outstanding job taking my scribbled notes of Ardebil and turning them into a wonderful map.

Most of all I'm grateful to my husband Tony, whose support, encouragement and love keep me going when I can't find the words. And thank you for giving me space to work, and for being there for me when it's not going well.

And lastly, thanks be to God, who gave me what ability I have to string words together into a story.

ABOUT THE AUTHOR

Evelyn Puerto entered the world around the time of the unveiling of the microchip, the introduction of Japanese cars to the US, and postage stamps that cost four cents. Her Saturday morning friends were Mighty Mouse, Dudley Do-Right and the Jetsons.

Growing up, school was merely an interruption of her exploration of the worlds of Grimm's Fairy Tales, Louisa May Alcott and, later, JRR Tolkien.

When she married late in life, inherited three stepdaughters, a pair of step-grandsons, and a psychotic cat. Currently she writes from South Carolina.

She's the author of the award-winning **Beyond the Rapids** and the multiple award winning Outlawed Myth series. To learn more or to check out some of her short fiction visit evelynpuerto.com. Or keep up with her on social media.

tiktok.com/@evelyn.puerto.aut

instagram.com/theevelynpuerto

bookbub.com/profile/evelyn-puerto

facebook.com/Author.Evelyn.Puerto